I0688464

PLEASURE

VS

PAIN

Vol 1

LAKEISHA KING

Cover design by Rabia Amir
Illustration by Dwayne Jones
Layout by Daiana Morales

Dedications

I want to first thank my Heavenly Father, whom I love so, dear! He provided the will and the strength for me to complete a childhood dream and allowed me to heal in the process throughout my own situation. I am here today because of His grace and love.

I would like to thank my father and mother for the time they spent together making me! My dad, for all the mornings that we prayed and rejoiced in the Lord. All the harmonious moments and funny stories he shared with me and my siblings. Also, just taking the time to listen to my poetry and excerpts from my first book, Daddy it means so much to me.

I want to thank my husband for being by my side through thick and thin, literally! For fighting for me at all cost, for being my rock, my best friend, and my husband. To my daughters for being the apples of my eye. My first baby, so sweet, charismatic, and sharp, you blow my mind with your intelligence and beauty.

My second baby, I love you, darling with your quirky humor and loving nature. You are so smart, and it's a pleasure to watch you and your twin grow together. My third baby (twinB), with your bubbly personality and the ability to plan our futures, I look forward to watching all of you grow into the beautiful women of God I know you will be.

My cousin Keilyn Ellis for the helpful and cutthroat feedback. Tiffani Mitchell, for being willing to listen to my book hot off the press and sharing all the exciting moments with me. Oh, and almost 28 years of friendship, Tiffani!! Erika Galtney for her stellar insight and constant motivation. Zoe, Zonaira, Keila Mendez(s) for helping me figure out how to do things that my brain would not allow me to figure out (lol) and pushing me to continue, despite the many roadblocks. To the wonderful artist, Dwayne Jones, for the opportunity to use such a beautiful piece of your work for my cover. My siblings and friends that are not mentioned but are dear to my heart and anyone who supported me on this journey, thank you all and may you all be blessed!

I

Disclaimer

Be advised this book contains violence, abuse, and explicit sexual content. Please read at your own discretion.

Table Of contents

Chapter 1

I was sitting on the porch while my mother prepared her famous home-cooked biscuit, eggs, sausage, and bacon breakfast. The aroma tickled my nose and taunted my stomach while I watched Tyrell, my cute new neighbor that lived across the street, throw rocks at innocent little animals. My curiosity began to intrigue me, and I wanted to go over there to ask if I could join him. Right before I mustered up enough strength to journey over there, my mother called,

"Treasure, get in here and eat your breakfast!"

She didn't have to say nothing but a word before I sprang up and headed towards the front door. Reaching my destination before entering the house, I couldn't resist turning around to face my curiosity, when a rigid rock hit me smack right on the side of my head. When the impact registered in my brain, my first thought was to scream in pain, but instead, I just giggled. Tyrell fell on his back in laughter and suddenly stopped dead in his tracks when he saw I was laughing right along with him. He quickly threatened to pick up another rock before I entered the house to join my mother for breakfast. For the first time at the age of eight, I was confronted with my pleasure versus pain theory, with someone other than my mother. Feeling a little too thrilled to be hit by a rock instead of being rejected, I sat down at the kitchen table with a massive grin on my face. My mother ignored my silly grin and immediately noticed the blood that was threatening to ooze from the small erosion on my forehead.

She anxiously asked, "Child, what in God's name, happened to your forehead?"

A mischievous smile appeared upon my face when I answered, "Oh, nothing momma, I just tripped and fell. I'm alright. "Trying to get her to believe my little black lie, I batted my eyelashes innocently.

She looked at me with her loving brown eyes and said, "Baby, you have got to be more careful."

I just giggled and said, "Momma, it didn't hurt that bad."

Almost escaping my mother's wrath, she looked at me with confusion and disappointment as she got up from the table to continue her morning cleaning.

She looked at my forehead closely and said, "I hope that rock didn't hit you too hard." With that said, I thought she was done until I finished eating and got up to watch my favorite Saturday cartoons. She surprised me by grabbing my shoulder, saying, "You better stay away from that little boy Tyrell, you hear me?"

Startled, I nodded my head yes, the whole time trying to figure out how the heck she knew. Convinced, she would soon be so occupied by working, cleaning, raising me, and trying to find a man she would quickly forget about my forced agreement.

My mother raised me all by herself, for all I know, she went to the sperm clinic and had me with a tube of man juice, as she would call it. I know most parents don't talk about sex to their eight-year-old kids, but my mother and I were very close. She frequently murmured how my father was a dog full of man juice that poured every woman he could a cup if he got the opportunity. If it weren't for her stories, I wouldn't have known she didn't do it the old fashion way. With the way my mother felt about my father, I could never see her loving another man or letting one pour her a cup of man juice. She was strong and confident in being able to raise me while living a successful, comfortable life. She always told me I was her treasure and warned me about allowing myself to be overpowered or lured by a man. I saw my mother as an inspiration to be a strong Black woman who makes her own rules and decisions, while other women live beneath the shadows of their husbands. When I looked at her, I would see a beautiful caramel woman with the prettiest hazel eyes, the shiniest black hair, and dimples the size of nickels. She had the pearliest white teeth with full lips to compliment them. The curves of her voluptuous breast and wide hips, made me hope I had her essence when I got older. I was definitely blessed with her shiny black hair, hazel eyes, and pearly white teeth. My complexion is far darker than hers, resembling a milk chocolate Hershey bar. At the age of eight, I couldn't quite tell what curves my body would have. All I knew is that I loved my mother with all my heart. I swore she did things for me other mothers wouldn't dare do for their daughters. She did my hair, my toes, and cooked my favorite meals. The best part was the beautiful cakes she made me. My favorite one was the one she called mud cake with rich vanilla ice cream, buried with mounds of crushed Oreos invaded by candy gummy worms. My mother is my one and only true friend that I would truly be lost without. Just the thought of her being angry with me would bring me great sadness and worry. Anytime I would do something to make her upset, I would dread any hurtful, mean words that would pierce my ears or my heart. I would pray she spared me any internal pain and whipped me instead so that the pain would only last so long; she knew I was sensitive and catered to my needs and emotions, I just knew she and I would be friends forever.

I love school and I would always finish my work first and rush to pick one of the books to read. My teacher knew how much I loved to read and would always let me take one home for the week and promised me that I could always use one as long as I went to school. I would go home and read my book outside on the porch and occasionally, depending on Tyrell's activity, use it as a shield. Over the last three years, my feelings grew to be a little more than a curiosity for Tyrell. I would occasionally watch him from the porch, and sometimes if I look up at the right time, we would make eye contact, but I would quickly break it by looking down. I was excited about my eleventh birthday coming up on March 5th, and then Summer would be around the corner. I looked forward to going to fifth grade, the one thing I was looking forward to, was spending another year in school with Tyrell. I hadn't got a chance to know him since my mom makes sure if I'm not reading, I'm doing something inside the house. With me and my mom's relationship, I never really felt the desire to make new friendships with anyone but Tyrell. My mom and I celebrated my eleventh birthday by going to the movies. Although it was a little out of character, we ate out, and she surprised me when we got home with my favorite mud cake. It wasn't my favorite birthday, but I was convinced I had plenty more to look forward to.

My mom and I had a golden summer; she showed me all her favorite things she used to do when she was a kid growing up in this house. We had a beautiful two-story, three-bedroom house with a huge backyard with lots of flowers and trees. She showed me all the stuff they planted when she was a little girl. I was amazed and asked her a million questions, talking until we fell asleep.

I went back to school hoping Tyrell and I said at least one word to each other, but Tyrell hung out with a group of kids that wore the best clothes and were the best in sports. A little intimidated and scared of being ridiculed, I never approached him. I would still go home and sit outside every chance I got to see if he was playing basketball or mowing the lawn. My mom didn't really seem to mind how long I stayed outside anymore like she used to. I guess she didn't notice, since she was on the phone all the time or suddenly going out right before I went to bed. I must say that I was shocked, I had never seen my mom get dressed the way she did lately or seem so carefree about everything; especially me, her treasure. I didn't pay much attention to her weird behavior; I figured it was a phase that would soon pass. I wasn't the least bit worried until one night after staying up without parental guidance watching grown-up shows, drinking as many sodas I wanted, and eating all the junk food my belly could store, I heard the door open. Exhausted from my rampage, I refrained from getting up running to the door with my gummy bear filled legs to greet my mother, when I heard my mother giggle like one of the flirty teenage girls in some of the movies. Following her echoing laughter in my ear, I heard the deep cunning voice of a man. My legs stiffened, and my bladder expanded. I thought I would explode from shock and anger. I demanded my legs to take me up the stairs, so I could use the bathroom and make it to my room before they saw me. As if I had a genie, I got my wish and made it upstairs like the matrix to use the restroom and jump into bed to pretend it was all just a dream. In all the years I have been alive, I have never seen my mom bring a man home or have any indication of intending to do so. I was hurt, feeling a sense of invasion from this mystery man, my sleep was far from peaceful.

After that spontaneous act of my mother, I thought her strange behavior would decrease, and things would go back to the way they were. Just when I thought my mother's self-regarding acts were coming to an end, I started to realize the distorted story was just beginning to unfold. My mother's new friend's name, or shall I say boyfriend's name, was Ken. He was this tall, dark man with very dominant features and a muscular body that made him far more than just fine. He had an extremely deep voice, but a childish smile that made him look mischievous. He was very casual with me, speaking every time he saw me and going out of his way to make sure I liked him. My mother carried on as if we had rehearsed a drill to prepare me for such a drastic change. After my introduction to Ken, she tried to avoid talking about him. When he wasn't there, she seemed to be yearning for him and his presence.

One Saturday morning, my mother and I sat down to eat a small breakfast in silence. She seemed to be in a hurry making me very nervous, wondering what could possibly be on her mind. I couldn't take the silence anymore between the woman who used to be my best friend and suddenly asked,

"Mom, what's the problem? What's wrong with you?"

I really wanted to ask her *what the hell did he do to you to make you so sprung?* But I knew she would slap whatever taste buds I had on my tongue completely off. She looked at me as if she forgot I was sitting there across from her and produced a strange smile and said,

"Oh, I forgot to tell you, Ken's bringing his four kids over to meet us."

She left me there with my mouth hanging open long enough for drool to roll off of my bottom lip. I couldn't believe Ken had kids to bring to the picture. Not just one, not two, not even three, but four children. I had to go to my room to gather my thoughts, with my mind spinning. I needed to escape the reality of my mother cleaning with urgency upon the arrival of Ken's litter.

My mind started to drift off to how happy my mother and I were before Ken's rude interruption. She used to be so confident and attentive to the environment we created. Now she was distant, as if to be reserving all her love and affection for Ken. And now his four kids that were added to the equation. When Ken was around, she seemed to be in a trance doting on his every word and need. I didn't want to be judgmental, but she was more like his slave than his woman. I was far from being tickled pink to meet his children like my mother was, I just wanted to go to sleep and wake up from this nightmare.

I was sleeping when I was rudely awakened by my mother's piercing voice, informing me to come down because Ken and his family were on their way. I reluctantly got out of bed and went to the bathroom to make sure there were no traces of sleep or sadness.

My mother yelled from downstairs, "Treasure, come down here; they're here."

Debating on whether or not I should stay in the bathroom for the rest of my life, I hesitantly opened the door. Reaching the top of the stairway to stare down at Ken's four colorful children, I slowly descended the stairs. My mom's face was lit up like a Christmas tree at the sight of Ken's offspring and embraced all four of them. Finally, reaching the bottom of the stairs, I immediately felt jealousy invade my heart.

When I saw that Ken was grinning at me, the jealousy was dismissed by shock when Ken grabbed me and said, "Treasure, come give daddy a big hug."

His words were disturbing, causing me to have a case of nausea, that could result in me puking all over his shoes. He squeezed me for a longer time than I expected, or should I say, longer than I wanted him to. Maybe because it was four of them and only one of me, I was relieved when we were finished with our little hugging session. Everybody just looked at each other like what's next, with silly expressions on their faces. Ken broke the awkward silence by pointing his finger to his obviously oldest son, who was the darkest one, with huge dark brown eyes and the prettiest curly black hair.

Ken began to explain, "This is Chino, my money-maker, he's going to make me a fortune someday. Look how big he is, he just turned fourteen March 10th."

Chino just smiled and said, "Hi."

Ken then pointed to his second oldest she was light-skinned with long pretty brown hair, and bright green eyes. Ken said, "this is my beautiful daughter Cassidy; she's going to grow up to be gorgeous and have all the finer things in life. She just turned thirteen January 2nd."

The whole time I just thought to myself about how much pride he had in his kids. Ken had two younger ones to introduce us to; believe me from the smirks on their faces, I knew I would regret ever meeting them. My mind started drifting to the reasoning of his little bibliography for his children when my concentration was broken. Ken's deep voice abruptly entered my thoughts by saying,

"Sénar's pretty good at explaining himself and his purpose here on earth." He pointed at Sénar and said, "Why don't you introduce yourself?"

With confidence, he puffed his chest out and said, "My name is Sénar, and I just turned twelve March 26th."

As if to say I have spoken, he beamed the brightest smile. His true emotions were in his eyes, which reflected hatred and envy. At that moment, my heart seemed to have an encounter with fear and worry. Sénar's stare made me uncomfortable, and I started to get impatient. I didn't care who any of them were or when their birthdays were; I just wanted to get back to watching cartoons and thinking about Tyrell.

Once again, Ken bellowed, "Last but not least, this is my sweet, beautiful baby Sabrina, she turned eleven on June 12th. She's my delicate little princess, who can dance and sing so angelic, I'm going to put her on TV."

He was so caught up in his own words that when I looked at my mom, she was hanging on the same rope. Until everyone's eyes were on me, anticipating my mom's or my Oscar-winning introduction. When my mom finally realized what everybody was waiting on, she came out of her trance and began speaking,

"Oh, this is my baby Treasure; she's the only treasure I had in my life until Ken came along…" That would have been it if I didn't clear my throat, "oh…uh, Treasure baby, why don't you tell them your age."

When I looked at Sabrina, that little bitch was giggling; I wanted to slap her immediately. Irritated and now bored, I opened my mouth to say, "I just turned eleven March 5th."

The look on Sénar's dark butterscotch face frightened me. He looked very mischievous and pleased to consume the information that I had just given. Sénar had jet black hair with full lips that belonged on the cover of some magazine. Although he was a very handsome kid with unique grey eyes, there was something devilish and extremely dark lurking within them.

Sabrina broke the silence with her whining, "Daddy, what are we doing? I thought we were going to go to the movies?"

Ken then looked at my mother, "Hey, angel baby, would you and Treasure like to go to the movies with us?"

I was hoping my mother looked at the disappointed faces of Ken's kids and just said no. It wasn't but half a second when my mother replied, "Oh yes, we would love to go!"

Little did she know, she was only speaking for herself when she answered. She looked at me and said, "Grab your coat, Treasure."

I reluctantly went to go get my coat while I could hear Cassidy and Sabrina snickering. I got my coat and was the last one out the door when my mom yelled,

"Make sure you lock the door Treasure!" As if she knew I was lagging on purpose.

Ken had this white Suburban that looked like he had just bought it. With that thought running through my head, he confirmed it by saying,

"You like angel baby, I bought it for us."

I don't know if I was the only one that kept catching on to his little remarks, but I was really starting to worry. Cassidy and Sénar argued about who was going to sit by the window when Sabrina offered to sit in the middle. All of them except Chino tried to avoid sitting next to me. He let me get the back seat that was on the closest side, and he went around. Out of all of them, Chino was the only one worth trying to get to know, the other three were nothing but trouble. On the way to the movies, everyone was chattering in their own little worlds, while I sat there observing the atmosphere. Chino was the only one who noticed I was left out of everything that evening, not even my mom noticed. This was just the beginning of the new family life that had been perfectly planned without my knowledge. It wasn't even a week before they moved in with me having to share my room with Cassidy and Sabrina. Chino and Sénar shared the other room that was specifically supposed to be a project for mom and me to experiment on. I knew in my heart that this would be one of the worst things that ever happened in my life.

Chapter 2

When Ken and his kids moved in, my life changed drastically. I knew that it would, but I just wasn't ready to deal with five different personalities, when I was still trying to figure out who I was. Cassidy and Sabrina were the biggest bitches I had ever met. They constantly complained and talked about me behind my back every chance they got. Mom and Ken didn't notice because they were too busy playing in their fantasy world. I hated the fact that I had to share a room with Cassidy and Sabrina. One of them would have been bad enough, but both made it almost unbearable. They constantly double-teamed me, it was impossible to win an argument when it's two against one, even on my birthday. I didn't have any friends or associates outside of school and only went outside to see Tyrell. So, I didn't have anybody to invite to my house for my birthday. All I did was watch TV and try to avoid pretty much everybody in the house. On the day of my twelfth birthday, Cassidy and Sabrina decided to invite their friends over to spend the night. I was a little offended that my mother agreed to let them have a slumber party on my birthday. Besides, every night is a slumber party for Cassidy and Sabrina. I went upstairs to get a book just in case there was nothing on TV later, only to hear Sabrina's exaggerated sigh as soon as I opened the room door.

Sabrina impatiently said, "You know, you're not allowed to come in the room tonight, right?"

I quickly responded out of anger, "Just in case you haven't realized this; it used to be my room in the first place."

Sabrina then made a smart remark, "Right, used to be, as in past tense, besides why don't you celebrate your birthday with the TV?"

Sabrina gave her suggestion with a counterfeit smile as if she really thought it was a really good idea. I calmly answered, "You know what, you're right, even though it's my room, that's a good idea. I would definitely rather spend the night without you two breathing around me."

The expressions I left on their faces, looked like I had mooned them with the words *eat me* on my ass. I started giggling while I retrieved my book, blanket, and pillow. I went downstairs filled with rage to my solitary birthday party to watch TV and read until I fell asleep, having to block out the laughter and voices of the real party. I woke up to the smiling faces of Cassidy and Sabrina's friends. They were all surrounding me while laughing and pointing. With a sense of urgency, I jumped up to hear their laughter grow louder and louder. Following the little boney fingers of their friends, I looked down to see that I had blood all over my pajama pants. It looked like someone repeatedly stabbed me in my private area and legs. I panicked and ran to the bathroom to pull down my panties. My heart beating like it wanted to emerge from my chest; I finally got my pants down. My heart skipped a beat when my flowered underwear was white as snow in the crotch part, while the rest of it was full of red contents. I thought it was blood, even though I hadn't started my period, I thought today was the day. Realizing it couldn't be blood, I smelled my pajama pants to discover it was tomato sauce. I immediately ran out of the bathroom to tell my mom, only to run into Sénar.

He just stood there, as if to be guarding the door, with an evil smile across his face, and said, "Happy birthday Treasure!"

Instead of running to my mom, I burst out into tears and ran to my room. My body was vibrating from the intensity of my crying. I could still hear the girls mocking laughter, along with Sénar's roaring laughter mixed in. At that very moment, I realized that rock didn't hurt half as much as what Sénar and his sisters did to me. I believe this was when I started to appreciate physical pain much more.

For the next two years of my life, I had to deal with Cassidy and Sabrina's stupidity. I learned how to tune them out and occasionally caught them off guard, with catty remarks. Chino was so distant, he never said much, he was always reading or writing. Sénar, on the other hand, was planning on ruining my life somehow. I began to think Sénar liked me, and that's why he got so much pleasure out of making my life miserable. I would catch him staring at me and peaking in our room at night. For a minute, I was kind of flattered. I was thirteen years old now but had a voluptuous body for my age that my mother commented on half the time. Even if it wasn't her, it was the whispering group of girls at school. The sad part was that Sabrina was in that whispering group of girls. It was bad enough that she got on my last nerve at home. To make it worse, Sénar went there too and hung out with a group of the best athletes in the school. Tyrell just happened to be one of them, which for some reason, scared me. I was glad Cassidy was in ninth grade and went to a different school along with Chino. I already had to deal with Sabrina more than I wanted to, except for the short fifty-five- minute classes that separated us.

When she saw me, she would always say the nastiest remark she could possibly think of. I think she was jealous of me because she always commented on my body or my looks. She thought that I was fat just because I had bigger titties than both her and her sister put together. Neither one of them owned a cute shape; they were shaped like iron boards with absolutely no curves. The only things they possessed were pretty eyes, long wavy hair, and a light skin tone. They thought they were the most beautiful girls in the world. The guys at school didn't help since they had Sabrina's head swollen like an overfilled water balloon. Sabrina happened to see me sitting at the lunch table, minding my own business, that skank just had to make her way over to me to say,

"Ooh look, one of your titties is falling out and believe me, you don't need any more accidents."

She and some of the same girls from the party started laughing. I just ignored them and pretended they were little summer mosquitoesflying around me. Before they left to prey on their next victim, Sabrina says,

"Maybe we could have another party this year, since your birthday is around the corner."

That did it, I wanted to slap her silly, but she walked off before my anger reached its peak. Each time I was reminded about the party, I winced in pain of the horrifying memory. The day they planned that horrible prank was one of the most embarrassing and hurtful days of my life. My internal wounds are still healing, and my self-esteem is still bruised.

When I got home from school, everyone was in their rooms, and the house was dead quiet. I decided to get my book and go read outside on the porch. Before I opened my book, I saw Tyrell come outside with no shirt and some basketball shorts on. The feeling that invaded my body was foreign, and I allowed my mind to wander off to wherever it took me. Sénar rudely interrupted my thoughts by asking,

"What the hell you need the book for if you are reading Tyrell's ass?"

Snapping out of the trance I so often found my mom in; I was embarrassed and tried to hide my face in the book. Sénar stood there, glaring at me for so long; I thought he would give in and slap me. He finally smacked his lips out of irritation and went across the street to Tyrell's house. I watched as they gave each other a high five and started laughing. They talked for a minute while I continued reading and trying to avoid eye contact with either one of them. Sénar came back across the street with that horrible sardonic smile he flashed before or after doing something horrible to me. I looked across the street to see Tyrell smiling so wide I could see it from where I was sitting. I couldn't help but blush, wondering what Sénar's crazy ass told him. When it was time for dinner, everyone sat at the table with blank expressions on their faces. I could feel Sénar's eyes on me the whole time while looking down at my plate and trying to avoid looking at Sabrina or anyone else. After dinner, I was on my way to my room when Sénar stopped me to tell me,

"Tyrell wants to see you tomorrow under the bleachers after school."

Instantly my curiosity kicked in, and I asked, "Why does Tyrell want to meet me there, out of all places? What did you tell him Sénar?"

He just gave me one of his famous smiles while trying to reach for one of my breasts, but before he reached them, I slapped his hand away. I ran to my room, ignoring Sabrina's nasty little sigh when I entered the room. Cassidy was on the cordless phone, entertaining whoever it was with her phony personality.

Sabrina then says to me, "You'll never get Tyrell, he's too fine. You may have big titties and a big gorilla booty, but you're still not a woman! You haven't even had your period yet, and Tyrell wants a real woman like me."

I started to ignore her until she said, "We probably got your hopes up high that time we played that joke on you on your birthday."

She then busted out in hysterical laughter. That did it, I retorted with a fiery attitude, "Just because you bleed once a month doesn't make you more of a woman than me. You wish you had a body like mine. You probably don't know what breasts look like since you or your sister don't have any!"

Cassidy dropped the phone and countered by saying, "Bitch, you are not all that with your nappy ass hair, you wish you looked like my sister and me! You black ass heifer!"

I didn't say anything else since their choice of harsh words were piercing to my heart. What they did to me on my birthday was the most hurtful thing that anyone has ever done to me, there was no physical pain that could top that. They continued to talk crap all night, I had to do everything in my power to tune them out. I was on the verge of having a nervous and mental breakdown.

The next day at school, I tried to make the day past as quickly as possible. I was anticipating my acquaintance with Tyrell, who I was in love with ever since the day I laid eyes on him. I still wondered what the hell Sénar told Tyrell yesterday when he caught me staring at him.

At lunch, Sabrina's lanky ass came to my table and said, "Well, maybe today you can put your body to use since you're a loner. But then again, nobody even looks at you."

I just ignored her until she disappeared when I noticed Tyrell staring at me. He was in a group of guys that Sénar happened to be a part of. All of their attention was concentrated on me, so I pretended not to notice them. I got up when the bell rang and walked past Tyrell with an innocent smile. Sénar was glaring at both of us with envy in his eyes.

The school day was almost over, with the last minutes dragging slowly. When the bell rang to go home, my heart started beating so fast; I was beginning to lose my breath. My mind was full of fear, and my body full of anticipation. I was so nervous, I fumbled my books and bit my bottom lip the whole way there. When I finally got there, I saw that the bleachers were completely empty, I lost hope so quick I turned around to see Sénar standing behind me. He must have been following me the whole time without me noticing. He was slowly walking toward me, flashing that cynical smile he gave when he already has or about to do something to hurt me, but to please himself. My first instinct was to run like all hell, but fear mixed with a little curiosity came over me, and I couldn't move. When he reached me, he grabbed me by my shirt and shook the crap out of me until he saw that I was letting him.

He looked into my eyes and asked, "What the hell are you doing here? Did you really want to see Tyrell that bad? What were you going to do with him?"

I looked at him at a lost for words because I had lost track of how many questions he'd asked. When I finally tried to say something, he took me by my shirt again and slammed me against one of the bleachers so hard; I thought it would hit him back.

I looked at him and asked, "Why are you so mad? You told me to come, I-"

He quickly cut in and said, "Shut up!"

His face so close to mine, I could inhale the carbon monoxide from his breath into my nose. Sénar's face grimaced with anger before yelling, "Don't say shit!"

Then pushing me so hard, I fell to the ground before he ran off like an angry child. Despite the brutal contact with the ground, the only thing I felt when Sénar left was confusion, that I just couldn't understand. The whole way home, my mind was tortured with the possibilities of what could happen when I got home. I was more afraid of Sénar's words and awful pranks than I was of his violent streaks. I could feel the pain in my back and shoulders as a result of being used as an assault weapon to the bleachers. With all the things Ken's little demons put me through, sometimes the physical abuse was a relief or an escape that I would take any day.

When I finally arrived home after taking the smallest steps possible without looking crazy or high, I saw Sabrina emerging from Tyrell's house. My first thought was to yell across the street and interrogate them like Sénar had done to me earlier, but instead, I just put my head down in disappointment. I entered the house to witness Chino and Sénar quietly talking in the kitchen. I turned to the opening door to see Sabrina walk in the house with a look of disappointment on her face. When she noticed me, she looked at me with so much disdain; I had to turn away only to see Sénar with the same look on his face. Those were two people that I knew that would go to desperate measures to destroy me. I went to my room in a hurry to read a book to escape reality and its wicked forces.

Chapter 3

I never understood Sénar, he was so mean to me, but at the same time over protective. Ever since that day under the bleachers, he has been so cruel to me. I tried my best to ignore him and keep my mind focused on Tyrell. I couldn't help wondering what would have happened if Tyrell was there instead of Sénar. I couldn't figure out whether it was a setup, since when I went home that day Sabrina was exiting Tyrell's house. I wondered what happened between those two since I never saw them communicate again after that. Sabrina didn't even talk shit to me that night, which was quite unusual. Sénar was more physical than he was before, always shoving or bumping into me every chance he got. Whenever Sénar was violent with me, I got this weird sensation that trickled down my spine, it kind of scared me. Whenever Sénar would corner me, I would feel so helpless, and fear would fill my heart. I never felt that way when dealing with anyone else, so I did everything I could to avoid Sénar as much as possible. In my confused little heart, no one could physically hurt me enough, but one could break my heart with words.

One day I was in the library reading a book, for real this time for one of the first times in a while to escape the world. My 14th birthday was coming up, and I was so excited about my last year of middle school. I knew Tyrell would be leaving to go to high school, but I knew I would find a way to get through it. I wondered when my period would come because Cassidy and Sabrina's already came long ago. Cassidy always referred to me as a little girl based on my age and the fact that I haven't had my period yet, but she never mentioned Sabrina's age. The two of them also figured since I wasn't involved with anyone, I was still just a little girl. The only person who intrigued me was Tyrell, with his beautiful eyes and his Adonis face. While I was caught up in my thoughts of Tyrell, I happened to look up to see him walk by. I was looking at him when he saw me, making eye contact for a second, but this time I didn't break it. He looked like he wanted to say something, but he kept walking instead. He was so freaking fine, one thing for sure, I couldn't even read my book anymore. I couldn't stop looking at him; everything about him gave me butterflies in my stomach. He walked to a random bookshelf to pick out a book, from where I was sitting, it looked like he just picked any book and sat down. Sitting at the end of my table, he pretended to intently read like I did almost every day since I was eight.

When I saw his attempt to pretend, he was reading, I did everything in my power to not laugh, by suppressing the laughter that wanted to burst out of me. When he positioned the book really high like I did when I felt him staring at me, I couldn't help but burst into a peal of uncontrollable laughter. Instantly offended by my outburst of laughter, Tyrell lowered his book to ask,

"What's so damn funny?"

Through the laughter that was occupying my mouth, I managed to say, "I don't know, I just couldn't help it."

He then replied, "I still don't see what is so damn funny. You know what, you're weird as hell, and you tend to laugh at all the wrong things."

Knowing he was referring to him throwing the rock that hit me almost five and a half years ago, I was pretty offended by his remark. My feelings were hurt; I looked down at my book to hide my emotions. Tyrell, sensing my disappointment, he quickly responded,

"Well, well, well, Treasure does have normal emotions to some extent."

Even though Tyrell was only 14 going on 15, he was mature and intelligent for his age, which is probably why he was so quiet. He softened up a little,

"Would you like to walk home with me?"

Shocking the heck out of me, I almost couldn't answer. My mind questioned reality, as I cautiously answered, "Yeah."

When I finally came to my senses, I rephrased my answer to, "Sure, why not? Whenever you are ready."

After my new answer, I immediately felt like a puppet. He looked at me with a mischievous smile that instantly made my cheeks feel like they would explode from excitement. When Tyrell got up, as he walked towards me, with the same curiosity that invaded my mind that day on the porch five and a half years ago, crept back into my mind. He was so tall and handsome that I couldn't help but wonder what it would be like to have him kiss me like I saw Sabrina kissing her 40th boyfriend.

Sabrina and Cassidy were fast asses, and they thought it made them more of a woman than me. However, the only thing it made was the definition of a yamp, which is a young tramp. Cassidy was only 15 and had been sexually active for at least three years. Sabrina, on the other hand, was only 13 and had been sexually active for almost three years herself, which by the way, was completely disgusting. They talked about their sex lives like it was something to be proud of at their age. Little did they know I thought it really made me think they were pathetic in their attempt to be women.

We walked home that afternoon, talking about our future plans. I didn't know Tyrell was so serious about sports, he raved on and on about football, explaining how he wanted to play at a popular university so he could be drafted into the pros. He told me how Sénar asked him if he wanted to practice with him and his friend sometimes. The mere sound of Sénar's name made me quiver inside with fear. I tried not to show my emotions by switching the subject.

I asked, "Do you have a girlfriend?"

The question made him blush and surprised the hell out of me. My lips didn't listen to a damn thing, my mind said. He took so long to answer, I started to wish I could have taken it back, but that thought soon faded when he replied, "No but it's probably not a bad idea."

I started smiling, and I couldn't wait to find out what happened next. He suddenly stopped walking then grabbing my hand, he turned to face me. He looked deeply into my eyes, with his mysterious eyes, I could have melted like the wicked witch in the Wizard of Oz and probably would have started drooling if he hadn't kissed me. The warm sensation of his lips gently caressing mine gave me the oddest feeling I've ever felt. My coochie got so moist; I was pondering what could possibly be that warm and slimy. When the kissing massage was over, I still had my eyes closed, when Tyrell asked,

"Are you awake?"

I snapped out of my trance and quickly responded, "Oh…..uh.. yeah, I am."

He started laughing and said, "Well, maybe we should be heading home." When he mentioned the word home, I dreaded seeing Cassidy and Sabrina. I just knew Sénar would have a million questions to where I had been, and to what I was doing when I got home. Tyrell walked me to the front door and quickly kissed me on the lips before turning around to go home.

Before leaving, he asked, "Can I stop by in the morning to pick you up?"

I nodded yeah and answered, "Yes" with a sense of urgency. I opened the door, hoping Sénar was not anywhere around to see him kiss me or to hear my answer.

Once inside, I saw Sénar standing right by the window, scaring the living crap out of me. I jumped back to make out his facial expression, with the lack of light that was present, I couldn't tell if he was hurt or mad. His mouth that usually curled in that evil smile was poked out, and his eyes were glassy.

I asked out of pure concern, "Sénar, what's wrong with you?"

He glared at me for a very long time before he responded, "You would not understand if I told you! You are a stupid broad-" Before he could finish, Chino walked in the door.

He looked at me and then at Sénar, shaking his head as he passed us up on his way up the steps. Before turning away, Sénar flashed the most disturbing look my way before going up the steps, leaving me there dumbfounded. I immediately started crying; I knew my heart would shatter into little pieces if Sénar had finished saying whatever he was going to say before Chino had walked in. I dreaded painful words and the cruel pranks they played on me. There was something that kept me from hating Sénar, but that same thing is what fueled my hatred for Cassidy and Sabrina.

When I got upstairs, I tried to wipe away the evidence of my tears before entering the room with Cassidy and Sabrina. They stop talking when I entered the room and took pleasure in seeing that I was hurt.

"Awe, what's the matter baby?"

For a minute, Cassidy almost sounded sincere when Sabrina's nasty little voice chimed in,

"Oh, she probably looked in the mirror and realize how ugly she really is."

Sabrina paused for a moment before saying, "Or better yet, maybe Tyrell must have told her how fat she is and that he didn't want her black ass!"

They both begin to laugh so hard that I ran out of the room after only grabbing a nightgown. I ran to the bathroom and locked the door with tears streaming down my face; my heart still sore from being pierced by Sénar's harsh words. I ran some hot bath water and continued to cry in unison with the flowing water, as my mind was poisoned with the mocking laughter of Cassidy and Sabrina.

I caught myself before I completely fell asleep in the tub, just in time to hear a knock at the door. I jumped out of the tub, almost breaking my neck with the lack of friction between my feet and the wet tile. I searched for my bra and panties but failed to find them. I even forgot to bring a towel in the process of escaping Cassidy and Sabrina's wrath. I had no choice but to put my flimsy white gown over my wet body. Opening the door to see Sénar's eyes widen at the sight of my nightgown sticking to my body in all my private places. My chocolate nipples exposed by the flimsy nightgown plastered on to them like wet tissue paper. I was embarrassed, I tried covering my breast and private areas. When he began to form that smile, I was so accustomed to, I tried to run back into the bathroom, but he grabbed my nightgown, restricting any more distance between us. He pulled me to him with so much force; he shocked me with the amount of strength that he had. I could feel his penis harden against my vagina, and I gasped with panic. His smile grew even wider when he saw that my nipples were at full erection, causing me to look away in shame. I was paralyzed, I couldn't move, a part of me curious about what was going to happen next and another part of me was scared shitless. Before Sénar could go any further, he released me at the sound of a door creeping open. Chino emerged out of their room, rubbing the sleep out of his eyes, so he could adjust to the bright light bursting out of the bathroom.

He looked at Sénar and then at me, noticing my body parts exposed, in my now wet nightgown, then took a look for himself. Impressed, he pushed Sénar out of the way and went to the restroom. Sénar rushed me up against the wall, squeezing my breast so hard, I threatened to scream when he stuck his tongue into my mouth, pulling my hair while pressing himself against me. He quickly let me go when Chino came out of the bathroom.

Chino looked at me with concern, "Shouldn't you be asleep? There ain't nothing but trouble out here this time of night."

He then retreated to his room; I quickly took the opportunity to run to my room. The warning he gave was as if he knew Sénar's intentions and acted as if we were in the wilderness in the woods or something. That night I went to bed confused, wondering why that same slimy substance found its way all over my coochie again. I also wondered what in the heck kind of kiss that was Sénar had given me and what the hell was happening to my coochie. I wanted to talk about it with my mom, but I was afraid our gap in communication was far too wide. I guess I will have to figure it out somehow on my own. I let my mind drift to Tyrell and went to bed dreaming about him.

Chapter 4

The night Sénar waited for me to emerge out of the bathroom, I will never forget for as long as I live. I was so confused and distraught while my body plagued by many mixed emotions. I didn't know what Sénar wanted from me, I was in love with Tyrell, and I was definitely convinced I wanted to spend the rest of my life with him. My 14th birthday was coming up Friday, and I was really excited, I knew Sabrina and Sénar would be up to no good, so I was going to ask Tyrell if he wanted to spend it with me. Since we had such a lovely time on Tyrell's 15th birthday. Tyrell and I were really starting to get to know one another better while we walked to and from school every day. When Tyrell and I spent time together, I felt like I was dreaming or on vacation from the real world. The only time I had to deal with reality, was when I reluctantly returned home to see that Ken had traded my mom in for a lost teenage girl that was madly in love with him and that he had let his offspring take over. I felt jealousy take over the day my mom came in with Ken for the first time. I knew that it was not a good sign, seeing that her behavior had already started changing before bringing him home. We used to talk all the time about everything because we were very close. When Ken moved in with his kids, she changed drastically, and all that came to a screeching halt. My mother had forgotten all about me, moving into her dreamworld, leaving me behind to deal with Ken's little demons. Happiness was so far away; the only time I felt a glimpse of happiness, was when I was with Tyrell. Deep down inside, I was lost, the path my mother used to light for me, was now dark with the evil Ken had brought into the house. I never thought my life could be so crucially affected if she fell in love. I decided to stop focusing on my mother's newfound love and focus on my own. However, there's no way I would leave my mom behind; I would take her with me no matter how much she Ignored me.

I didn't regret one second of the time I spent with Tyrell. Sénar always had a look of disgust when he would catch us holding hands or even talking for that matter. He was probably contemplating ways to tear us apart and shatter the only world I enjoyed being in. I would always mention all the horrible things Cassidy and Sabrina did to me over the years, but for some reason, my tongue refused to confess the evil things that Sénar had done to me. I was ashamed and convinced that no one would believe me, or even accuse me of bringing it upon myself. One day after school, Tyrell and I decided to go to the park for a while. We just wanted to be where no one would be able to see us or know where we were.

We sat down on one of the benches, and he asked, "What if I told you I really like you and wanted to......"

He paused, and I urged him to go on by fluttering my eyelashes at him. He continued,

"Well since we see each other every day, I was wondering if you wanted to go out?"

My brain froze, and my heart skipped a beat when I realized what his question meant. He looked disappointed in my reaction, and before I could reply, he said, "Never-mind that was a stupid idea."

Tears threatened to emerge out from under my eyelids and dance all over my face. I tried to sound as happy as I could, "Sure, I would love to....... but does that mean people would know?"

The question seemed to catch him off guard, and he replied, "Well, if you want, we could be boyfriend and girlfriend without telling anyone. Anyways we are going to different schools soon, so we shouldn't have to worry about anyone being in our business anyway."

Little did he know, he would be going to school with Sénar, which was the main person I was worried about. I was happy but weary, "I would love to be your girlfriend, but I would prefer if no one knew about it."

When I said that, I had one person in mind, and that was Sénar. I was more afraid of what he would say more than what he would do. Sénar's actions never really left me with any physical pain that wouldn't subside, but his words would often destroy whatever self-esteem I tried to build while growing up with Cassidy and Sabrina. I was afraid to tell Tyrell the real reason why I didn't want anyone to know because I thought Tyrell would think that I was crazy or that I was weak. When I got lost in my own thoughts, Tyrell broke my concentration by asking,

"Who are you afraid of anyway? Is there someone in particular that makes you want to hide our feelings for each other?"

The next words that emerged out of my mouth shocked me, "No, I just don't think my mother would approve of me dating at such a young age."

I knew damn well my mom's head was so high in the clouds that she didn't give a rat's ass about what I did. My mother was continuing to drift further and further from reality daily. Sadly, that reality she left behind; I was all alone. I prayed every night that my mother would realize how lonely and lost I was and return to planet Earth where I was suffering. But my prayers were left unanswered, and every time I entered the house, I was reminded of that. Tyrell looked at me with confusion and frustration before mentioning,

"Cassidy and Sabrina always talk to guys and a whole lot more than that."

He saw my eyes widen with interest at what he was going to say, so he just dropped it, saying, "Well, if you think it's best, we won't tell anyone."

I was relieved and wanted to change the subject, "Well, my birthday is coming up this weekend." feeling a little shy, I fidgeted a bit before finishing my question, "Would you like to spend it with me?"

He looked at me with his breathtaking smile, responding, "Sure anything for my girl."

I was so flattered that I produced the most genuine smile that I hadn't been able to find in a long time. He grabbed me and kissed me so hard; I felt to see if my teeth were still there when we were done kissing. My body was overfilled with excitement and curiosity as to why he never tried anything else, but I kept my curiosity to myself.

I was growing up and had confused feelings about my sexual attraction. My body would always betray me at the wrong times. When Sénar played his cruel jokes on me, my heart would shatter into little pieces, and with each horrible thing he said would make it harder to put the pieces back together. However, his curiosity with my body or the violent ways he would approach me in the past would secretly arouse me, even when fear was present. Whenever he would corner me, a part of me wanted to run like hell, and the other part of me was plagued with curiosity. I started to worry when I didn't feel that dangerous curiosity with Tyrell. I guess with Tyrell, everything just seems to flow naturally, registering in my brain as normal or too good to be true.

On my 14th birthday, Tyrell and I slowly walked home from school hand in hand. When we finally reached my house, I went inside to put my backpack away, when I realized no one was home. For a moment, it seemed like my house, that was haunted by little demons and a lost angel, was cured. Although I was excited about my newfound peace, I knew it would be rudely interrupted sooner or later by either one of them. Sénar was the only one of them, besides my mother that would have an effect on me for the rest of my life. Cassidy and Sabrina try to destroy me, but they were just jealous used up little brats. Deep down inside, I think Sénar knew he had that effect on me, and that's why he got so much pleasure out of torturing me. I snapped back into reality, realizing Tyrell was waiting for me downstairs. I grabbed my jacket and ran back down the steps to see Tyrell there, anticipating my return.

Feeling a little shy, I asked, "So what do you want to do now?"

I was really wondering why there was no one at my house. Tyrell anxiously answered, "Well, there is no one at my house either. My mom and dad went to a class, and they won't be back until tonight." My smile came shining through, and we bolted across the street to his house.

When we entered his house, my heart was racing from all the excitement; I had to hunch over to catch my breath. When I started to gain back some of my composure, I looked out the window to see Ken and my mother with all of Ken's offspring, jump out of the car like The Brady Bunch. My heartbeat immediately decreased; tears began to burn my eyelids. Tyrell's soft touch fell upon my shoulder; my head lowered as my tears became violent like a storm throwing me to my knees. Tyrell immediately looked out the window to see the Reject Brady Bunch go into the house with cakes and pizza. The first thought should've been they were celebrating my birthday, but Tyrell and I both knew that they were talking and laughing without them even thinking about me.

I refused to go home and deal with my paper like family. Tyrell saw the disappointment in my puffy eyes and instantly grew happy. I was confused when he grabbed me, saying, "Come on Treasure!"

Almost ripping my arm off, we ran through the kitchen to grab some keys and raced to the garage. I felt like my mind was spinning out of control when he opened the garage door. Before my eyes, there was a shiny black Lincoln with plush black leather seats, a wooden dashboard, and a comfortable, roomy interior. A confused smile appeared on my face when Tyrell appeared to be feeling cocky; he asked, "You like it?" Nodding my head in agreement, he blurted out in excitement, "Get in!"

I reluctantly got in the car, immediately asking, "Wait, what are you doing?"

When he started the car, I blurted out, "Wait, do you know how to drive?" He rolled his eyes sarcastically, "Yes, I know how to drive, the question you should be asking is if I'm supposed to be driving. Because then the answer would be no."

He said with a smirk on his face. I started giggling when Tyrell assured me, "But have no fear I got a permit when I turned 15. My dad said when I turn 16, I can get my license, and he'll give this car to me."

Worried, I asked, "Can we get in trouble?"

He had a daredevil look in his eyes and said, "Yeah, but it's worth it! I'm going to take you to the drive-in movies."

Raising my eyebrows from all the surprises, I wanted to ask what a drive-in movie was, but I decided to use my common sense. Besides, my curiosity always gets me in trouble anyway.

On the way to the drive-in movies, the eagerness shown in Tyrell's face made me grasp my seatbelt to ensure it was secure. I was as nervous as a driving instructor; to break the tension, I asked, "Won't your mom and dad be angry if they find out?"

I was really worried and didn't want him to get in any type of trouble. He shrugged his shoulders, "Treasure, my parents are cool; they will understand that my lady was in distress."

He tried not to sound like he was bragging, but it only made me think of the new, improved Black Reject Brady Bunch with faces full of smiles that entered my house earlier. Little did they know that my smile was turned upside down into a frown at the sight of them. I begin to feel sadness ease its way back into my happy picture that Tyrell tried to paint. I allowed my eyes to close for comfort and tear control. Darkness was starting to take over when my eyes popped open from the tickling sensation of the fluorescent lights from the biggest TV I ever saw in my life. Immediately my heartbeat started to speed up, and the joy that I so rarely felt started to embrace me. A big hefty man walked up peering into the car with his perverted beady eyes and asked,

"Tickets for two?" His eyes accusingly darted to the backseat. Feeling accused, Tyrell pulled out a ten-dollar bill ignoring his antics,

"Yes, only two." He said mockingly, looking at me out of the corner of his eye to make sure I didn't magically disappear.

I thought about how much money my mom pulled out for a matinee on my 11th birthday it was almost double the money he had to pay, and that was three years ago. I was under the impression that was why we never went again at her expense. Well, at least that was the reason I was more comfortable with, instead of the reason being that I was replaced by Ken.

When we pulled in front of the giant screen to park, I was stoked at the thought of being alone with Tyrell, somewhere without any faces or voices that I hated. The lights that lit up our pupils left me in awe for a second. I was once again lost in my own thoughts when Tyrell grabbed my shoulder to pull me out of Lala Land. For a second, I wanted to go back to reach for my mom's hand, but she was long gone. Tyrell instantly try to keep my attention by asking me,

"Have you ever been to the drive-in movies before?"

I think he knew the answer but was just trying to spark a conversation. I answered bitterly, "No, sadly, I haven't been much of anywhere in the last couple of years, except the places I'm forced to go only to be outcasted."

To avoid 21 questions, I told him how much I appreciated him taking me out of hell's hands. I really wanted him to know that this was the best birthday I've had in my adolescent years, where I actually enjoyed myself. The smile he beamed at me, was so bright I would have to be a completely different person, with a completely different life, to produce a smile that bright. A twinge of jealousy struck my heart, knowing how easy it was for him to produce that smile, even though I was trying to cheer up, he could see that my thoughts were consuming me. He took hold of my hand and asked me,

"Would you mind if I gave the birthday girl a big, wet, and juicy kiss?"

My eyes felt like they would burst right out of my head with excitement that my heart instantly felt. He said, "Close your eyes."

I hesitated for a quick second but obeyed his command. The moment I closed my eyes in anticipation, I entered a world full of pleasure, where pain didn't exist. It put a bit of fear in my heart to feel my body tingle with such pleasure as his hands gently wandered my tense body. He kissed me softly, and slowly while his hands inched closer to forbidden places that had never been caressed, only violently grabbed, I could feel my body's hesitation. The weirdest thought entered my mind, causing confusion in this passionate moment. I simply wondered when the pain would arrive, and the longer I waited, the more impatient I got. Since I wasn't feeling the thrill of the aggression picking up, only his gentle caressing, I just wanted him to hold me to ensure he really desired me.

Somehow with his mouth still on mine, I asked him, "Can you hold me in your arms?"

His answer was a dream come true, "Yes I'll hold you in my arms forever and ever……"

We giggled and cuddled throughout the whole movie. I was hoping our night would go on forever and ever, but our night was cut short when Tyrell's car phone rang. His parents called wondering where he was and when he was coming home. They asked him nicely to bring the car back home. Tears threatened to rip through my eyelids at the thought of having to return to hell's arms.

On our way home, Tyrell held my hand in his hand the whole ride home. Just by the way he looked at me, I could tell he could sense my agony. The closer we got to the house, the more excuses and stories that I planned to use danced across my mind. Although I knew my little black lies would not satisfy Sénar's or my mom's curiosity about where I had been. I was more afraid of what Sénar would say than my own mother. I figured she would be so wrapped in Ken's web she would not even care.

As Tyrell reached the turn that would take us down the street we lived on; he started to slow down. He stopped pleading with me with his eyes, "I hope you enjoyed tonight and don't let the evil Reject Brady Bunch ruin your birthday." He then leaned over and kissed me gently on the lips. I felt like I was dreaming while the reality I had to face at home was screaming accusations in my ear way from around the corner. I relaxed and allowed him to hold me for a few moments before we turned the corner and pulled into his driveway.

When I arrived home, in my heart I knew my birthday would somehow be destroyed, yet the person who didn't just rain on my parade, but completely destroyed it was the last person I thought it would be. As soon as I entered the house, I could hear Ken's little demons arguing with the voice of an angel. The first three voices were Cassidy, Sénar, and Sabrina, they were having a heated argument, while Chino threw his comments in it in a civilized manner. The other three were too ignorant to understand the reasoning of effective communication. Within the first forty seconds of walking into their argument, I could already read in between the lines. Sénar was highly upset, accusing his sisters of being whores. He complained that half of his boys, if not all them, had been involved with either Cassidy or Sabrina or even both of them. They argued they weren't whores and that half of it was lies. Cassidy's argument had a little thought to it, as she claimed she had grown out of her promiscuous stage, while Sabrina argued she wasn't a whore but that she just loved guys, and they loved her. Sénar's anger bolted to the top when he realized I had just walked in the door for the first time in my life at 9:30 at night. He looked at me with disgust and continued to spit fire at Cassidy and Sabrina.

Although the daggers that Sénar shot through me with his eyes hurt, they weren't enough to steal my joy of finally having a birthday that I enjoyed. I quickly got tired of hearing them argue and went into the kitchen to grab something to drink when I heard a snap crackle and pop. I looked at my cup to ensure I didn't pour a cup of Rice Krispies. It wasn't but 2.5 seconds before Sabrina yelped in

35

anger mixed with pain, to confirm my hypothesis of someone getting smacked a couple of times. On that note, I knew something serious would happen, I looked around the kitchen to see the aftermath of what should have been my birthday celebration. Empty pizza boxes littered the counter with a half-eaten cake, with my name nowhere on it. A sense of sadness mixed with urgency came over me. To avoid the potential possibility of arguing by quietly scurrying my way up the steps. I felt relief, as I was on my way up the steps undisturbed. I looked upstairs to see my mom at the top of the stairs; in a way I have never seen her before. The way her eyes pierced my heart, she appeared as if she was demon- possessed.

Frightened and confused, I walked up the steps to try and comfort her. "What's wrong, mama?" I asked while getting closer. I slowly walked towards my mom, and her response seemed to have the effect of sharp knives ripping the flesh of my back, "Where the fuck were you?" She yelled at me, with anger that was far beyond being mad.

In all the years she raised me, I had never heard her use a curse word. The one day of my life she did use a curse word, it was shockingly to me, that one seeped out of her mouth. Before I could answer her, she struck me across the face so hard that it felt like little pieces of broken glass were plastered to her palm. Immediately, the tears that were already building up after the way she cursed at me forced their way from behind my eyelids and onto my face. I was hoping her next move was to slap me again, instead of saying the things that were dashing across her mind and spilling out of her mouth. My hopes were crushed when she decided to continue her tongue lashing,

"You were out being a little whore, weren't you? I told you I didn't want you talking to Tyrell-" Before I could answer her, I heard a horrifying loud scream coming from downstairs, causing my mom to snap back into reality. Guilt seemed to strike her heart like she had me with her words, more so than her actions.

Immediately, Ken emerged out of his room glaring at my mom while he towered over us. When my mother gave the impression of a melting wick candle, I knew exactly where her unexplained anger manifested from. He looked like he would strike my mother next, before turning his attention to the commotion going on downstairs. Sabrina's cries and screams rang our ears after the unmistakable sound effects of another slap were heard. The sad part was, it wasn't a sound effect. Sénar had really hauled off and slapped Sabrina so hard across her face, she looked like she went to a carnival to get it professionally painted on. We all ran down the steps, just in time to stop Sénar from whipping Sabrina's ass. Ken grabbed Sénar holding him back, while Sénar screamed in rage,

"How could you? How could you? You are such a little whore!" Ken threw Sénar to the ground.

Ken demanded, "Why are you putting your hands on your sister?" As if he didn't hear Sénar refer to Sabrina as a whore, he pretended like he didn't know what the problem was. Silence took over, while it competed with Sénar's heavy breathing. Ken looked around before asking,

"What the hell is going on here? I won't ask again or……"

Sabrina blurted out, "Sénar believes his friends over Cassidy and me!"

Cassidy feeling like she didn't need to be mentioned, she smacked her lips in disappointment. Sabrina, feeling guilty, continued, "Daddy none of this is true! I swear! It's just rumors!"

Sénar jumped up from the floor, yelling, "You're a lying little whore Sabrina!"

Ken winced at hearing Sénar call his little angel, a whore. Ken roared in anger, "Go to your room Sénar! And I don't ever want to hear you talk to your blood that way again!"

Ken dismissed everyone to their rooms, as Sénar stormed up the steps. Everyone dispersed from the living room and headed to their rooms. On the way to my room, I couldn't help but wonder what Ken meant by saying,

"To your blood."

Did that mean he could talk to me and my mom anyway he wanted too? I sure hoped not; I had enough problems with Sénar as it is. That night everyone went to bed with disturbing thoughts. The only positive was that I wasn't alone this time. I went to sleep, hearing someone else's sobs other than my own.

Chapter 5

The next morning Cassidy and Sabrina were still sleeping after having what seemed like a scene from *Jerry Springer* take place in our living room last night. I looked over to observe Sabrina sleeping like a baby with Sénar's handprint plastered onto her face, as evidence that she had the crap slapped out of her. I muffled my laughter, careful not to wake them up from their slumber. Instead, I occupied my mind with the anticipation of wanting to see Tyrell and how much I couldn't wait to see him. I decided to take a bath first to relieve some of the stress and to refresh my own slapped face by splashing cool water on it while waiting on the water to get hot. I was excited about Tyrell and I becoming boyfriend and girlfriend. When the water was finally starting to get warmer, I drifted into my thoughts about all the things that we would do with each other eventually. I thought about how he kissed me last night at the drive-in movies, while gently caressing my body all over. I started to get aroused as I pretended my hands were Tyrell's hands touching me more aggressively. With the now hot water pooling around my coochie and lower extremities, I thought about how good it felt against my skin. Sitting under the faucet with the thrashing water pressing against my hands. I cupped my hands together, letting the water overflow all over me as I hunched over to get closer to the flowing water. I couldn't help but wonder what it would feel like to put my whole coochie under the flowing water. I scooted awkwardly into a position where the water could fall directly on my coochie with my legs stretched upward against the wall of the bathtub. I laid back and enjoyed the thrashing hot water as it messaged my little man in the boat. I let the thoughts of Tyrell consume me as I caressed my breast. Quietly moaning from the unbearable sensation traveling through my body.

Sensations I never felt before started to intensify, causing my heartbeat to increase and my muscles to tense up. Unbearable pleasure rippling through my body as I envisioned Tyrell kissing me with his traveling hands all over my body. Sénar's sadistic smile flashed in my mind, feeling like I would explode into a million pieces, I pushed myself from under the water with the force of my legs, before reaching a level of intensity I couldn't bear. I turned the water off to compose myself as I caught my breath. I was frantically wondered what would've happened if I didn't push back. I quickly got out of the bathtub to get dressed. As I open the door to leave, Sénar snatched me up swiftly, pressing me against the wall. Trying not to make too much noise, he gestured his finger to his lips, "Shush". My heart still racing and afraid, I held my breath to refrain from screaming. He put his hand behind my neck and slid his other hand under my shirt. Feeling the warmth of my breasts in his hand, I could feel him brace himself as he was trying to stay focused.

He quietly asked me in my ear, "Are you dating Tyrell?"

Immediately alarmed, I felt his grip tighten on my neck as he moved in closer and pressed his hardened member against my body. Both nervous and too afraid to answer him, I closed my eyes to keep from looking him in his eyes.

He asked me again, "Are you and Tyrell together?"

He was grinding against me, making it impossible to concentrate, as I felt like my knees would buckle from fear. He grinded faster and harder, holding my neck tightly while awaiting my answer. Panicking, I was thinking of a response when he kissed me deeply before I could answer. Grappling my breast and thrusting his body against mine, he tried to stay focus on the question he asked me. Sénar's breathing increased while forcefully kissing me, apparently fighting the urge to release something raging inside of him. Unable to control what was happening to him, he reluctantly released me. Quickly escaping into the bathroom to handle his business, whatever that was. Leaving me in the hallway, both distressed and relieved, I bolted for my room to pull myself together. Terrified, I felt like I had been caught red-handed and ran out the front door to Tyrell's house.

After my incident with Sénar, I felt like my secret relationship was in jeopardy of being exposed. I was afraid that Sénar would confront me again since he didn't get the answer he wanted. I decided to leave in a hurry before I encountered my mother or any other demon in the house. I walked rapidly across the street to Tyrell's house. When I knocked on the door, Tyrell answered, I could not stress enough the fact that we had to leave in a hurry. I told him I wanted to leave before my mom figured out that I was gone. He believed me, although the real reason I wanted to leave was to be gone before Sénar exited the bathroom and came looking for me. Sénar put so much fear in my heart, but I refused to tell anyone. Besides, I can't think of one person who would care or not take it completely out of proportion.

Tyrell instantly rushed to get his keys and his jacket. As soon as I heard the beeping of the alarm along with the clicking of the doors unlocking, I ran like the wind to get into the car. Tyrell got into the car with the biggest grin on his face that I have ever seen him have. As we backed out of the driveway, I could not fight the urge to look back, feeling like I was being watched. Just as I had thought, Sénar was standing in the window looking like a crazed man with his hair all wild as if he had rushed out of the bathroom. I gasped, covering my mouth to disguise my intense worry. With the music playing, I thought Tyrell would not notice, but he asked,

"What's wrong?"

With a mixture of disappointment and concern. Thinking about the way Sénar's eyes cut into me like swords dripping with hatred and betrayal, I couldn't respond without tearing up. Tyrell then grabbed my hand with great efforts to comfort me; when I looked up at him, his wide grin had been replaced with a poked-out lip. I looked down with a sense of guilt, knowing I would have to lie to him about what really was wrong with me. I tried my best to give him the most genuine smile I could muster up and replied,

"Oh nothing, my family just won starring roles on the *Family Feud* show, but without the prizes."

He tried to maintain his composure but still reluctantly giggled a bit. We both could not help but bust out laughing together at my analogy.

He then said, "Well, why don't you forget about the bad news because I have some really good news. As a matter of fact, this might help you escape the Reject Brady Bunch more often."

We were now in full-blown laughter in unison, allowing me the ability to be eager to find out about this good news he was talking about. I always referred to my family as the Reject Brady Bunch, being it was just too many different step siblings to be Cinderella. Instantly, I felt some sunshine on my stormy day and responded by saying,

"Well, anything is good news when it involves getting away from the Reject Brady Bunch."

Accumulating his huge grin that had transformed into a poked-out lip earlier, he blurted out,

"I'm going to get my license soon when I turn sixteen. My dad said the car is officially mine, so that means we can do more things. Until then, we will just sneak out sometimes."

He said that with his chest all poked out as if he was standing on a golden throne. Although he was a little arrogant, I could not help but be more excited for him.

I whispered, "What kind of things?"

Thinking about this morning's pleasure and feeling a little naughty. He looked at me and said, "Whatever you want, babe."

Happy with his answer, I grabbed his hand and squeezed it. Hesitating to let his hand go, I guided it to my upper thigh, wanting to feel the warmth from his muscular hand. He couldn't resist moving it higher to my hot spot in between my legs that was even hotter with the thoughts of this morning taunting me. I couldn't help but reminisce on the pleasure I received this morning at the thought of him. As for Sénar stealing the starring role at the end, still had me baffled, right along with the nail marks I inflicted on my breast. I couldn't explain any of it being that none of it was familiar. I had never touched myself like that or thought about things to that degree. Deep in thought, I didn't want to pick my brain about it now while in the presence of the one who triggered it in the first place. All I know is that the ending result was something I wanted to do again and again. I wanted Tyrell to take it to another level; I wanted some aggression. What scared me the most is that I actually wanted him to do some of the things Sénar did to me every chance he got.

Tyrell interrupted my thoughts with, "What's going on in that mind of yours?"

Caught off guard as it was so easy for me to drift off into daydreaming since it's what I did on a daily basis to escape my family. I tried to answer him as quickly as possible,

"Oh, nothing."

Feeling ashamed, I clenched my legs together, squeezing his hand. Sensing the tension, he changed the subject, "Well, since I have a car, my dad says he will help me get a job. He said if I keep my grades up, he doesn't have a problem with me working." Filled with so much joy for him, I could not help but put my confused thoughts away and let happiness consume me.

Tyrell and I pulled into a huge parking lot of a big park with beautiful trees and magical looking ponds. Instantly pleased with the sight of the magnificent scenery, I realized I couldn't remember ever seeing such beautiful things, let alone a park like this. We got out of the car, and he saw the awe in my eyes which made him beam a smile so bright, I couldn't help but run to him to grab him and kiss him. Shocked at my aggression, he pushed me off him as if I was some crazed woman trying to take advantage of him. Confused and a little hurt by his reaction, I tried to camouflage with the door of the car. To quickly break the ice Tyrell asked,

"Damn Treasure, that's what you were plottin' on the way over here?" With a small laugh, he continued, "I wish I was in on the plot, so I would know to run or surrender." I couldn't do anything else but laugh at his attempt to make me feel comfortable again. He stroked my hair and kissed me gently, then whispered, "Let's get a better view."

Tyrell and I slowly walked down the paths that were meant for jogging until we found the perfect spot to spend our evening. The spot we picked had healthy, fully leaved trees that produced the best breeze and the most amazing scenery I ever saw. To be fifteen, Tyrell was so clever and romantic the knit basket he was carrying had our whole afternoon laid out in it. I almost sat my goofy self-down on the grass. I was so excited about what could be in the basket until Tyrell stopped me,

"Just wait, I have our seat in here."

He placed the basket on the grass and opened the flaps to remove a checkered red and white blanket that was just like the tablecloths they had in the movies. This wasn't just an ordinary blanket; it was tough enough to keep little sharp blades of grass from poking our behinds and soft enough to lay our heads upon comfortably. Now a little embarrassed for being too anxious, I still couldn't help plopping my behind right down on the blanket with a huge silly grin. In love with the breeze and the softness of the blanket, I laid down, allowing a million thoughts to run through my mind. I was very relaxed while I watched Tyrell pull out what seemed to be a feast right before my eyes. He started out with a container filled with egg salad whipped to my pleasure and fresh wheat bread with poppy seeds along the edges.

Then to flatter the sandwiches, he had some French onion Sun Chips I've yet to taste. My mouth-watering with anticipation of our meal he had laid out, I couldn't help but blurt out,

"Wow!"

He looked at me with a mischievous smile and said, "Wait, I'm not even done yet."

He then pulled another container with grapes, strawberries, and kiwis cut to perfection with a bottle of whip cream to sweeten the meal. My eyes grew big at the display, and just when I thought our picnic couldn't get any better, Tyrell pulled out a bottle of Moët. My eyes couldn't get any bigger, so my mouth dropped open in shock, suddenly remembering all the rappers talk about Crystal and Moët. I would have been happy with apple cider, let alone Moët. I couldn't help but ask,

"Wait, now how did you manage to get that?" My eyes targeting the Moët bottle.

Tyrell answered, "Oh, hush, it doesn't matter; what matters is that we're about to enjoy a picnic with a little bit of something extra, that's all." He asked, "Why you scared?"

I quickly answered, "No."

Curiosity filled my brain as Tyrell pulled out the Champaign glasses handing me one while asking, "So are you hungry now, or do we want to chat a little before we eat?"

Being that I was so confused and overwhelmed at the same time, I didn't know whether to choose the forbidden surprise or the delicious lunch he prepared. Lost in thought, my stomachs growl answered the question for my mind. I snapped out of my trance and spoke, "Well, we could eat so we could enjoy our dessert."

Tyrell agreed, giving me a kiss on my cheek before preparing our sandwiches. I kept occasionally pinching myself to see if I was dreaming because no one, not even my mother, did anything to make me feel this special lately. Tyrell handed me my sandwich on a paper plate while he prepared his food, we just sat there grinning at one another while listening to the bird's chirp and the wind softly blowing. We ate and talked about our plans now that he had a car.

He caught me off guard when he asked, "So, what are some of your plans when you graduate?"

Gosh, I was only in the eighth grade going to the ninth soon, and Tyrell was only going to be a sophomore. I didn't quite know what I wanted to do yet, always so worried about surviving my crazy ass household. It never occurred to me that my education was one of the only ways I could be freed from my evil family. So deep in my thoughts, I had totally forgotten about the beautiful picnic before me, I allowed my thoughts of my future to consume me. I had to choose quickly and stick to it if I ever wanted to get away from my family for good. Whit Tyrell to do; I felt lost for a minute. When Tyrell found me, I was floating away in my mind badgering myself to come up with a good enough answer when he tugged on my hand.

Feeling my frustration, he said, "Treasure it was only a question, take it easy, you don't have to worry about that now. That's the beauty of being young; we still have our parents to support us."

In my own thoughts, I knew he was only speaking for himself. I really did need to figure out a plan to escape my scandalous family, or I could be tortured longer that I had to be. We finished with our sandwiches, so Tyrell opened the container with our succulent dessert waiting to be devoured.

He wanted to change the subject, so he asked, "So why do you think Sabrina and Cassidy hate you so much?"

Not that the subject was any better, but at least someone was concerned. I thought for a moment before replying, "Ummm... to be honest; I think they are just evil and unhappy with themselves, so they look for my negatives to make them feel better about themselves. They are also probably jealous that they have to spend hours in the mirror to look normal and not like pale bumpy little creatures. Unlike myself, I just have to brush my teeth and wash my face, and I'm good."

I flashed my pearly withes and batted my eyelashes. Tyrell smiled and said, "Yeah, you got that right baby!"

Making me feel really confident about myself, I continued to talk crap about raggedy Sue and raggedy Anne. I continued, "They play horrible jokes on me and they always double team me. They also throw their sex lives in my face like it's something to be proud of. They really bother me, but I'm learning ways to ignore them as much as possible."

Tyrell, interested in the juicy gossip, urged me to go on, "So what does your mom say about all of this?"

Feeling sadness trying to invade my heart, I quickly answered, "My mom doesn't care about anybody but Ken. Ever since Ken brought himself and his demons to our house, my mom has been in a trance. My mom and I used to be so close; now, sometimes, I feel like I don't even know her anymore. I really miss all the fun we used to have together. I wish Ken would unleash the spell he has over her."

I looked down at the blanket to hide my sadness when Tyrell embraced me. I didn't want any pity, I just wanted to change the subject, but Tyrell still had questions. He was fishing for something, but I couldn't quite figure out what it was.

That quickly changed when Tyrell asked, "So what about Chino and Sénar, don't they have roles in this story?"

BINGO, he didn't want to know about Chino, he really wanted to know about Sénar. A little uncomfortable, I answered, "Chino pretty much stays to himself most of the time or is never home. He doesn't bother me at all. As a matter of fact, he's the angel in the little pack of demons." I paused for a moment; I wanted to choose my words carefully because the fear Sénar installed in me kept me from hating him but fueled the flames of hatred I had for Cassidy and Sabrina. I answered, "Oh, Sénar is tremendously nosey and extremely crazy. I just try to avoid him as much as possible."

I tried to make my answer as short as I could by shoving a huge strawberry in my mouth to keep it occupied. Suspicious, he stared at me before he continued,

"Well, that guy talks about you a lot."

A part of me wanted to break down and tell him the truth about Sénar harassing me in so many different ways and on so many different occasions. What stopped me was the fear of him blaming me for letting him get away with it or even that I secretly enjoyed it, since I never told anyone, not that anyone would care or listen. Tyrell could see that I was at a loss for words, so he decided to change the subject again, although he wanted to know all about Sénar. Tyrell started to talk about our future as if he could see it; I couldn't help but join his wishful thinking about our future without all the negatives present. I grabbed Tyrell's hand and went on the journey with him to Lala Land.

Tyrell asked with a funny accent, "Would you like some Moët Madame?"

I quickly answered, "Heck yeah!"

I anxiously grabbed my glass for him to pour me a cup, wondering what it tastes like and the effects it would have. Tyrell poured himself a glass, and we toasted to a loving future. I loved the way the bubbles from the Moët tickled and danced upon my taste buds. We talked and laughed while we drank; I was having an awesome time. The Moët was really starting to kick in, and I found myself thinking naughty thoughts and reminiscing on my experience in the shower this morning. I started licking my lips and holding my legs closed tightly as if to capture the excitement. Tyrell was lying on the side of me with his hands behind his head, looking sexier than ever, before he decided to roll over and place his hand on my stomach. He looked me in my eyes and asked if he could kiss me, already feeling excited.

I said, "Please do."

Without even having to think about it. The Moët playing with my emotions and kindling the flames to my lust; I allowed him to place his lips on mine. For some reason, his lips felt softer and warmer than ever before. My lips seemed to melt beneath his allowing a passage for his tongue to slip through. Although a little shocked, I was still at ease, permitting him to caress my breast, I lie there in pure ecstasy with my mind drifting off, leaving my body to take over. We lied there fondling each other exploring new territories, with both of our bodies reaching its peak Tyrell kissed me long and gently before rolling over on his back.

Tyrell said, "Wow, Treasure, you're so soft and lovely. I have to stop, or I was going to explode."

Not sure what he meant by that because I also was feeling like I was going to lose control. Tyrell asked if it was ok to ask me a personal question; I was still in quite a daze but still managed to say yes.

He then asked, "Are you still a virgin?"

Feeling a little offended, I embraced myself and answered, "Well, of course, I'm still a virgin, why?"

He replied, "Oh, well...I just wanted to know."

Now a little curious myself, I asked, "Why? Aren't you still a virgin?" He then answered, "No."

Confused, I didn't know what to say or exactly how I should feel. Suddenly the confusion went away when my buzz started to speak for me, "Well, sorry I'm not as experienced as you, but I would prefer to wait till the time is right." I said that as if I knew what the hell I was talking about. Whenever that was going to be, I kind of felt a little shallow when he replied,

"Well, I think you are right, besides I'm not as experienced as you think. I've had a couple of experiences, but only a couple."

Feeling a little jealous, I had to inquire, "A couple, meaning two or three?"

Tyrell began to answer, "Well, I.. " He paused, looked down, and then back at me, "I only had sex twice and oral sex once."

Shocked, I screeched, "Oral sex!"

He saw me wipe my lips with disgust and quickly responded, "No, no, no, I let this girl do it to me!"

Already highly disappointed, I was really starting to get upset. Tyrell saw that I was angry and started to explain himself by telling me that the girl he had sex with was older and that she had gone off to college somewhere really far. Then he told me that a girl with no age range and no name kept bugging him to give him oral sex, so he gave into temptation by allowing her to do it for him. He was very adamant in the girl bugging him to do a lot more, but he didn't want to have sex with her because he didn't have any feelings for her. I was very curious to whom the girl was, but he refused to tell me. We had to change the subject in order to enjoy the rest of our evening

Being that my buzz was still present from drinking most of the Moët, I didn't want anything else to mess the mood up. I accepted Tyrell's sexcapades and decided maybe we should have some of our own. I know I was only fourteen, but I really looked forward to losing my virginity to Tyrell. I was going to the ninth grade very soon, and now that he was going to have a car, we could spend a lot of time together over the summer. Savoring the taste of Tyrell's lips at the thought of us indulging in sexual activities and spending more time together, I couldn't help but think about the indescribable pleasures I experienced this morning again. I was so busy thinking about me and Tyrell I almost forgot we were there in the flesh. Tyrell grabbed my shoulder,

"Hey, what are you thinking about?" He asked with a silly grin as if he could read my thoughts from the expression on my face. Completely embarrassed and caught off guard, I started to stutter,

"Oh, uh um nothing.'"

Feeling caught thinking nasty thoughts, I started to giggle to release some of my tension. Tyrell just shook his head and asked,

"So are you ready to go, I don't want you to get in any trouble."

As if to burst the protective bubble that separated me from the reality of having to return home, my smile quickly turned upside down. Remembering that I was still a little Black girl named Treasure with a crazy-ass family, I sadly answered,

"Yeah, I guess you got a point."

He heard the reluctance in my voice and hugged me from behind to comfort me; he whispered in my ear, "Don't worry, we'll have much better nights in the future." With that reassurance, I was ready to face the negative forces that awaited me at my house.

Tyrell and I drove back to the house captured in our own thoughts; by the grins, on our faces, I'm pretty sure we were having similar thoughts. Before we pulled up onto our street as routine, we kissed and hugged each other and said goodnight. Thinking that driving onto our street with the lights off would help, we pulled into his driveway. I jumped out of the car and took one last look at Tyrell, feeling tempted to sneak another kiss, until I looked at my house to see a shadow in the window. Instead, I decided to run for my door. I waved to Tyrell once I reached my front door and disappeared into the house.

As soon as I entered the house, the hairs on the back of my neck raised. The Moët started to seep out of my pores, along with the sweat beads that invaded my forehead. Sénar was standing behind me with a stare of a scolding parent. I didn't have to turn around to know that he was standing behind me. Sénar grabbed my shoulder with such force he made me do a 360 degree turn around.

He then asked, "Where the fuck you been?" Scared shitless, I fumbled my words only to be interrupted, "You know what I don't even care, get the fuck out of my sight!"

As to be dismissed as the weakest link, I hurried up the steps without even looking back; I just couldn't endure the evil he had in his eyes. With my emotions in a whirl, I wanted to think positive thoughts, but Sénar made sure I went to sleep with guilt in my heart. Afraid of taking a shower, I went to bed reeking of Moët and excitement. Cassidy and Sabrina were sleeping, thank God, I took my clothes off, slipped into a T-shirt and some panties, and went to sleep.

The next morning, I woke up feeling a little groggy. I sat up in my bed, rubbing my eyes to erase the buildup that accumulated while I was asleep. Only to clearly see that Cassidy and Sabrina weren't there.

It was Sunday I debated with myself as if they were gone or lurking around the house somewhere. I searched for some sweats to throw on to confirm what time it was since I'm normally the first one awake. I opened the door with caution; I used my ears as a detective for movement and my eyes for any shadows that might be present. When I felt safe, I ran to the bathroom, almost stubbing my toe against the frame, trying to close the door behind me. I pulled my sweats and panties down and sat on the toilet. Still a little groggy, I rubbed the fog out of my eyes to see a burgundy discoloration in my underwear.

Flashes of the memory of the cruel joke Sénar and his evil sisters played on me, I panicked. I quickly grabbed a piece of tissue, wrapping it around my fingers while almost hoping it was a joke, afraid of what the next step would be if it wasn't. I wiped with urgency, trying to collect enough evidence of my possible introduction to womanhood. When I put the tissue before my eyes, it was full of red gook that I was more than sure wasn't ketchup. Nausea swept over me as I gasped at my discovery; my coochie was definitely going through some changes. I wasn't prepared for this at all. I raked my brain for the next step to take. I started to make a bundle of tissue to protect my panties from any more red dye. Then I remembered duh…. that's what maxi pads were for. Hoping and wishing there were some under the bathroom sink, for once, my wish was granted, but there definitely was a catch 22. They were brand spanking new and hadn't been opened yet. So that meant I had to open them, and one of the evil sisters would figure out it was me. Looking down at my underwear, I realized I had no choice. I wanted to hurry and brush my teeth and wash my face so that I could escape yet another reality. My stomach growling in anticipation for breakfast, I exited the bathroom with a blank expression. Still not knowing what awaited me downstairs, I prepared myself for pretty much anything.

When I reached the bottom of the steps, the aroma of food cooking taunted my stomach. I almost formed a smile, thinking it was my mother cooking one of her famous breakfasts that I loved so much.

I thought my mouth would hit the floor when I saw Sénar cooking in his basketball shorts and no shirt. Although my stomach was still growling, my first instinct was to run back up the steps, but Sénar sensing my presents turned around to face me and my confused expression.

He then spoke, "Although you really pissed me off last night, I figured I would make us breakfast since everyone is gone."

Lost for words, I just stood there afraid to move or say anything wrong since there was no one else here (not that it would matter), to interrupt any cruel intentions he might have in mind. He sensed my discomfort and told me to have a seat. Reluctantly, I walked over to the table to pull out a chair for myself. I knew it would only benefit me to play along if he was behaving like he was. I smelled bacon; I think eggs and a hint of toast. Not wanting to make the situation any more awkward than what it was, I tried to start a conversation,

"So, where did everyone go?"

He turned around as if he was happy to announce and replied, "They all went to the mall except for Chino, you know his nerdy ass went to the library."

I just looked at him with a blank expression, and he continued, "They probably assumed you didn't want to go, since you *never* wake up this late."

Never was definitely emphasized in his little comment. Feeling a little bitchy, I said, "Well, they were finally right about something."

He turned around with his eyes partially squinted, "Well, well, well, Treasure woke up on the wrong side of the bed this morning. After your drunken night, you would think you'd be full of smiles."

A little irritated with his sarcasm and the situation. I responded, "For your information, I had a lovely time last night until I had to return home to hell's house."

The silly grin he had on his face instantly turned into a smirk, "Well, I don't want to hear that shit; I could have given you a better night! Look, do you want breakfast or not?"

Cautious of my next remark, I had to soften up a little, "Yeah, why not? Besides, I don't want to argue."

He said, "Argue? Who said anything about arguing? You're the one that woke up with a stick up your ass!"

Little did he know it was more like something crawled up my coochie with sharp blades and went ballistic. Ok, a little grotesque, but I was still in complete shock. Caught in my thoughts, Sénar cleared his throat to gain back my attention. I snapped back into reality and looked in his direction to see that he was staring dead at me. Looking at his bare chest along with his naturally rippled stomach and muscular arms, had me shrug my shoulders then look away. Feeling a little guilty and naughty, I didn't want to give off the wrong impression. Sénar feeling a little offended as to have read my thoughts, he placed my plate down in front of me and said,

"Well, considering how late you were out last night, maybe something did go up your ass." He sat down across from me with accusing eyes, making me feel smaller than my fork.

Finally, grasping the meaning behind his statement, I quickly defended myself, "I'm not a little whore like your sisters, so don't get it twisted. Some people can have a good time without pouncing on each other. Besides, I'm still a virgin if you know what that means."

Treasure number two had come out once again to speak for me because I couldn't believe the words that seeped out of my mouth. Sénar looked like I had stabbed him with my fork. His eyes grew big, and he responded,

"Hot damn, you're feisty this morning, but I kinda like it!"

He looked down at his plate, grabbing his toast and arranging his bacon and eggs to make his sandwich, I could tell he was more than satisfied with my answer. I looked down at my plate, and I thought the conversation was over until he responded, "Just don't get beside yourself, little momma, cuz daddy would love to chastise you."

Feeling that I said enough, I let his comment bounce off and said my blessings over my food. I arranged my sandwich and took a bite;

the spices he used in the eggs made them spicy, but quite tasty. I didn't think eggs could be so bold; they were very different. I actually really liked them. To break the silence that usually took place when people are stuffing their faces, I decided to break the silence,

"Dang Sénar, I didn't know you could cook."

He got up to get some orange juice and turned around to say, "There's a lot you don't know about me." He said that with his famous smile.

He poured me a cup of orange juice and sat back down across from me, never taking his eyes off me for a second. I drank my orange juice and finished the last of my breakfast, and I looked up to catch Sénar, still gazing at me. Feeling a little uncomfortable, I grabbed my dishes and asked him for his; it was the least I could do since he cooked a hung-over woman breakfast. I washed the dishes while he cleaned the table. He asked with anticipation,

"Treasure, what are you doing today?"

I was at a loss for an answer, stammering a little. I replied, "Oh…. um well, I have some homework, and…….uh, I was probably going to the mall later."

Trying to sound busy, although I had no plans. He then responded, disappointed, "Oh, I guess well, maybe I'll ask Julie if she wants to go to the movies or something."

Trying to sound interested, I said, "Oh, that's cool, I hope you have fun."

He smacked his lips with frustration and said, "I guess you're going to the mall with your punk ass boyfriend."

A little upset, I said, "Dang, why does he have to be all that?"

Sénar looked at me like I was stupid and turned away to walk off. Really curious, I walked behind him to ask, "What's your problem, Sénar?"

He looked at me like I was a lost dog begging for food before he answered, "You just don't get it. Maybe you are a little girl like my sisters said…….whatever dude, I'm leaving."

Dismissing me with his hand as he grabbed the cordless phone. I stood there, dumbfounded for a minute before going to my room. When I got to my room, I grabbed a book by Sista Soldier called '*The Coldest Winter Ever*'; it was a really good book so far. I read until my eyes started to burn and decided to take a nap.

When I woke up, I emerged out of my room to see that everyone was still gone. I went downstairs to grab something to drink and called Tyrell.

He answered the phone, "Hey Treasure, I've been waiting for your call all day."

Shocked, I asked, "How did you know it was me?"

He quickly answered, "I'm a psychic." I smacked my lips with disbelief. He said, "I'm just kidding Treasure, I have caller ID silly."

Feeling quite stupid, I replied, "Oh."

He quickly changed the subject, "So how was your morning?"

Not wanting to go into specific details, I shortly answered, "Ok."

He then asked, "Do you want to come over for a little while?"

I answered, "Sure, only for a little while, I have to try and make it back before my mom gets home."

He then said, "Well, come on over."

I hung the phone up and ran across the street like a runaway slave. Tyrell opened the door with a huge grin on his face, "Wow, a dream come true living across the street from my hot girlfriend."

I couldn't help but blush, "Oh, stop it Tyrell, you're so silly."

He moved to the side to let me in and followed me around with his eyes. He asked, "Are you hungry?"

Remembering the breakfast Sénar cooked for me that just happened to wear off during my nap. I answered, "Yeah, I am kind of hungry."

Knowing damn well, I was starving and couldn't wait to taste what chef #2 was going to prepare. I was starting to feel like Queen Sheba when he brought our lunch; it was a Tombstone supreme pizza freshly baked. He placed it on the table in front of us, along with some sodas for us to drink. We ate while we watched reruns of *Fresh Prince*, laughing at Will's crazy ass the whole time. Occasionally on commercials, I would catch Tyrell staring at me out of the corner of my eye like Sénar would often stare at me. I started to ask him if there was something on my face until he rushed me. Passionately kissing me while squeezing my breast, I just laid there, allowing him to have his way with me. Fondling me and licking my lips, I was in a blissful state filled with burning lust. Kissing me one last time before tugging at his pants and trying to pull himself together, he looked at me and said,

"I'm so sorry, Treasure, you're just so sexy, pretty and sweet, I just can't help myself. Am I making you uncomfortable?"

Feeling my erect nipples press against my shirt, I sat there trying to think of an answer. Tyrell assuming that he was making me uncomfortable said,

"All you have to do is tell me if I'm moving too fast, I'll slow down, I promise."

Realizing he was talking to me and still waiting on an answer, I quickly opened my mouth, "Ummm, it's fine." Noticing the time, I continued to reassure him, "No, really, it's fine. I really care about you, and I think you're sexy too."

Embarrassed, I still quickly grabbed him and kissed him before running towards the door with him following behind me. He grabbed my hand and kissed it, "I'll be there tomorrow to pick you up 7:00 AM on the dot." He said that beaming a bright cheesy smile, I smiled back, nodding my head in a yes gesture and left to go home.

Seeing that all the lights were all off, I figured no one made it home yet and felt a major relief. I opened the door to see Julie on top of Sénar grinding and sticking her tongue down his throat. Sénar realizing that it was me pushed Julie off him as if I was his wife catching him in the act of infidelity. Julie hit the floor, trying my best to compress my giggles; I pretended as if they weren't just humping each other and managed just to smile. Before dismissing myself, I couldn't help but look at Julie's expression on her face; it was a mixture of hurt, anger, and confusion. With that, I hurried up the stairs noticing that Sénar never took his eyes off me the whole time, as if he were a lion snacking on prey until he saw something tastier. Feeling both worried and flattered, I entered my room with the intention of going straight to bed; today was an interesting day.

It wasn't long before Sénar dismissed Julie and ran up the stairs to knock at my door to harass me. I rubbed my eyes while I stood in the doorway to indicate that I was tired. I could smell the alcohol on Sénar's breath along with the stench of smoke. He clumsily put his arm on the door and asked if he could come in as if he really cared what my answer was. Looking at him, I could tell that he was extremely intoxicated, I quickly said,

"No, Sénar I'm going to sleep. Have you been drinking?"

He grabbed me and stuck his tongue so far down my throat; I could have given him the results to a sobriety test. He picked me up, almost throwing me on my bed and started aggressively fondling me. Sénar was sucking on my bottom lip while slightly biting it and forcefully trying to pull my breast out of my shirt. I panicked, trying to push him off me, but he was much stronger, not even budging. He was moaning and calling my name as if he was worshiping me; I could feel his penis harden through the padding that protected my coochie. I felt his hands travel down my stomach to the top of my pants, making me lock my lips and squeeze my legs together as tight as I could. So, he started nibbling at my neck and the top of my breast. He grew even more excited when he saw that my nipples had betrayed me once again and tried to expose them by trying to rip my clothes off.

I thought I would faint until we both heard the front door close. Relieved, my legs rested, and I let down my weak forces, while Sénar listened to clues as to who it might be. When he realized it was just Chino from the quiet entrance, he grinded his now fully erected penis against my padded coochie and squeezed my breast so hard, I threatened to scream. To keep me from screaming, Sénar occupied my mouth with his tongue while continuing to grind and squeeze until he shivered like a wet puppy on a cold day. It grew immensely hot in between my legs as if he had released some hot fluid in his pants, Sénar quickly got up and ran out of my room. He just left me there feeling like a victim; I checked my clothes to see if they were intact, grabbed a nightgown careful not to forget my bra and panties, and ran to the bathroom. I took my clothes off willingly and got into the bathtub, not caring that I was bleeding like a butchered sheep. I stayed in the water until I heard a mixture of voices. They were home, never feeling so relieved to hear my evil stepsisters voices I jumped out of the bathtub to get dressed. I hesitated to grab another maxi from the recently opened pack, but I grabbed it anyway.

While getting dressed, I overheard the excitement in Sabrina's voice as she talked about the party, they were going to throw in a couple of weeks for the end of the school year. I opened the door to hear Sabrina curiously ask,

"Where's Sénar?"

Wanting to tell him about the party. Chino looked at me and said, "That nigga is sleeping like a baby."

Sabrina looked at me and rolled her eyes. I just walked past her like she was a fly on the wall. I could feel all their eyes on me as I went into the dungeon, we called our room. I went to sleep quickly to avoid having to listen to Cassidy and Sabrina's bullshit. I couldn't wait to be freed by Tyrell's smile and presence. I went to bed, trying to avoid thinking about Sénar's drunken behavior or his behavior in general.

Chapter 6

The next day I woke up at a quarter to 6:00 trying to get an early start before my evil fake sisters took over the bathroom. I crept around the room, trying to find a cute outfit, then brushed my teeth and washed my face, and rushed downstairs to call Tyrell. Tyrell answered the phone, sounding a little groggy,

"Hey Treasure.......did I oversleep?"

I answered, "No, I'm just up a little earlier; you want me to call you later?"

He snapped out of his sleepy stage and answered, "No, no, no, just come over. I'll get up and get dressed."

I asked, "Right now?"

He said, "Yeah, right now."

With that said, I grabbed a shiny red apple and rushed over to Tyrell's house. Tyrell opened the door in his boxers, I tried not to look down, but when I saw his manhood rising to the right side of his boxers, I had to grab my mouth in order to avoid making a fool of myself. When Tyrell saw my reaction to is morning erection, he blushed in embarrassment and said,

"Oh, I'm sorry I can't help that it's up every morning before me."

I just giggled and shook my head as he moved aside to let me in. Once I was inside, Tyrell closed the door and asked if I wanted to come upstairs. Secretly wanting to see his room anyway, I said, "Sure."

He led the way upstairs, and I anxiously followed. When he opened the door to his room, I was pleasantly surprised to see that his room was cleaner than my room and definitely cleaner than Sénar's and Chino's. He had huge posters of Janet Jackson and Beyoncé along with a bunch of other sexy no name women plastered all over his walls. His clothes neatly placed on hangers, shoes perfectly arranged by colors beneath his clothes, and his dresser carefully organized with his colognes. My eyes darted all over the dresser, and I spotted a picture of myself that Tyrell cut out of the yearbook. I was flattered to see that he had a picture of me posted in his neat little world. Tyrell took this opportunity to jump in the shower as I just sat on the bed and laid back. Allowing myself to get comfortable, I couldn't help but daydream about my and Tyrell's future together. I was in a trance that was soon broken by Tyrell entering the room with a towel around his waist and little droplets of water plastered to his bare chest.

Feeling warm and tingly all over I braced myself as he looked me in the eyes with that mysterious grin, he often gave me when he was thinking something naughty. Being that it was so early, we had a lot of time on our hands; I started to get nervous thinking about how we were going to spend that idle time. To break the tension, he turned to the closet to look for an outfit to wear when he found one, he laid it across the bed and sat down next to me. With the towel still wrapped around his waist, I was nervous, yet excited at the same time. I looked at him in his eyes and proceeded to kiss him passionately, surprised at my aggression, I continued my promiscuous curiosity. Caressing his chest with my hands feeling extremely naughty and bold, I slowly eased my way on top of him. I could feel his manhood harden against my thighs. I couldn't help but place my hand upon his throbbing erection. A memory of Sénar and his sexual rage flashed through my mind making me even more enticed. Tyrell grabbed my fluffy booty cheeks, squeezing them while moaning as I suckled on his neck and fondled his private parts. My heart was racing as our sexual regions were gyrating and pulsating against one another. Tyrell's moans turned high pitch as he squeezed harder and harder until it felt like a fire was unleashed between us. Tyrell going through some kind of episode jumped up and headed for the bathroom while I tried to pull myself together. Tyrell came out of the bathroom with a huge grin on his face, smiling from ear to ear. I couldn't help but break out with my own silly grin as we headed downstairs.

He asked if I was hungry, and of course, I said, "Yeah." He put some waffles in a toaster and some frozen sausages in the microwave. We ate our breakfast and jumped in the car to journey our way to school. On the way to school, Tyrell brought up the summer and how he wanted to have a lot of fun since he had a car and a part-time job. I told him that sounded like a great idea and that I couldn't be happier to spend my summer doing anything else. He told me he couldn't wait till I came to his school because he would be able to see me all day. Feeling really flattered, I grabbed his hand and kissed him on his cheek. He had no idea what was in store for us because we all would be going to the same school; me, him, Sabrina, Cassidy, Chino, and worst of all, Sénar. Hell, I didn't even know what was in store I just knew it was going to be a lot of drama.

We pulled up to the school to see Sabrina and her little clan of skanks standing in front of his school, trying to make some extra lunch money. Tyrell and I looked at one another with the same look of disgust on our faces. We both didn't care that they were standing there; we leaned into each other and kissed like we wouldn't see each other till next year. I smiled at him and said,

"Ok, I'll see you later."

He reached into his pocket and gave me a five-dollar bill and said, "Here, this will keep you from standing in front of the school."

We both started laughing because we must have been thinking the same thing. I got out of the car feeling really special. I walked past Sabrina, and her friends with my head held high, smirking at their pathetic attempts to be cute. Of course, Sabrina had to open her mouth and say,

"That bitch ain't' got shit on me. If I wanted Tyrell, I could take him. That nigga doesn't know he messin' with a little girl when he could have a woman."

Her and her friends started laughing, but I didn't want to spoil my good mood by interacting with Sabrina's stupid ass, so I kept walking and ignored her. Besides, I knew Tyrell didn't want her ugly skinny ass anywhere near him. I was confident enough to know that he had more class than that. School went by kind of fast, being that the end of the school year was coming up; we were preparing for tests and school activities. I couldn't wait for when the school year was over so that me and Tyrell could have the whole summer to spend together. I was daydreaming when I was interrupted by the school intercom,

"Eighth graders get ready for the yearbook nominations! Look your best tomorrow; you could be on the front of the yearbook and not even know it! We have lots of voting to do, so get your friends to vote for you."

With that said, the class burst out into groups of chatter. I continued to daydream when this boy yelled out, "Hell yeah, Treasure should be voted for best looking!"

Shocked, I turned around to see the majority of the male classmates nodding their heads in agreement. I was flattered, I had no idea anybody noticed me I just smiled and gathered my books so when the bell rang, I could jet out of here like the matrix. When the last bell rang for school to get out the group of boys were eyeing me as I walked towards the door, I heard one of them say,

"Yeah that's Sabrina's sister, she doesn't look nothing like Sabrina but she still fine as hell."

Feeling like an object on display, I hurried to the school gates to wait for Tyrell to come and pick me up. One of the boys walked up to me and asked, "Aye, you got a boyfriend?"

I said, "Yeah, I got a boyfriend."

Trying to avoid prolonging the conversation, I started to look for Tyrell pulling up.

He then said, "My name is David, and I know your boyfriend don't go here; whoever he is, he's a lucky boy."

He said that and smiled at me, I said, "Thank you."

To avoid being rude. Tyrell pulled up as he was turning to walk away, and I jumped in the car and closed the door. David had turned around to see who I got in the car with I looked down to avoid eye contact. I turned to see Tyrell looking at me with a puzzled look on his face.

Tyrell asked, "Who was that guy?"

I started giggling, "Just some boy who wanted to know if I had a boyfriend."

Tyrell said, "Well, what did you tell him?"

I looked at him like he was crazy, "Duh, I told him yes I had a boyfriend, what do you think I have amnesia?"

He looked at me like I was crazy, "Well, I ain't ever seen you talk to no boys when I was going there, so I think I have a right to be concerned. Besides, he sure was all up in the car."

I didn't say anything afraid I would say the wrong thing. He seemed to let the jealousy subside and said, "Well, as long as he knows, and you know you're, my woman, that's all that matters."

He said that with a cocky smirk and slouched in his driver seat like a gangster. I just chuckled a little and gave him my batting eyelashes instead of a comment. We drove home listening to the radio; it felt good to belong to someone and have them be possessive over me besides Sénar. When we got home, Tyrell kissed me and told me to call him as soon as I got myself settled in. I agreed to do so and went home a little worried about the different possibilities with Sénar and Sabrina.

I went inside the house with a huge smile, trying to avoid both Sénar and Sabrina. However, things didn't work out that way, Sénar came out of the kitchen the minute I walked in the door. Chewing on an apple and looking at me like he would pounce on me if I tried to move.

He quickly asked, "Where the fuck were you at this morning?"

At lost for words because he and I both knew where I was, I just looked at him with a dumbfounded expression on my face. Feeling like I was in trouble, I was afraid to move or say anything. Sénar just standing there staring at me made me feel extremely uncomfortable, I didn't know what was going through his mind. Sabrina came through the door and said,

"You know what Treasure, your fat ass should be the one walking, maybe I'll steal your boyfriend so we can watch you walk home."

I looked at her happy to break eye contact with Sénar and said, "You know what Sabrina, I'm tired of your ass speakin' up on my man. I know your skinny butt is jealous, but you are going to have to get over it. Besides, Tyrell doesn't like whores who have been passed around like a chain letter."

Sabrina's mouth dropped open and said, "Bitch, you are not all that! You are overweight, and your hair is nappy as hell! And if you know like I know, you would watch your back because, like I said, any man in their right mind would rather be with me than you any day!"

Filled with anger, I said, "Well, prove it until then, keep lying to yourself!"

I took this opportunity to run up the stairs and escape Sénar's wrath. I went into the room and slammed the door behind me. Thank God there weren't any demons waiting in my room; I just wanted to relax without hearing Sénar or Sabrina's bull crap. I changed into some more comfortable clothing and called Tyrell to get my mind off of the people who seemed to be trying to destroy my life on a daily basis.

Tyrell answered the phone with a jolly tone, "Hey baby, what are you doin'?"

I answered, "Oh nothing, I just changed into some comfortable clothes, and I'm in my room chilling, trying to avoid Sabrina's stupid ass."

He laughed, "I don't know how you do it. I don't know if I would rather live in pure silence with no siblings or in a house with the evil rejects of Brady Bunch."

We both just laughed, but I assured him he would rather live in silence. Starting to feel a little sad, I told him, "I would give anything to have my home and relationship with my mom back to the way it used to be before Ken's family came into the picture. I mean, me and my mom used to be such good friends, now I don't even know who she is anymore. That's not even the worst of it because I don't know who she will become. She used to be so independent, confident, and strong before Ken came to cast a spell upon her. I would never imagine my life or my mom's life would be disoriented because of some man."

Tyrell was extremely quiet on the other end of the phone. I asked, "Are you there, Tyrell?"

He quickly responded, "Yes, Treasure, baby, I'm here. I was just listening to your sorrows; I'm so sorry, I never thought about how much pain you were in. I always thought maybe you were just dealing with the everyday problems of getting along with siblings that everybody goes through when they have a mixed family. But not only have you gained enemies in this process, but you've lost your best friend."

There was a silent pause for a minute as reality started to sink in for the both of us. I could feel my eyelids burning with the tears that were stored behind them. Tyrell trying to make me feel better said, "Don't worry, Treasure everything will be ok. Have you tried talking to your mom and telling her how you feel?"

Not wanting to answer afraid of my own answer, I said, "No, my mom doesn't seem to have time. As a matter of fact, she doesn't seem like she lives in the same world as I do. The only person she seems to care about is Ken. She left me to fend for myself; I can't even think the last time we made eye contact. Look, this is getting depressing, there's got to be something else to talk about."

Tyrell said, "Yeah, you're right. Besides, it was just a suggestion you'll do it when the time is right... So, can you get out?"

I answered, "Well, I don't know, let me see what's going on, and I'll give you a call back to let you know."

Tyrell agreed to wait on my call. I went downstairs to see what was going on and was shocked to see my mom in the kitchen, getting ready to prepare dinner. I hurried to run back upstairs and called Tyrell back, "Hey, I was just calling to tell you that I'll see you in the morning because my mom is cooking, and I kind of want to talk to her while I have the opportunity."

He said, "That's cool. I'll see you tomorrow. Good luck with your mom. Goodnight."

I appreciated his understanding and said, "Thanks, goodnight."

I walked into the kitchen and said, "Hey mom, how are you doing today?"

She turned around to look at me like she almost couldn't recognize my voice. She answered, "Oh, I'm fine; thanks for asking."

I was contemplating what I would say next when I just blurted, "Well, aren't you going to ask how I'm doing? How come we don't talk anymore? Did you completely forget about me? Is there something I've done wrong?"

Almost losing my breath at the fifth question, I was able to catch it when I saw the lost look on her face. She looked like the naive teenage girl she had turned into since Ken's been around. My mother turned her back to me to continue preparing dinner as if to paint a smile on her face; she then turned back around to say,

"Well, Treasure, I assume you're doing well, since you defiantly still see Tyrell after I specifically asked you not to. We don't talk anymore since you run to Tyrell's house every chance you get. No, I haven't forgotten about you. Is that all you think about now. And yes, you have done something wrong you've refused to get along or except Ken and his family."

Tears fluidly rushed to the nearest exits of my eyes, "Well, obviously you were listening when I asked you all those questions, but you couldn't possibly be listening when you gave me the answers that Lucifer helped you come up with!"

She snapped at me, "Look, little girl, I have spent the last fourteen years of my life raising you, and I finally found a man that wants to be with me. I'm not going to give him up for anyone, especially a self-centered little brat like yourself."

Clearly, she was bringing Tyrell up to justify her behavior, but I don't know who she was or who she had become. All I know is that I have lost total respect and liking that I had for her now; I only love her because she is my mother. I really didn't want to make her my enemy, but she obviously wanted to be since she had no regard for my feelings, whatsoever. To avoid a heated argument, I picked my face up off the floor and went to the living room to watch TV to find an escape from my reality. I almost wish I hadn't even asked her all those questions. I would rather wonder than to be told to go fuck myself, in less colorful words. Sénar saw me in the living room watching TV and decided to come in there to join me.

I'm not sure if I sighed out loud, but he scratched his head and asked, "So what is the occasion, don't you have a second home?"

I looked at him, "Must you always come to me with sarcasm or anger; don't you have anything else better to do like …..Julie?"

He looked at me and smiled, "I'd rather do you!"

I quickly replied, "Well, as flattering as that is supposed to be, I think I'll past."

He smirked, "I'll get you to comply one day, you'll see." He said that like a fortune teller rather than a threat.

I just looked at him like he was speaking another language and continued to watch TV. Ken came home, and as if she had radar, my mother came running out of the kitchen to grab his jacket and keys like some desperate servant. Sénar and I watched them like they were plastered on the TV.

Without a hello or a thank you, Ken asked, "Is the dinner ready?"

My mom replied, "Oh yes, honey, it's almost done. I'm just waiting on the bread."

Ken gruffly said, "Well, hurry up and bring it upstairs; I'm tired." With that said, Ken nodded his head at us and went up the stairs.

Sénar continued to watch TV, and I was still in awe the way he just treated my mother. Disgusted, I asked Sénar, "Would you treat your woman like that?"

He sighed before answering, "No. Not if it were you, and I didn't have to chase you around the world."

Feeling that the conversation was going in the wrong direction, I almost regretted asking him that until he said, "If you're wondering why my dad treats your mom like that, it's because that's how he treats all of his women, till he gets tired of them. What can I say? He's a pimp. So no, I don't want to be like him, Treasure."

I rolled my eyes at him and said, "Good because I wouldn't let no man treat me like that anyway."

I got up off the couch to go make myself a plate, and Sénar followed me. He sat down at the table, then said, "Make my plate woman!"

We both looked at each other and started laughing. I made his plate only because he made me breakfast the other day, and we sat down and ate together. "Why didn't Treasure's black ass make our plates?"

Sabrina asked with an attitude with Cassidy standing behind her.

I retorted, "Maybe because you have two brittle hands and only one person in this house has a maid, and it damn sure ain't you."

Sabrina smacked her lips and put her hand up, "Whatever bitch, you'll end up just like your mom, cuz y'all ain't cute like us."

I smirked at her when I replied, "Yeah, I'm sure that's why he's with my mom and not yours." Sabrina looked at me like she wanted to cry.

Cassidy replied to me with the nastiest attitude she could muster, "Why don't you shut up! You don't know shit! Sabrina's mom died, and you need to watch your mouth before you get slapped in it."

Sénar looked down at his plate as if he knew I had crossed the line. I felt a little guilty and said, "I'm sorry, I didn't know-"

Sabrina cut me off, "I don't want your stupid apology, maybe your mom will end up the same way!"

70

Sabrina turned her back to me as she prepared her food. I felt way too much tension as I raked my plate and ran upstairs. I called Tyrell to tell him goodnight and forced myself to go to sleep before Cassidy and Sabrina came upstairs.

The next morning, I got up at my normal time to get dressed for school and somehow still managed to get up before everyone else. I called Tyrell to see if he was up and if it was ok for me to come over. He said I could come over to eat breakfast only if I was going to be a good girl. I hung up the phone with a huge grin on my face thinking about how naughty I was yesterday and left for his house. I knocked on Tyrell's door, almost hoping to see him in his boxers again, but to my disappointment, he was fully clothed. He invited me in and led me to the kitchen where our breakfast was hot and ready to eat. He made breakfast burritos filled with bacon, eggs, and salsa. The burritos were delicious to my surprise, and I was more than satisfied. We ate and talked about the school year ending and what different activities that were going to take place at our schools. I told him about the yearbook and the dance that was coming up. I also told him I had no intention of going to since we couldn't bring anybody that didn't attend our school. He told me if I wanted to, I could go, but I explained that I would prefer to spend it with him. We finished up and headed for the door holding hands.

Once I got to school, I noticed everybody chattering with excitement about the yearbook nominations. I could care less, so I decided not to vote. By lunchtime, everyone that was nominated for the different categories would be announced at lunch, and people would be called to take pictures. I went to my class and refused to get involved with any conversation or questions involving the yearbook. I went to lunch happy the day was halfway over. When I was almost finished with lunch, one of the popular girls approached the stage. My eyes couldn't help but roll to the back of my head when she cleared her throat and announced that she would be giving the results. The first category was Most popular, the second was best dressed and, third was best personality, Sabrina's name had been called for all three categories. I was highly disgusted and decided to gather my things when I heard her say the next category,

"Best looking the girl with the highest vote is Treasure Lee, then Sabrina Brady ....."

She went on and on with the list. Still, in shock, I hadn't realized that she had called my name a second time for most likely to succeed. I wasn't shocked Sabrina's name wasn't called for that one. I dropped my head and rushed out of the cafeteria to my next classroom. It was fourth period, and they were going to start calling the people that were nominated for the yearbook categories because I was towards the end, I knew I had time to let everything sink in. I thought about Sabrina's ignorant ass being there and me having to take a picture with her. Just the thought of having to deal with her made me irritated. I knew Sabrina wasn't happy about me being nominated for anything, and she would try her best to start something. I wasn't looking forward to her drama, but it did feel good to know that people found me attractive and thought I had a bright future ahead of me. Lost in my thoughts, I heard my name and others to go to the library for pictures.

So, I gathered my things and headed to the library while trying to avoid eye contact with anyone. When I arrived at the library, Sabrina and all her little girlfriends were already there, forming their circle of bullshit. When they noticed that I walked in, Sabrina started laughing, "Um. You could leave; they made a mistake. They thought it was the blackest and the most stupidest."

Her and her friends continued to laugh. I just looked at them like they were speaking a different language and found a spot as far away from them as possible. When everybody they had called arrived, the photographers told all the nominees from the best-looking category to position their selves for a picture. I reluctantly walked toward the group of girls I hated and the popular boys to be awkwardly placed somewhere in the picture. Trying my best not to focus on all the laughter and snickering Sabrina's crowd was producing, I found a spot next to one of the cutest boys in the school. His name was Riley, and he gave me a welcoming smile and looked at Sabrina, giving her a disgusted look. We took three pictures before moving to the next topic. Because you actually needed to have brains to be in the next picture, Sabrina nor anyone in her crowd were nominated. Riley just happened to be one of the people who was nominated for this subject. Sabrina and her friends were instructed to leave.

Feeling a little bitchy, I blurted, "Too bad there wasn't a category for the sluttiest because you and your friends would have been runners up."

Riley and the rest of the guys that were still lingering started to laugh harder than I expected being that they probably knew from firsthand experience. We took the pictures and returned to our classes. I couldn't wait till school was over so I could see my baby, Tyrell. Finally, the bell rang, and all I could think about was getting into the car with Tyrell. As flattering as it was to be nominated for something, I was glad the school year was over I looked forward to spending the summer with Tyrell.

It was early June when our summer started, and Tyrell would spend his mornings working while I tried my best to avoid Ken's offspring. Tyrell came up with a pretty good idea for me to go to summer school, so both our mornings would be filled with positive activities. I agreed to pretty much anything if that meant escaping my household. Besides, I got a head start on some of the ninth-grade curriculum and how high school functioned. Tyrell would pick me up after school on his lunch break, and we would go back to his job. Tyrell worked at the movie theatre, and I would sneak into movies until Tyrell was off work. When he got off, we usually grabbed something to eat and spent the rest of the afternoon talking and laughing. Every time I returned home, I avoided everyone by reading or doing homework from summer school. One day after Tyrell and I returned home from hanging out; I entered the house to see that it was quiet and vacant. A sense of relief came over me, and I hummed all the way to my room, only to hear a quiet moaning coming from Sénar and Chino's room. I couldn't help but be nosey, so I went closer to see if I could get an idea of what was going on.

I got closer to their room, close enough to hear Sénar clearly asking, "Yeah, you like this shit, don't you! What's my name? What's my name?"

I then heard a young female's voice reply, "Uhhhhh, ohhhh Sénar!"

I could hear a smacking noise; I quickly grabbed my mouth to keep from being heard and ran into my room. Confused, shocked, and a little worried, my mixed emotions made it hard for me to make a clear decision on what I wanted to do. I didn't want Sénar to know I heard them or that I was even home. So, I went to my room, closed the door quietly, and picked a book to read. I chose to read a book called *G Spot; it* started off as such a good book I found myself lost in what seemed like another world. I was rudely interrupted by Sénar, uninvited, opening my door with a huge grin on his face. Hesitant to acknowledge him, it was hard to ignore the silly grin that occupied his face, making him look like an animated character.

I figured his face had to hurt from the exaggerated smile he finally managed to ask, "How long have you been here?"

I looked at him like he was annoying me, "I've been here long enough if you must know."

As to read between the lines, he started laughing and said, "Well, you know you could have been in there, but you are always playing hard to get."

Before I could respond, he closed the door leaving me with a mouth full of words I had to swallow. I started to think about his comments and gestures and wondered if he was serious or was it one of his playful antics. Careful not to go too deep in thought about it, I went to bed that night wondering what was to come.

Chapter 7

This summer flew by so quickly with summer school and my escapades with Tyrell. He and I had become very close, allowing our relationship to mature. Exploring new territories and breaking a couple of boundaries. Tyrell and I were ready to start the new school year together. He tried his best to explain to me that being a freshman sucked and that he would do everything he could to make it easier for me. Feeling confident, I explained to him that I would be fine, especially since high school was versatile in activities and age. I looked forward to the change and decided I would do everything I could to avoid my unwanted step-siblings, especially Sabrina. Apparently, Sabrina was still highly upset about me being nominated because she still talked crap every chance she got. I had to ignore her during the summer to avoid physically hurting her since she never really gave me a chance to talk. Both Sabrina and Cassidy made sure I spent most of my summer away.

I woke up Sunday morning to the phone ringing; I hurried to the phone having a feeling it was Tyrell. I picked up the phone and said, "Hello?"

Tyrell sounding eager to talk, "Hey Treasure, get dressed, we're going out in approximately thirty minutes."

Careful not to burst his bubble, "You do remember that we have to go to school tomorrow, right?"

He sighed, "I know."

He replied like a disappointed child. He quickly regained his happiness, "Well, don't worry, you'll love this surprise!"

Letting my guard down, I was convinced that I should be happy getting dressed to be on my way to Tyrell's house. I hurried to the room to get dressed. When I opened the door, I heard Sabrina and Cassidy raving about their new wardrobe, Ken and my mother took them to get. They were trying to make me jealous but being that I had never been a materialistic person, it didn't bother me as much as they wanted it to. Deep down inside, I was still upset that my mother made sure those brats had clothes when they are just as skinny as they were the year before. My mother didn't even consider me, and that hurt, making me realize that I needed a job soon. Being that I matured in many ways, I did need some undergarments and maybe some new shirts so that I wouldn't have cleavage in everything I wore. I didn't even want to dwell on that, I just got my things and headed down the steps. When I got downstairs, Ken was sitting on the couch for one of the first times that I could recall. He looked at me like I was some stranger descending from the stairs.

Not knowing exactly what to do or what to say, I just stood there for a minute until he said, "Good morning, Treasure."

A little shocked, I quickly said, "Good morning Ken."

While heading for the door. Ken shrieked, "Wait Treasure!" I hesitated to turn around to face him. He said, "Hey, your mother and I took the girls shopping, and you weren't here, so did you want to go?"

Hoping he didn't mean with him, I said, "Well, there's a couple of things I need that I can get while I'm out today."

Hopefully, insinuating that I had plans to go anyway. He went into his wallet and pulled out two crisp bills with the face of Benjamin Franklin in the middle of them and said, "Well, hopefully, this will cover what you want, and if not, all you have to do is ask."

In awe, because Ken never really said much to me, I accepted the money and gave him a dry thank you and headed for the door. My mind in a whirl I crossed the street to Tyrell's house with the money in my pocket.

Tyrell opened the door with a huge smile on his face. "Are you ready to go?" He asked with so much enthusiasm I couldn't help but giggle before saying,

"Yes, I'm ready."

We jumped into his car with smiles on our faces, and our eyes filled with anticipation. "Where are we going?" I asked.

He said, "I'm not telling, you'll see."

With that said, I just lay back in my seat and allowed myself to relax. I couldn't help thinking about Ken and his vain effort to make me feel like he really cared and just why my own mother didn't care enough to be the one to make sure I got my school clothes. I could feel myself getting a little angry, so I switched the channel in my brain to what Tyrell had in mind. We pulled up to the mall, and I thought what could be so great and surprising about the mall.

We got out, and Tyrell asked, "Soooo, where's your favorite place to shop?"

Not catching on, I replied, "I don't know, I never really thought about it. I don't come to the mall that often."

He said, "Well, don't worry, I will help you find some outfits and take you to every store in here until you're satisfied."

Confused, I asked, "How did you know I had money to shop?"

Tyrell looked at me, "Well, I didn't know you had money, but even if you did, I'm taking my baby girl shopping. You can get anything you want, just promise not to break me." He said with a sarcastic smile.

I was stunned, first Ken's unexplained generosity, and now Tyrell wants to take me on a shopping spree. I needed to pinch myself to make sure I wasn't dreaming. Tyrell saw my confused expression and said, "Look, just save the money you have. I've been saving all summer for this, and I've been waiting to do something really special for you. Don't worry; I won't go broke. I managed to save a lot of money."

Still feeling a little awkward, I couldn't help but smile at the idea of Tyrell wanting to spoil me rotten. I loosened my butt cheeks a little and decided to have some fun. We went to store after store playing dress-up. I tried on a bunch of different outfits watching Tyrell's eyes light up at the sight of me in all the latest gear, flaunting my new curves and pearly whites. We were having so much fun we lost track of time, almost forgetting we were just kids with some extra money. It was getting late; we had so many bags; it was time to go put them in the car and go back in for one more round. We placed the bags in the car and went back into the mall to finish shopping.

Tyrell asked, "So we have so many clothes what else is there to get?"

Almost feeling a little embarrassed, I replied, "Well, I need some underclothes, and maybe a couple of pairs of shoes..... But I have some money; I'll get that stuff."

Tyrell looked at me like I was crazy, "Oh, hell no, I definitely want to buy the lucky garments that get to touch your most intimate body parts."

Blushing and feeling a little naughty, "Well, you won't be so lucky to see what they look like now, but we'll work something out."

He giggled and urged me to go to the lingerie first. We went to Fredrick's and a couple of other stores to get undergarments. I got something special without Tyrell noticing; I was going to surprise him one day. I got some sandals and a couple pairs of sneakers, and we were done shopping for the day. Tyrell and I wobbled to the car with the remaining bags and gladly rested our exhausted feet once we got in the car. We were drained of energy but managed to stop at Chilli's to get some food and talk about how excited we were about going to school tomorrow.

After eating we journeyed our way back to our homes with our bellies full and our bodies tired, Tyrell said, "Thank you so much I really enjoyed myself. I can't explain to you enough how much fun I had today."

I smiled, "Tyrell, you really made me feel special today."

He looked me in my eyes and said, "You have no idea how lucky I am to have a girl like you. This is only the beginning of the things I want to do for you. You mean so much to me, I don't ever want to see you suffer, not even in your own home. You don't deserve to be neglected or abused in any way. I'm going to do my best to take care of you."

We hugged and kissed like it was going to be our last time seeing one another. I told him I would call him first thing in the morning. We kissed one more time, and we got out with so many bags, I didn't know how I would get all of them in the house by myself. So, I thought I would be bold and asked,

"Hey Tyrell, you want to help me bring these in the house?"

Confused Tyrell asked, "Are you sure, Treasure?"

I replied, "Yeah, there's no way I can get all this stuff in by myself, besides what's the worst that could happen?"

I thought of a million things that could go wrong, but I didn't care too much, I did it anyway. We got to the door, and I took a deep breath before opening the door to see Sabrina, Cassidy, Sénar, and Chino sitting in the living room watching TV. Everyone turned their attention towards me and Tyrell holding more bags than Santa's helpers. Trying to pretend everyone was invisible, I directed Tyrell to bring the bags up to the bottom of the steps. We put the bags down, and we headed for the door as everyone avoided speaking to each other. Tyrell and I went outside to say goodnight. We joyfully kissed before turning away to go our separate ways. Reluctant to face everybody and their questioning looks, I hurried in the house to put my clothes away. Having to walk past Sabrina and Cassidy's snickering along with Sénar's dirty looks. I just avoided eye contact with everyone, even Chino. I walked to the stairway and struggled to pick up as many bags as my arms would permit. I hauled all the stuff I could up the steps to my room, not hesitating to drop all the stuff in the middle of the floor.

I had to catch my breath and try to muster up enough strength to get the rest of the stuff remaining. As I walk towards the door, I saw Sénar carrying the rest of the stuff towards my room with a puzzled look on his face. Secretly grateful for the help that saved me two more trips up and down the steps, I knew the interrogation process was going to begin. Sénar dropped the bags on the floor, never taking his eyes off me.

He asked, "What the hell is all of this? You won the lotto or something?"

Trying not to laugh, I responded, "I went shopping."

Keeping it short and straight to the point, Sénar looked at me like he wanted to slap me, "Don't play with me, Treasure. Where you get the money?"

Overjoyed with happiness that I didn't want him to steal, I answered, "Tyrell took me shopping."

Sénar allowed his eyes to roll into the back of his head and said, "You mean that chump took you to get all of this stuff? I don't believe that shit."

Feeling a little offended and accused of telling a lie, I quickly obtained an attitude, "Some people have jobs, and some people know how to treat a woman."

Sénar looked at me and said, "Well, you must have given him some, cuz ain't nobody going spend that much money on a female that ain't givin' up the good stuff."

Offended once again, I asked, "Did you ever take Julie on a shopping spree before or after you humped her?"

He scrunched his face up and said, "Hell, nah!"

After his strong response, I smirked at him and said, "My point exactly."

He looked at me and said, "Well, maybe if you let me hit it, then I would take you shopping."

I rolled my eyes at Sénar, "Look, keep your suggestions to yourself. I managed to have a boyfriend who doesn't care about sex."

Sénar laughed, "That nigga is gay if he ain't trying to fuck, sorry to break the news to you, sweetheart."

I quickly corrected him and said, "Believe me, Tyrell is far from gay, and I don't have to discuss any of this with you. I wasn't all up in you and Julie's business."

Sénar then said, "Well, obviously, you were if you know, I fucked her."

Not having a quick enough come back, I just smacked my lips and told him to get out. He looked down, and out of all the bags he carried up, he just happened to pick up the Frederick's bag to look inside. His eyes grew big, and he formed that evil smile I grew accustomed to and said,

"Ooh weee, I wish I could see you in this."

Embarrassed, I snatched the bag from him and embraced myself. He moved towards me and stopped when he heard his sisters getting closer. Sénar winked at me and left the room in a hurry. Sabrina came in with her nasty attitude kicking my bags as she entered. Pissed off at her childish behavior I asked,

"What the hell is your problem kicking my stuff like that?"

She looked at me and responded, "Well move your shit bitch this ain't just your room!"

Sensing her jealousy, I just grabbed my bags and pulled them on to my side of the room. I just stared at her like I wanted to beat her ass, which I truly did desire to do so. Cassidy came in feeling the tension, and instead of keeping her mouth closed, she added to it,

"Damn, I guess Tyrell's trying to tell you that you need a new wardrobe without hurting your feelings."

Feeling cocky, I said, "Yeah, he thinks I'm hot and wanted to buy me a whole new wardrobe, to show off my bomb ass body to make all you skinny bitches jealous. Don't hate, maybe you shouldn't be sluts, and guys might think of doing special things like that for you."

The both of them looked at me with anger threatening to reach a boiling point. Sabrina said, "Whatever bitch you ain't all that! Your black as hell, and you're fat, so I don't know who lied to you."

I rolled my eyes at them both and said, "Right, that's why your own brothers think you're whores, and not only that, I rather be my size than boney like you guys."

Sabrina kept coming back for more, "You wish you were as cute as us, and if I was you, I would watch my back, cuz I know a lot of females who don't like your ass!"

Not the least bit threatened I responded, "I'm sure it's because of you because I don't mess with nobody, I'm with Tyrell all the time."

Cassidy, just looking back and forth, finally decided to say something, "Well, I don't like your ass and never have, so maybe they just know you're stupid from looking at you."

Getting awfully tired of hearing their bullshit, I said, "You know you guys can talk amongst yourselves because I'm going to bed."

Totally ignoring them and choosing an outfit for school for the next day, I put all my bags to the side and went to sleep.

Monday morning was finally here. I was so excited I was the first one up and dressed. It was still early, but I knew Tyrell was excited, so I called him to see if he was awake,

"Hello?" I said in a low tone, Tyrell happily said, "Treasure, hey baby. You dressed already?"

I said, "Yeah, are you?"

Tyrell responded, "Yeah, but I can't wait to see what you have on.

Blushing to myself, I said, "Well, I'm going to come now. Is that ok?"

Tyrell quickly answered, "Yeah, come right over!"

With that said, I went right over there, filled with enthusiasm to start the first day of school. I knocked on his door with major confidence wearing a red tight fitted Puma shirt and my seven jeans that fit perfectly around my curves along with my Red Puma shoes. Tyrell opened the door cheesin' like he was posing for the paparazzi with his blue FUBU jersey and denim blue FUBU jeans. To top it off, he had a brand-new crisp pair of white K SWISS and a silver chain dangling around his neck. He was so excited about his new gear he forgot to check out mine.

He asked, "You ready to go because I'm ready."

Looking at him like he was crazy. I answered, "Yeah."

Sensing his urge to rush as he got his stuff, leaving me outside for the first time, then came out to open the garage. His smile grew bigger as the garage rose higher and higher. He pushed the alarm to his shiny black Lincoln once the doors were unlocked, we both got in. Tyrell looked like he was having trouble controlling himself; he jabbed the keys in the ignition with urgency. Before putting the car in drive, he turned the radio on. I could instantly tell he had some sort of system put in from the vibrations and extra-base that boomed through the speakers.

His smile lit up like a Christmas tree as he asked, "You like?"

Caught a little off guard, I answered, "Yeah, it's nice."

Excited, he said, "You ain't seen nothing yet! Wait until we turn the corner, I'll show you what it really could do."

When we turned the corner to the main street, Tyrell cranked up the sound so loud it made my ears pop. The rapper B.G. was blaring in the stereo 'Bling Bling.' I felt kind of out of place, but once I allowed myself to relax a bit, I couldn't help but bob my head to the music. We stopped at McDonald›s to eat breakfast. We sat in the car to eat our sausage McMuffins and hash browns. We talked about school, along with all the other things running across our minds. Occasionally being interrupted by Tyrell turning his car on and off to keep the battery from dying. Once we were done eating, Tyrell pulled out a box that was perfectly wrapped in pink gift paper, claiming it was a surprise that he knew I would love. Shocked once again, I was speechless and a little curious as to what he was trying to prove with the shopping spree and all the surprises he was pulling out of his ass. He handed me the box, urging me to open it.

I took the box and tore the wrapping off it to see a box that usually contained some kind of jewelry of some sort. I couldn't help but let the excitement reach my fingertips as I rushed to see the contents. I anxiously removed the silver string holding it together. I thought I would cry when I saw a beautiful gold necklace with a charm attached to it with Tyrell's name on it. I was a bit confused until Tyrell pulled his chain out of his shirt with my name dangling in the middle. I started laughing, filled with an unexplainable feeling of pure flattery and confidence. I blurted out, "This is so sweet! I don't know what made you think of this, but it's beautiful. Thank you so much!" I reached out to give him a big hug. Tyrell probably feeling like he was next to me on the top of the world, he smiled at me and then kissed me so hard when he released me, I had to check to see if my mouth was still attached to my face. "Now everybody will know that we are together and that you're mine and I'm yours." He said that with his chest puffed out and a cocky smirk on his face. Feeling anxious, I was ready to go to school and experience my first day of high school. We left McDonald's on our journey to Pacific High, with our minds being tickled with happy thoughts.

Tyrell and I pulled up to school with the music vibrating other vehicles and our confidence showing in the smiles upon our faces. Tyrell parked in the student parking lot, and I noticed a numerous amount of people somewhat breaking their necks to see who Tyrell was with. Once Tyrell parked, we both got out of the car to retrieve our backpacks from the back seat. Tyrell then met me in front of the car, so he could show me around the campus. One of Tyrell's fellow athlete friends came up to him and said,

"Ooh weee, you got a fresh one!"

Tyrell just ignored the comment and continued showing me around. We walked to where my first-period class would be and just talked a while before the bell rang. I was excited about English being my first class. I knew I would be writing and reading more since I was in the highest English they had for ninth graders. I knew Sabrina wouldn't be in any of my classes because I only had college prep classes. Besides, Sabrina didn't come to school to learn; she came to mingle and fraternize with as many boys as she could manage. Sabrina and I were the total opposite of each other; I actually enjoyed reading and writing. All of the classes I had were preparing me for college, and I couldn't wait to get acquainted with my teachers. Most people call me a teacher's pet, but I never bought an apple or anything, all I brought was an open mind and listening ears. When I got to my first period English class, I had an old white man with a long beard and long ponytail for a teacher. He looked like he escaped from the '70s and was in hiding from the fashion police.

He stood in front of the class and said, "Hello, everyone, I am Mr. Hartywells. I will be your English teacher this year. I will most definitely be the best English teacher you ever had, so I expect some of you to be the worst students I ever had."

He continued with his speech while I laughed inside at his corny sarcasm. Mr. Hartywells wasn't so bad. He was borderline funny, and he seemed like he would make this class pretty interesting this year. My next class was Algebra, which was pretty damn easy for me. My math teacher was a fat white woman named Mrs. Clarkson. She was boring and straight to the point, letting everyone know she wouldn't hesitate to flunk anyone. I didn't really care for her, but it didn't matter. I was really good at math, so I would just do my work and ignore her negativity. My next class was Biology, and my teacher's name just happened to be named Mrs. Stein. She seemed like she would go straight by the book, and her class would be a drag. I had second lunch, so I had to go to my fourth period while half of the school ate lunch.

My fourth-period class was History, which was my least favorite since the majority of it was bullshit due to the white man's selective memory. Mr. Swayer was a young white dude full of attitude. Due to the fact that he had the wackest subject to teach to kids, who really didn't give a rat's ass about the material that was selected, only to fill our minds with reasoning to why America was the way it was today.

I couldn't wait until his class was over, so I could go to lunch and see Tyrell, being that I hadn't seen him since my first-period class. History finally coming to an end when the bell rang, I thought that I would yell *thank ya, Jesus*, like I was at the average urban Black church. I gathered my things that were much heavier with the books being added to the weight. I hurried towards the cafeteria to look around for Tyrell. I saw him in line with his boys and hesitated before walking over there. Tyrell stopped talking to his friends to meet me halfway, he kissed me quickly on the lips and asked me what I wanted for lunch. A little caught off guard; he told me the options they had for lunch. I told him to bring me a pizza and some chips, he seemed happy to go get our lunch as I occupied a table for us.

To keep myself busy, I pulled out My English curriculum for the semester and overheard some giggling approaching. I looked up to see a flock of stupid skanks surrounding their ringleader Sabrina, as they all looked at me with dislike and disgust. I just rolled my eyes at them when I noticed Tyrell coming towards our table with our food. I just pretended like Sabrina and her crew just magically disappeared, when Tyrell started arranging our lunch for us. However, those skanks magically stood right there, looking at us before they walked to our table.

As if they rehearsed, they all purred in unison, "Hi Tyrell." While batting their eyes flirtatiously. I looked at these desperate girls like they were crazy when Sabrina noticed she said,

"Bitch, what are you looking at?"

Tyrell turned around quickly, saying, "Hi, but do you guys mind?"

Sabrina snapped back, "Yeah, we do mind because you could do way better than her."

Sabrina and her girls started agreeing amongst themselves. Tyrell rolled his eyes and ignored them and looked at me with a plea of humbleness. I bit my tongue, but when they walked away, I let Tyrell have it. Staring holes into him, I asked,

"Why can you speak to them, but I can't?"

He looked at me as if he didn't know who I was and answered, "Well, I didn't know it would bother you that much if I spoke to them, but since it did, I'll make sure I don't next time. Anyway, I just didn't want any drama on the first day of school."

I just stared at him, and to avoid hurting his feelings, I bit into my pizza. Tyrell couldn't help but ask, "Damn, you really don't like Sabrina, huh?"

I looked at him like he had asked what my name was, before responding, "Look, Tyrell, just drop it because you out of all people should know that I dislike Sabrina more than anyone else on this Earth."

Feeling my anger almost reaching its boiling point, I looked down at my food and forced myself to take another bite. Tyrell took my advice and changed the subject,

"So, what do you want to do after school?"

Still a little agitated, I responded, "I really don't care, whatever you want to do."

With that said, we finished our lunch and kissed shortly before going to our next class. Just my luck, P.E. was next, and Sabrina's pale stupid ass just happened to be in my class. I just ignored the fact that she was there and walked to my P.E teacher Mrs. Caderrn to retrieve my gym clothes. I looked at the green and gray garments and almost laughed.

I asked, "Umm, what size is that?"

The teacher looked at me like I was trying to get smart and responded, "Sorry, hotcakes, but this is the smallest that we carry."

A little confused, I didn't know whether to be offended or flattered. I regained my focus and told her, "Well, I think that I would be more comfortable if I wore a bigger size."

Almost relieved, the teacher then said, "Well, that's a different one!"

She gladly reached in her box and pulled out a bigger gym suit. I grabbed the shorts and a T-shirt along with the piece of paper with the combination to my locker. Trying to avoid conflict, I just quickly undressed and put my P.E clothes on. After changing into the brightly colored green and pale gray uniform, I thanked the Lord I asked for a bigger size. The shorts definitely did my ass justice, and the fact that they were bright green just made it even more noticeable. I self-consciously left the locker room, wishing I was invisible like the girl from Incredibles. Everyone had numbers they were assigned to for roll call, so I looked for number 22 and quickly sat down, trying to avoid making eye contact with anyone. The teacher waited for all the conceited females that were trying to show off their extra small P.E. uniforms. All the guys whispering to each other their ratings on the girls playing show and tell. Mrs. Caderrn clearing her throat, began to call roll call. When she called my name, I quickly answered, "Here." I heard a girl say, "Eew."

I turned around to face one of Sabrina's partners in crime and gave her a look that could kill Hercules. Her name was Jessica, and I knew she hated me just as much as Sabrina, being that she supposedly dated Tyrell in the past. I turned my attention back to Mrs. Caderrn as she explained the activities that we would need to participate in for the year. Out of all the things she explained, all I really heard was a swimming course that I really didn't want to participate in. Soon enough, the P.E. session was over after some stretches and exercises. Glad to be on my way to the last class, which was Drama, I thought to myself that it couldn't possibly be more dramatic than I dealt with on a daily basis. Mr. Gassan was the drama teacher and started the class off by beaming a bright smile while he carefully looked over his students. He paused for a minute when his eyes grazed my face; I noticed he was very young to be a teacher and quite cute if I might add. I could tell by the flirtatious giggles that the girls in the class had similar thoughts. He carefully explained that everyone would participate in acting and scene writing, whether they had talent or not. He ignored the giggles of all the little horny girls whose hormones showed in their actions.

When the class was over, I was relieved to be freed of the newfound territory. I couldn't wait to see Tyrell and tell him how my day went; since he would be the only one who cared. I knew this school year would be crazy, having 99 problems and bitches being more than one.

Chapter 8

Tyrell and I stopped at a neighborhood park on the way home to talk about our first day of school. I told him how I was concerned about the potential problem I would have with Sabrina and her pack of wolves. He just snickered like it was cute, but it was far uglier than he could imagine. Mainly because I had reached a point of no return, and I refused to be Sabrina's target of destruction. Tyrell looked me in my eyes and reassured me that he would do everything he could do to protect me, by keeping me out of harm's way. The truth was Sabrina I could handle, but Sénar was a totally different ball game, that I had no skills in. I couldn't tell him the things Sénar put me through without him feeling a violation of our relationship. I was afraid to tell anyone for fear that I would be blamed for it instead. I was even afraid that I could be looked at as a troublemaker, who was threatening to blemish Sénar's reputation. Being that he had a choice to date and sexually satisfy himself with any girl he wanted, but me.

Tyrell looked at my facial expression while I started to drift away into my thoughts, and he asked, "You believe me, right?"

Not wanting to hurt his feelings, I falsely answered, "Yeah, I do."

With that said, we decided to head home with my mind drifting once again into thoughts of what was to come of this school year, and this now foreign place, I still had to call home.

When I entered the house, the negative energy, I felt tugged at my insides made me feel nervous as I walked towards the steps. The house was quiet, but I felt a presence that was unmistakably strong. I slowly crept up the steps to my room to find that it was empty. An emotion of relief moved through me only to be quickly ejected from the sound of a slamming door. I quickly turned around to face Sénar standing in the doorway, staring dead at me, with that crazed look in his eyes. Not even thinking twice, I quickly guarded myself and looked away. He slowly walked towards me, taking pleasure in my fear and asked,

"Dang, what's wrong with you?"

His tone was sarcastic as I looked down to avoid eye contact. He inched closer to me as my body tensed up with every inch of him getting closer to me. Eventually, I couldn't help but make eye contact to plead with him to just leave me alone. Unfortunately, in some sick way, it turned him on, and he started to rub my thigh while inching closer to my neck. I could feel him breathing on my neck and his hand rising to my coochie. He slowly began to lick my neck regardless of my reluctance to allow him. Trying to fight the feeling of the eerie pleasure that trickled down my spine, I couldn't help but allow a moan to seep out of my lips. He reacted to it by grabbing my crotch and squeezing it while continuing to caress my neck with his tongue. Afraid of the feelings lingering in my body, I tried to push him off me, only to be forced to lay down. He then took his other hand and caressed my breast while moaning in my ear. He then tried to force his tongue in my mouth as I fought my own feelings that were longing to be expressed; I reminded myself this was an uninvited approach. I pushed against him in a vain attempt to release myself, which only made him more excited. I could feel his penis harden as he pressed against my coochie with so much pressure, I couldn't decide whether it hurt or felt good. Using one hand to hold me down and the other desperately trying to unbutton my jeans, fear overcame all emotion. He succeeded at pulling my pants down while trying to control me at the same time. My mind was in a whirl of wonder to if he was going to really violate me in my own home.

He whispered, "Damn Treasure, I want you so bad. I wish you were mine."

He caressed my thighs as he continued to wrestle my pants off me. On the verge of tears, I silently prayed that the Lord would free me and bring Sénar to his senses. Sénar still continued his rage of sexual passion despite my fear and the tears threatening to emerge. Freaking helpless and weak, my tears broke loose from there cage streaming down my cheeks in my last attempt of a genuine plea. Sénar looked at me with frustration as conviction invaded his heart, and he released me. Grabbing his manhood, he sighed before saying, "You're gonna like this shit, as a matter of fact, you're going to miss this shit one day, you just wait and see."

With that said, he left the room, slamming the door behind him. A feeling of relief came over me, and I couldn't help but allow the tears to fall until my eyelids were exhausted enough to go to sleep.

I was emotionally and physically drained; I slept all the way through until the morning. I woke up early enough to be able to take a relaxing bath. While everyone was still sleeping, I grabbed all my belongings and went to the bathroom as quietly as possible. When I got to the bathroom, I noticed the light glowing under the door. Something intrigued me to put my ear to the door just in time to hear Sénar saying my name and moaning like he had done in one of our sexual encounters. Until he sounded like he was releasing some kind of demon. I clenched my things and bit my bottom lip to avoid gasping. Quickly coming to my senses, I fumbled my belongings and tried to run back to the room when I heard the sound of the door opening. I tried to avoid turning around when Sénar swiftly grabbed me from behind and whispered into my ear,

"Just who I wanted to see."

I closed my eyes and awaited his next move. He gently kissed me on the neck and said, "Your turn." He snickered as he released me, leaving me standing there with my eyes still closed.

I opened my eyes, confused, and yet relieved at the same time. I ran for the bathroom, locking the door behind me as fast as I could. I undressed with a sense of curiosity. Inspecting myself as I undressed to see what Sénar could possibly be so fascinated with. I saw my perfectly rounded breasts with chocolate drops for nipples in the center of them. My stomach smooth and narrowing to a small, perfected waistline. I then turned around to see my voluptuous buttocks shaped like an upside-down heart being held up by my thick chocolaty thighs. I could not help but touch myself all over, then coming to the center of my anatomy, which I was trying to understand. Looking at my private area with a sense of pride so perfect, so sacred, and so beautiful. I could understand why someone would want to enter a place so beautiful and warm. With sweet juices lining the walls and at the temperature of perfection, I realized my fingers were inside of me. I gasped and tried to snap out of my trance. I remembered I was supposed to be bathing myself, instead of playing with myself. With that thought, I stopped my shenanigans and jumped in the bathtub.

Feeling a little naughty, I placed my coochie under the hot water with the pressure as high as it would go. I let my head fall back and rest on my shoulders. The pleasure was unbelievable, causing my mind to wander into thoughts of pleasure. Tyrell's face came into play, and I began grabbing my breast and licking my lips. Moaning quietly and trying to stay focus. Tyrell's image of him emerging from the shower danced across my mind bringing me closer to the feeling of pleasure. The closer I got to my climax, the harder I grabbed my breast, and the closer I came to releasing some of my sweet juices with the flow of the water. Almost reaching my peak, I almost moved to avoid exploding, but I placed one of my hands on my thigh to reinforce my stay. Flashes of Sénar grabbing my thighs and my breast flew through my mind like a projector. My grip grew stronger on both my thigh and my breast. Sénar's face appeared, and before I knew it, I busted all over the place almost one with the water. I quickly sat up and tried to pull myself together, confused at why every time I have an orgasm, I see Sénar's face first. I washed up with my cocoa butter caress and got out to get dressed.

To avoid everyone, I got dressed and headed to Tyrell's house. Tyrell opened the door before I had a chance to ring the doorbell with a huge grin on his face. He grabbed me and hugged me as if It had been years since we've seen each other. I just went along with it and hugged him back.

Tyrell held me in his arms and said, "Hey baby, how u doin'?"

I laughed, almost pushing him away in an attempt to gain control. He tugged at my hand, pulling me upstairs, curious to what he had in mind, I eagerly followed. When we reached his room, he swiftly closed the door behind us and kissed me. He put his arms around my waist, caressing the small of my back with his hands, and kissed me softly. He whirled me around and laid me on his bed and continued kissing me. He parted my lips with his tongue and massaged my lips with his while his hands slowly wandered my body. He placed his body on top of mine and centered himself in the middle of my thighs. He caressed my breast and whispered he loved me into my ear, which added to the feeling of ecstasy I was enduring. Instead of my heart racing, I was in a trance awaiting more pleasure to be released. I laid there, allowing him to taunt and touch me wherever he wanted. He kissed the nape of my neck and the top of my breast, making my coochie throb.

Then he whispered, "We have to go get some breakfast and go to school."

I shook my head in confusion and asked, "What?"

He looked at me with a huge smile, "Don't trip; we have plenty of time for that."

He grabbed his backpack and urged me to come with him. We got into the car while backing out; I saw Sénar getting in the car with one of his little girlfriends. Tyrell looked at me out of the corner of his eye as if he would catch me with a look of jealousy on my face, but instead, he got nothing. He gripped the steering wheel tighter and bit his lip in frustration.

He hesitated before asking me, "So you always talk about Cassidy and Sabrina, but you never talk about Sénar or Chino. What's up with them?"

I was completely caught off guard, but I still knew he didn't care about Chino; he was concerned with Sénar. I asked, "Um, what, like, what do you mean?"

He looked at me like I insulted him. I hesitated before answering, "Well, Sénar's an asshole, and Chino stays to himself."

Trying to keep the answer short feeling under pressure, I folded my hands. Tyrell asked, "Well, how is Sénar an asshole?"

I was starting to feel uncomfortable and replied, "Tyrell, he's just really stupid, he's always picking on me, and he's really mean to me. Look, I don't want to talk about it, please."

Tyrell was getting impatient, "Why? I'm your man, and I could take care of dat shit!"

He instantly turned into a thug as if he was going to do some serious damage. I looked at him like he was scaring me and pleaded with him, "Look, Tyrell, I don't want any problems because I have to live with these people, you won't be there to protect me then."

He looked at me as if I was hiding something and said, "Well, I think Sénar likes you. He's always talking about you, and I see the way he looks at you, and I don't like that shit! So, if you tell me you don't like it either, then I'll do something about it."

I looked at him with an attitude and replied, "Well, I never noticed it, and I don't want to accumulate any more problems than I already have, so can we change the subject?"

On the verge of tears, I put my face in my hands. Tyrell quickly turned back into the boy I liked again and said, "I'm sorry, Treasure I'm just worried about you. All of them are some scandalous, conniving bastards!"

My eyes widened in surprise; he was just as furious as if he had his own encounters with them. We both just remained quiet, overwhelmed by our own thoughts and frustrations. We decided just to eat breakfast and went to school right after. When we got there, we quickly kissed and went our separate ways. I went to class, feeling very strange like something crazy was going to happen. I tried to stay focused on my work and what was going on, but I kept thinking of Tyrell and Sénar. I was worried that they would somehow clash, and I would be the one to blame. I couldn't help but wonder who would win a battle between the two. In addition to that, I felt guilty knowing I would be secretly rooting for both. Tyrell is my boyfriend, and I have deep feelings for him, but Sénar and I have a weird relationship. I can't decide if he is a threat or a challenge. I knew I was creating a situation for myself if I kept accepting the fact that Sénar molests me every chance he got. It pained me because deep down inside, I yearned for his attention and used it for fuel to understand my sexuality.

Hearing the bell ring, I knew I had spent the entire period racking my brain about this situation. I couldn't concentrate on anything but how Sénar and Tyrell seemed to be the only two people in my life that cared about me. That seemed to be all I've really thought about lately. I couldn't help but feel guilty that I hadn't been thinking about my mom for the last couple of days. I didn't want to be anything like her, or I would be just as guilty of neglecting our relationship. So, I promised myself that I would try to connect with my mom even if I failed to do so, I would at least try every day. I went to my next class with my brain relieved of the drama from mine, and my alter ego's boyfriend. I thought about my mom and how close we could become, and I couldn't help but smile while my teacher rambled on, probably thinking I was smiling at her. Besides, biology was the least of my worries; I couldn't help but wonder what happened to my mother and why she seemed so distant and far away from me. I felt like I had lost her, and someone bought a replacement, but that wasn't realistic. I started to think about how, or when, or even if she ever showed any signs of this drastic change that consumed her, so suddenly. Before I could fathom the next thought, the bell rang.

As if my day couldn't get any more mind-boggling, I had history next, which added to the fuel of the hate I had for ignorance. I knew I would be able to conclude in this class because I would do everything I could to block my teacher out for the sake of my understanding. After replaying the years of my childhood, I shared with my mother; I realized her strength came from her being independent. She was not in a relationship, and she was happy or thought she was happy. She couldn't stop telling me what not to fall for and how not to let men do this and that, but she never told me what to fall for. Surely Ken couldn't be what she wanted to fall for or the example she wanted for me. Either Ken was really good or really evil. My mother was just so lost and distant, I couldn't help but wonder what it would take for her to find her way back to me. Besides, I wanted her to know that no matter how much she neglected me in the last few years that I was still here for her, no matter what, and she had no reason to be afraid. I started making excuses for my mom like maybe Ken forced his way into my mother's life and was holding her captive against her will. The bell rang and believe it or not; I was very happy to be left with that thought instead of possibly facing the fact that my mother's neglect was by choice.

I was eager to get to the cafeteria and see Tyrell when suddenly a weird rush of urgency came over me. It grew more urgent when I saw a crowd of people gathering in front of the cafeteria and could recognize the voices causing the commotion. It wasn't just any two guys; it was Tyrell and Sénar. I immediately ran towards the growing crowd, pushing and shoving people, creating my own battles on the way to the commotion.

I heard Tyrell, "Treasure is my girl, so you need to back up, and when you lookin' at her, keep ya compliments to ya self homeboy!"

He yelled at Sénar with his chest puffed out. Sénar smirked and gave him a devious look and replied, "It's my mothafuckin' eyes, and I do what the fuck I want with em' homeboy. Besides, I live with her so I could look at her whenever the fuck I want!"

Sénar boasted while grabbing his crotch. Before I could say anything, Tyrell dropped everything but his keys. With the end of the key sticking out of the side of his fist, he swung and hit Sénar across the right side of his face opening a flesh wound immediately. The whole crowd oohed and awed at the sight of the blood. When Sénar saw the blood, he seemed to be amused and gave a smile that could have fooled the devil. Then when he saw me, he gave me the most sadistic smile he had ever given me. He then charged Tyrell and punched him so hard blood sprayed the crowd. I screamed in horror at the sight of all the blood that was smeared across their hands and faces. They both looked like they wanted one another to die as if they were fighting for their lives. Tyrell picked Sénar up and slammed him on the ground, and I ran to try and get him off. Tyrell turned around and flung me like a rubber band across the pavement as Sénar was getting back up. Security rushed the both of them, throwing Sénar to the ground and restraining Tyrell. As I was still trying to get up, security rushed me, grabbing me by my hands and forcing me to walk forward like I had been fighting too. Everybody in school seemed to be there watching as the three of us were being hauled off with blood all over them and security dragging me behind them. I was so embarrassed, and as if things couldn't get any worse, I saw Sabrina and her little clique pointing and laughing while yelling crap at me. Oh my gosh, I even saw Cassidy there with her little boyfriend pointing her finger at me. I was even more shocked when I saw Chino standing there, shaking his head like he had done that night in the hallway.

We were taken to the office, and they sat us down in three different corners while we waited to see the principle. The principle's name was Mr. Bell; he was this short stubby black guy with a sarcastic attitude, and no matter what the subject, kept a smile on his face.

He said, "Let me guess you've been leading these boys on, and finally, they caught on to it?"

Mr. Bell assumed he had it all figured out. Offended, I looked at him and responded, "For your information, I haven't led anyone on.

Tyrell is my boyfriend and has been for the last year. As far as Sénar, he is just my stepbrother."

Mr. Bell smiled and said, "Well, obviously, your stepbrother wants to be more than a stepbrother." He laughed to himself before he continued, "Well, Treasure, considering your placement here, I assume you are here for educational purposes and not to be a troublemaker. With that said, I will keep my eye on you after you come back from your week vacation."

I looked at him with a blank expression to mask the anger and hurt from revealing itself. More upset about missing a week of my class than getting in trouble for something I did not encourage in any way. Trying to convince myself that this was solely a personal issue they had, I just happen to be their scapegoat. I was beginning to accept everything when a slap from reality got a lick in on me when I realized Mr. Bell was calling my house. He spoke calmly when explaining the ordeal. I was racking my brain, trying to listen for hints of whether it was Ken or my mother on the other end. I was kind of hoping it was Ken, so I wouldn't have to face my mother's scrutiny in front of Ken or Sénar. I was promptly dismissed and led out of his office by security. Sénar was going in after me with a smirk and a hint of revenge in his eyes. Tyrell's eyes were more apologetic and filled with anger. I have never seen Tyrell angry like that; it was kind of sexy to know he had a rough side. Sénar came out by himself with his cell phone to his ear, talking all loud, telling someone to come and pick him up. The security just stood there, watching us wait for our rides.

My mom pulled up to the school with an evil scowl on her face; my heartbeat immediately picked up speed. I slowly walked to the car when I saw this beautiful white girl in a red convertible pull up and wave at Sénar. I was shocked because she looked like she was in her early twenties. I got in the car with a dumbfounded expression on my face and tried to avoid eye contact with my mom. I turned around to see Sénar leaving with that woman and Tyrell coming out. Before I could turn around to face my mom, my face was forced to turn back with the hot palm of my mother's hand. Hurt and shocked, I grabbed my face and winced just in case another one was coming.

She yelled, "That's for getting in here and avoiding looking at me. Treasure this is not how I raised you to be whoring around having young horny boys fighting all over you." She said with a concerned look on her face. I couldn't help feeling like I had my old mom back; she was driving and talking the same as my mom.

I looked at her with apologetic eyes and said, "Momma, I'm not having sex or anything like that. I love Tyrell. Sénar and him fighting doesn't have nothing to do with me."

She looked at me like she didn't know who I was and with an attitude responded, "Well, I don't know Treasure, you have all the evidence pointing in a different direction. You need to occupy your time with something else besides boys, and I'll make sure of that."

Before we got home, I couldn't help but ask her why she had been neglecting me. I asked, "Mom, why are you so distant with me since Ken has come along?"

She looked at me like I was crazy and imagining things then said, "Oh, so you are going to try and make me look like the bad guy? First of all, I didn't pick you up to talk about my behavior. Second, you've spent so much time sneaking around clinging to Tyrell, now look where it has gotten you. Besides, Ken and I are getting married, so just learn to accept him and I, are one."

She said this in an overly defensive way as we pulled into the driveway. Taken by surprise, I didn't respond as she exited the car in a hurry before slamming the door. A little confused and relieved at the same time to not get in more trouble. I looked across the street to see a vacant driveway and wondered what the hell I was going to do for a whole week without school.

Chapter 9

Almost afraid to enter the house after having been suspended, then having my mom tell me to basically get over my feelings of being neglected due to her and Ken's relationship. I cautiously opened the door to hear my mother climbing the steps with what sounded like wind chimes with her. I decided to turn around and go back outside just in time to see Sénar pull up outside with one of his Barbie dolls. He spotted me as soon as I came outside. He got out of the car without even so much looking at the girl who brought him home to say goodbye; he kept his eyes on me the whole time. He was getting taller, bigger; he looked so mature and rough with his new beauty mark on his face. I couldn't help but wonder what it would be like to be a beneficiary of his sexual wrath instead of a victim. I was looking at him like I had never seen him before as he walked up to me and pushed me against the door. He kissed me for the first time so passionately, I didn't fight him because he had never been so gentle, at the same time as powerful. I started to put my hands around his neck when Tyrell approached the corner, driving like a maniac, I threw Sénar off me so fast that he and I both were shocked.

Of course, neither of our guards were as strong as they would usually be. I moved Sénar out the way when he came charging behind me as Tyrell parked his car in the middle of the street and jumped out. The two of them looked like two Pitbulls trying to strangle each other. I wanted to scream but refrained from doing so to prevent attention from being brought to us. I tried my best to pull them apart, but it wasn't even fazing either of them. I just fell to the ground and started crying. Some of the tears were real, but the majority of them were bogus. They never let go of each other while watching me act like a child having a tantrum in the middle of the street. They both looked at each other then finally unleashed each other at the same time, never taking their eyes off one another. They looked at me and then at one another, debating if they should continue their war until death do them part. They glared at each other for what seemed like an eternity and backed away from each other far enough for the other one to feel safe enough to turn their back on one another.

Tyrell turned to me, "Get up and get in the car!" He grunted at me with not an ounce of love left in his voice.

We drove around in silence for so long, I couldn't help but start fidgeting because I was afraid of him driving so fast that it seemed like he wasn't ever planning on having to brake. When we approached a red light, I didn't know whether to be relieved or afraid for my life. He continued to keep his speed as if he was color blind; I couldn't help but let a cry escape my lips,

"Tyrell, please!"

He ignored me and kept racing for the light. I closed my eyes and silently prayed that the Lord would somehow come and rescue me from this deranged kid who was once my loving boyfriend. The hurt and anger in Tyrell's eyes was a side of him I had never seen. I found myself wondering who he was mad at, Sénar, or me. Tyrell cut the corner without completely breaking; my eyes widened when the car careened onto the opposite side of the street, striking the curb, causing the tire to pop. Tyrell's face went from anger to fear quickly as he tried to regain control of his Lincoln from going side to side until little sparks kicked up from the rim. I put my hands over my face waiting for the next impact that would probably kill us. Tyrell was now looking like a flailing sailor in a windstorm trying to maintain his composure. He braked until we came to a screeching halt on the right side of the street that we should have never left from.

Not knowing what to say, being we were both in a fragile state, I couldn't let my anger escape me before letting him know how disappointed I was with his behavior lately. I turned slowly to look at him in his eyes when I saw that they were still filled with fear; I felt it was the best time to let him have it.

"What the hell is wrong with you? You almost killed us! You're acting like a barbarian fighting in school. You could have gotten kicked off the football team! You're always questioning me as if I'm doing something wrong-"

Fury rushed back into his eyes, "Well, are you?"

He interrupted my long list of disapprovals of his behavior. Before I could answer him, he continued, "Fuck that shit, who the hell side are you on? You are my woman, so I thought, and you should be on my side no matter what! Fuck Sénar's bitch ass! First, he is an asshole, and now I'm the one in the wrong for standing up for you? You are looking at me like this is all my fault! Well, if my beef with him is my fault, then your battle with him is your fault too!"

He said that with conviction in his voice that made me whimper. He got out of the car without even looking at me and then headed for his trunk. I was dumbfounded; I didn't know what to say or whether to get out or not. I slowly got out of the car, and cautiously walked towards the trunk. I was still unaware of what he would do, so I asked the safest question I could think of,

"Tyrell, do you still love me?"

He looked at me like I asked him a trick question. He answered, "Well, should I? You don't even know who the hell side you're on."

He hissed at me while snatching the spare tire out of his trunk. He left me at the trunk, wondering while he grabbed all the tools that he needed to replace the shredded tire. I never thought I would have to convince Tyrell that I didn't have feelings for Sénar, hell I had problems trying to convince myself that I didn't. I walked over to where he was and tried to avoid crying before saying,

"Tyrell, I love you, and I waited a long time for this opportunity. I used to sit and wish you would just talk to me. I don't want to be with anyone else but you Tyrell."

He glared at me before he responded, "How can I be sure when you guys live in the same house, and I see the way he looks at you! Then you hold back things that he does and says to you. I know it!"

He yelled at me, trying to stay in control of what he was doing at the same time. I thought for a second before answering, knowing what he was saying was true, and the more I lied, the more guilty I would become.

I said, "Well, Tyrell, what do you want me to do?"

He looked at me like I should know the answer. Feeling like a cornered mouse, I just backed up a little to take a good look at him and said, "You know what, is this all having a relationship has to offer? Because if so, I'm cool."

I rolled my eyes as far back into my head as possible. Where the attitude came from, I didn't know, but I was starting to feel like he was blaming everything on me as if he didn't have a starring role in the drama. He looked at me with anger present in his eyes until he saw how serious I was; he quickly changed his facial expression. I couldn't help but wonder if this was the end, I didn't want to lose him, but I had enough drama in my life and needed him as an escape instead of him adding to it. Exhausted from all the unnecessary arguing, I was ready to go; I didn't even know where to because there was no place to hide anymore. The drama just seemed to be in everything that involved me. Concerned with myself and not with Tyrell, I drifted away into my thoughts, almost forgetting that we were together stuck on the side of the road, replacing a blown-up tire. Tyrell snapped, "Treasure!"

Rushing me back to reality, startled, I looked at him like he was a stranger. His eyes were still cold; I just turned away. I tried to hold in my tears of frustration and confusion. Tyrell came up and grabbed my shoulder, turning me around to face him; it took everything in my power to look Tyrell in his eyes. He looked at me for a long time, and I was mesmerized by the love that took over the anger in his eyes.

He asked me, "Treasure, do you love me?"

I looked at him and kissed him so passionately to assure myself, then I answered, "Yes, I do love you, Tyrell."

I couldn't help but cry because I was feeling a bit overwhelmed with the emotions that rushed in and out of my body. Tyrell grabbed the back of my neck, and we kissed each other like we would never see each other again. Then Tyrell started to apologize and bury his head in my chest. I felt sorry for him, grabbing him and hugging him to assure him that I would always be here for him. We got in the car and began to drive back home. There was nothing else to talk about; we just wanted to wake up and start all over again. Tyrell pulled up to my house and parked the car. He turned to look at me in my eyes to tell me he loved me, but that I scared him sometimes because he was afraid of losing me. I told him I loved him, kissed him good night, and walked into my house without looking back.

Once inside, my heart's steady beat began to increase with the anxiety that I had of what was to come this night, let alone the rest of the week. I tried to creep up the stairs when I heard a door shut, I almost turned around to go back downstairs, but I just kept going up. When I reached the top, my mother was standing there with her eyes bloodshot and reeking of alcohol.

She glared at me with a look of disgust on her face, "Where the hell have you been, Treasure?" She slurred and raised her drink in the air, moving it in a motion to form an invisible question mark.

I looked at her and cautiously answered, "Oh, momma, I just went for a walk."

She looked at me like I was a bum on the street, "Oh, really? You are a god damn liar, just like your damn daddy! Get the fuck outta my face, you little yamp! I better not catch you sniffing around my man, because you're nothing but a little sneaky lying whore!"

She pushed me out of her way before the tears could stream down my face. I didn't understand why she hated me so much; I could hear her carrying on downstairs to herself. I was so confused and exhausted. Sénar came and rushed out of his room toward me. When I saw him, I just broke down and fell to my knees; I couldn't take any more abuse at this moment. Sénar ran up to me and picked me up off the floor; I wasn't sure if I should be thankful or scared.

He grabbed my chin and said, "Treasure your mom didn't mean that; she was just drunk. She loves my dad, but he can be a jerk, don't cry please."

I slapped him across his face, hitting the cut Tyrell put there earlier. Blood oozed from his wound, and tears almost flooded his eyes. I almost yelled at Sénar at the top of my lungs when I asked, "And you're not Sénar?"

He was shocked and hurt; he released me then ran to his room, leaving me there alone. I turned to go to my room when all I could hear is music and laughter. I turned around and went to the bathroom instead. I sat on the toilet and cried for about an hour until my tears seemed to run out. When I came out of the bathroom, the house was dark and quiet, a bit timid but still relieved I went downstairs quietly and fell asleep on the couch. I curled up in a fetal position on the couch and actually felt safe for once in a long time. Subconsciously hearing the front door open and close, the feeling of the cold air grazing my skin. I cradled myself to keep warm. When I suddenly felt someone rubbing my thighs and starting to grope my breast. The person was really strong and muscular. I slowly opened my eyes to see a manly figure hovering over me.

I panicked when I heard him speak, "Get up and open your mouth, I want my dick sucked!"

He grabbed the back of my head and tried to pull me forward; I pushed him back, jerking my head free at the same time. He got mad and backhanded me so hard, I whimpered in the corner of the couch while he hovered over me, holding something in his hand. Suddenly the lights came on, and before I could look and see who it was, I noticed this thick brown penis right in my face centimeters away from my mouth.

I quickly looked back to see my mom stumbling down the stairs yelling, "Ken, is that you?"

Rubbing her eyes as she tried to see what was going on. Ken hurried and tried to put his penis back in his pants.

My mom yelled, "Treasure is that you! What the fuck are you doing down here?"

She ran down the steps as Ken fixed himself and seemed to catch her in mid-air as she was charging for me.

He said, "Baby, I thought she was you. It was dark, Angel baby, I didn't know!"

He grabbed her and caressed her hair; she seemed to melt in his arms. She looked at me with pure evil in her eyes and said, "I'ma fix you, you little bitch!"

Ken snatched her up, "Come on, baby let's go, I told you, I thought that was you waiting on me, let me show you what I got for you."

She took her eyes off me and let Ken bring her up the steps. Sénar was in the kitchen the whole time. He emerged from the dark and looked at me like I was some sort of freak show, then went up the steps turning the light off behind him. I sat there in the dark frozen, barely blinking horrified until I saw the sunrise.

When the morning came, I felt like I had been on the battlefield bruised, petrified and paranoid. I couldn't even move. I could hear all the hustle and bustle of everyone getting ready to go to school. Chino was the first one downstairs. He went into the kitchen to grab an apple, a cup of juice and came to sit next to me.

He asked, "Damn girl, what's wrong with you? It looks like you seen a ghost."

He wasn't being funny either, I had seen a demon not a ghost and I was imprisoned by the memory of what happened. I couldn't even respond. He looked at me and said, "Damn girl, I thought we was cool. Well I'll see you later ma. Stay out of trouble or out of trouble's way, whichever."

He got up and left me there taking one last look at me, before returning his cup to the kitchen and leaving for school. I just sat there waiting for Sabrina and Cassidy to leave so that I could go to my room. I was exhausted and traumatized with last night's events that took place. I couldn't even allow myself to feel that everything would be ok. Sabrina came down the steps with her phone glued to her ear and yapping her gums. The sight of her made my stomach churn and the way she looked at me I'm sure her's was turning to. She couldn't help but smack her lips and roll her eyes as far back into her head as they would possibly go. I hated Sabrina so much, she was so competitive, cocky, and always making nothing into something. She was messy and liked to argue to get attention, it was like she had to hear her voice over any other voice, oh and she had to get the last word. I was patient and calm with her, but I knew one day her mouth was going to get her in a lot of trouble, if not by me then by someone else. I was ready, she had no idea what was coming, I was getting fed up with her mouth and drama. I was just waiting on her to cross the line with her mouth on a day that I didn't feel like conjuring up ways to make her feel stupid, then I would meet her with a knuckle sandwich just to my liking. I looked at her and smiled at the thought of punching her in her mouth.

She smacked her lips and rolled her eyes again before leaving. The thought of plucking one of her eyes out the socket wouldn't be such a bad ideal either. I was reaching my boiling point and I couldn't think of anyone else to burn with my wrath that would be more deserving then Sabrina. Cassidy came down next and looked at me like damn where you been, but she just kept walking out the door. I let out a sigh like a mother that had just cooked, cleaned, and sent her children off to school. I laid there for a moment gathering my thoughts when I heard more footsteps. I jumped up to see who it was, and it was Sénar. I let out another sigh of relief which was quite awkward being that I'd rather see him then my mom or Ken. He looked at me like he wanted to say something but didn't. I was so drained; I probably was better off not hearing it anyway. He just turned away going to the kitchen instead. I grabbed my stuff and booked it upstairs.

When I got to my room, I gently closed the door and fell on top of my bed like I was a homesick kid. I laid there thinking how I was going to make it through this week without school with everything going on around me. Before I knew it, I drifted off into a deep sleep. I could incoherently hear a voice that sounded familiar saying,

"Oh yeah, well let me call you back."

Cassidy put her stuff down lightly allowing me to hold on to part of my sleep and left the room. Almost reaching the point of sleep I was in before I was quietly interrupted, I heard the door swing open and Sabrina's loudmouth,

"So, I don't care if she sleep! Who the fuck is she, I'm not about to be quiet for that bitch!"

I was ejected out my sleep like a victim in a car crash. I jumped up and sat up on the bed trying to regain all of my senses when I could still hear Sabrina running her mouth. She said, "Oh what she gonna do? I ain't scared of that bitch! This is my room too and if she doesn't like it, then she could do something about it!"

Her last remark was louder than the rest, I regained my clear eyesight and met her eyes with mine. Sabrina looked at me and got all hype when she asked, "What bitch you feelin' froggy?"

I got up and she got even more hype and again asked, "You feeling froggy bitch? Then leap!"

Right when she said leap, I followed her orders by lunging at her and punching her dead in her mouth. Cassidy happened to walk in right when my fist connected with Sabrina's lips. We were all shocked but before anyone could react, I drilled Sabrina so hard with my flying fist that Cassidy started to feel guilty and tried getting me off Sabrina. Cassidy yelled for help summoning Sénar and Chino. They came running in the room with their eyes bulging with disbelief. I held Sabrina captive by her neck against the wall, while she sporadically let out cries to get me off her because I was letting her have it. She was flailing her arms wildly and finally connected one of her tiny balled up fist of fear to my lip, causing me to go even harder on her. Chino moved Cassidy out the way and Sénar came up from behind me and grabbed me,

"Treasure let go! Let go of her neck!"

I couldn't let go; my hand had a mind of its own. Sénar grabbed my fingers and forcefully peeled them off her neck and picked me up throwing me on the bed. I was trying to resist his strength because I was not finish with her. I could hear Chino yelling at Sabrina, "Calm down sis, calm down! You need to chill!"

Sénar was wrestling me down to the bed trying to restrain me, "Damn girl, I didn't know you were this strong, or this mad. Calm down Treasure!"

I was bucking like a wild horse every time I heard Sabrina run her mouth. There was so much yelling and tussling that only one thing could make us stop, Ken asked, "What the fuck is going on in here?"

Everyone froze for a minute when we heard Ken's questioning voice bellow through the room like a horn. I couldn't see him I was face down on the bed, but I could definitely hear him. I instantly stop resisting when I heard his voice and the tingling feeling of fear invaded my blood stream. Sénar felt me go limp beneath him and loosened his grip but remained on top of me for a minute. He then released me and stood up to face his dad.

With rage in his voice and violence in his eyes Ken asked, "I said what the fuck is going on in here, somebody better start fucking talking!"

I sat up and moved back into the corner of my bed and put my knees to my chest, the suspense was really killing me. It was all eyes on Ken, except for a quick second when Sénar looked back at me as if to check on me, not once looking at Sabrina. Ken got ready to make moves when Sabrina burst into tears, "Daddy! Treasure attacked me; I swear she tried to kill me! I didn't even do nothing I was just coming in here to put my stuff down when she jumped up and attacked me, Cassidy saw it!"

Cassidy looked like a deer caught in head lights, when Ken looked at her and then at me. His eyes threatening me without words, he tried to avoid speaking to me directly he put his attention back on Cassidy. She fidgeted a little and looked at the ground and then at Sénar as if she wanted him to help her. I couldn't really understand the situation I was still angry and scared, feeling out numbered.

Sénar said, "Man that's a got damn lie Sabrina, we all know you better than that. You came in here talking shit and got yo' ass whipped."

He tried to be funny to loosen up the situation, but it just made Ken more furious. Ken roared, "Look boy, this ain't no motherfuckin' game! I'm not fuckin playin, so keep your stupid little comments to yourself. I ain't taken your word either, I know who's back you got, so shut the fuck up, I ain't talking to you!"

Sénar closed his mouth, but he tensed up giving Ken a threatening look. Ken just turned away from Sénar to show him he could care less about him puffing up. He looked at Cassidy as if she was Sabrina's keeper,

"What happened Cassidy?"

She looked at me in the corner but quickly turned away, "Ummmm." She hesitated a moment, "Uhh, I heard Sabrina up here trippin', then when I heard the commotion. I ran up here and they were fighting. I don't know who hit who first."

All three of us were just as shocked as we were when I socked Sabrina in her mouth. Sabrina broke loose from Chino and ran to her dad clinging on to him, "Daddy that's not true, it's not true!" She yelled as she looked at Cassidy and then flashed on her, "You are such a liar; I can't believe you gonna lie for this bitch! You're a fucking trader! I hate you! I fuckin' hate you!"

Ken snatched Sabrina up and shook her slightly, "Sabrina calm the fuck down, everybody downstairs now!"

Everybody started to move when I debated with myself if he was talking to me too. Everybody left the room, Ken in the doorway glared at me like I was some sort of threat to him and his family as he slammed the door. I heard him yell, "Come get your fuckin daughter!"

My mom quickly rushed in shortly after. The little bit of rage I had left, I stored aside just in case I needed it to defend myself from my mom. She hurried over to me, "Treasure what the hell has gotten into you lately? You're not the Treasure I raised, what have you done with her?"

She put her hand on my shoulder and looked at me like she once loved me. I didn't know whether to cry on her shoulder or slap her for acting brand new, like she had been the same mother that had raised and loved me once upon a time.

I looked at her and said, "You know mom you haven't exactly been the same either. You could care less how I'm feeling or what I'm going through, you just left me out here to rot with your newfound family!"

I lashed out at her with tears rolling out of my eyes like an over filled bucket. I had no idea how she was going to react but after all the things that went down today, I didn't even care anymore. She looked at me as her anger increased until she too started crying. She buried her face in my bosom and cried like a baby. I couldn't help but console her, although we haven't hugged each other in what seemed like a lifetime.

I said, "Momma, don't cry please I love you so much, I would never stop loving you no matter what." I tried to ensure her my love was unconditional and would remain that way.

She looked at me like a lost child, "Treasure I'm sorry I haven't been there for you, I was so wrapped up in Ken, it's like I forgot who I was. I should be a mother before I'm anything else. I haven't had anyone but you to love me since my mother died and your father left me. I was afraid to lose Ken because he requires more attention than a child and I didn't want him to stray. That's no excuse, but I love him and he's so attractive that I tend to feel insecure at times. He reminds me so much of your father it scares me, and I don't want to be left again."

She was crying softly. I just looked at her with pity, but I always thought of my mother as a strong independent woman. Wanting to console her I said,

"Momma, no man should make you feel like you're not enough. You are one of the most beautiful women I have ever seen in my life. I want us to be close again momma. I miss you I feel like you've left me, but you are just in the other room. I want you to be a part of my life as I'm growing. You've missed so much that I really thought you would be there for."

I was trying not to cry because I didn't want her to think I was trying to make her feel bad, I just wanted her to know that I felt like she left me and that she was the first person to break my heart. My mom broke down once again, she was opening up like a whore's legs.

She poured her heart out, "Treasure when Ken came into my life, I was so lonely. I confided in you about everything you were my only friend, but of course you know there was certain needs that I needed to be met that you or no female friend could supply me with. I was lost because I had convinced myself that I didn't need a man and I became bitter. Ken brought me back to my womanhood and I hadn't felt like that in so long that I couldn't let it go again. Then I was worried that you would be a problem, but I found out he had custody of his children. I just thought he was perfect and that if he didn't leave his kids, then he wouldn't leave me. The older you get, the more you remind me of myself and your father, something I didn't want to go back to thinking about. I would sometime see his face in yours and think he had come back through you to haunt me, especially when I drink. The very thing I'm afraid of I did to you and I'm so sorry. I'm a terrible person for what I've done to you, I hope you can forgive me and love me still."

I looked at her and fell in love with her all over again, she was my mother and not some stuck-up teenage girl anymore who only cared about getting a piece of penis. I instantly forgave her and forgot about the last three dreadful years of my life. I said, "Momma, I forgive you and I love you so much, just promise me you won't ever leave me again. Please?"

She looked at me and without hesitation replied, "Baby, I promise not to ever leave your side again." She kissed me then looked at me like I thought I was slick then asked, "Ok, I am very happy we had this talk but what the hell happen in here earlier?"

I looked down and then back up, she had a smirk on her face I had never seen before. I started to lie but if she was the woman, she said she would go back to being, I knew she would understand. I replied, "Well, Momma after last night and the earlier events I was so tired. I felt like it was me against the world. What happen last night with Ken, momma really scared me." I paused to see her facial expression. She was looking at me like I was trying to change the subject. So, I tried to stay on track, "Ok, I was tired and because I'm suspended from school for the next week, I was just overwhelmed with all the stuff going on in my life. So, I came upstairs to take a nap. When Cassidy came in, I guess she saw that I was sleeping so she came in quietly and probably told Sabrina I was sleeping. Oh, my goodness Momma, she came in here talking mess and making noise on purpose and calling me out in my sleep. So, I got up because I was going to leave to avoid conflict, like I've been doing but she got in my face. So, I punched her and never stopped until Sénar came to get me off her."

Her smirk grew into a full-blown smile. She said, "That's what that little bitch gets messin' with my baby, hell I never liked her ass anyway."

Shocked but satisfied we both started giggling like little schoolgirls over juicy gossip. When Ken opened the door and saw us having the best time we've had since he's been here, he grew jealous instantly. The veins popped out of his neck and forehead,

"What the fuck! I'm downstairs chastising my kids and you guys are up here giggling? While my daughter looks and feels like she was assaulted?"

My mom looked like a kid again that had got caught ditching or something. I just looked at Ken like he was some dumb boy bugging me and my friend, making Ken even more furious. He cut his eyes at us,

"Check this shit out, get y'all ass up and get downstairs now!"

From the look in Ken's eyes, I almost jumped up before my mom. We scurried toward the steps like scared little children. He sounded like an ol' G pimp talking to his hoes. Even though I was out after my mom, I still hurried down the stairs after leaving the two of them in the same vicinity. I walked into the kitchen and sat down at the extended table. I was feeling myself because I didn't feel alone anymore, I had everybody on my side. I was mistaken when I realized everybody at the table was focused on me, even the woman I had just reconnected with. I tried not to show a sudden change of mood and bluffed by looking at everyone like I was trying to figure out what the hell everyone was looking at.

Sénar spoke first, "Well, Mrs. Treasure." He looked at me through his sarcastic eyes, "What shall we do? You are the root of the problem, are you not?"

I knew Sénar was testing me and he wasn't talking about Sabrina. Then Ken stepped in like he knew where this conversation was going, in the opposite direction in which he wanted to go.

Ken ignored Sénar, "Treasure, you seem to be a pretty popular subject lately so what are you planning to do about it? I mean I can make some suggestions." Ken said to me with sarcasm that would have made me upset, if I wasn't feeling so cocky about bombing on Sabrina.

I squinted my eyes at everyone, "I don't know Ken, your kids seem to really like me or really not like me, so it makes me a little popular here I guess, but in the real-world people tend to mind their business and leave me alone."

Sénar thought it was cute while the other three stooges looked at me as if I was about to dig a hole too deep to get out of. My mom kind of just blended in, trying to steer clear of Ken's wrath. Ken looked at me and licked his lips before responding,

"Well we have a smart ass on our hands, now don't we Angel baby?"

My mom eagerly nodded in agreement and went back to her Lala Land. Ken said, "Well I think I've been considerably nice to you. Are you trying to take advantage of me?"

What I was thinking must have been written on my forehead because my mom gave me a pleading look to hold my tongue. I answered, "No Ken I am not, I just want to be left alone. I don't bother anybody, and I don't want to sleep in a room with someone who hates me."

I did everything I could not to start tearing up, but they strolled down my face any way. My mom wanted to get up to come to me, but Ken's glare challenged her to do so. Sénar winced in agitation with his father while Cassidy and Chino remained emotionless.

Sabrina scrunched up her face, "Whatever don't try to play all innocent now. You were the one trying to kill me stupid bitch! Look at my face and neck!"

She started crying as if we were having a crying contest. My mom finally spoke, "You know what, I never say much to anyone around here. I keep to myself and deal with my man, but I will not sit around and watch my daughter get bullied anymore. Sabrina you've given Treasure grief since the day you stepped foot in my house, and I allowed it to go on long enough. You got what you deserved. You don't respect me or my daughter and barely yourself for-"

Ken cut in, "Well, where the fuck is this shit going? The one time you do speak, you want to put my daughter down. And it's your house now, huh?"

My mom resumed her position as a quiet invisible person while Ken finished, "I had enough of this shit! Sabrina pack your bags we are leaving."

Everyone confused and lost we all started to sit on the edge of our seats. My mother was the only one who got up, "Baby where are you going?"

She grabbed at his shirt, he threw her hands off him and walked away as she followed him like a lost puppy. Sabrina started crying, "Daddy where? Where are we going, I'm so sorry daddy please don't make me go!"

Chino finally had enough and spoke up, "Dad what's up? where are you guys going?"

Ken turned to Sabrina and said, "I'm not going to tell you again, get your shit all of it and let's go."

Sabrina went up the steps quickly trying to hide her embarrassment and pain. I had no sympathy for her, I could careless where she went as long as it was as far away from me as possible. I couldn't wait, even though Cassidy was cool I could see she deeply regretted taking my side and for all I cared she could go to. Chino looked at me for the first time like he hated me and wanted me to go instead. Cassidy just avoided eye contact. Ken came back an sat at the table everyone waiting to hear the details,

"I'm taking Sabrina to her aunt's house since she seems to be the problem."

He said dryly. My mother immediately tensed up for a second before she quickly came to her senses, "Wait I'm going with you."

Ken stopped her dead in her tracks, "Nah, you ain't going with me. I think you've done and said enough." Ken barked at her.

My mom started to cry and ran to her room like a grounded adolescent child. Ken didn't care to hear how anybody felt so before anyone could open their mouths, he left the room. Everybody had a dumbfounded expression on their face except for Chino. If looks could kill, I probably would have dropped dead right then and there. I had never seen an ounce of anger in Chino's face until tonight. Chino was furious he got up in a hurry and threw his chair against the table and left. Sénar and Cassidy looked at each other and then at me like they wanted to know what was next. I felt obligated to say something.

I said, "Ok, I don't want you guys to think this was my intentions because it wasn't."

To be fair, I looked at them both to see if they had any objections to my claim. They both nodded in agreement, so I continued with a little more encouragement, "I just want to be drama free. I don't have anything against either of you."

I made it very clear I was talking about them and not anyone who wasn't sitting there at the time. I asked, "Cassidy, do you think we can be civil to another and live together without any grudges about our history with one another?"

She looked back as if to ensure herself that no one could hear her answer. She replied, "Yeah Treasure, but don't get to comfortable calling the shots cause Sabrina leaving wasn't my intentions either. Oh, and I'm older."

She just had to throw that in there, but I found a way to agree.

I said, "Ok, that's cool, I hear you Cassidy. Sénar, are you going to just try and make it impossible to go to school with all this beef between you and Tyrell because-"

Sénar cut in, "Treasure you cute but you ain't that cute, I can't help that this Swagga Mac Dagga makes ya boy insecure as hell. I don't blame him, but I'm done with him. He ain't shit and he won't last, I guarantee you."

He said it like he knew something that I didn't, but I just let it slide. I agreed, "Ok well do we have an alliance that will keep us from killing each other?"

Everyone laughed and agreed. We all got up and went our separate ways. I went outside to sit on the porch while Cassidy and Sénar went upstairs to say their goodbyes to Sabrina. I didn't care to see it because

I'm pretty sure they had to tell her something she wanted to hear. It was getting late the sun was going down, I could see a shadow in the window of Tyrell's house. That's when it dawned on me that I had not called Tyrell all day. I saw him look out his window then close the curtains and turn his light off. If I knew that I wouldn't have to answer to anybody then I would have run over there, but I think I had enough drama today that would last a lifetime. I waited until I saw Ken come out of the door when he saw me, he grabbed his crotch area and looked at me like I was some whore on a street corner. Confused, I just looked away and tried to ignore whoever or whatever else was next to come. I could hear other footsteps following him out the door. Chino, Sénar then Sabrina came out with bags in a single file line. It almost looked similar to a funeral burial. I avoided eye contact with everybody.

As Sabrina came out, I got up to go inside when Sabrina turned around and said, "I got you bitch! This shit ain't over, I'll be back."

With that said she turned her back on me and got in the car. Sénar turned around after waving goodbye and walked back towards the house with his eyes all over me. I could see Chino hugging Sabrina as Sénar inched closer. He walked up to me and said,

"Oooh you good and real sneaky, I like that shit."

I looked at him like he was crazy before glancing towards Chino coming toward us in a hurry. He walked up to the door and looked at me and Sénar then said,

"Y'all some cold motherfuckers. Man, y'all make me sick."

He slammed the door behind him. Sénar looked at me and said, "Wow." Before going inside. I looked back one time at Tyrell's house just in time to see the curtain shut again. Still tired and completely through with everybody and everything, I was hoping Cassidy would give me the chance to continue sleeping again. I needed rest to face the new beginning of the reality that was unfolding before me. I had in a sense lost three people but had gained three more and my mother was the only one, I cared to see left standing.

Chapter 10

I couldn't help but wonder why Chino was so angry with me. I mean, Sabrina had brought us all problems and shame at one time or another. He should be relieved that I got rid of her for the sake of some sort of peace in this house. Sénar didn't mind he couldn't stand her ass; she stayed screwing all his friends. Cassidy was surprised but looked relieved. Chino was the only one who seemed to be affected by it in a negative way. I just laid there looking at the wall with my back to Cassidy while she rummaged through her things as she tried to get prepared for school. I could hear her shuffling around, looking for things that Sabrina probably packed.

Cassidy mumbled under her breath, "That bitch."

I giggled a little, and then Cassidy asked, "Treasure you're awake?"

I hesitated a little before I responded, "Yeah."

I rolled over so that I could face her. The first thing I noticed was how pretty her face was without the scowl on it.

She said, "Sheesh, I was hoping for more space, but damn I didn't want her to take my shit to get it." We both laughed.

She then asked, "So how long are you suspended for?"

I smacked my lips and answered, "Just a week. I can't wait to go back. Man, I didn't even do nothing."

Cassidy looked at me like I was crazy, "Girl, please, you know you were all up in the Kool-Aid with that, but it's cool shit happens, right?"

Cassidy grabbed her stuff for school and headed for the door. Before she walked out of the door, I said, "Wait! Cassidy, what made you stick up for me?"

She turned to face me then replied, "I didn't stick up for you, Sabrina had that shit coming, and I'm tired of fighting her battles for her. She needs to chill out, I would have whooped her ass too but just don't pull that shit with me. If you cool, I'll be cool."

I nodded my head in agreement and said, "Yeah, I feel you; we'll be straight."

With that said, Cassidy left for school. I went back to sleep until I heard a knock at the door. I asked, "Who is it?" but there was no answer. I reluctantly got up and opened the door, but there was no one there. Irritated, I gathered my things to go to the bathroom. Then I heard another knock; I opened the door to see Sénar standing there grinning.

"What do you want?" He looked at me like I was tripping then said, "Damn, what's your problem?"

I looked at him like he was stupid and snapped at him, "Don't act like you didn't just knock on the door a second ago and didn't say anything."

He looked at me again like I was losing my mind or something. Sénar said, "No, I didn't you buggin', man, whatever your ass is crazy. You're one confused female. You don't know what you want!"

He turned away all puffed up, so I just grabbed my things and went to the bathroom to take a hot relaxing bath. I felt bad because Sénar was right. I was confused, and I didn't know what I wanted or how I felt, I was a mess. I had to let off some steam by releasing the warm liquid that filled my bladder over the night; it was very relieving. I took my clothes off and examined myself in the mirror. I felt like I was looking at another girl's body; it was definitely looking mighty nice. My breast were budding more, and my nipples were hard, with little goosebumps on them. My waist was slender, my thighs and hips were spreading,

I couldn't help but turn around to see my other assets. My butt was round and smooth, still looking like an upside-down chocolate heart.

I couldn't help but squeeze my cheeks before dipping one of my legs into the hot water filling the tub. I laid my head back and allowed the tension to seep out of my pores and my mind to wonder. The first thoughts that surfaced was how nice it felt to have my mother come to me and confide in me. I had a good feeling about her opening up to me. I heard her side of the story, and although it wasn't right, I felt her pain. I forgive her, and I want to be there for her and her to be there for me. I felt a feeling of love embrace me, and I wrapped my arms around myself, so I could hold on to the feeling longer. Before sweeping myself off my own feet, I had to come back to reality and think of what I was going to do when I got out of here. I thought about Tyrell and how he would react, being that we hadn't talked at all yesterday and all the events that took place in the last couple of days. I was hoping he would just be happy to see me. I was ready to face reality, and its many obstacles spread out throughout my life. The first thing I wanted to do was go and see Tyrell, so that we could be clear on where we stand with one another. I definitely wanted things to work out, but I knew the drama was far from over. I rushed out of the tub and quickly got dressed. By the time I finished dressing, I had a one-track mind. I was on a mission to regain the love and trust of Tyrell. I was feeling good about the situation. I grabbed my things and bolted for Tyrell's house.

I knocked on Tyrell's door, he answered it like he thought the person was going to play ding dong ditch or something. I couldn't help but giggle before asking,

"Dang, what's wrong with you?"

He looked at me like I was a reoccurring Jehovah Witness before he replied, "What Treasure?"

Lost for words I just looked at him a little shocked by his tone. Before I could say anything else, Tyrell said, "That's the first thing you could think of asking me, after your ass just forgot about me?"

I looked at him and smiled thinking he was playing; I went towards him to hug him. He pushed my arms away with so much force and anger. I was not only shocked but drawn back by his behavior. Tyrell continued, "Look Treasure, don't come over here frontin' and shit like things are all good."

Extremely hurt and tears burning my eyelids begging me to release them, I turned to run back home when Tyrell snatched me by my arm, damn near dragging me inside his house. He slammed the door, alarmed I snatched my arm away from him and looked at him as if he was a stranger. We stood there for a moment sizing each other up as if we were preparing for battle. Fear and anger gripped me, and I asked,

"Tyrell what the hell is wrong with you?"

He looked at me like he hated me. I did everything I could to fight back the tears from pouring on to my face. He was definitely not Tyrell at this moment, a part of me wanted to run. He looked at me and said, "What the fuck Treasure, you haven't even called me or come over to see me. I thought you loved me but I'm obviously the least important person to you. What, are you mad cuz I whooped your little side man's ass?"

Offended and feeling insulted I turned to leave. As I was opening the door Tyrell rushed toward me spinning me around and using my body to slam the door shut. My emotions a complete mess, my anticipation and happiness turned to instinct and sadness. I was devastated not knowing what to do or what to think, I felt helpless. Tyrell's face was so close to mine, I had no choice but to look at him.

He spoke in a tone I had yet to hear and said, "Treasure you are not to play with my emotions. You don't want to be with me then tell me. If you don't love me then don't. So, what is it?"

I didn't know how to answer, I was still in shock and very afraid of his next move. He was still holding me against the door. I quickly came to my senses and answered, "Yes Tyrell, I want to be with you, and I do love you, but you are really scaring me. Why are you so angry at me? Yesterday was crazy, I couldn't come or call. I-"

Tyrell quickly cut me off, "What, that doesn't even sound right. What or who could possibly have had you hymned up all day like that?"

He looked at me like I held the key to life or something. I felt I needed to tell him everything that happened yesterday. I said, "Well, I was tired, so I went to sleep until late afternoon." I paused as I was distracted by Tyrell moving back a little, so that he could have direct eye contact with me. I continued, "Well, I was sleeping when Sabrina's dumb ass barged into the room talking major shit, damn near yelling at the top of her lungs. I got up out of my sleep and she continued to test me, so I punched her in her mouth." I had Tyrell's full attention as he anxiously anticipated the rest of my story. I continued, "So, we fought until Ken came in and made everything worse forcing everyone to sit at the table, leaving me in the room like an outcast. Then my mom came in after to talk to me. We had a conversation that was so deep, I would have never expected it." Almost out of breath, I sucked a nice amount of air in to finish my story. "Then while me and my mom were finally getting to where we needed to be, Ken busts in and orders us downstairs like we had family court or something. When we got down there everyone was looking at me like I was giving my plea. Then we had a huge debate on whose fault it was and what the repercussions would be. Everyone was on the same page because Sabrina was definitely the problem, I was shocked because everybody was on my side except Ken and Chino."

Tyrell smirked, causing me to choose my next words carefully. I continued, "Then Ken came to the conclusion that Sabrina would move with her aunty. Although I was happy, Chino was really upset about it and he did not hide it." Out of breath I allowed Tyrell to soak everything in while I contemplated my closing speech. He looked at me as if he was giving me permission to continue on. I said, "Ok, so after all of that Sabrina reluctantly packed her things while sobbing and begging her daddy not to make her go. I sat outside to avoid any more confrontations. That's when I saw you, Lord knows I wanted to go over there, but I was afraid of getting in trouble. Ken and the whole clan came outside to see Sabrina off. So, to avoid any more issues, I just took that opportunity to go inside and go to sleep."

Tyrell looked at me as if he was deciding whether to believe my story. I was tired of his interrogation process, I decided to take control of the next conversation. So, before he could say anything, I quickly told him, "Look Tyrell, the last couple of days have been really crazy. There's been so much going on that we need to be here for each other not against each other, so please remember that we are in this together. Yesterday was crazy, but today is a new day and I'm here, aren't I?"

He looked at me like I was trying to be his counselor. He frowned his eyebrows at me and said, "Yo, Treasure don't try to seem all innocent and shit, then try to be a peacemaker now. You just remember that all the stuff you just told me, still involves ya boy Sénar too."

With that said, he grabbed me like he missed me and kissed me like he loved me. Tyrell then said, "Let's go upstairs, so I can get dressed."

I grinned like a kid in a candy store, damn near with a hop skip and a jump because I loved being there when Tyrell was getting dressed. Tyrell opened the door to his room and led me inside. Excited, I went straight to the bed to get comfortable. He looked at me with this sexy look in his eyes that made me feel extra naughty. He air kissed me and grabbed his crotch while licking his lips. Squirming and cheesing I couldn't resist him and said, "Tyrell you are driving me crazy! Get over here." I begged him as he smiled and turned to his closet.

He said, "Hold on, let me get my clothes I'm going to wear." I smacked my lips looking at him like he was crazy, mainly because he was serious. He smiled mischievously and went to his closet to pick his clothes. He then laid them on the ironing board and bent down to plug the iron in. I couldn't believe he was going to leave me hanging like that for real. He saw the expression on my face and started busting out laughing and said, "I'm just playing Treasure."

He pounced on me as I giggled and playfully pushed him off me. I said, "You're a big goof!"

We started passionately kissing, I could feel myself melting in his arms as he mounted his body on top of mine. I just laid there as if he was going to use my body as a tool for his pleasures. I could feel my heartbeat speed up as he licked my lips before parting them with his tongue. He grabbed my hand and put it on his hot throbbing penis. I wanted to pull away but instead I squeezed it. When he moaned, I snatch my hand back and Tyrell asked, "Why you stop!"

Caught off guard I asked, "Did it hurt?"

He snickered and said, "Nah girl, that shit feels good."

Blushing I could feel some of the blood leave my coochie and flood my cheeks. Looking in his lustful eyes I reached for the log feeling object in his pants. I could feel the blood pumping through it, my nipples hardened as he brushed his fingers across my shirt and use his other hand to grope my butt cheeks. I wrapped my legs around his upper thigh squeezing his body closer to mine. I wanted more than an acquaintance, I wanted him to come in. I caressed and messaged his hardened member as he humped and moaned. I got excited when a moan seeped out of my mouth when he gently grabbed my breast. For a moment, I thought this was it, this was the moment that I would become a woman. I felt like I was going to explode as I endured all the pleasure coming from so many places inside me. I could feel hotness in his shorts like he had an explosion of his own. As the hotness spread in his pants, his face became distorted as he gasped for air and then started whimpering like a hurt animal. I didn't know whether to apologize or be jealous. Our faces were masked by our emotions and thoughts, his being embarrassment and mine being dumbfounded. He quickly jumped and grabbed another pair of boxers then ran back into the bathroom. My hands were a little moist from the extreme heat of whatever happened in Tyrell's boxers. I couldn't help but wonder if the same thing that happened to me when I reached my peak of pleasure, had just happened to him. I just laid back and wondered what our private parts were really capable of. Putting my hand on my sticky throbbing coochie, spreading the juices around in a circular motion. I could feel tingling sensations throughout my body, I was lost in my own little world losing track of time.

Tyrell walked in without me noticing and asked, "What are you doing?"

Startled, I started to snatch my hands out of my pants, but he quickly prevented me from doing so, then said, "I don't care, don't stop."

With that silly grin on his face he started kissing my neck and rubbing my breast. I kept rubbing in a circular motion even though my fingers were hurting. With each suckle at my nipple, I rubbed more vigorously until I felt an explosion ripple through me. I pushed Tyrell off me and snatched my hands out of my pants to make sure my fingers hadn't shattered into a million pieces. My heart was beating so fast and the pulsation in my coochie was starting to subside when I looked over at Tyrell, he was grinning from ear to ear.

He asked, "Whoa what was that? We need to do that more often."

Still unsure of what happened and feeling embarrassed, I nodded in agreement. He got up to finish dressing and I ran to the bathroom with sticky funny smelling hands. I examined my hands again and grabbed tissue to wipe all the slimy stuff off my coochie. I couldn't help but smell it, but it didn't really smell like anything, so I tossed the tissue in the toilet and flushed it. I looked in the mirror and I was still in one piece, but I felt awesome. I walked out of the bathroom with a Kool- Aid smile ready for the rest of the day. When I came out the restroom Tyrell stood there waiting for me with this killer smile, looking fresh to death. He had on a pair of crispy white K SWISS, some blue khaki pants and a brand-new white tee. He looked so handsome with his sexy smile and chocolate brown skin. He was perfect and I loved him, even though he was getting way too jealous. I decided to take it as a compliment because it just meant I was super important to him. We left the house and got into the car. We were still driving on a donut tire after experiencing his crazy crash course of emotions, we pulled into a shop so that he could get his tire replaced. We got out of the car and I stood by the entrance of the tire shop while Tyrell talked to the tire guy. The whole time he was talking to him, the tire guy just stared at me. I was feeling uncomfortable, even Tyrell had to ask,

"Aye man, are you hearing me?"

The dude had an accent and replied, "I hear you bro, it's thirty bucks."

As if to get to the point, he just kept staring at me until Tyrell looked back to see what he was staring at. When he saw me patiently waiting for him to hurry up, he smiled but then became entirely irritated with the tire guy.

The tire dude said, "Like aye bro, she fine as hell, my bad let me get your tire on so you and your pretty lady can be on your way."

Tyrell gave him the money and walked off to avoid having one of his fits. He walked up to me and said, "Damn Treasure, I wish I could put you in my pocket. You so fine, you got me wanting to beat the shit out of the tire dude."

He started laughing and twirling me around then he pulled me in to hug him. The tire guy was still gawking and licking his lips while trying to stay focused on his job. I asked, "So, what are we about to do?"

He looked me in my eyes and just stared at me, then answered, "I don't know baby, but you got me so deep in my feelings, I don't even care. Shit, I just want to live long enough to get some sheesh!"

We both started laughing when the tire dude happily broke up our laughing fest and said, "Aye bro, you done."

Tyrell opened my door to secure me just in case the dude was going to steal me. He then jumped in the driver side with a big grin on his face. I grabbed Tyrell's leg with a loving gesture. He exhaled and shook his head then said,

"Look babe, you are fine as hell and it seems to me that Sénar ain't the only one who be wanting to taste my chocolate. Hell, I haven't even tasted it yet." He smirked at me before he continued, "I just want to know you belong to me. I hate that you live with that fucking crazy ass Sénar, but I just need to know that there ain't no bullshit going on between you two."

I was irritated because I understood his frustration, but I really didn't know what to do any more. I couldn't tell him he would never understand, so I just looked at him with pleading eyes and said, "Tyrell, things are really awkward at my house but with Sabrina gone hopefully things will be better-"

He interrupted me saying, "Look we ain't talking about Sabrina, we are talking about Sénar!" He yelled at me, I grimaced and held my composure.

When his nose was starting to flare, I quickly responded, "You didn't even let me finish, what I was going to say." Rolling my eyes and trying to control my attitude from ripping out of me I continued, "What I was saying is that Sénar has several girlfriends he is not worried about me, and even if he was I am not worried about him."

I was sure to quickly add that before he needed to remind me, he did not look convinced. He just gripped his steering wheel to relieve his anger, so to prevent another driving incident, I quickly reminded him that he was mine and I was his. I pulled my shirt down exposing my entire breast with his beautiful name placed in between the two of my breasts. The grip he had on the steering wheel instantly released, causing the car to drift to the side. He put one hand back firmly on the steering wheel and reached out to grab one of my breasts. He then ran his hand over his name gleaming confidently above my breast as it hung from the chain he bought. He smiled that sexy smile and quickly found a place to pull over to have his way with me. He kissed me so passionately and squeezed my breast and whispered, "All mine."

I kissed him back and said, "You are damn right!"

We giggled and reminisced on all the fun times we had together. He vowed that he would do his best to control his jealousy but that he was just tired of everybody commenting on me and my beauty.

Tyrell said, "I guess I have to learn to take it as a compliment."

He looked embarrassed for his behavior and grabbed my hand to kiss it. We found a taco truck and decided we would give it a try. We ordered ten tacos of all the different meats and found a park to chill at. I must say the tacos were better than any taco I had ever had in my life. Tyrell and I debated on if I should get an equal number of tacos since I am a girl. Shoot, I got my four tacos and was ready to fight for the fifth. The sun was setting, and we started to head back to the house.

He looked at me and said, "It's not so bad being suspended."

I slapped his shoulder playfully and we laughed all the way home. We kissed goodnight, then he broke the news that he would be working the next few days. He said his parents were upset and told him that if he fought again, he would lose his car for a couple of months to get his act together.

He smacked his lips and said, "Shidd they ain't never home anyway, so I ain't worried about it."

I didn't laugh because he was too cocky sometimes, he appeared to never want to take any responsibility for his actions. I realized he was a spoiled brat. He had it so good, I was almost jealous of him for a second. I kissed him and got out of the car and crossed the street. When I got inside everyone was downstairs including my mom. They were looking at me like I had a sign held up with the words *look at me* across it. I waved to acknowledge everyone and tried to run up the steps. When Ken called my name, I hesitated and thought about running but I knew it was a terrible idea.

I reluctantly answered, "Yes?"

Still facing the steps afraid to turn around to face all the beady eyeballs that were staring at my profile, as I tried to escape. When he didn't respond I repeated, "Yes, Ken?" I asked unsure of the response he wanted.

He responded, "Come sit down at the table, we all need to talk."

I held the large breath I wanted to exhale and let it out slowly to avoid appearing disrespectful. I sat down at the table and tried to look as innocent as possible.

Ken said, "Your mom and I had a trip planned and I was looking forward to it. All up until I heard this nonsense that took place this past week. I work too damn hard to come home to a bunch of dumb asses that can't act civilized. Everyone is old enough to know right from wrong. The next time we have anything like this take place in this house there will be some serious consequences."

He looked at everyone, even my mom nodded her head like she was a kid. Chino responded, "Where you gonna send Treasure's ass?"

Ken slapped the table and said, "Shut the fuck up boy, I ain't playing no games. I am serious the next ass whipping that's going to happen, is coming from me!"

Chino said, "I haven't done anything. I mind my business and get good grades, so I am not the problem." Chino smacked his lips then glared at me then at Sénar and rolled his eyes at Cassidy. He didn't even acknowledge my mom.

Ken smirked and looked at him and replied, "So what! You want a cookie lil' nigga? I am saying keep it that way or else." Ken looked at me and said, "Treasure, you are a growing young lady and I see you got a couple of admirers but don't let it go to your head. I want you to respect this household. I have had way too much drama coming from you and this little boyfriend of yours."

Sénar smirked and rolled his eyes. I started to say something, but Ken cut me off and said, "Maybe I need to meet him and let him know my expectations, because if I have any more problems, I will make sure y'all never see each other again."

The look in his eyes was so cold and sadistic, I could see where Sénar got them cold ass looks from. My throat tightened and I was silenced by his eyes. I looked down at my lap so no one would see the tears wailing up behind my eyelids. Sénar snickered and Ken slapped the table again, then put his attention on Sénar.

Ken said, "You are next boy! If I keep having problems out of your ass, I am going to send you so far away, your head will spin!"

Chino jumped up and said, "Now we gotta send away another one of ours!" Chino yelled with his fist balled up, Ken jumped up and Chino whimpered back down into his chair. Sénar's face was stone cold with no emotion. He sat quietly because he knew he was doing too much and did not want to get sent away. Cassidy was so silent, I almost forgot she was there. Ken looked at her and smiled and she smiled back nervously.

Ken then said, "Cassidy, I see you already slowed your roll so just keep slowin' it because I don't wanna have to school you too."

She knew not to argue as she was getting a pass and just responded, "Yes daddy."

He smiled and gave me a look as if that was the proper response, with a similar sadistic smile like Sénar flashed before or after his sexual devious acts. Sénar instantly became enraged with jealousy, as fear gripped me after the horrific encounter, I had with Ken flashed across my mind. I looked down to avoid both of their eye contact. Ken got up from the table and beckoned my mom to follow, by just getting up. She was behind him like a little puppy. As soon as Ken and my mom left the room, Chino cursed under his breath and gave me his own sadistic look before leaving the table. Sénar gave him an eye as if to say *I wish you would.* Cassidy just shook her head and left without saying a word, I thought to myself damn she sure is a lot quieter without Sabrina's rowdy behind. Sénar and I were the only ones left at the table. I was overwhelmed, I could barely move as Sénar looked at me long and hard. I wish I was Cleopatra and could read minds.

He just stared at me until I snapped, "What are you looking at Sénar?"

He just stared at me more intense and quickly got up from his chair, causing me to flinch in fear. Sénar laughed at me and then walked pass me leaving me with confused anticipation of what was going to happen next. He disappeared going upstairs like everyone else, I waited a while before I went up the stairs. I was exhausted feeling on edge, normally he would never pass up an opportunity like this to grab me or say something inappropriate. I was almost offended by his lack of actions.

The week went by slowly but smoothly, everyone seemed to take Ken's pep talk pretty seriously. No one wanted to see how he would fulfill his threats. I wondered how long it would last before someone did something stupid. The last three days Tyrell had been at work and I sat in my room reading my books while Cassidy ran the streets with her friends. Even Sénar and Chino were gone or either in their rooms. My mom occasionally floated out of her room to make food for Ken and maybe to grab a cup or bottle from the fridge. She was happy when I saw her. Ken had been home for the last couple of days, so the house was well behaved. I just sank into the background, like I did best. It was Friday and I was missing Tyrell; I could not wait to see him. I called him and his mom answered the phone, I almost hung up because I was not expecting to hear any voice but his.

She said, "Hello?" I breathed into the phone like a weirdo, until she said, "Hello is anyone there?"

I cleared my throat and said, "Hello Mrs. Carter."

She responded, "Good morning darling, how may I help you?"

I thought to myself what else would I be calling for before I said, "Hi, is Tyrell home?"

She responded, "Oh no sweetie, him and his dad went out this morning they won't be back 'til later. I'll tell him you called, what's your name?"

I almost flashed and asked her well who else calls him, but I sweetly responded, "Oh this is Treasure, thanks."

I must admit I was a little offended, but I knew both his parents worked a lot, so I tried not to let it bother me. I huffed and puffed and thought what the hell am I supposed to do for a third day without him. My mom and Ken were even gone. Chino was coming out of the room the same time as I was, he rolled his eyes at me.

I couldn't help but ask, "Chino, where's everyone at?"

He looked at me and barked his reply, "Like you really care! ... Your other boyfriend is asleep, and I don't know where the love birds flew to. You should know about your own roommate, so don't ask silly questions; I don't want to be tied in your little web."

I winced because I could hear the hate in his voice. He looked like he regretted his words when he seen my response and just kept walking while shaking his head. Cassidy was still sleeping and from the looks of it she was not getting up anytime soon. I was so bored, I almost thought about going to bug Sénar, but I knew I would be out of line, so I just grabbed a book and sat on the couch. I read until I fell asleep. I woke up to the smell of eggs and bacon and a hint of cinnamon. I followed my nose to the kitchen, not caring who was responsible for the aroma that hypnotized my nose to float into the kitchen. Sénar was in the kitchen listening to some music on his Walkman. He was grooving too, in his own little world. I was watching him get it, when he turned around to see that I was cheesing as I watched him dance. He reacted like a naked lady being caught in the shower. I giggled causing him to blush because he had no idea, I was watching him the whole time. He looked at me licking his lips flirtatiously and kept on with his cooking, just no more dancing. I was disappointed because I was enjoying the show.

Cassidy came downstairs and saw me watching Sénar cook, she was also intrigued to investigate the smell too. She looked at me and just smirked like she knew something that I didn't. She walked up to Sénar with his back turned and slapped him in the back of the head. He turned around ready to pounce, he slapped her with a spatula and looked embarrassed because he had a devious look on his face, until he realized it was her. She started laughing then snatched bacon and some French toast before she ran out of the kitchen. Accidentally bumping into me on her way out the door, she then put up the peace sign before leaving. She obviously was late to school because she should have been gone. She was a junior now so she could get away with that because they had different rules for them. When the door closed, is when I realized me and Sénar were officially alone in the house. The second the door closed Sénar was behind me with his sadistic grin on his face. I started to bolt out the door after Cassidy but Sénar already had his arms wrapped around me. I could feel his erection on my behind and feel his breath on my neck.

I went limp, he picked me up from behind and carried me into the kitchen. He released me then turned me around to face him with a huge grin on his face, he then picked me up, sitting me on the counter. He spread my legs with force, I tried with all my might to close them back. He took the plugs out of his ear and looked me in my eyes. I was stiff as a board; I didn't want to do or say anything to set him off. In a seductive voice he asked, "Are you hungry?"

Before I could answer, my stomach had an audible growl that answered for me. Sénar laughed then quickly kissed me before turning back to the stove just in time to flip his French toast, to replace the one Cassidy snatched earlier. I felt like a baby placed on the counter afraid to jump down. He looked back to ensure I had not moved while he fixed our plates. I sat on the counter like a good little girl and he moved around the kitchen like the busy mother. When he had everything set up, he came back to resume his place in between my legs.

He winked at me and said, "Let's eat ma."

He picked me up like a little girl and squeezed my butt cheeks while carefully standing me on my feet. I quickly turned around to walk toward the table. SMACK! My ass rippled and vibrated from the force of Sénar's hand slapping my ass jolting me forward. I quickly sat down with an instinct to cool the warm hand print I felt on my butt cheek.

He said, "Damn, you got a fat ass girl, umph!"

I was annoyed and a tad bit flattered but refused to show it. I could not help but say, "You are so rude Sénar!" He rolled his eyes and retorted, "You know you like that shit!"

I smacked my lips and sighed. He ate his food while I cautiously took my time eating mine to prolong the process as much as possible. He did not take his eyes off me the whole time. I don't know how he found his food with his fork because he never once took his eyes off me. I was starting to get uncomfortable because I was running out of food, which I must say was delicious. He was done eating and impatiently waiting for me to finish. I stopped to drink my orange juice and purposely took my time.

He was irritated and barked, "Man, hurry up!" Startled, I jumped then asked, "Why are you in such a rush?' It's not like we have to go to school."

He looked at me like I was dumb, then snatched my plate with the food on it. He put his plate on top of mine, handed it to me, then shooed me into the kitchen to clean and put the dishes away. I raked my plate wishing I would have just eaten my last couple of bites, I washed the plates putting them to dry. He was waiting on me with his arms crossed. I stood there reluctant to move as I had no idea what was next and needed to be cautious because no one was home. He licked his lips and grabbed his crotch and told me to come to him. I was so scared, I stood there for a second wondering what my options were.

He then asked, "You want me to carry you?" I shook my head no like a defiant child and reluctantly inched towards him. "Good girl." He whispered.

I took a deep breath and tried to walk around him. Sénar put his finger up wagging it in my face and said, "Ahhh, ahh, ahh, no, no, no." He snickered and grabbed my waist pulling me to him then said, "I don't know when I'll have this opportunity again." He grabbed my neck and kissed me so passionately. I couldn't stop him because he had full control of my body. He let me go and looked at me and said,

"I won't tell." He yanked my hand and pulled me upstairs, damn near dragging me like a rag doll. I braced myself not wanting to trip on the stairs, my heart was beating so fast I thought it would burst out of my chest. He threw me on my bed and didn't even bother to close the door. He jumped on top of me, I pushed him off me then curled up into a ball for protection.

He sighed, "Damn why do you have to make shit so difficult?" His eyes turned dark before he pulled me by my feet and spread my legs apart forcing himself in between them, then wrestling my shirt off me. My blue lace bra barely covered my chocolate nipples, he gawked at me as I tried to cover them. He was in awe as he looked like he wanted to rip it off. He said, "Take it off unless you want me to tear it off." I thought about the bra being one of my favorites and that I wanted to show Tyrell since he bought it for me. I didn't want him to rip my bra and I knew he would, I started to cry.

When Sénar reached for one of my straps to my bra I scooted back and said, "Ok ok ok…" He stopped, but appeared impatient as I asked him, "If I take it off, will you leave me alone?"

He smirked before he answered, "Yeah…..nah you have to let me suck on them."

I opted out by shaking my head no, prompting him to eagerly snatch down my bra exposing one of my breasts. He rushed to put his mouth on it as we heard keys in the door. He grunted, "Fuuuuuck!" He quickly got up looking back at me to get one more look before leaving my room. I hurried to fix my bra and to put my shirt back on, then laid in my bed like I was sleeping. My mind was racing, I was so happy to hear Ken's voice. My mom was silent while Ken was telling her to go and put his favorite outfit on. I laid in the bed thinking how lucky I was that they came home. I couldn't help but wonder what would have happened if they didn't come home. Sheesh Sénar did all sorts of things when they were here, so I just knew he would have done whatever he wanted. I had to get out of the house because he was sure to come back. I looked for an outfit and paced my room thinking about where I would go or what I would do. Sheesh, I had no friends and there was no telling when Tyrell was coming back.

When I opened my room door, Sénar was standing there. I tried to close the door, but he stopped it from closing. We could hear Ken and my mom in the room sounding like teenagers having fun. My stomach churned as Sénar warned, "To be continued."

He looked agitated before he headed downstairs. I came out my room to watch him leave. When he opened the front door to go out, I ran down to see where he was going. I saw the red convertible outside with the pretty white woman from the other day waiting for him, he got in the car and left with her. He probably needed to relieve himself because he was so excited earlier, he thought he would have his way with me, and no one was here to be able to stop him. I felt so lucky to be saved as I walked back to my room. When I got to the top of the stairs Ken came out their room without a shirt on. I looked away as I walked towards my room, with Ken now behind me I heard him say,

"Damn I know your ass is driving Sénar crazy! I bet you glad to see me, huh?" I turned around and he was smiling like his sadistic ass son. My mom opened their door, "Don't forget the wine babe...Treasure what are you doing here?"

I thought, *did she forget already that I was suspended?* I answered quickly, "Oh, I am going to the library now momma."

Instead of going in my room, I ran down the steps and hurried out the door to get as far away from the house as possible. I was walking down the street with nowhere to go, I even forgot to grab some money. I figured I would just walk around like a nomad for a couple of hours. I was walking with my head down when an expedition pulled up. This fine ass dark skinned man with the most beautiful smile I had ever seen rolled his window down. I kept walking when I heard Tyrell's voice, he came from around the front of the car. I was so happy to see him I ran to him and kissed him.

His dad chuckled and said, "You got some good taste boy!"

He beamed a smile like his dad's. Tyrell asked, "Where are you going baby?"

I answered, "I needed to get out of the house. I didn't know where I was going actually."

He looked at me with concern, "Are you ok?"

I answered, "Yeah, I'm cool. I called you but your mom said you were with your dad."

Tyrell eagerly introduced me to him, "Hey dad, this my baby girl, Treasure."

I waved at his dad then smiled and he smiled back. Tyrell told me to get in the car and we went back to his house. His dad was bumping shoulders with Tyrell and he was trying not to be embarrassed. The dad sensed our need for alone time, so he took his mom on a date and left us there alone. Tyrell and I ordered pizza and looked for some wine to drink. I was so excited when he found some Sangria because the last time, we drank we had so much fun. He looked for some fancy glasses and poured us a cup each. We drank and went way back to when he first saw me an threw a rock at my forehead. We laughed so hard because for the life of him, he would not tell me why. That was the first time I realized an interesting concept, sometimes first comes pain, then comes pleasure. We were bored of watching TV and went to his room to playhouse. Feeling the wine, I ran upstairs first.

Before Tyrell entered the room, I removed my shirt to flaunt my blue bra Sénar tried to rip off me earlier. He stopped dead in his tracks and just stared at me with lustful eyes, he then rushed me and started kissing me. He clumsily tried to take my bra off, I got tired of waiting and helped him take it off. When he saw my breast, he just put his face in the middle of them. I could see his member grow through his pants, and I got excited. He laid me down on his bed and climbed on top of me. He started to hump me and squeeze my breast, it felt so good. I started to moan and take his shirt off, he looked at me with confusion but just went with the flow. I tugged at his pants and then took my pants off to show off my voluptuous thighs. He started to rub my thighs, then

142

put his hand in between my legs to feel the warmth of my excitement. Then moving his fingers around the outside of my panties making me even more excited. Yearning for more, I tugged at his pants again. He resisted a little but still allowed me to take them off.

He was hesitant to go further, but I urged him by kissing him while pulling him to me. He got up to turn the lights off, leaving the bathroom light on. When he came back, I rubbed the outside of his boxers and squeezed his member. I got a wave of courage and pulled him on top of me. He pulled his member out and rubbed it on the outside of my panties. I was so horny, I thought I would shove it inside of me for him. I felt like I was the aggressive one and pushing towards feeling him inside of me. I started to think about Sénar and if it were him in this position, how he would have already been inside of me by now. I shook the thought out of my mind and tried to focus. I had no fear at this time and wanted to feel what it felt like. He pushed my panties to the side and put the tip of his member in. I felt a pain like I never felt before, it felt like all the air left my body when I yelped in pain. Tyrell pulled himself back and stopped like he was scared.

He asked, "Are you ok? Did I hurt you?" I didn't know what to say because it hurt so bad, that I didn't know whether to lie, or say no, or just keep going. He stopped, then said, "No, you are drunk, and we shouldn't be doing this."

He stopped and started to get dress. I lay there in pain but still horny. I looked down and saw blood, I freaked out and he did too. We were both silent and uncomfortable, he told me to get dressed in authority. I quickly got dressed and pouted because I felt like I was in trouble. He left the room and I followed him. He told me to go home and sober up, he quickly kissed me then sent me on my marry way. I was so confused and annoyed. I thought about what happened and couldn't understand why people made such a big deal about sex, when it was more fun to mess around then to actually have sex. Although we didn't go through with it, we were really close. I felt like I messed up, I was so embarrassed, I went home, ran upstairs and passed out.

Chapter 11

The next morning, I woke up with a headache that felt like a little man in my head was playing the drums. Through blurred vision and the will to see despite the uninvited music in my head, I saw Cassidy combing her hair and eyeing me out the corner of her eye. She looked at me with a smirk and greeted me with,

"Ump humph, what were you doing last night?"

I immediately cleared my throat to make an easier passage for my lie to flow through, while I searched for a suitable answer. We Both laughed for different reasons and immediately warranted a possibility of friendship. I sighed in discomfort and told her, "I made some bad decisions and I am currently paying for them."

She laughed and told me that I was just a rookie at being fast. She really took pride in being an experienced fast ass teenager along with her sister. Now that Sabrina and her poisonous wrath was gone, Cassidy was definitely home more and not as outgoing.

She then said, "Now that I don't have a secondary witness to my bullshit stories, I choose my escapades wisely. I usually only drank so Sabrina wouldn't feel alone."

I asked her, "Are you assuming I drank?"

She looked at me as if I was stepping on her toes for trying to play her. Then she said, "Unless you are sleeping with rubbing alcohol you definitely had some liquor."

I looked down before responding, "I did not think it was going to be this bad."

She then said, "You might want to get some practice with people you can trust to not take advantage of you. I know that sounds weird, but drinking can really get you in a situation you are not ready for."

I thought to myself whoa is she really giving me advice. Sheesh one damn time of having some fun with Tyrell had her thinking that I am really trying to make this part of my life. I laughed out loud as she cleared her throat and asked, "What's so damn funny?"

I looked at her like I forgot she was even there; she smacked her lips dismissing my opportunity to respond. I felt bad, so I hopped up to sit on my bed and asked, "Why are you so defensive?"

She looked at me offended and said, "Look, I was trying to school your ass, but you're acting like you got it all together, so I will not be wasting my time. I was trying to be nice to yo dumb ass."

I almost flashed on her until I realized I did kind of zone out for a second. I said, "My bad, I was still dazed, I did not mean anything by it. And I appreciate the advice, so chill out."

She looked at me with don't tell her what to do written all over her face. I proceeded to ignore all her attitude, "I just had a couple of drinks with Tyrell, thank God he lives across the street or I probably would have ended up in a ditch somewhere hahaha."

Me and Cassidy laughed so loud that Sénar popped his head into our room and said, "Dayumm what's that smell?"

Cassidy yelled, "Get your nosey ass out of here boy!"

He quickly closed the door before eying me with suspicion. I quickly looked away to avoid eye contact with him. Cassidy looked at me when he closed the door and asked, "Why are you so scared of his ass, he ain't shit. He hella crazy, but we all are. If you can handle us, you can handle his ass too."

I thought about how many times he cornered me or how I tried to fend for myself and ended up on the floor or worse. She just looked at me waiting once again for me to respond, I quickly answered her, "I am not scared of him, he is nosey though."

We both laughed again, but mine was forced and hoped we would change the subject. Sénar was violent and careless towards me. He had some sick obsession with me, and I was afraid to tell anyone. I was so scared of him, every time I thought about standing up for myself, I cowered, and I would just hope he stopped before I was not able to take it any longer. She then asked what I was doing this Saturday afternoon and mentioned the mall. I thought about my crazy night with Tyrell and I wasn't ready to face him yet. So, when she asked me if I wanted to go, it wasn't long before I agreed to go with her. I jumped up to take a shower grabbing some clothes and ran out of the room to the bathroom. Soon as the door opened, someone rushed me from the side and pushed me into the bathroom. Sénar was standing in front of me with his nostrils flaring and his eyes red with fury. I whimpered at the sight of him, then quickly remembered what Cassidy said.

Mustering up the remainder of drunkenness left, I said, "Get out boy and mind your business!"

Sénar snatched me so hard by my shirt, I felt my bra strap cut into my back and shoulders. He warned me, "Don't ever talk to me like that again! Don't forget who I am!" He ripped my shirt exposing my bra and bulging breast. He looked me up and down and said, "We gonna finish this conversation, when you have some respect of who you are talking to."

He left me there shivering out of fear. I was at lost for words, not that anyone would listen to them anyways. I just sat on the edge of the bathtub and cried for what seemed like an eternity, then I heard Cassidy knock on the door.

She asked, "Girl what are you doing? I don't hear no water running and I would like to go to the bathroom before I go. Hurry up!"

I turned the water on and snapped back into reality, so I could get ready as fast as possible. I did not want to get left and have to deal with Sénar or even Tyrell. I was still uncertain about last night and was not ready to face what happened. I took a shower as fast as I could and quickly ran to the room to get dressed. As I was putting all my clothes on and putting lotion on my body, I looked up and Cassidy was staring at me with a complexed look on her face.

I looked at her and asked her, "Are you ok?"

She also seemed to be in a trance and was unaware of it. She then looked at me as if I was the one tripping then said, "I am fine, you are just taking a long time."

She never took her eyes off me. I felt a little uncomfortable but continued to get ready, leaving some body parts with no lotion. She then asked, "Are you sure you want to go?"

I answered, "Yeah, why not?" She shrugged her shoulders while grabbing her Gucci purse and headed for the door, I had no choice to follow like a puppy. When we got outside some cute older guy was driving the car and we jumped in the back seat. There was a pretty caramel skin girl with curly hair and big pretty hoop earrings in the back seat. Her hoops were sparkling, and I am pretty sure they were expensive. She saw me eyeing her earrings and smirked,

"You like them girl? They super cute huh and expensive too. Just like I like it."

She was pretty, she had jet black curly hair and blue eyes. I had never seen anyone like her in my life. Her skin glowed and glistened, her lips were pretty and pink. I caught myself looking at her like Cassidy was looking at me earlier. They both giggled and told the driver to take us to the mall. Her name was Nevaeh and she was a year older than Cassidy. They were both holding their digital cameras in their hands and taking pictures of themselves. I thought to myself how in the hell can they afford such things at our age. I didn't even have a pager and they totally had digital cameras. As we were driving, I noticed the guy in the front eyeing me from the rear-view mirror. I smiled at him in an innocent manner because I did not need another creep looking at me in any type of sexual way. I was starting to realize that men seemed to be all thinking of what they can get out of you sexually, and that was the furthest thing from my mind right now.

When we got to the mall, Nevaeh told the driver to pick us up at 8:00pm. It was barely one o' clock in the afternoon. I thought to myself, what in the hellified tosis could we do for seven hours at the mall? I was damn near ready to tell them that I don't think I could last seven hours at the mall before I heard Cassidy on the phone with her boyfriend Tony. We went inside the mall where there was a large amount of people walking around. There were clusters of people boys and girls of all types, lots of chattering and laughing everywhere. I was trying to look around without being obvious hoping no one from school would notice me with my arch enemy's sister and her beautiful friend. I totally hoped too soon, one of Sabrina's raggedy ass friends came up to Cassidy,

"Hey girl wassup? Where is Sabrina?"

She looked at me as if I had some sort of disease and waited for a response from Cassidy. After looking her up and down as if she didn't know her, Cassidy answered,

"I don't know that's your friend, right?"

The girl smacked her lips and Cassidy immediately checked her, "I am not Sabrina's keeper little girl, so bye!"

The girl dared not say another word and tapped her friend on the shoulder as their cue to leave. Cassidy was irritated, I could see it in her face. The girl's name was Jessica and she was whispering to her friend, eyeing me and giving me a stank face. She was with Sabrina when we got into it at school. Cassidy's phone rang and it was her boyfriend Tony, she summoned me and Nevaeh to follow her. When we got outside there was a fresh ass black SS Impala. The guy in the car was fine, but he was a grown ass man.

He looked at me then asked, "Who is Miss. Chocolate Drop you got with you?"

Cassidy kissed him on the mouth and said, "What are you worried about her for?"

He must have met Nevaeh before he nodded what's up to her and pulled off. I did not say a word, I was shocked that this grown ass man was picking us up and he was not a driver. He pulled up to a house and there was a bunch of dudes in the garage smoking and playing a game of dominoes. They all stopped and looked at us like we were sparkling like Nevaeh's earrings, I was so nervous I had to go pee. I squirmed a bit but didn't say anything. One of the guys asked, "Wassup shawty?"

I looked at him and said, "Hello, my name is Treasure."

He laughed and said, "I see, you lookin' like a whole bunch of jewels."

He laughed along with all the other guys in the garage then said, "I'm Markese, I never seen you before."

Nevaeh went to sit on one of the other guy's lap and they kissed. I was so uncomfortable because there was like two other guys there and they were looking at me like I had something they wanted. To break the silence, I asked to use the bathroom. Cassidy smacked her lips and jumped off her boyfriend's lap to show me where the bathroom was. She did not hesitate to school me on the way,

"Look Treasure, don't be super needy and don't start acting brand new."

I looked at her with a confused look, "What do you mean brand new?"

She rolled her eyes, "Like don't be acting like you a little girl and shit."

I looked at her careful not to make her mad, "Ummm, ok."

But in my head, I was thinking I am a little girl, I am definitely not a grown woman and these men are grown ass men. I went to the bathroom and tried to come up with a game plan on how I was going to act. I flushed the toilet and took a deep breath while I washed my hands. I decided I would learn to play dominoes and beat them so bad; they would not want to touch me. I walked into the garage and everyone stopped what they were doing, to look at me as if they were waiting for me to return.

I was a bit uncomfortable, but I managed to say, "Can I play dominoes with y'all?"

They started laughing and one of them looked me up and down. Markese asked, "Do you know how to play?"

He asked like he was talking about something sexual. I smirked and said, "Nah but I am willing to learn."

I had a little flirty attitude, but I was genuinely talking about dominoes. Markese was really cute, he was a dark-skinned dude with a nice goatee and pretty white teeth. He had corn rows and he had on a crisp white tee with some black jeans. His shoes were the cleanest shoes out of all them and he seemed to be nice enough to teach me. He wanted to be funny, so he tapped his lap and said,

"Sit here girl, I'll show you how to play."

Everyone laughed, but me. I had to think fast, I swiftly replied, "Then I would surely win, so I'll just sit next to you, so you will have a chance to win after I learn."

Everybody started to laugh again but uncomfortably. I found an empty chair and pulled it up to the table and offered to watch them play a round. I realized it was basically a color-coded math game with a twist of strategy. All I needed to know was the rules of what we could and couldn't do and I would pretty much have it down pat. I was concentrating hard trying to figure out the strategy of the game when I almost jumped out of my chair, when one of the guys named Debo smacked the table so hard then yelled, "Domino nigga!"

They all threw the dominoes on the table out of frustration and the game was over. Apparently, domino meant the person who has one domino left on their turn, if able to play their last domino, all other players must give their remaining dominoes to the person who dominoed as points. I was ready, they started a new game and I grabbed my dominoes with eagerness. I looked at my hand and felt a little self-conscious but tried not to let them know. Markese, which was the cute dark skin guy who could not keep his eyes off me, asked me if I had big six.

I stuttered, "Wwwhat's big six?"

Everyone laughed, and his homie threw it on the table, it was twelve because the six was on both sides. A light bulb went off in my head and I realized all numbers had a double-sided domino. When it was my turn, I saw the opportunity to get 15 points. I slammed the six/ three domino on the table connecting the six leaving the three, then said, "Fifteen!" The guys laughed because they called it a rape case and had no idea, they were speaking their futures having all of us little girls there, but I chose to keep it at fifteen along with my soon to be age. That's pretty much how the game went, I was whipping them so bad. Markese appeared agitated and started to roll what they were calling a blunt. It was a green and sticky plant he pulled out of a baggy. He licked the cigar looking at me and then cut it down the middle. He then put the plant in it and rolled it back up to where it looked like it did originally. He lit it and then passed it to his boy and then asked if I smoked. I shook my head no with a look of disgust on my face.

Everyone hit it except me when Nevaeh said, "Hit it once girl, it won't kill you."

She was smiling so pretty and appeared to be extremely happy when saying it. I started to decline but she passed it to me anyway. I put it to my lips and coughed before I even inhaled. Everyone laughed, Markese then took it from me to show me how to smoke it. I did as he said and coughed so hard, I thought I was going to pass out. I immediately felt like I was in a movie. Everyone's face was a little more animated and clearer. It was like I had glasses on and could see exceptionally well.

Markese asked, "You cool shawty?"

I looked at him and started laughing because he looked like Popeye the Sailor Man with the blunt in his mouth as he was speaking. I was laughing and could not stop it was like the funniest thing in the world at the moment.

Cassidy said, "Ah shit, she's high already."

She shook her head, and everyone started laughing in unison. Markese put some music on and started to shuffle around the dominoes again. Nevaeh and Cassidy got up with their dudes and left into the house. It was just me and the other three guys left in the garage. I was too busy giggling to realize the danger that put me in, but I liked Markese. He was cool, but the other two were older and a little creepy. I just knew I was unusually happy, and it felt kind of nice that I could not stop smiling. Markese appeared to be the only one I could see myself trying to get to know. The rest were old ass dudes looking for prey. Markese on the other hand, seemed more down to earth and not as thirsty as the rest. He was funny and still had a youthful sense to him. I asked him if I was playing well and he smirked,

"You aiight."

It was just me, Markese and the other two creepy dudes left in the garage. I started to feel a little uncomfortable, so I made sure to let Markese know I liked him and not in any special way, but I trusted him more than the other dudes. One of the creepy dudes went inside and Markese kept looking at me out of the corner of his eye. He decided to play 21 questions, he asked,

"How old are you?"

I thought about lying but then I decided just not to tell the whole truth instead, and maybe they would not try and get at me. I told a little black lie,

"I am fifteen, I have a birthday coming up."

It sounded better than saying I was just fourteen years old. Markese made a face saying, "Dayuuum girl, you a lil' youngin' huh?"

We both laughed. The other guy had come back in time to hear my age but did not seem the least bit bothered by it. He just licked his lips never taking his eyes off me, he was making me nervous. I asked Markese what time it was, and he told me it was 3:00PM. I almost passed out because 8:00PM was so far away. I started to panic thinking what would I possibly do all the way until then. I tried not to show how nervous I was because I did not want to be targeted by the girls or the guys. I just started to think what I could possibly do to entertain them until then.

Markese saw me thinking hard and asked, "Damn girl, what you over there thinking about?"

Feeling a little pressure, I quickly responded, "Um nothing, I just wanted to know what game we were playing next?"

The guys all laughed at me like I was a comedian, then it got really quiet and they all just stared at me. I was so anxious, Markese was nice enough to break the silence,

"Damn girl you like games huh, you ain't even mastered dominoes yet. If you win the next game, then it's up to you what we do next but if one of us wins, it's up to us what we do next."

I was not ok with the alternatives given to me because they all looked like they already knew what they wanted to do. Although I knew whatever they wanted to do, I didn't want to do but I just agreed to get them to stop staring at me like a piece of meat. Markese shuffled the dominoes with a smile on his face while the other dude named Aarnez came back and was just staring at me in a very sexual way. I was so uncomfortable I hid my dominoes with the container they came in as if they were naked. I felt more comfortable holding my dominoes securely in the box as I was not a pro or had big enough hands to hold them without them falling all over the place. I played like my life depended on it, scoring left and right. Markese and Aarnez were really agitated as they were both losing terribly. They made eye contact as if to give a signal to one another that they may need to team up against me, so I was really cautious on my next few plays. I was so nervous Cassidy and Nevaeh never came back out. I wondered what in the hell could they be doing that took them so long to come back. Markese scored and called thirty points which I did not even think was possible.

I became very paranoid thinking they were working together to win so they could have their way with me. I saw an opportunity to score thirty-five points which helped me calm down a bit. I only needed forty points to win and I was determined to get those forty points.

They were also determined to keep me from getting them. The game was very intense. I played the last six and neither of them could play, so I got to go again. I scored fifteen points then Markese could play but Aarnez couldn't. Then Arnez yelled,

"Damn! I knocked again!"

Apparently to knock means he couldn't play and to domino meant that you were playing your last domino. So, I dominoed and made sure to smack the table as hard as possible while taking all their dominoes. When counting my points, I smiled when it added up to exactly twenty-five giving me the win. They all stared at me with annoyed expressions. I didn't want to be too boastful and they just did what they wanted to anyways. A car pulled up with loud music and a massive vibration rattle the garage. Markese dug into his pockets for something. A guy got out the car and walked towards him, they gave each other a handshake and said what's up to one another.

The guy that walked up looked at me then said, "Damn yo, I ain't never seen her before, she a bad lil' chocolate thang."

He said licking his lips, Markese smiled at me, "Yeah she knows it to."

I smiled to avoid appearing agitated, I was not a thing and I was not feeling the vibe at all. Markese just sat back down and the other guy looked at me and said, "Damn I wish I could take you with me."

I just sat there with a blank expression because there was not one thing that I could have said that would not result in a bad reaction. These were real life thugs or drug dealers. I realized at that moment I was not watching TV or reading a book, this was really happening. The guy talking was referred to as Tyrone. I had zoned out for a second until I heard, "Damn you don't hear me talking to you?"

I looked at him like he did a magic trick and appeared before me, then I responded, "Oh yeah, I heard you."

He looked at me like I was mentally retarded and walked off. Perfect, that's what I was hoping for. I really needed to figure out how I was going to get out of here. Nevaeh came outside to the garage giggling with her dude. She totally ignored me and asked, "Where's the blunt?"

Markese responded, "Ask yo' nigga!"

Her dude laughed and told her to go get the weed, slapping her on the ass. He looked at me and asked, "So, what y'all asses do this whole time?" Markese smacked his lips and ignored him. Aarnez answered, "Nothing but play games n shit!"

Markese shrugged his shoulders. Nevaeh came back and sat on her dude's lap as he laughed at his friends while grabbing Nevaeh's ass. They all looked upset as I did everything I could to avoid eye contact with all of them, but it made me wonder what kind of girls usually accompany them. Whatever type of girls did, I was absolutely sure I was not one of them. Nevaeh's dude's name was Slim, and he rolled a blunt looking at me out the corner of his eye. I was squirming in my seat waiting for Cassidy to come out. Slim closed the garage and lit the blunt. He passed it to me first making Nevaeh pout. I did not want it, but he made it very clear to take it or else. I hit the blunt and passed it to Nevaeh, she snatched it from me and blew smoke in my face. Still coughing from the hit, I took and now off the smoke she blew in my face, I got up to catch my breath.

Slim said, "Aye Markese put the music on, she got a fat ass!"

Nevaeh smacked her lips, "Slim why are you worried about her ass for?"

He laughed and said, "Aye, I'm just helping my boys out. I know they been thinking about that ass the whole time."

Cassidy heard Slim's comment as she came out and said, "Boy she got a boyfriend."

As her dude followed behind her. Slim laughed, "So he ain't here. So, what's yo name Treasure, right?"

Feeling high, I shook my head slowly to nod in agreement. Slim asked, "Y'all be fuckin and shit?"

I shook my head slowly to disagree. Slim laughed, "Let my boy Markese show you how."

Slim and Nevaeh laughed, but Cassidy just looked like she made a mistake. Cassidy feeling guilty said, "Aye, Slim chill."

Cassidy's dude Tony quickly checked her saying, "Aye man, shut the fuck up! Don't be talking to da homie like that."

Cassidy looked nervous and didn't say another word. Slim told me, "Aye dance for my nigga Markese tho."

Cassidy started to squirm as she saw the fear in my eyes. I said, "I have to use the bathroom and then I'll dance."

I smiled then went to the bathroom, Cassidy offered to come but I told her I remembered where it was. I went inside and bolted for the front door. I ran out and looked to the right and then to the left, running toward the left since it was an open street. The sun was setting, and I just walked as fast as I could, not looking back. I had no idea where I was, I just walked until I saw a main street. I heard a couple of honks from horny men as I walked looking for safety. My heart was beating rapidly, I was so high everything seemed to be a cartoon or slow motion. I was wondering why I couldn't see as well as I did earlier or why I wasn't laughing. I guess the situation had a lot to do with the circumstances, because I had the biggest knot in my stomach as I was paranoid with the possibilities. Different scenarios played in my head as I wondered the streets looking for a familiar street name. Finally finding a street name, Foothill. I walked all the way to the street that would take me home. I started to feel like I might possibly make it home alive. I walked and walked until I could see our cul-de-sac, I wanted to run, but I was so tired all I could do was walk briskly until I reached the house. I was amazed that I made it home.

It was almost 7 o'clock in the evening, it took me almost two hours to walk home, at least that's what it felt like. I walked in the door out of breath and tired. I sat on the stairs catching my breath, I noticed Sénar and this girl coming down the stairs. I had never been so happy to see Sénar, but his girlfriend was not happy to see me. She looked me up and down with attitude, I responded with,

"Nice to meet you too."

I started giggling and pulling at Sénar's pants in a playful manner. The girlfriend started to trip, but Sénar told her to shut up and rushed her out the door. He closed the door in her face mid-sentence, we heard her yelling outside the door. Sénar called my name, "Treasure!"

I answered, "Here."

Like we were in school taking attendance. He looked at me and grabbed my face, "Why are your eyes so red? Are you high?"

I slapped his face and said, "BINGO."

Pulling his cheeks. He slapped my hands away annoyed. He snatched me up off the steps like a little kid putting me over his shoulder and bringing me up the steps. Chino heard the commotion peeking out of his room.

I looked at Chino and said, "Peekaboo!"

And started laughing so hard, Sénar put me down and told me to shut up. Chino looked at us both like we were crazy and closed his door, Sénar made sure no one else heard us and closed the door behind us. He threw me on the bed and asked a million questions about where I was and who I was with. I answered him and played in his hair, he was just looking at me like the silly girl that I was, getting mad at some of the details. I wasn't even afraid of him for once, I was so happy to see him instead of all the strange men who were trying to take advantage of me. Sénar was mad with Cassidy and asked me where she was, I was feeling so loopy I shrugged my shoulders and told him how happy I was that I made it home. He shook his head in anger but then looked at me with his sadistic smile, I stopped talking and he said, "Me too."

He kissed me and I kissed him back. He was so aroused, he pushed me back and rubbed his hands all over me. I didn't stop him, so he stopped himself and just looked at me. He appeared to be contemplating if he should take advantage of me in the state that I was in. I ran my fingers through his hair and wrapped my legs around him, he looked like he was going to explode. He grabbed his crotch and bit his lip, "Damn girl stop playing, you are really faded huh?"

I asked, "What? I am fading?"

I looked down expecting to see my body fading away. Sénar laughed, "Girl you are high as hell. I wonder what y'all was smoking."

I put my fingers to my lips, "Shhhhh."

He gazed at me like never before and kissed me again. Sénar said, "I like this Treasure too. She likes me more."

He said cheesing. When we heard the front door, Sénar ran out of the room. I could hear him and Cassidy arguing. Cassidy came in the room and looked at me like I betrayed her. I laughed at her then she asked, "What the fuck are you laughing at?"

I ignored her. Cassidy asked, "Why you leave like that?"

I waved my hand at her, "You know why." She looked back to see Sénar at the door, so she knew better. She pouted as Sénar looked at her like he wanted to slap her. I laughed at Cassidy and went to sleep.

I woke up the next morning feeling like I had slept for days. Cassidy was already gone, I wanted to tell her off. She left me with those crazy old ass men and was going to let them do whatever they pleased to me. I was never going anywhere with her ass again. Sénar had his fun too, but I was happy that he didn't do the things I know he could have. All I remember is being super nice to him; I was so embarrassed. I just wanted to get dressed and go see Tyrell. I got my stuff to get dressed and showered. On my way out, Sénar saw me and shook his head. I looked away in embarrassment. I went to the room and gathered my things to go to Tyrell's house. When I heard the phone ring, I ran down the stairs to get the phone.

Tyrell immediately asked, "Where the hell were you yesterday?"

I told him I went to the mall with Cassidy and left out the whole other part of the story. I told him I was on my way. He said he would see me in the morning before school because he had to work. I was disappointed, I wanted to see him, but yesterday's shenanigans still needed to be dealt with, as I totally put it somewhere in a compartment to deal with it later. I just know that weed is something special if used in the right environment. I say that because there were some pretty spectacular things that took place that I could not explore because of the circumstances I was in. I would definitely try it again in a more secure environment. My birthday was coming up and thought that it would be a good day to try it with Tyrell if he was willing to try it with me.

Chino was coming down the stairs on his way to the library when I stopped him and asked, "What do you do at the library all day?"

He looked at me like I was retarded and needed some additional help. Chino answered, "Ummmm, read."

I laughed and said, "I know silly, but the whole time? What are you reading?"

He looked upstairs and appeared to be uneasy before he responded, "I don't know, books and poetry and stuff. Maybe I'll get you one, so you can learn something and use your brain more wisely."

He heard the door to his room opening and quickly rushed out the door before Sénar saw him talking to me. Sénar looked down and saw me standing there looking dumbfounded. For the life of me, I could not figure out why Chino seemed to be afraid of Sénar, sheesh, he was the older brother. Sénar came downstairs slowly, keeping his eyes intently on me. I didn't know whether to run or wait for him, besides where would I run to? I had enough of running through a maze to find safety after last night; I was still trying to find the compartment that I stored my emotions in for that incident. I was still in my own thoughts when Sénar reached me, grabbing me by the front of my shorts. He whispered, "Where's the Treasure from last night? I wanna play with her."

I was ashamed and offended at the same time. He was implying that I was someone different, and for the most part, I was, last night was just me with no inhibitions. I ignored his request, "I don't know what you're talking about, Sénar."

I attempted to turn around and go to the kitchen, before I could he grabbed me, "Uh uh, don't act like you don't know what I'm talking about."

He had that sadistic ass smile like he was ready to pounce on me and pull the Treasure I was out of me to play with her. I was nervous and did not know how to respond to him because he was so unpredictable. I just froze, becoming a victim to make him feel sorry for me. I told him the first thing that came to my mind, "I was scared of all those old ass men, ok? So, when I ran and got home, I was just happy to see a familiar face, and it happened to be yours…"

His feelings looked hurt, "Well, what if it was Chino, would you have been all over him?"

He looked at me long and hard while he waited for my answer. I quickly answered, "No." I looked down, feeling ashamed then continued, "Look, Sénar, I was just happy to see you…., can we just forget about it now and eat something tasty?"

He rolled his eyes, "What is it with women and food? Well, if I make you something to eat, what are you gonna do for me?"

I looked at him having a flashback from last night's domino game, and sighed, "I don't know, I can't cook-"

Sénar cut me off, "I'll think of something."

He winked his eye at me. I just knew I was in for some more shenanigans; I just could not get a break, I followed behind him with my stomach growling. After eating his marvelous meal, I tried to sneak away. Sénar said, "You are cold-blooded Treasure. I'm going to need you to do something for me too."

I smacked my lips and folded my arms, "Like what Sénar?"

He smiled mischievously, "I don't know I'll give you a choice to come up with something."

I rolled my eyes and tried to think of something that was not sexual and said, "I know, I can clean your room."

I was serious because I knew he could use it, and there was time for me to actually do a good job. Besides, I would be busy, and he would have to leave me alone. He was shocked; I guess he didn't think I could think of something so clever, and he knew he needed it.

He smiled, "Ok." I was so relieved that it was easy. I started to walk up the steps, he added his conditions, "But I get to watch you, and you have to take your shirt off."

I knew there was a catch 22. I started to complain, but he cut me off, "You wanna keep them shorts on?"

I frowned and decided to go with the first suggestion. When we got to his room, he put his ear to our parent's door and didn't hear anything, so we snuck in his room. Once in there, I was disappointed it wasn't dirtier than I thought, but it could use a wipe down and some reorganizing. I took my shirt off and neatly folded it on Sénar's bed and turned around to see what he was going to do while I cleaned his part of the room, he was sitting on Chino's bed cheesing. I rolled my eyes and started with his dresser rearranging things and throwing stuff away.

He was said, "Aye, don't be throwing no numbers away." He was laughing and watching my every move. I was washing down the dresser, and my breast was jiggling with every motion. Sénar was licking his lips and grabbing his crotch. I sighed in disgust because guys were so shallow sometimes, was sex all they really think about? I looked at his dresser, and it was spotless and neat; I was proud of myself. The next part was his bed area; there were gold Magnum x large condoms everywhere in one corner and magazines in another. I saw a picture of me on the side of his bed from the best-looking category from my school the year before; I tried to act like I didn't notice. But he jumped up to his defense,

"Aye, I like that picture, so just leave it there."

He said with an embarrassed smile. I blushed, "Your girlfriends might see it though, that's not the appropriate place for it."

I put it on his dresser in the corner at the bottom where it was not as noticeable. I told him, "I ain't touching nothing in that corner where all the condom wrappers are."

He looked at the towels and napkins; he blushed as he picked up all the wrappers and towels himself. He tossed the towels and clothes in the hamper and looked at his side of the room, then at Chino's side and smiled, "Ok, it looks great."

I grabbed my shirt to put it back on. He took my shirt and said, "Let me see them, and I'll let you go."

I said, "No!" I tried to get my shirt back, and he held it in the air, causing me to jump for it like a dog doing tricks. I realized that was quite the show for him and stopped crossing my arms,

"Why do you have to be so difficult, Sénar? You have so many girlfriends. Why you always messing with me?"

He smiled, "None of them ain't you though."

I smirked, "Duh…. look, you know I have a boyfriend-"

Sénar cut me off, "I don't give a fuck about that nigga! His ass is lame as fuck! If you were my girl, you would not be doing this for nobody."

Feeling ashamed, he was right; I needed to get my ass out of his room. I got my feelings hurt and ran out without my shirt and went to my room, closing the door. I quickly found another shirt; I sat on my bed and saw a book on it I had never seen before. The book was called *God Don't Like Ugly* by Mary Monroe. I was excited there was a note that read happy early birthday and remember God don't like ugly; it wasn't signed, but I knew it was from Chino, which meant he knew I was in the room with Sénar and just didn't come in. Ugh, he probably thinks I am nuts. I laid in my bed and opened the book and started to read it. I read a couple of chapters until I smelled food. I went downstairs; it sounded like a house with a family in it, so I joined the Reject Brady Bunch for dinner and went to sleep reading.

School was much better this week; me and Tyrell ate our lunch and avoided all drama by eating outside. I went to some of his practices to watch him in action, and I must say he was pretty good. I stayed as far away from Sénar as I possibly could and ignored Cassidy since she put me in a dangerous situation. Tyrell and I stayed in our own world, and I did my best to not be a victim to Sénar as it was really hard living with him to avoid the pitfalls.

Finally, my birthday was approaching. I was so excited. Tyrell always makes my birthdays super special. I was turning fifteen, and I was so happy, I felt like Tyrell, and I were really maturing along with our relationship. We were becoming more aware of our bodies and comfortable with the changes we were experiencing. We would mess around and not get too bashful and explore things at a rate we were both comfortable with. Although sometimes I wanted to speed things up, ever since that night, we explored sex for the first time we totally avoided that part. It was like he was scared to take it to the next level. I was too, but I knew eventually it would happen we just didn't want to rush anything.

Chapter 12

Sunday morning, I woke up to a quiet room. The breathing of another human was not present, giving me a sense of calmness. A slight smile formed on my face at the thought of having it like this all the time. When I looked around the room, I suddenly felt like the secure little girl I was when it was just my mother and me. I started to cry at the memory being shredded to pieces at the arrival of Ken and his little demon children. My tears suddenly came to a halt when the woman I was becoming took over and realized it was something I needed to get over already. I gathered some clothes to take a shower while wiping the evidence of tears away. I was tired of crying, I just wanted to see Tyrell today, and hopefully, it would make things better. We were having some difficulties in our relationship lately, and things were rocky. Tyrell was mad at me every other day for one thing or another. Usually, it had something to do with Sénar or some other idiot voicing their opinions on my body. He was always searching for a reason to bring Sénar up, and it always caused an argument. After the fight they had at the beginning of the school year, I really thought for a second their feud was over. It had been months, and we all managed to go to school without killing each other or making another scene. Sometimes I convinced myself that he just wanted to break up with me so he could date one of his little groupies. To this day, I really believe Tyrell messed with Sabrina, he just refuses to admit to it, and she's not here to rub it in my face anymore.

On my way to the shower, the house was so quiet; I thought this was the perfect time to take a shower and yell when relieving all my frustration. A devious smile appeared across my face as I thought about my love affair with hot water; I was having behind Tyrell's back. If Tyrell knew he would be jealous of the sparkling new shower head that magically appeared out of nowhere, and somehow, he would link it to Sénar. I laughed at the imaginary argument he would present to link it to Sénar. I could hear Lauryn Hill song *"Killing Me Softly"*, taking over the thoughts running through my mind and improving my mood as I ran the water. I decided to take a bath and let the water run while I examined my chocolate body in the mirror. I noticed my swollen breast, my tiny waist, my wide hips, and my big butt still resembling an upside-down heart. I was mesmerized by the smoothness and even tone of my silky brown skin. Admiring the natural shine, my skin had with glimmers of golden flakes sparkling through, as I slipped one of my feet into the tub. I eased in allowing the feeling of relaxation to travel through my body as it was being engulfed by the water. It felt like hot silk clinging to my body as I allowed the water to consume me, my thoughts drifted to Tyrell, and the feeling of his soft kisses smothering my neck.

Now at ease, I thought about the hassle I would have to go through to get my body positioned under the faucet when the sparkling showerhead seemed to sparkle just for me. I briskly got up to retrieve the showerhead and pulled the plunger to release the raging water through the shower. I laid back and placed the showerhead in between my legs, feeling the strong pressure of the water as it battered my little man in the boat. As the gushing water tantalized my coochie, my mind drifted to Tyrell, sucking on my neck and squeezing my breast. I could feel a rush of blood travel to my coochie as if to compete with the heat of the water. I was panting and squeezing my breast with one hand while holding the showerhead in place with the other. Imagining Tyrell's touch, squeezing my breast even harder. As I almost reached my peak, Sénar's face flashed across my mind with his sadistic smile, throwing me into a violent whirlwind of ecstasy. Yelling out in pleasure, instantaneously, covering my mouth to try to muffle my scream. I clenched the showerhead so hard between my legs; I thought it would shatter into a million pieces. My body uncontrollably convulsed wildly before shivering and then going limp. I released the showerhead from my legs' deadly grip and pulled myself up, to prevent myself from drowning in my own juices mixed with the water.

Quickly turning the water off and carefully listening to make sure no one heard me. Relief came over me when I didn't hear a sound. I quickly washed up and was attentive to making sure I washed away the slimy fluids that were now oozing from me. I looked in the mirror to ensure I was intact, I dried off and got dressed. I had on a matching yellow bra and panty set that I could not wait to flaunt in front of Tyrell. My florescent shirt fit tightly against my breast along with a short green skirt that I had on. Feeling confident, I opened the door and gasped when I saw Sénar standing there, smiling with anticipation. I tried to close the door when he pushed against it knocking me back and slipping in. Sénar picked me up and locked the door behind him. I started to scream, but he grabbed the back of my neck and stuck his tongue so deep in my mouth, I almost choked. When he released me, he pressed my face against his chest so tightly; I couldn't open my mouth to scream as he slid his hands up my skirt. He moved my panties to the side and slid his fingers into my coochie with ease, as it was still wet and now pulsating.

He whispered in my ear, "Ooh, it's juicy just like I like it."

Easing his fingers in deeply, I struggled to suck in air with the restricted space between my mouth and his chest. He held me tight and whispered, "You like my little gift I bought you?"

Not giving me a chance to answer, Sénar continued to swirl his fingers in and out of me. Panic aligned with my racing thoughts of what gift he was talking about. As my worry increased, I had no idea what he was going to do to me. I suddenly remembered the sparkling showerhead that seemed to appear in my bathroom magically. He kept my face pressed against his chest while his fingers invaded my insides. I wanted him to stop, but my body did not want him to stop. He let my face go and stuck his tongue deep into my mouth again while thrusting his fingers in and out of me rapidly. Unintentionally I moaned, as he slowed down his thrusts, pushing his fingers deeper inside of me and moving his tongue all around my mouth with excitement. Trying to fight the urge to moan, my mouth fell open Involuntarily, allowing me to pant for air when I felt the heat rise in my coochie. A wave of pleasure took over me, Sénar's laugh enraged me but fueled my passion. Until my coochie became hot, clenching his fingers and gushing out hot fluid that caused my body to quiver. He pulled me close to him, celebrating with his own moaning. Pulling his fingers out of me and grabbing my hand to place it on his throbbing penis. He clamped my hand down, forcing me to squeeze until he released a hot thick liquid all over my hands and thighs.

Both of our juices were running down my thigh. I gasped in shock and tried to snatch my hand back unsuccessfully, as he used my hand to empty out the rest of his own fluid. My mouth now gaping open with shock, he kissed me quickly and whispered,

"Now both our hands are wet. Hmmm Thanks, ma!"

He quickly zipped his pants and exited the bathroom. Sénar left me there in a bewildered state with fluids dripping down my hand and thigh. Flabbergasted and shivering, I quickly snapped out of it running to lock the door behind him. There was a clear slimy fluid coming from me, mixing in with his thick milky white fluid that oozed down my legs and on my hand. I instantly thought of man juice and panicked, grabbing tissue urgently, wiping it off my thighs. I couldn't help but think, oh no, am I going to get pregnant! Sex Ed class memories quickly consoled me but did not completely wipe out the thought of little tadpoles swimming into my coochie. I quickly undressed and jumped back in the shower, using the showerhead to wash away all the evidence of Sénar's man juice and my liquids of betrayal. I sat in the pool of water, letting the water from the shower hit my face and hair. I was a mess and could not believe what just happened. My tears fell down my face because I felt like I had betrayed Tyrell and myself. I should have stopped him; I should have fought harder. I badgered myself with these thoughts, dropping my face into my hands and cried uncontrollably. Now in a daze, letting my tears mix in with the water until I heard a knock at the door, making my heart skip a beat.

Chino demanded impatiently, "Damn, hurry up!! She-esh, you've been in there forever!"

I quickly dried off, putting everything back on except my soiled underwear. I almost opened the door when I saw the mess on the counter and some evidence on the floor. I used my towel to clean the counter and the floor. Balling the towel and my soiled underwear into a ball, keeping it a safe distance from me, I opened the door and exited the bathroom. Chino looked at me weird and rushed me out of the way. I got to my room and sat on my bed, confused, I laid down and cried myself to sleep.

I woke up with urgency checking the time, it was almost noon. I told Tyrell I would be there in the morning. I jumped out of bed and looked for a pair of panties to match my bra or the flowers on my shirt, since my original ones were ruined. I found a suitable pair and rushed out my room towards the bathroom to fix my hair. Sénar was coming out of the bathroom with a towel on, freshly showered.

He beamed a cocky smile, "Damn ma, you want some more?"

I could not help but notice his curly hair, dark bronze skin and muscles with droplets of water still clinging to him. The towel snug around his waist with the imprint of the culprit that threw up man juice on me protruding threw the towel. I quickly looked up to see him flash his pearly whites with sarcasm, "Well?"

Embarrassed I carefully tried pushing past him practically begging him with my eyes, "Please move Sénar?"

He snickered allowing me to past him but without passing up the opportunity to slide his hands up the back of my skirt, almost giving me a mini stroke before I could turn around to close the door. My hair was frizzy, and my eyes were puffy from crying. I looked a complete mess, I applied as much gel as possible to help tame my still damp coils of hair. I splashed my face with cold water until the redness in my eyes disappeared and the puffiness under my eyes shrank. I grabbed my hoops and purse and sprinted across the street to Tyrell's house. Tyrell practically answered the door before I could knock.

"What the fuck took you so long?" He barked at me with his arms crossed, demanding an answer before even saying hi to me. I just sighed because I was not in the mood to deal with his jealous fit. He lashed out, "Oh and you got an attitude too?"

I just pouted and looked as helpless as possible, letting him know my attitude was gone and I was just happy to see him. I grabbed him and squeezed him so hard, kissing him all over his face. Telling him I was so happy to see him. He blushed and flashed his million-dollar smile,

"Damn girl, I am happy to see you too. Bring yo' fine ass over here!"

He hugged me and squeezed my booty as I melted in his arms; grateful I didn't have to come up with a story to explain why I was so late. He slapped my behind, I giggled running up the stairs with him chasing behind me. He playfully threw me on his bed and smothered my face with kisses.

He stopped abruptly to ask, "Why do you have so much gel in your hair? You gonna' mess my pillowcase up."

We both laughed as he kissed me again. He rubbed my thigh in the same place I had man juice on it earlier and my stomach churned. To disguise my discomfort, I quickly asked, "So what are we doing today?"

He looked at me as if I was rushing him and answered, "I don't know. Why, are you in a rush?"

He was really on the edge, so I was very careful with my response, "No… I was just excited to see what we were going to do. I just wanna' have some fun and get some good food. You know my birthday is coming up next week and I was just excited that's all."

He looked deeply in my eyes and appeared to be searching for something. Tyrell gave me a side look then said, "Um no. Since you already missed the show."

Fully dressed and flexing his muscles in his new fit, I giggled and squeezed his butt making him jump. We played and tussled until we were satisfied and gathered our things to leave. Walking out the door to see Sénar cheesing at us as he walked towards the convertible parked in front of the house. There was a new young lady I had never seen. She jumped out of the car to hug him. Me and Tyrell's eyes widened for different reasons. She was stacked, she had poppin' lip gloss, big titties, a big fat ass and the prettiest brown skin that appeared to be oiled to perfection. Even Tyrell was mesmerized by how hot she was. I on the other hand, could care less about that hood rat. I just saw Sénar's eyes fixated on me, while Tyrell was fixated on her booty as she wrapped her arms around Sénar's neck. Sénar wasn't the least bit bothered by her tugging and kissing on him, as he was looking at me with intensity. Feeling anxious, I squeezed Tyrell's arm to break his concentration off her chocolate booty and the phenomenal presentation of her body, that had Tyrell in his boy feelings.

Tyrell immediately fixed his gaze on Sénar, whose gaze was on me. He became so tensed and bothered that Sénar finally acknowledged him with a glare of hatred and then a smirk as if to say *let's trade.* Tyrell looked at me to see my expression, but I was ready to meet his gaze with my loyalty screaming let's go. My loyalty to him fueled his confidence to strut me on his arm as he opened the car door for me. Sénar smiled his famous smile then slapped his video vixen's ass, causing it to jiggle massively as she squealed with excitement. I just sighed in disgust and clung to Tyrell as he urgently pushed me in the car. Sénar walked to the driver's side of the convertible to lean on her car. When Tyrell got into the car he paused and looked at me in silence. I was uncomfortable but did everything in my power to not look bothered by his stare.

Tyrell blurted out, "What the fuck!"

Confused by his outburst I looked at him and asked, "What's wrong Tyrell?"

He sighed in frustration and asked, "Why the fuck is Sénar always hating? He got that bad ass bitch, but it seems to me, he really just wants you!"

I was at loss for words, not only was he telling the truth, he did not hesitate to let it be known that the video vixen was a bad ass bitch. I quickly responded, "I don't know what you are talking about."

He instantly filled with rage before asking, "What the fuck took you so long to come over?"

I got nervous because he was already convinced it had something to do with Sénar. My eyes pleaded with him, "Look Tyrell, I overslept, and I had to take extra time getting my hair right. It was a mess. Please don't let this mess our day up. He has a million girlfriends; he is not thinking about me!"

Tyrell looked at me as if I had shit on my face and asked, "Oh, really? Then why that nigga try to kill me? Why is he always looking at you, like you are the only fucking girl in the world to him?"

I almost blushed at the thought of him only having eyes for me, no matter how hot the girl he was with was, but I quickly dismissed that thought when Tyrell was impatiently waiting on my answer. I said, "All I know is that you're my man, I don't know what he feels, and I don't care. I'm yours and I mean all yours."

I tried to convince both him and me. He looked at me smacking his lips, gripping his steering wheel, forcefully throwing the car in gear and skirting out of the driveway. As he was ready to drive forward, he yelled, "Ugh, I can't stand that mothafucka!"

I grabbed his leg pleading with him to calm down. He was looking in his rear-view mirror with his nostrils flared like he wanted to go back and beat Sénar's face in. I tried to grab his hand to beg him to let it go but he snatched it away from me, using it to turn his wheel around to viciously make a U-turn. The girl was starting her car as we rolled back up to her car. She gave me a nasty look, while Tyrell and Sénar locked eyes.

Sénar asked, "What's up, chump?"

I grabbed Tyrell's arm and Sénar jumped out of her car. Tyrell snatched his arm from me, threw his car in park and jumped out of the car to meet Sénar. I ran out of the passenger side running toward the two of them as they glared at one another. Sénar looked me up and down smiling the first genuine smile I had ever seen him have. Tyrell pushed me out of Sénar's eyesight behind him, and lunged at Sénar like a bull, punching him in the mouth. Tyrell then with all his might punched Sénar again in his right cheek, opening a cut under his eye and sending Sénar into a rage. Sénar stopping Tyrell's next attempt to punch him again, by grabbing him and body slamming him onto the ground. Sénar hovered over Tyrell to punch him, but I yelled,

"Please don't Sénar!"

He looked at me with his sadistic smile and punched Tyrell so hard that Tyrell's head hit the concrete, I screamed in horror. Ready to unload an ass whipping of a lifetime onto Tyrell, I leaped toward Sénar grabbing his hand. He stopped to stare at me and spit blood out from his busted lip with a crazed look in his eyes. His glare softened a bit and the girl snatched his hand away from me.

Sénar said, "You better be glad you are so cute!" Tyrell instantly tried to jump up but Sénar kicked him back down with a fresh pair of Nikes, leaving an imprint on Tyrell's white tee shirt. He slapped his video vixen on the ass again, and she ran to the passenger side of her car. Sénar jumped in the driver's seat skirting off, leaving me trying to help Tyrell off the ground. Tyrell pushed me off him with a swollen eye and a Nike shoe print on his chest. He jumped up without brushing the gravel off him and parked his car in the driveway. He got out of the car slamming the door so hard, it shook the entire car. I ran towards him as he looked like he wanted to cry. Once inside the house, I tried to console him by wrapping my arms around him. He pushed me so hard, I fell back awkwardly landing on my wrist, hearing a popping sound when I landed. I screamed so loud both of us winced in pain, as he rushed to my side to help me. I looked at my wrist and it was grossly twisted. I started to wail because the pain was beyond anything I ever felt in my life.

I was angry, hurt and scared. Tyrell forgot about his own battle wounds and tried to grab my right wrist. I snatched it away bringing it to my chest and covering it for protection. I was trying to stifle my cries by biting my lip as a distraction from the pain ripping through the bone of my wrist. Tyrell was being dramatic and begging me to see it. when I saw his mom appear at the top of the stairs rubbing her eyes as if she had just woken up.

"What's all the commotion about?"

She focused her eyes to clearly see me sitting on the floor rocking myself back and forth. She looked at me with confusion and asked, "What happened?" As she rushed down the steps, Tyrell looked at me with pleading eyes as if to say please don't tell on him. I narrowed my eyes at him and managed to grimace in pain before answering her,

"I fell on my wrist."

I avoided eye contact with her to conceal my bold face lie. When we finally made eye contact it was as if we were meeting for the first time. She instantly believed me for the sake of administering help without getting too much into the details of how I fell. She turned into mommy nurse and she asked me questions pertaining to my injury. She gently asked me if she could see it as I was still covering it for protection unknowingly. She asked me questions about my pain as she gently observed my wrist. With her being a nurse, she thoroughly evaluated the situation groggily to the best of her ability. She was honest and sincere when telling me it was impossible for her to know if it was broken without an X-ray. Immediately I started to cry because

I thought of the trouble it would cause my mom to take me to the hospital.

I asked her if she thought it was broken and she sighed, "I really think you need an X-ray honey."

They offered to take me to the hospital, I looked down and asked, "What if I don't want to go to the hospital?"

She looked confused and asked, "Why don't you want to go to the hospital?"

I looked frustrated because I could not go into detail and shatter their perfect little lives, even if I wanted to because I was in too much pain. I got up using my left arm to holster me up, hoping not to shatter my left arm with all my weight bearing down on it, when Tyrell rushed to help me get up.

Tyrell panicked, "Where are you going Treasure?"

The mom feeling Tyrell's desperation she offered to take me to the hospital again. I shook my head in refusal to going and said, "I am just going to go home and put ice on it and go to sleep."

I managed to produce a small smile hoping they would let me leave peacefully. Tyrell and his mom looked helpless as I walked towards the door.

Tyrell's mom said, "Wait let me wrap it for you sweetie."

I graciously accepted her offer and Tyrell sighed in relief. She ran upstairs to get the first aid kit with all the fixings to wrap my wrist. I sat in their beautiful kitchen in awe at how clean and perfect everything was as I never noticed before. His mom was coming down with the first aid kit and I noticed how pretty she really was. She was petite with a perfect set of white teeth to compliment her pretty smile. Her lips were full but compact on her caramel brown oval shaped face.

She spoke to me in a gentle caring voice, she smiled before asking, "So, you are the famous Treasure that has my Tyrell's head in the clouds?"

Tyrell sighed, "Mom, please."

She giggled and carefully checked to make sure she didn't wrap my wrist too tight, to avoid cutting circulation. I watched her intently just in case I had to do it myself. When she was done, she insisted I go to the doctor for an X-ray, but Tyrell interrupted her and said, "We were going to go to the movies, you think she will be ok mom?"

His mom looked like a mom for the first time and not a nurse on duty. She answered, "Tyrell, it's really up to her sweetie. I don't think it's really a good idea." She said searching Tyrell's face to see if he understood. She quickly looked closer and asked, "Honey, what happened to your face?"

She lifted her hand to touch the side of his face that Sénar had brutally punched earlier. Tyrell quickly objected, "Nothing mom, I'm fine."

She kissed him softly and responded, "Ok sweetie I have a double, so I have to get some rest."

She could tell neither of us wanted to talk about it and she looked too exhausted to interrogate us, as she turned to ascend the steps into her own Lala Land. Before turning the corner, she looked at Tyrell lovingly and said, "Stay out of trouble you two."

As she disappeared Tyrell seemed relieved, she didn't force him to go further into an explanation. He looked embarrassed and remorseful just for a moment. Which didn't last long once he remembered why his face was battered and that he had a Nike shoe print on his shirt. Rage filled his eyes again alarming me that I should leave. I got up slowly and carefully headed for the door, when he noticed he quickly blocked my exit.

Tyrell asked, "Treasure, where are you going? What? You gonna tell your little boyfriend on me?"

I started crying because he just wouldn't let it go, even though I was possibly cradling a broken wrist. He looked like he wanted to hurt me, I was so weak I could not fight him even if I wanted to. I just whimpered against the wall, trying to avoid passing out from the overwhelming emotions swimming with the flow of my tears. He grabbed me and was careful not to touch my wrist.

He pleaded with me, "Treasure don't leave! I am sorry, I just hate Sénar. I hate that you live with him. I hate how he looks at you……It almost makes me hate you!"

He was so frustrated when the words spewed out of his mouth it gave me the burst of energy, I needed to push him out of the way. Opening the door to run out, he grabbed the back of my arm, and I whimpered in pain. He swirled me around and kissed me. "Please don't leave me Treasure." He begged me as he kissed me passionately confessing his love for me.

A mixture of pain and pleasure filled my body. With my adrenaline increasing the feeling of nausea gripped me, I almost fainted. Tyrell felt my body go limp in his arms, struggling to hold me up, he called my name to bring me back to reality as if I was drifting away. I managed to weakly ask, "Tyrell take me home, please?"

Trying to gain my strength back to walk, he walked me across the street as my legs felt like al dente noodles. When we got to the door, I checked the door with my left hand desperately praying it was unlocked. The door opened and Chino was standing there looking at the two of us like we were trying to break into his home. He saw my pale face and bandaged arm and looked at Tyrell accusingly. Before Tyrell or Chino could say anything I quickly interjected, "Thanks baby, I love you and will call you later."

Tyrell looked relieved and had a hint of fear in his eyes. He quickly kissed me and made sure I made it inside before turning to cross the street back to his house. I struggled to stand on my own but managed to close the door with my back, I used the door to muster up the strength to walk. Just seeing the stairs took the strength I mustered up, I started to faint when Chino caught me keeping me from falling. Chino picked me up and carried me to the couch, observing me with a look of concern, he asked, "What happened Treasure ….are you ok?"

He touched my sweat beaded forehead and started to panic. He kept calling my name repeatedly, but his voice sounded like it was getting further away, I wanted to respond but I was too weak. He ran upstairs to get my mom and she rushed down the stairs. "Treasure!" I jolted at the sound of her voice, "What happened baby?" She was checking my body and grabbed my wrist when I yelled in pain, she let it go.

She yelled, "Chino go get my keys and help me get her to the car!"

She was frantic and running around to get her purse. As we were leaving Sénar and his video vixen pulled up as Chino was carrying me to the car. I was clinging onto Chino for dear life as I did not want to see Sénar or Tyrell in my moment of distress. Sénar jumped out of the car and rushed to my side. He looked worried and asked Chino what happened, Chino looked at him with a look of perplexity and concern shrugging his shoulders. Sénar and Chino jumped in the car with my mom and we all went to the hospital. The car ride was in an awkward silence until Chino said something, "Treasure are you ok?"

My mouth was dry, and I was feeling weak, "Uh huh, I am ok."

I managed to say, trying to convince everyone including myself. No one asked what happened, we all just continued to sit in silence during the drive. We got to the hospital and Chino hesitated to get me out of the car since Sénar was there now, but Sénar did nothing to object. Sénar had a guilty expression on his face and Chino knew it was ok to pick me up. He carried me into the waiting room, him and Sénar sat down one on each side of me.

Sénar whispered, "Did Tyrell do this to you?"

He asked hoping Chino did not hear him, but he heard him. They both anxiously waited for my answer. I did not want any more drama, so I answered, "No." Emotionless. He scanned my body for signs of abuse and pulled my skirt down, so my thighs were properly covered. Him and Chino looked at one another as to agree that I was lying, but Sénar knew he couldn't incriminate Tyrell without incriminating himself. Sénar just sighed in disbelief but didn't say a word. My mom returned with a nurse that took me back for vitals. The nurse looked concerned because my blood pressure was low, but my heartbeat was sky high. They rushed me to the back and ordered X-rays. They gave me something for pain and gave me a room. My mom called Ken from her cellphone letting him know where she was and that the boys were with her, just in case she needed an alibi since she was always there waiting on him when he got home.

The doctor came in and interrupted her conversation, forcing her conversation to abruptly end. She gave the doctor her full attention. The doctor explained, "Treasure has broken her right wrist. It's a pretty clean break so it can take up to eight weeks to heal. We will put a cast on it and want to see her back in six to eight weeks." He looked at me and in a skeptical tone he asked, "Pretty hard fall you had there huh?"

I answered, "Yeah." I just laid there in disbelief that all this was happening.

The doctor out of concern added, "She probably went into shock from the pain…she should of came in right away, do you know what happen to her?"

My mom felt a little offended by the question and responded, "She said she fell, and I believe her."

The doctor stared at me for a moment before leaving the room. His nursing staff came back to administer a shot and start the process to put the cast on. I was so embarrassed, but whatever they gave me for pain had me feeling really good. I was overwhelmed and did not want to think of anything but going to sleep. We all rode back in silence. Ken was standing at the door like he had radar when we pulled up. I was still feeling a little dazed from the medications and the events of the day. Chino offered to help me out of the car, but Ken came to the door of the car to ask if I was ok. I responded yes and he picked me up carrying me inside, my mom followed closely behind with a twinge of jealousy threatening to emerge. He took me to my room and laid me on the bed. My mom, Chino and Sénar were like little puppies at the door.

Ken asked me, "What happened Treasure?" Everyone listened intently…. Sénar was the only one who looked worried because he was hoping I didn't tell on him. Sénar knew if I told what really happened, he would be on his way out the door. I was tempted to tell the truth but Sénar would not be the only one affected, so I stuck to my story of falling.

I answered, "I was getting out of the car, when my foot got caught in the door. I fell and had to use my arm to break my fall." I was so convincing that I thought Ken would not pry, Ken then said,

"You need to be more careful…are you sure you are not hiding anything?"

He looked behind him to see that Sénar was anticipating my answer as well,

"No Ken, I really just got my foot stuck in the door. I'll be fine… I didn't think it was broken. I am sorry for all the inconvenience." I started yawning to indicate I was tired. Ken not really believing me, scanned my body to ensure that I was undamaged everywhere else and noticed my little mini skirt in the process.

He shook his head, "You need to stay around here for a while Treasure."

Ken was implying away from Tyrell; Ken gave me the eye to make sure that I understood him. I shook my head in agreement to show I understood, like a good little girl. As he headed for the door, he looked back again at my little Minnie skirt and smirked at Sénar. "Good night Treasure." He said with authority before my mom and the other two said goodnight. Chino and Sénar turned away when the door shut, I was out like a light. I woke up the next morning with Cassidy looking over me waiting for my eyes to open.

"Girl what happened?"

She was being nosey rather than concerned. I wanted to tell her to mind her business, but I had no energy to defend myself in case she got feisty. I looked down at my arm to make sure yesterday wasn't just a nightmare and there it was, looking back at me with a hard cast protecting it.

"I fell and broke my wrist." I said dryly.

She looked at me like I was lying and smacked her lips then said, "I thought we were cool. Why you lyin'?"

I looked at her with my mouth snarled, "I don't have to lie to you! I told you what happened because you asked, so if you don't believe me then too bad."

She looked at me like I was trash, then responded, "Whatever, I don't give a damn anyway!" She said closing the door with an attitude.

I thought to myself about how we were finally getting along and I did not need the extra drama, but I wasn't telling her nothing different. Yesterday was the worst day ever on so many levels, I just wanted to sleep the rest of my life away. I just laid in my bed not wanting to face reality. I figured I would sleep the next eight weeks away and I would never notice my wrist being broken. There was a knock at the door, I was hoping it was my mom, but the hope went away when I told them to come in. Sénar was standing in the doorway with a long face. He looked so guilty, which he was, I closed my eyes and pretended to be sleeping.

Sénar said, "Treasure stop playing it's late and I know you ain't sleeping still."

I never opened my eyes; I was playing dead. He came in and sat on the edge of my bed, I still had the same clothes on he violated me in. Sénar demanded, "Treasure get up, wash your ass and come downstairs."

I wanted to laugh because he was trying to act like he had some authority, but I knew he was mad I had not changed from yesterday. I just laid there until he left, I was still mad at him and Tyrell. They were like little kids fighting over a toy until it broke, literally. I just wanted to be left alone. The next knock had me irritated, instead of saying to come in I told them to go away.

My mom opened the door without me knowing it was her until I heard her voice, "Treasure, why are you still in bed? You haven't even showered or ate anything." I thought how she even managed to know all of that when she never noticed any other time. She also demanded, "Get up Treasure…Now!" I got up slowly avoiding eye contact. She grabbed my face and said, "Snap out of it Treasure!"

I wanted to snap at her and ask how she had the nerve to say anything to me about anything, but I knew it would end terribly. So, I got up and started looking for something to wear so that I could take a shower. With her arms folded she asked, "What happened yesterday?"

I thought about when I was a little girl and Tyrell threw the rock at my head and she knew I was lying about what happened. I hesitated before trying to do a better job this time, "Mom, I was getting out of the car and my foot got stuck and I fell on my wrist." I was going to say it enough until I believed it, so no one could tell I was lying.

Her arms still crossed when she said, "Treasure, what really happened?"

Irritated now because I thought I did a pretty good job, "I told you mom I fell. I didn't want to bother anyone, I thought it was just a sprain. Tyrell's mom offered to take me, but I told her no because I thought I was fine." I added that to the story so she would know there was another adult to collaborate my story. She had no choice but to accept my story because I wasn't changing it. She reached for me and I made no effort to welcome her.

She said, "Treasure baby, I am here for you if you need me." looked at her like I believed her since she pretended to believe me, that was the least I could do for her. She gave me a quick hug and left. I gathered my things to take a bath since I could not risk wetting my cast. I ran my bath water and looked at myself in the mirror. I was disgusted with what I saw, I was a mess. My hair was wild, my eyes were puffy, and the cast just looked so awkward on my pretty brown skin. I took a deep breath and got into the bathtub. I let my body soak with my arm hanging over the edge and tried my best not to cry. What was I going to do about school? What would everyone think? What was Tyrell thinking? His mom probably thinks we're crazy. I laughed at the thoughts that probably ran through her head. I was already in a better mood. Sheesh, washing your ass, definitely does a body and mind good. I struggled a bit to get out, but I managed to without incident. I got dressed, taking longer than usual having to adjust to my new handicap. I started to go back to my room, but I smelled food. It wasn't breakfast either. I went down the steps slowly and peeked my head around the corner to see who was in the kitchen. What do you know, it was half of the Reject Brady Bunch starring, chef Sénar, Cassidy and Chino. They both sat at the counter watching Sénar cook. It smelled like tacos. I was so hungry, I didn't care what it was, I just wanted some.

Sénar turned around, "Well, well, well, look who has risen."

Cassidy and Chino turned around and looked at me like a specimen. Cassidy rolled her eyes at me letting me know she was not feeling me. I totally ignored her and focused my attention on Chino.

I said, "Thanks Chino for helping yesterday, I really appreciate it."

Chino thought long and hard before his response being, that Cassidy was an instigator, Sénar was a jealous crazed maniac and I was the culprit who got his sister sent away. He tried not to blush and dryly responded, "It's cool."

And turned back to see Sénar's facial expression. Sénar pretended to look hurt by holding the spatula in one hand and putting the other on his hip. Cassidy and Chino couldn't help laughing at Sénar's silly antics and his pretending to be hurt.

"Oh, and thanks Sénar." I said sarcastically.

Tension suddenly thickened when Sénar snapped, "I'm not the one who broke your arm!"

I winced at his harsh words and wanted to yell back the million things he did do, but Chino and Cassidy were waiting on my response like they were watching a soap opera. Biting my tongue and fighting the urge to cry, I felt forced to apologize to avoid conflict and not reveal what really happened. I looked at Sénar's fresh wounds on his lip and cheek and I reluctantly responded,

"I know! I am sorry, thanks for coming with us Sénar." I said that feeling defeated and embarrassed.

To break the ice, Sénar said, "Good, now let's eat!"

With his spatula in the air like an old lady on Thanksgiving. Chino and Sabrina laughed at their silly brother, who appeared to be a normal funny guy at the moment. He made me my plate first and asked, "You need me to feed you?" He was being seductive but still silly, Cassidy rolled her eyes and Chino laughed.

I smiled, "No thank you, Chef Sénar." He beamed a smile that put me at ease for once.

Cassidy said, "Make mine too, chef Sénar!"

Chino knew better than to ask, he made his own tacos. Sénar made Cassidy's because she asked, but he didn't want to. He made his and stood in the kitchen eating his tacos while watching me eat mine awkwardly with my left hand. I tried not to make a mess, but it was really awkward and uncomfortable. Everyone noticed my difficulty and tried not to make it obvious. I was feeling embarrassed already, so I just stuffed my mouth instead of eating properly, besides they were really good.

Sénar looked agitated with my discomfort and made a joke, "Hey I offered to feed you." He said and then smirked at me.

Cassidy and Chino were done and took that as a cue to leave. They washed their plates and went on with their day. When they left Sénar approached me and asked, "Treasure, you want me to beat his ass again?"

I looked down at my messy plate to avoid responding. Sénar was too impatient to wait for my answer, he asked, "Did he do that to you? Don't lie either." I looked at my plate and stuffed my mouth again to avoid answering his question. He was so furious that he snatched my plate from me and looked me in my eyes, "Answer me Treasure."

To avoid crying I got an attitude instead, "Why do you even care? I never tell him what you do to me!"

He looked guilty for a second before responding, "Whatever, then you would have to tell him you liked it too." I was offended and pissed off at the same time. I got up to leave but he stopped me and said, "Look I know I ain't perfect but if he puts his hands on you again, I will hurt his ass."

I believed him, so I answered, "I fell, he didn't hit me. I fell that's all."

Sénar didn't believe me he just shook his head and said, "That's the kind of guy you make me compete with? He's a lil' chump anyway. He ain't gonna last long. He knows deep down inside; you belong to me."

He turned around to let me know our conversation was over, he cleaned my plate and left me in the kitchen. I was so confused how could he be so sure of himself, when Tyrell was my man and he was so insecure. I sat there in my own thoughts when Chino came in the kitchen to get something to drink, he noticed me lost in my own thoughts.

Chino said, "Hey, you're welcome Treasure. You know you really are a beautiful girl, so I understand why you cause so much drama. Just be careful because someone is always going to end up on the short end of the stick and it ain't gonna be Sénar."

He said with concern and sincerity. Cassidy was in the room and I did not feel like being bothered with her, so I took the opportunity to take over the living room since it was empty. I watched TV for the first time in forever. Reruns of *Fresh Prince of Bel Air* was on, then I saw an upcoming TV show that looked like something I would watch premiering in a couple of months named *Girlfriends*. I was anticipating watching it in the future, it looked like a cool show. I settled for reruns of *Living Single* and laughed my butt off at the silly cast. I thought about Tyrell, so I decided to call him. Tyrell answered the phone and I was silent for a moment.

He called my name, "Treasure?"

I responded, "Yeah, it's me."

He paused then asked, "So how did y'all trip to the hospital go?"

He said it with an attitude. I was caught off guard, I should have known he was watching everything.

To avoid persecution, I responded, "Well my wrist is broken."

He took a long time to respond, then replied dryly, "Oh."

Infuriated with his answer, I said, "Oh?... Is that it?"

I waited for his response. He replied, "Well, what am I supposed to say to that?"

Frustrated with his nonchalant attitude, I responded, "I don't know, like maybe, I am sorry Treasure for breaking your wrist!"

Tyrell barked, "How about I'm done fighting over your fucking ass, he can have your ass!"

The sound of the phone slamming and the dial tone made sure I was unable to respond. I called back but the line was busy. I could not control my tears they were running down my face, I tried the redial button for what felt like a hundred times. I could not believe him, not only did he hang up in my face, but he broke up with me. I was devastated I thought things could not get worse but apparently, they just did. I could not deal with this level of stress, I went to my room and ignored Cassidy's rude question as to why I barged in the room. I got in my bed and went to sleep, not caring if I ever woke up again.

Chapter 13

It was Monday morning; I was still groggy from crying myself to sleep last night after Tyrell broke up with me and ignored all my phone calls. I was devastated. I did not want to get out of bed, let alone go to school and face the reality of having a broken wrist, a broken heart, and a broken ego. Hell, I didn't even know how I was going to get to school. Ever since the first day of school, I rode with Tyrell every morning to school after having our little morning fun time. I started to cry, causing Cassidy to toss and turn in her bed uncomfortably. I just laid there with an extra hour of torture as to how my life was completely over. I had to pull it together and get myself ready before everyone else. I called Tyrell, and the phone just rang and rang until I hung up. I was infuriated and hurt. I could not believe I am the one with the broken arm and broken heart. I started to get angry and had sinister thoughts on how to get back at him. I was not ready to meet another Treasure; I'd much rather be the silly one from the other night. No one would want to deal with the Treasure that was brewing in me from all the crazy trauma that I had been through for almost four years. I was about to turn fifteen on Saturday, and I felt like I could go on a killing spree. Starting with Tyrell and ending with Sabrina and whatever unfortunate souls that would end up in the middle somewhere. I was exhausted at the thought of the effort I would have to put forth to do something as crazy as my thoughts, and settled on the fact, that it would be easier to just take my own life. Instead of contemplating on how I would take others' lives. I shut down my murderous rage and looked for an outfit.

I was determined to get through today without crying or feeling sorry for myself. I quickly got dressed and headed for the door. I walked to school for the first time, ignoring all the honks and looks from other walking kids on the way to school. Girls and boys snickering and pointing, having never seen me walk before and the fact that I had a cast on my arm. I was so embarrassed, having to talk myself out of turning around and running home. When I got to my first class, it was like there was a mass letter that went out that I had walked to school, and my arm was broken. People were gawking at me like I was an estranged celebrity. I completely ignored everyone and pretended like I was normal, even though I could not do any work. All my teachers looked at me with pity, going out of their way to make accom- modations for me, knowing I was a good student. I was not going to let this stop my 4.0 GPA, especially when I only had less than three months left. The only teacher that was a pure ass was my P.E. teacher. Forcing me to walk the track since I could not engage in all the other physical activities. I was fine with that; it gave me time to think and get away from everyone else. Me and all the other P.E. misfits walked the track while everyone else came to their own conclusions about what happened to me.

Lunchtime, I sat by myself when Sénar came up to me and asked, "Where's your punk ass boyfriend at?"

Everyone was watching. I answered him in a whisper, "I don't know, Sénar. Please my day already sucks, please do not make it worse."

He didn't say another word walking off with a trail of young girls behind him. I was so over today; it wasn't until Sénar had asked me about Tyrell, that I realized Tyrell didn't come to school. I was actually concerned about him for a second until I remembered his swollen eye that probably had a lot to do with him not coming. I thought about his custom-made Nike shirt and laughed for the first time today. I made it through the school day without crying and walked home quickly before the crowd of kids had a chance to join me. When I arrived home, I looked across the street and didn't see Tyrell's car. I wondered where he could be and dismissed the thought as quickly as it came. I was so tired and exhausted from monitoring my emotions all day. I went to my room and fell asleep.

I woke up to the smell of food and wondered who was cooking; I was almost hoping it was Sénar since his food was always so good. Just like that, magic, Sénar had his shirt off cooking some fried chicken and French fries. He smiled when he saw me and put his hand down, gesturing me to have a seat. He was abnormally nice, making me a little uncomfortable, but I sat down, eager to taste his food. I bit my lip, deep in thought of how fine he was and how he could cook his ass off.

He turned around to catch me in my sinful thoughts and smirked, "Oh, now you want a piece of big daddy, huh?"

Embarrassed and irritated, I smacked my lips. "Boy, please." I said, rolling my eyes. Cassidy and Chino came in, coming straight to the kitchen to witness me and Sénar's connection.

Cassidy rolled her eyes, and Chino smiled in admiration of Sénar and said, "Damn bro, it smells good in here!"

Sénar cheesed and responded, "You already know, I have to feed the crippled."

He said, eyeing me. I just sighed and rolled my eyes again. Chino looked at me with sincerity, "You good, Treasure?"

I looked at him and nodded my head in a yeah gesture. Sénar turned around and looked annoyed with his question, and Cassidy just looked like she was annoyed with all of us.

Cassidy got up from the counter. "Call me when it's done; I ain't' trying to watch the Chef Sénar show tonight." She said, looking at me accusingly.

I just ignored her and waited patiently for my food. Sénar was loving catering to my food desires, and Chino just seemed to enjoy the show. The food was so good, I almost forgot my wrist was broken, licking my fingers to get the flavor off them. Sénar was watching me as I licked my fingers in pure pleasure. Chino noticed Sénar's reaction giggling to himself and then shook his head. Chino finished his food and left me and Sénar in the kitchen. Sénar waited for me to finish and took my plate to wash it for me.

He looked at me for a minute and hesitated before saying, "I got you, ma! I am going to feed you and take care of you until you're better because you got work to do." He said, insinuating I had chores pending, as he rubbed my thigh on the way out. Cassidy came down to make her plate; I got up, leaving her in the kitchen by herself.

The next couple of days got easier; I walked to school and walked home. I ignored the rumors and dumb ass questions people tried to ask me. I didn't call Tyrell anymore, I just went to school, ate, and slept. Thursday morning, I got up to get dressed, and the phone rung once and then stopped. I thought about who it could be, a part of me was hoping it was Tyrell, and the other part of me didn't care. I didn't bother calling him to find out. I brushed my teeth and got ready for school. I left the house early and saw Tyrell come out of the house to catch me. I kept walking like I didn't see him. He jumped in his car and drove down the street to catch up to me.

I just kept walking as he yelled, "Treasure!"

I ignored him until he parked his car, jumping out and walking up to me. I kept walking until he grabbed my arm, forcefully turning me around to face him. Avoiding eye contact with him, I asked him with an attitude, "What?"

He smacked his lips and took a deep breath before he said, "Treasure, I am sorry. I didn't mean to hurt you."

I rolled my eyes at him and tried to keep myself from crying. Still angry at him, I responded, "I thought you were done with me? Now I am just supposed to forget everything that happened? How embarrassing it was for me this week?"

He didn't know what to say; he just got frustrated. I took this opportunity to turn around and keep walking like he wasn't standing there looking at me. He got so mad; he screeched off in his car in the direction of the school. I didn't care; I was not going to be his little puppy like my mom was to Ken. He broke my wrist, he dumped me, and then he discarded me like a piece of paper. I was beyond pissed; I decided I was going to make him suffer instead.

I went through my day, just like every other day this week. Except I had to avoid Tyrell and ignore people's whispers. All the girls huddling around him at lunch made it super easy to avoid him. He was staring at me while trying not to be rude to his groupies. He watched Sénar laugh and enjoyed the distance between the two of us. I felt like they were both staring holes into me. All the girls were annoyed with knowing both Tyrell and Sénar were single, but they were both focused on me. Everyone just kept making stuff up and asking me about the both of them, hoping to get the scoop before anyone else. I mean, girls that never spoke to me were trying to be my friend. Cassidy was so annoyed with questions and all the buzz about me. At home, she completely ignored me and let me know that I was not all that. She started to act like her, and Sabrina would act before Sabrina left. It was getting overwhelming because my birthday was coming up, and I so wanted to spend it with Tyrell. Just like my last couple of birthdays since we've been together, but my pride was in the way.

Friday morning, I was almost ready to give in, but I wanted to see how long I could last or how hard Tyrell would try, knowing my birthday was the next day. He passed me up slowly, as he drove to school and watched my every move. Making sure I didn't talk to anyone and no one dared to talk to me except Sénar, of course. Sénar saw me sitting down, eating my lunch, and minding my business.

He walked up to me, knowing Tyrell was watching and asked, "Any special request for dinner tonight, special lady?"

The girls behind him were whispering about him being able to cook. I rolled my eyes; at the show, he was putting on. He smiled because he knew I was annoyed, but he also knew I loved his cooking.

In an attempt to get rid of him and also ensure my dinner was not jeopardized, I answered, "Sénar, it doesn't matter your food is always satisfying."

I said it almost smiling as I looked up to see Tyrell standing there, looking like he wanted to kill Sénar and me for talking to me. They sized each other up, forcing me to pay attention to both of their next moves.

Tyrell said, "Treasure, we need to talk now!"

Sénar cut him off, "Look, homeboy, I know you see we were having a conversation."

Ready to pounce on each other, a young girl grabbed Tyrell asking him if she could have his number. While another girl I had seen at the house before grabbed Sénar's arm, tugging on him in a flirtatious manner. I used the opportunity to get up and walk away as I wanted no part in the shenanigans that could take place. I had enough trouble this year, and I was finishing without getting hurt or suspended again. They both mad dogged each other, as I walked away, allowing themselves to be captured by their little distractions. I, being the main attraction, walked away. I managed to get through the rest of the school day without any other crazy moments.

When I got home, the phone rang; I just walked up the stairs needing a moment to breathe and think about my day, let alone the week. I knew I could not go on like this much longer; it was too hectic. Tyrell was about to lose his scruples, and Sénar was fully enjoying my breakup. I did not want him to get used to this bull crap when I knew I wanted to be back with Tyrell. I could hear lots of voices mixed with excitement, enticing me to see what all the commotion was about. Sénar and Chino were high fiving and celebrating something while talking with their dad.

I almost turned around to go back to my room, when Ken and I caught eye contact. "Hey Treasure." He said with a genuine smile, causing Sénar to turn around to notice me staring at them all from upstairs. He summoned me down the steps; reluctantly, I made my way down. Chino was smiling so wide his smile it outshined the other two. Ken spoke with pride, "My boy Chino here got his license! He is a fine young man. I am so proud of him. He is graduating this year and stays out of trouble." He said with a smirk looking at Sénar and me.

I was having flashbacks of his award-winning speech the first night I met his offspring and had to refrain from rolling my eyes deep into the back of my head. Ken continued, "To show my appreciation." He opened the door as my mom was pulling a blue Toyota Tacoma truck into the driveway. Chino ran outside with so much excitement, while Sénar and I were still trying to figure out which emotion to use.

It was my birthday tomorrow and Chino's next week. For the life of me, I couldn't figure out why they didn't just wait for his birthday instead of making mine about him. I had to fight my envious feelings towards the situation and force a smile onto my face. My mom got out hugging Chino, telling him happy early birthday and congratulations. Chino got in to check out his new ride smiling from ear to ear, Sénar went to join him in his celebration. I was annoyed, but I managed to still be happy for him, making my way to check out his ride. Chino jumped out to hug Ken, then he and Sénar jumped in to go for their first joy ride. They offered me to go, but I declined, not knowing the risks I'd be taking. I headed back to the house, passing Ken and my mom. Ken stopped me saying,

"Treasure, I didn't forget about you; I know your birthday is tomorrow. Let's clear our schedules tomorrow so we can all hang out."

I smiled at his attempt to make me feel special; he failed miserably, thinking that I really wanted to spend it with them. He pulled out two crisps hundred-dollar bills and told me to buy myself something nice. I laughed, thinking they love early birthday gifts, recalling the book Chino gave me and the showerhead Sénar bought me. I can't complain because they were both pretty exceptional gifts that brought enlightenment and pleasure. I smiled genuinely and headed inside after saying thank you. I sat on the couch to watch some TV when Cassidy came home, she looked in my direction and reluctantly nodded her head to say hello before running up the steps. She came back down quickly and asked where her brothers were.

I answered dryly, "They went for a joy ride in Chino's new truck."

She smiled and said, "Damn, you sound like a hater." She said it in a joking way.

Cassidy looked out the door to see Chino and Sénar pull up; she grew excited, meeting them outside to congratulate Chino. They all came back in happy with each other, just like every other one of my birthdays.

Feeling salty, I started to head upstairs when Chino stopped me and asked, "Where are you going? We have to celebrate Treasure; we're about to get krunk for our birthdays!" He sounded silly, but genuine enough not to go upstairs and be a brat. Chino saw Sénar looking at him sideways and put his hands out as if to present his brother, saying,

"Chef Sénar has a show for us!"

Everyone started laughing and headed to the kitchen. Sénar washed his hands like a professional and started getting the food ready to prepare. While Chino and Cassidy talked about how it felt to have a new car and to be graduating soon.

Sénar asked, "You know we are all going somewhere tomorrow, right?"

As if to confirm that I was going and to confirm what Ken had told me earlier. In reality, he was saying I wasn't seeing Tyrell tomorrow like I normally did on my birthdays. Annoyed by him telling me what I was doing on my birthday, I shrugged my shoulders, feeling the sadness of the reality that me and Tyrell were broken up.

Sénar feeling cocky, "Don't worry, you'll be with big daddy tomorrow." He said, flexing with a big old goofy smile.

Chino and Cassidy shook their heads and continued their conversation, irritated I rolled my eyes and smacked my lips. Sénar made enough fajitas for the whole family, and my mom and Ken joined us for dinner. Everyone was in a good mood, and we actually looked like a normal functioning family. I was the only one who wished I was with Tyrell instead of pretending to be part of the Reject Brady Bunch.

My mom saw me drifting away in my thoughts and said, "Treasure baby, can you get our dessert out of the fridge?"

I looked at her thinking, *wow the first thing she said to me all day, was to go fetch dessert.* I tried to keep my attitude to a minimum while getting up to go to the fridge. I opened the fridge and almost passed out when I saw a bucket in the fridge. I grabbed it to check the contents and felt like a little girl on my birthday. I tried not to cry and couldn't help but smile the biggest smile I've had in this house in a long time. My mom smiled as she could see my reaction, regardless of my attempt to conceal my excitement.

I brought it to the table, and Cassidy asked, "What the heck is dessert doing in a bucket?"

I laughed and told her what it was; Sénar jumped up to grab it. I slapped his hand away and shocked the both of us. Everyone laughed even Sénar, although he was a little embarrassed. I grabbed the little bucket of gummy worms in the treasure chest on top, putting it to the side carefully. To make up for my slap, I sweetly asked Sénar to grab plates and spoons for everyone. Cassidy rolled her eyes, but everyone else giggled. He humbly did as I asked without letting his arousal show by my sweettalking. Everyone ate the cake and was surprised by the delicious mud cake that happened to come out of a bucket. Everyone looked satisfied with the delicious dinner and a surprise dessert. I grabbed my gummy worms to secure them and offered to clean the dishes, forgetting my wrist was broke. Everyone looked at me like I was crazy, and we all burst into laughter.

Sénar sighed and said, "Yeah, right, Cassidy is going to do them."

Cassidy looked at him like she wanted to kill him. He laughed and got up, saying, "Dang, must I do everything?" He said it in a sarcastic voice.

Chino and Cassidy bought their plates to the sink, and I followed. My mom bought hers and Ken's plate, and then they both went upstairs. After Ken and my mom left, Cassidy and Chino ran out, giggling. I acted like I was going to run too, and Sénar grabbed me by my pants, "Uh uh, you ain't going nowhere."

I sighed and turned around to him, rushing me with a passionate kiss. I resisted, he let me go and then stared deeply into my eyes. I was stunned and unwillingly aroused. I quickly turned to help clean off the table, and he ran dishwater without saying anything. He washed the dishes, and I put them away in silence. When we were done, he left me without saying a word. I was so confused; tonight, was like no other and ended with an awkward silence. I just shook my head and went upstairs to go to sleep.

The morning came, and me and Cassidy were the last ones up. I could hear hustle-bustle in the hallway and on the stairs. I smelled bacon and sausage and thought, sheesh Sénar is at it again? I brushed my teeth and washed my face and headed downstairs, not even bothering to get dressed. I was not thrilled apparently, as everyone else was about the day. The phone rang, and I almost answered it when Sénar ran downstairs, snatching it from me answering it. It was probably Tyrell because the person hung up.

Sénar looked at me and said, "Don't even think about it." His eyes dared me to try him.

I responded with, "Fine, dang!" With an attitude, I went to the kitchen to follow the smell of the food. My mom was making her famous home-cooked biscuit, grits, eggs, sausage, and bacon breakfast. I thought I was hallucinating for a second. I sat down and watched my mom prepare breakfast, reminding me of the days I would sit and wait for her delicious food. With all these surprises, I was hoping she wasn't having a baby next.

Laughing to myself, she turned around to observe me in my thoughts. My mom asked, "What's so funny birthday, girl?"

I wouldn't dare tell her my thoughts, not wanting to give her any ideas. I lied, "Oh, nothing, Momma." She smirked at me and finished cooking.

She asked, "So, do you have a bathing suit to go to the beach in?"

She took me by surprise, is that what all the hustle and bustle was about? The boys were loading stuff into the trucks and appeared to be busy. Totally unprepared, I responded, "No."

She then responded without turning around, "Well, ask Chino to take you to Walmart and get you one, we're leaving after breakfast."

I didn't respond. I needed to take everything in; everything was so abnormally normal. I waited for breakfast to be done when Chino and Sénar came in, my mom told them to eat and asked Chino to take me to Walmart. Sénar looked uncomfortable, and Chino quickly asked, "Sénar, you want to go with us to Walmart?"

He shook his head no, "Nah, I have to get the rest of the food ready and packed."

He quickly ate his food and busied himself with packing up food and utensils. Chino was a bit uncomfortable as we were ready to leave, Sénar called out to Chino, "Aye, get more ice and don't try no funny shit."

Chino nervously laughed, and I rolled my eyes. We got in his new truck to go to Walmart. He started his truck with a smile and looked to make sure I had put my seatbelt on. After driving off, we sat in silence for a couple of minutes before he said, "Happy birthday, Treasure."

I smiled and responded, "Thank you, Chino."

He was nervous and intently kept his eyes on the road. I asked, "Well, how does it feel to be graduating and to have a new car?"

He blushed and said, "It's cool, it all seemed to happen so fast. I'm about to be eighteen!" He proudly said.

I asked him what his plans were. I noticed how tall he had gotten and how much older he looked from the day I first met him. He really was growing into a fine young man. He saw me staring at him, and he said, "Uh uh, don't look at me like that." He laughed then continued, "I am trying to make it to my eighteenth birthday."

I blushed and said, "What? I was looking at how much you've grown from a young grasshopper." We both laughed.

Chino replied, "Yeah, well, you have too." We were quiet again until he said, "Yeah, you're driving all the guys wild with your growth, especially Sénar."

I slapped him playfully and said, "Oh, shut up, Sénar's ass was already crazy!"

Chino retorted, "Yeah, crazy about you." He said that with conviction, I wanted to change the subject.

"Well, Chino, what are you going to do now since your graduating and stuff?"

Chino looked at me and answered, "I am still figuring it out sheesh, I still have a couple of months."

We both laughed as we pulled up to the Walmart parking lot. We went in and agreed to meet back at the front. I looked for a bathing suit that I felt was appropriate, which was pretty hard to find, being that everything looked like bras and panties. I found one with shorts, not that it helped cover my ass at all but was better than all the skimpy two pieces. The top was also more coverage but still had cleavage, making my breast look super-hot. It was the best I could do, grabbing a shawl as an attempt to help hide my assets. I bought a tank top, some shorts, and cute sandals. I met Chino at the front with two big bags of ice in his hands. We went to the register and put our stuff on the conveyor belt, and I grabbed the stick to separate our purchases.

Chino smacked his lips then said, "Put that back, I am not having the birthday girl buy anything, I got you…. just don't tell Sénar."

We both laughed, knowing he was serious as hell. We got back to the house, and Sénar tried to look like he wasn't waiting for us to come back. Chino and Sénar jumped in the truck summoning Cassidy and me to get in. I had a bag that Sénar securely tucked in the back of

Chino's truck. Chino put some music on, feeling like we were in a movie scene as the windows were down and the air was blowing in our faces. Sénar was being extra, yelling out the window, and celebrating like it was his birthday. Cassidy was on her phone, looking at something keeping herself occupied. Sénar was bored of yelling out the window, so he focused his attention on me.

He said, "Happy birthday, baby girl. You still getting in the water with that cast on." I ignored him until he turned around and asked, "What kind of bathing suit do you have on?" I looked at him, annoyed that he had the audacity to ask me such a vulgar question in front of his siblings. Sénar flashed his famous smile and licked his lips seductively while waiting for me to respond. Cassidy looked at Sénar like any other dude being inappropriate. Chino just shook his head, knowing his brother was crazy.

I answered, "A bathing suit Sénar, just a regular bathing suit."

He was satisfied with my answer knowing whatever it looked like it would look good. We listened to music bobbing our heads and enjoying the wind upon our faces. After tailgating my mom and Ken, we finally arrived. We found some decent parking and started to unload. Looking at all the stuff that needed to be unloaded, I appreciated my handicap at this time. Cassidy was mad when Sénar gave her some bags to hold along with her stuff, and when she left, he slapped my ass after giving me just my bag. I wanted to punch him for his immaturity and inappropriate behavior, but I was glad I was just holding my bag. I met up with my mom, and we walked with Cassidy to find a spot. We found the perfect spot with a grill and not too far from the water. We sat our things down and started to set up with the stuff that was already there. My mom mentioned my arm, but I ignored her because it was too late to act like she really cared. The boys were bringing our belongings to where we settled. I laid down my blanket and lay down to relax.

My mom and Cassidy had their beach attire already on as I laid down fully dressed. Ken saw my mom lying down and laid next to her, letting the boys do the rest of the work. They looked like teenagers all cuddled up and smooching. Cassidy was putting sunblock on and was nice enough to ask if I wanted some. I declined as my skin was naturally protected. Once the boys were done, they laid out their towels and joined us to relax. Sénar, of course, found his way next to me. I was still fully clothed while everybody looked ready to get in the water. Sénar appeared impatient and busied himself, getting everything positioned. Chino saw him and got up to help. Ken lay there fondling my mother while she just laid there like a beached whale. I laid there wondering how I ended up here with them, instead of Tyrell and started to get sad. My mom appeared to sense my sadness and asked us if we were ready for the water. I ignored her pretending to be resting when Cassidy kindly declined. Once everything was set up, Chino and Sénar sat back down to relax.

Sénar slapped my thigh and told me to get in the water, but I didn't budge. Everyone was just chilling, but Sénar started to complain. He got irritated and decided to go on a journey of his own, forcing Chino to come with him after asking Cassidy for her phone. They walked the beach while we all just lounged in the sun. Ken got up to grab himself a beer and a wine cooler for my mom. They sat up and talked about all the kids growing up and giggled while they reminisced. I was bored and irritated. I went to the bathroom to remove my shorts and top, putting the shawl over my shoulders. It was hot, but the shawl was used to help somewhat cover my bathing suit, although it was sheer. I walked back to our little gathering, and Chino noticed me walking towards them and elbowed Sénar, he looked at him and then in my direction. Sénar was in a trance when he saw me walking towards them and dropped the tongs, causing Ken to turn around to see what the hell had Sénar all tripped up.

Ken said, "Hey, the birthday girl is back."

He said it with a smirk as he looked for himself. Sénar not wanting to make a scene, tried to carry on with anticipation in seeing me take off my shawl, which I did not. Ken grabbed my mom and started playing around and dragging her to the water. She broke free and ran towards me. Ken grabbed the boys, and they ran towards the water.

My mom said, "Come on baby, let's get in the water; it's your birthday, let's have some fun."

She was genuinely making it hard for me to decline. I took my shawl off and headed to the water with her. Ken and the boys stopped their horsing around to admire us as we walked towards the water.

My mom said, "Treasure, you look beautiful, and I hope you are enjoying yourself."

I just looked at her; she looked so pretty and youthful as she was smiling with anticipation of getting in the water. We walked into the shallow water as the waves messaged our legs and feet. It felt so good I wanted to dive in before realizing I had a cast on. I saw Sénar run back to our area and grab something.

He ran towards me and called out, "Come here, Treasure!"

Enjoying the water, I was reluctant but went towards him anyway. He grabbed my cast and wrapped it with some Saran Wrap; he couldn't help but look at my water glistening body as he wrapped my wrist. I knew if the world wasn't watching, he would have kissed me and whisked me away. I cleared my throat after noticing Ken watching us, and quickly told him thank you and ran back to the water. Sénar ran to put it back and jumped back in the water with the beach ball. We all were like little kids throwing the ball around and splashing water everywhere. I was careful not to do too much with my cast despite Sénar's great efforts to protect it. We went back to our area, and Sénar got on the grill to prepare our food. My mom and Ken grabbed another drink for themselves. We put some music on, and Cassidy got up to look to see what was on the grill. I sat in the sun and daydreamed about Tyrell, wishing he was here with me. We ate and chilled in the sun until my mom was apparently feeling her buzz, as she kept giggling like a silly teenage girl. Ken and her were all over each other, while the rest of us just sat around in our own little worlds. I noticed Sénar kept his eyes on me wherever I was, his eyes were. I laid down and let the sun dry my wet body.

Ken and my mom announced that they were done for the day and told us to have fun. I thought about riding back with them, but I didn't want to be in their way. Cassidy and Sénar both looked happy they were leaving. It wasn't but thirty minutes after they left that we had extra company. Cassidy had one of her little guy friends, knowing better not to bring her grown-ass boyfriend. Sénar had two of his little groupies pull up to keep him and Chino company.

Cassidy's friend rolled a blunt and Sénar grabbed beers and wine coolers out for everyone, which I'm sure Ken left knowingly. I was skeptical but knew I would enjoy myself more if I loosened up a bit. I had a wine cooler and watched everyone mingle while they passed around the blunt. When it got to me, I wasn't sure I wanted to, but everyone insisted it was my birthday and to have fun. I hit it to the best of my ability and almost coughed up a lung, sending everyone into roaring laughter. I was instantly high, feeling a sense of euphoria. Sénar's little friend complained he wasn't paying attention to her as he was focused on me the entire time. He just ignored her, drank his beer, and listened to the music. Sénar made sure everyone else was enjoying themselves by cracking jokes and dancing. It was kind of fun; everyone was chilling until the sun went down. I was feeling great. I had a wine cooler in one hand and Saran Wrap on the other grooving to *Karupt, 'Gangsta'*.

Sénar had his eye on me, and Chino was watching Sénar try to hold himself together. The first commotion was one of Sénar's groupies named London, she was complaining about me and asking him to leave with her. He told her to leave, and she was enraged, pulling on him and demanding him to leave with her. He was embarrassed and ready to go off on her. Chino stepped in and asked her nicely to leave to avoid commotion as everyone else was enjoying themselves. She knew Sénar was mad as he appeared to be fuming, she tried to grab her friend, but she was hesitant to leave as her and Chino were feeling each other. Chino offered to take her home, and London left in a rage. The sun was starting to go down, and Cassidy and her friend left shortly after London left. On my third wine cooler, I was really relaxed and could care less who was there and who wasn't, I was actually enjoying myself. I laid there watching the sun go down with Sénar quietly lying on the other side of me. The moon was bright, and the stars were twinkling, and for a moment, I was just where I wanted to be.

The music was playing, while Chino and the girl giggled and flirted with each other. It was too cold to get back in the water, and I could feel my bladder expanding from all the wine coolers I consumed. I got up and went to the bathroom with my shawl to keep warm. Feeling a little buzzed, I peed with urgency. When I came out of the bathroom, Sénar pulled me by my arm; I almost stumbled before he caught me. For some reason, he had a blanket with him. He led me to a deserted part of the beach and laid the blanket down.

I was alarmed, but I didn't want to make him angry, but I asked, "What's that for?"

He responded, "It's to lay on, damn girl. Chino might finally get some squaiso, and I don't wanna mess it up for him, being in the way."

He was really serious too. I sat down on the blanket and wrapped my arms around my legs. I told him, "I wish I knew we were staying over here. I would have put my shorts back on."

Sénar rubbed my legs to keep them warm and asked me if it was ok. That was the first time he ever asked me anything like that, so I said, "Yeah, I guess, it's cold."

He scooted closer and laid next to me. He talked about Chino and how he was going to miss him when he left. He pulled me closer to him and said, "I don't know what's going on between you and Tyrell, but I really don't care. Normally, I would not care about a lot of things, but it's your birthday."

He inched closer to me, and I inched back starting to feel uncomfortable, he told me to relax, which was impossible. He gently pushed me back to refrain from forcing me but was still dominating what I did. I laid there stiff as a board he rubbed his hands all over my body and begged me to relax. I could not for the life of me. He positioned himself in a lying position by my legs, spreading my legs despite my attempt to close them back. He moved my bathing suit to the side. Since he had not mounted me, my defenses were only halfway up. He just looked at me with admiration and placed his face in between my thighs. I was so confused; I didn't know what he was going to do. Forcing my legs open wider, and he placed his mouth over my coochie. He flicked the little man in the boat with his tongue. Thinking I might pee in his mouth from the unbearable tickling sensation, I squeezed his head with my thighs.

Almost mad, he said, "Stop it." I was obedient and listened, trying to relax my legs but still had a nice grip on his head with my legs. He placed both his hands on my inner thigh to pry my legs open and kissed my coochie like he was in love with it. I thought I would die from pleasure. He pushed my legs down with force and told me to stop again. I thought to myself like I was supposed to be saying stop, but it felt so good. He sucked and nibbled on my little man in the boat, I was at a loss for words, emotions, and thoughts. I didn't even know what to call this, and I was trying not to pop his head open with the pressure from my legs. He placed his hand on my belly, pressing down and gently caressing it while he shoved his tongue in and out of me. I thought I would go into convulsions as my body twisted and turned until I shivered.

Sénar slid his body in between my legs and told me, "Damn Treasure, you look so damn good in that bathing suit." While rubbing his hands all over my breasts, I was still trying to recover from an obvious sexual seizure. I tried to pull myself together as he kissed my neck and gyrated his hips, pressing our privates together. I could feel his hard penis pressing against my now sensitive little man in the boat that he had nibbled and sucked on. I moaned and weakly resisted his muscular warm body mounting mine. He whispered in my ear while adjusting his pants or something, I couldn't tell. I was still tense and started to squirm to sit up.

Sénar laid me back down and whispered, "I am going to take it, and it will be mine forever." I could barely make out what he said before I felt him enter me, taking my breath away. I was pushed back by the sharp pain mixed with pleasure of him entering my wet and quivering insides. I realized it was all the way in, as he was gently thrusting deep inside of me. I tried to utter a plea for him to stop while pushing my hand against his chest and trying to catch my breath. He pressed me back down when I tried to get up; he passionately kissed me, gripping my body beneath his while thrusting himself in and out.

Sénar moaned in pleasure and said, "Oh, my goodness, this is better than I thought, oh shit!" He jumped off me and grabbed his man stick and shot his man juice all over the sand. Trying to catch his breath and looking at his now blood-stained man stick in shock as he noticed blood on the tip of it. Looking at me confused as I tried to cover myself with the blanket, he asked, "Treasure, you were still a virgin?" He sounded surprised and happy at the same time. I, on the other hand, was traumatized and felt bamboozled. I was still trying to register what happened; I didn't even know how to respond. He snatched the blanket off and rubbed his hand up my thigh, "Treasure, I didn't hurt you, right? I didn't know you were still a virgin." He kind of sounded remorseful. I couldn't say anything; I was at a loss for words. He grabbed my legs, playfully, "Treasure?" Deep in thought, he continued with, "Well, that nigga is crazy, that was the best pussy I ever had, and I want more. Shit, I knew you were mine, but now," He smiled sadistically, "that shit is mine forever. For real now."

I scooted back, and he pulled me forward, "Tyrell ain't ever slid up in that tight, sweet, and juicy place of yours?" He looked like he really needed to know; he called my name, "Treasure?" I felt like closing my ears and my legs forever. I didn't want to answer him; I just wanted to go home and go to sleep.

Sénar called my name with authority, and I snapped at him, "We were going to ok! But we didn't finish…What do you care? Thanks to you, I'm not a virgin anymore!" I said with tears welling up in my eyes. He had a mischievous smile on his face, "Well, he should have finished because I am your first, and I will be your last one day."

He grabbed my coochie forcefully, "This was mine first, and it's going to be mine forever, until it's only mine, forever." He looked me dead in my eyes with a burning desire that sent a chill up my spine. He scooped me up off the ground, squeezing me and kissing my neck while carefully standing me up on the ground. He wrapped the blanket tight around me and guided me back.

"Sénar, please don't tell anyone." I said, pleading with him and feeling a twinge of guilt.

He looked at me and pulled me into him, "I won't tell anybody; it'll be our little secret." He said sarcastically while licking his lips and squeezing my behind. I felt so vulnerable but didn't want to appear like anything was wrong with me when we got back to Chino. I just needed time to sort out my thoughts and emotions.

Chino and the girl were lying down cuddling when we walked up. Chino was smiling so big while the girl was rubbing his bare chest. Sénar's smile was bigger than Chino's, but when Chino noticed it prompted him to look at me. He scanned me up and down, searching for an emotion. I didn't want anyone to know what happened between me and Sénar, so I did my best to appear normal. He quickly looked relieved, but still looked a bit concerned. Before Sénar started to clean, he helped remove the Saran Wrap from my cast, while fighting the urge to kiss me. I looked away to conceal my true emotions. Sénar started to clean up, and Chino jumped up to help. I gathered my things and sat with the girl whose name was Mia and waited patiently.

She smiled at me and asked, "Hey, did you guys have fun?"

I looked at her as if to say, *damn you nosey*. I reluctantly responded, "Yeah, we just talked and stuff."

She giggled and said, "Oh, and stuff?"

I didn't want to be mean to her, but she was a bit too familiar. She then said, "Well, I had fun. Damn Chino is so fine, and he could fuck too." Her mouth was so vulgar it caught me off guard. She nudged me, "I know Sénar can fuck too. My homegirl is so sprung on him." She cleared her throat, realizing she might have offended me.

I rolled my eyes because I could care less; I wanted to get home and forget this ever happened. We headed back home to everyone in their feelings while the music played. Chino dropped his muse off then took Sénar and me home. I was the first one in the house going straight to my room and into my bed. I went to sleep trying to keep my mind off tonight and on getting Tyrell back.

I woke up to girls chattering and giggling. Sabrina was talking loud on purpose. I was hoping it was a nightmare I would wake up from, but I could hear her say Tyrell's name. I looked back at her, and she snapped,

"What is your black ass looking at? He ain't your man no more anyways." Flashing a nasty smile at me and resumed talking to Cassidy.

I quickly wondered who had told her and jumped out of bed. She jumped up just in case she was going to have to prepare for another ass whipping. I rolled my eyes and ignored her, as I was a professional eyeroller that said what I did not want to say with my eyes. Plus, there was a part of me that still felt guilty after last night. She lowered her voice as if now whatever she was saying was such a secret. I just left to take a shower and get away from my evil rivals.

When I got to the bathroom, I undressed carefully examining my body. My round breast and flat stomach stared back at me with Tyrell's name sparkling over my bare breasts. I ran my fingers across my necklace and longed for Tyrell. I turned the hot water on, letting it run all over my skin as I traveled through my thoughts. I tried to convince myself that last night was not my fault, and it was a horrible experience. I even tried to forget the melodious pleasure of having Sénar licking all over my coochie until I broke out into convulsions and the electricity that went through my body when he entered inside of me. The pain being overtaken by the rhythm of his thrusting in and out of me. I was feeling everything all over again. To control myself from the urge to masturbate, I got out and quickly got dressed.

Chino was in the hallway with Sénar behind him. With his eyes focusing intently on me, Sénar grabbed his crotch and licked his lips. I looked down in shame and hurried to my room. Sabrina and Cassidy must have gone downstairs, and I was relieved. I hated Sabrina's face and her voice; I just wanted my space. Feeling hungry, I went downstairs. Everyone was sitting at the nook while Sénar prepared breakfast. Sabrina smacked her lips as if to ask what I was doing there when to be fair; she was the one banished. She saw Sénar give me my plate and sighed. I did everything in my power to keep my mouth from confessing my hatred for her. Chino feeling my frustration asked everyone about the mall and the movies. I quickly declined while Cassidy and Sabrina happily agreed. Sabrina waited for Sénar's response. He shrugged his shoulders, and reluctantly agreed to go. He barely spoke to Sabrina but knew he had to go, being that she was visiting and leaving tonight. I ate and went to my room while everyone left for the mall and movies. I read until I fell asleep; I woke up to the smell of food and headed downstairs. Sénar was making tacos, and they were all just talking about the movie. After everyone ate, Chino took Sabrina home, and Cassidy rode with them. I hesitated to help Sénar with the dishes. I tried to go back to my room when he pulled me from behind into his body.

I froze and tried to wiggle away; he held me tighter grinding himself against me and said, "I can't stop thinking about you ma. Mmmm, you taste so good and feel even better."

I thought I would faint when he spun me around and picked me up, putting me on the counter, forcing himself in between my legs. I looked away when he tried to search my eyes. He pulled me close, and I pushed him away. He snatched me off the counter, agitated, "Oh, it's like that?" He pushed me against the counter and slid his hand up my shirt when we heard keys in the front door. He released me and walked away, leaving me there with my heart beating and my coochie throbbing with unwarranted anticipation. Overwhelmed and beyond tired, I ran upstairs to cry myself to sleep.

Chapter 14

I woke up with my eyes feeling tired from crying all night. I didn't know what to do or how to feel. I just wanted to go back to sleep. I wanted to avoid Sénar as much as possible and run into Tyrell's arms for safety, but I was still angry with him too. I wanted to blame him for what happened on my birthday to take the guilt away from myself. If we were together, I would have been with him instead of at the beach with the Reject Brady Bunch. Filling up with anger, I got dressed and forced myself to take on the day with my emotions on the verge of crumbling. I continued to avoid both Sénar and Tyrell as they were tearing me into pieces. The whole week I felt like a zombie and isolated myself as much as possible, refusing to eat some nights and going to bed early every night.

Tyrell was getting impatient by the second week of our breakup; he would stare at me so intensely. I would avoid him whenever I could, and he didn't care if I knew he was following me around.

One day after school, he waited for me and walked alongside me. It was extremely hot that day, and I was sweating. He wasn't saying anything, and we were getting further from the school. I couldn't help it with the heat and suspense.

I asked him, "Where's your car?"

He looked at me and responded, "It's at the school."

I looked perplexed as I was sweating; I was starting to wish we were in it. It was like he could read my mind. "So, walk back with me, and let's get it." He said looking at me desperately waiting for me to answer,

I tried not to roll my eyes by closing them instead then hesitantly agreed. We walked back to the car silently. Tyrell was careful not to say anything to mess up the chances of me getting into his car. When we reached the car, Tyrell opened the door for me, and there were several people who were being nosey. I got in and felt some relief knowing the air conditioning would be blowing, while the rest of the kids would be walking home in the heat. He was still silent as he started his car and drove off. I was cautious, I knew how emotional Tyrell could get, especially when driving, so I chose to sit in silence as well. He drove occasionally looking at me like he wanted to say something, but he was skeptical. I tried to remain neutral, as I was just glad not to be walking in the heat but dreaded the conversation we would have when our silence was broken.

We pulled up to a park we had never been to and parked the car. He left the car on to keep us cool then turned to face me. He stared at me long and hard before saying, "So, you don't even miss me. Have you already replaced me?"

I sighed because the conversation was not starting on a positive note. I chose my words wisely and replied, "Look, I don't want to argue I-"

Cutting me off; he said, "Treasure, I asked you a question."

Feeling the tension, I quickly answered, "Yes. I missed you, and no, I'd never replace you."

He rubbed me and kissed me so passionately; I couldn't help but melt into his arms, kissing him back. Not able to control himself, he took his seat belt off and mine to remove anything that would restrict our bodies from coming closer. Both of us knew we had a lot to talk about, but we took advantage of this moment to quickly fulfill our lustful desires. We fondled each other's bodies and kissed each other passionately like we were never going to see each other again. He stopped and told me how much he missed me while scanning my body to ensure I was intact. He rubbed my breast, gently squeezing them, running his finger around the nape of my neck. Moving my shirt down in search of something, he smiled when he found his name sparkling on the chain in between my chocolate breasts and put his face in between kissing them all over.

He looked me in my eyes and said, "Treasure, I need you to be mine again."

He looked at me with pleading eyes, he wanted to grab me again, but he started the car and headed back towards our houses. We pulled into the driveway of Tyrell's house, and he asked me to go inside with him. Everything went so smoothly; I decided to go in with him, not the least bit worried about the possible outcome.

Tyrell still quiet as he led me to his room, once in his room he set his keys down as I sat on the bed. He slowly walked towards me and joined me on the bed; our silence still awkwardly lingering between us.

He asked me, "Treasure, you still wanna be with me?"

I looked at him and nodded my head, yes, still trying to gauge his emotions. He is never this quiet or self-conscious, his cockiness was at a zero, and he appeared helpless.

Tyrell said, "I am sorry, Treasure; I wish none of this shit happened. The last two weeks have been miserable, and no matter what I tried to do to get you off my mind, nothing worked."

The look of guilt felt familiar and made me want to ask him what he had done, but I didn't want him to ask me anything just in case the look of guilt was contagious. Putting my head down lost in my own feelings of remorse and my racing thoughts. I finally looked up to see that he was staring at me, waiting for me to respond. I processed what he said, and I felt the same way, but I didn't want to make things too easy. I replied, "I missed you too, but you really hurt me when you left me hanging. I was just trying to comfort you; I love you, Tyrell."

He sighed and said, "Look, just stay away from Sénar." He paused and thought for a second, then added, "And everybody else too." We both chuckled. Deep in thought for a second, he confessed, "I just don't trust Sénar, that's all. Chino seems cool, but something about Sénar just rubs me the wrong way. I wish you could get rid of him like you did Sabrina's ass."

I knew that was my cue to ensure him by saying, "Tyrell, I want to be with you. Sénar is Ken's son, and there's nothing I can do about that. Sabrina had it coming; she just wouldn't let up."

I wanted to tell him about Ken's threats to send Sénar away too if he kept getting into trouble, but I didn't want to give him the incentive to continue their war, I continued my speech, "Look I am yours, I just want you to trust me. I don't like the situation either, but it's that much harder when we are arguing and fighting too. Promise me you won't just leave me hanging like that again."

He responded, "Shit, I don't want to lose you, and I need all my Treasure, so I promise, baby." He grabbed me and kissed me, squeezing me all over. And just like magic, we were on again.

Tyrell was so happy to be back with me, and I was so happy to be back with him. We made up for the lost time we experienced the last two weeks. Tyrell was concerned about my birthday and wanted details on how it went. We were lying on a blanket at a park with his hand holding his head up as he stared at me with inquisitive eyes. I was still trying to block out things from that day, or should I say night, I also didn't want to give the impression that it was too enjoyable. I started off with the story of Chino getting his car the day before my birthday and my mother being the one to drive his truck into the driveway. Tyrell was listening intently as I told him what we ate for dinner and how my mother made me mud cake after it being years of me having one. He smiled, but I could see he was feeling guilty for not being there and letting my family steal the show for making my day special. Then I told him about Ken and how he forced everyone to go to the beach on my birthday.

Tyrell sat up and asked, "Wait the beach? What did you wear? I mean, you have a cast on so you can't get in the water."

He was looking at me impatiently, waiting for an answer. I replied, "I wore a bathing suit, but I had shorts and a top on to cover it." Before he could interrupt me, I continued, "I didn't have on a skimpy bathing suit, it was short bottoms and a mid-way top, I also had a shawl, so I was decent. My mom forced me to get in the water, so I had to get in, but I didn't stay in long."

Tyrell looked agitated, "So, what did everybody else do?"

I answered, "Sénar and Chino walked the beach flirting with girls, Cassidy talked on the phone, I read a book, and my mom and Ken cuddled. Then Sénar had some girls come for him and Chino. We barbequed and then went home."

I rushed through it as quickly as possible and then mentioned Sabrina was there when we got back. He looked uncomfortable; it was like he wanted to pry for more details, but he also looked cautious.

He then asked, "It wasn't better than our celebrations, right?"

I smiled and answered, "Not even close, baby, you always make me feel so special. I was really sad we didn't get to spend it together."

Tyrell looked down, feeling regretful; I wanted to change the subject but still asked him what he did that weekend. He hesitated before answering, "Nothing, I just tried to keep myself busy to keep from crying over you." He said bitterly.

We both agreed it was the worst two weeks ever and never wanted to go through it again. Tyrell appeared hopeful and said, "Let's go get some tacos!"

He made sure to get eleven tacos, so I would get my five, and we laughed about our taco connection. We ate them in the car; the tacos were so delicious. We ate them while laughing at all the silly things people did and said the last two weeks. We made plans to ensure we had a good rest of the school year. He asked me to come to his games more often and even some of his practices. I agreed to the games, but I brought up all the groupies, and Tyrell understood why I didn't' want to go. I assured him I would make it to a couple just to make him happy.

The weeks flew by, with everyone being so busy preparing for the end of the school year. There was a lot of testing and basketball games to conclude our weeks. My house was busier than usual with Chino preparing to graduate, Cassidy bragging about becoming a senior, and Sénar trying to stay out of trouble so he could play sports and not get sent away. I even ate a couple of frozen dinners, which I was not happy about being that Chef Sénar was so busy with his girlfriends and basketball. He would come home exhausted and sometimes still managed to cook or was kind enough to make a chicken or tuna salad for sandwiches. He made it clear, he was serving the crippled. It was only a week left before my mom, and I would go check my wrist to have the cast removed, I couldn't wait. Although I had figured out how to maneuver with it, I was ready to get it off. I figured maybe I would learn how to cook since Sénar was Chef Sénar for the crippled, I needed to feed myself and not depend on his cooking. Tyrell also would take me to eat sometimes when I joined him for his practices, which was rare to avoid slapping one of his groupies. The girls were catty and totally purposely flirting with both Tyrell and Sénar. The cheerleaders were the worse. They were so conceited, prancing around in their little shorts and skirts, making sure the boys gave them the attention they seemed to live for. It was wack, and I could only take so much of it. I would rather go home and watch the *Parkers or Girlfriends* than to watch them in their desperate attempts to harvest attention.

My doctor's appointment was on a Friday this week, which was the same day of the game before the championship. I wanted to go, but I couldn't miss my doctor's appointment. Tyrell understood with a pouting look on his face. To give him some confidence, I grabbed his face and kissed him. "Make sure you guys win this game, so I'll have a championship game to come to."

He looked at me and then smiled so big and said, "I got you babe, I'm going to play my heart out so you can see me win the championship." He looked like he was daydreaming of a trophy; I giggled and thought to myself how it worked like a charm.

My mom told me my appointment was at 4:30 pm, so when she picked me up from school at 2:00 pm, I was confused. They called me from my classroom to the front office, and everyone started to whisper in their little groups. I remained unbothered; I was used to everyone being so damn nosey. My mom waited for me as I walked through the office. Mr. Bell happened to see us and stopped to acknowledge the fact that I was staying out of trouble then whispered Sénar's progress as well. I was so embarrassed and irritated that he felt the need to add Sénar's progress with mine. Why couldn't he have just left Sénar out of it? My mom smiled and thanked him for his positive report.

Trying not to pout, I asked, "Mom, why are you so early? I thought my appointment was at 4:30." She responded, "You have another appointment as well at 2:30."

I looked at her like she spoke another language an asked, "For what?"

She sighed before answering, "You are becoming a young lady, so I made an appointment for a physical and PAP smear."

I panicked, "A PAP smear. What is that, momma?"

I whined like a little girl, and she responded, "Treasure, it is normal you are fifteen, and the gynecologist checks to make sure you don't have any abnormalities in the cells of your cervix. All women get it to help monitor the risks of cervical cancer. Besides, you are a young lady, and you're growing up, and only God knows what else."

Offended, I looked at her like she was one of the catty girls from my school. She laughed, "Girl don't look at me like that you have a boyfriend, right?"

I wanted to ignore her question as I had an idea of where this was going. "Umm." I reluctantly answered.

She then continued, "Well, I don't want no grand babies. You two have been together despite my warnings, and I'm not taking any chances."

Already irritated with her secret agenda, I told her, "Well, Tyrell has not poured me a cup of man juice, so no need to worry about that." I said with an attitude.

She chuckled, "Girl, I haven't heard that in so long, well, it won't be long before he or someone else is trying to pour you a cup."

She was killing me with all these low blows, what did she mean or someone else? I was done talking to her as I did not want to get popped in the mouth on the day I was getting my cast removed. My doctor's appointment for the physical was so uncomfortable as I had to answer very personal questions in front of my mom. The doctor told me I could have her leave the room if necessary, to get accurate information. I thought about that being a set up for my mom to automatically assume I was having sex. I was almost honest; I was not having sex, and the experience I did have was complicated. Saying no to every question was very easy to say but very difficult for my doctor and mom to believe. The process where the lady stuck the plastic tool up my "*vagina*" as she called it, hurt like hell. To make matters worse, she scraped something off of somewhere, and it was very uncomfortable. I never felt so violated, and if I may, there was only pain, no pleasure whatsoever. Ugh and if things could not get any worse, she came in with a huge needle with some clear liquid inside of it and sat it down next to me. I was on the verge of having a nervous breakdown and running out of the room to safety.

My mom and the doctor tried not to laugh as I was squirming and uncomfortable, not knowing what was next or why there was a huge needle next to me. The doctor explained the needle and its purpose, "This is Depo Provera; it is a long-lasting birth control injection as a contraceptive method. You will need to come every three months for an injection to prevent pregnancy. Now, this is not to prevent sexually transmitted diseases, so it is advised you still use protection to protect yourself from HIV or any other sexually transmitted diseases. I will give you your first injection today and see you in three months."

I was embarrassed and angry because I did not sign up for a sex-ed lecture or birth control. If my mother just talked to me, she would know I wasn't having sex. I was in no mood to argue as my mother obviously had her mind made up. I reluctantly gave the doctor access to my top right butt cheek to inject some, "*I don't want no grand baby injection.*" The injection site was a smidgen of the pain I felt from my mother's betrayal. She just acted like this whole process was normal, like everyone's mom puts their daughters who aren't having sex on birth control and tells them it's a normal physical examination. We went to the next visit to a different department of the hospital to have my cast removed. The doctor asked my pain level, but I was in no mood for small talk, I just wanted this to all be over already. I said ok to everything in a trance, not wanting to even think about how I ended up in this situation or how this one would end. If matters couldn't get worse when he removed the cast, I almost passed out. I didn't recognize my chocolate wrist as it looked like someone switched it out for Cassidy or Sabrina's wrist. It was this puny, pale wrist, with hair I never saw, and it smelled like Sénar's feet after a long day of practice. I could have died and came back when I looked at what had become of my wrist. The doctor noticed my expressions and assured me that in two to three weeks, everything would be normal again. He told me to keep the area clean and moisturized. The doctor's last remark was so unnecessary when he said, "Oh, and keep it safe we don't need to see you in here again." My mom nodded in agreement, and we left with my new wrist and an uninvited butt injection.

The drive home I was livid, I could not believe she didn't even have the common courtesy to ask me if I was having sex or if I wanted a shot in my ass! I wanted to ask her why, but I was too infuriated mixed with disappointment. To make matters worse, she turned on her Christian music and tuned me out on the way home. When we got home, the house was quiet; my mom came in behind me without a word going straight up the steps. I was so mad that the thought of tripping her butt crossed my mind, but I couldn't afford any more injuries as a result of trying to trip my mother. I went to the kitchen and made a sandwich out of Sénar's delicious homemade chicken salad. It was so good; I felt like I would make love to my sandwich now knowing I couldn't get pregnant. I know it's silly, but it was that good, and I had to stop myself from eating another one. I quickly went upstairs and got my things to take a hot bath. I examined my arm to see if it had come back to life, but it still looked like it was hanging on to threads for its life. I just laid my head back to relax and tried to forget about the horrible day I had. It was still early enough to watch some of my shows before going to bed. In the middle of *Girlfriends*, I heard Cassidy, Chino, and Sénar come in the front door. I didn't hear Sénar's voice, but I heard Cassidy and Chino having a conversation. I looked up and saw Sénar's face, he looked upset, so I figured they must have lost the game. I asked, "Sénar, who won the game?"

He looked annoyed and answered, "Why don't you ask your ball, hoggin' ass boyfriend!" He stomped up the steps before I could respond to his nasty attitude. I finished my show and called Tyrell.

I could hear the excitement in his voice, "Hey babe, guess what?"

Confused about his excitement thinking they lost tonight, I responded, "What babe?"

Having to move the phone from my ear as he was yelling, "We won! We are going to the championship!"

I smiled, thinking about how awesome it must feel to have accomplished such a huge goal. I told him congratulations, and I couldn't wait to go to the big game. We talked a little, and I went to bed telling him I would see him tomorrow. I didn't want to damper his day with my shitty experiences I had earlier. I went to bed wondering why Sénar was so upset when they actually won. Maybe because Tyrell scored too many points. Sénar was such a tough guy, but such a crybaby when things didn't go his way, ugh I had enough drama for today. I closed my eyes and drifted into a deep sleep.

The next morning, I was excited to see Tyrell. I called him as soon as I woke up. His mom answered, "Good morning, Carter residents, how can I help you?"

I responded, "Good morning Mrs. Carter; is Tyrell there?"

She responded, "Hello Treasure, he is still sleeping darling, I'll tell him you called."

Disappointment set in, and I responded, "Ok, thanks."

The only positive was she didn't ask who I was. I was sad because I thought I would escape this hell hole first thing in the morning. I thought I should have just gone over there, and if he was sleeping, just go get in his bed and fall back asleep with him. I saw a car pull up in front of the house; I wondered who it was this early in the morning. A cute familiar looking dark caramel-skinned girl got out of the car and walked up to the door. I was looking out the window when Sénar was coming down the steps.

He asked, "Why are you being nosey?"

I looked at him like he was crazy, even though I guess I was being nosey. He looked nice; he had on a white button-up shirt with a black tie, some slacks, and some fancy shoes. Now, I was being nosey and asked, "Sheesh Sénar, where are you going?"

He looked at me and smirked before replying, "None of your business!"

He reached for one of my breasts, and I smacked his hand away before he successfully grabbed one. He opened the door to let his number gazillion girl toy in. She looked at him like he was worth a million bucks before grabbing him and kissing him with her arms around his neck. I just stood there waiting to be introduced, and Sénar looked at me like I was a lost puppy.

He reluctantly introduced her to me and said, "Aye babe, this is Treasure; let me make a sandwich before I leave."

She looked at me and introduced herself, "Hi, I am London, Sénar's girlfriend."

Even though Sénar's back was to the both of us, I knew he was rolling his eyes. We followed him to the kitchen and watched him take the chicken salad out of the fridge. Sénar shook his head and said, "Damn Treasure, you damn near kilt this shit."

I giggled because I forgot to mention I had another sandwich before bed last night. He asked London if she wanted one, she frowned her nose and declined. That was my cue to let him know that I definitely wanted one; she was crazy for turning it down. He laughed and left the container on the counter for me to make my own as they were on their way out the door. I ate my sandwich in peace and wondered why Sénar was dressed so nicely. London looked like I had seen her before, but this girl referred to herself as Sénar's girlfriend. It was like a forbidden term for them to use. I don't care if they had sex every day, the word, *girlfriend*, was like taboo for Sénar.

The phone rang, and I quickly answered, "Hello?"

Tyrell said, "Good morning, babe."

I happily replied the same to him. Tyrell then said, "I am so tired, come by, and let's chill here for a bit, and don't be mad if I fall asleep."

I happily responded, "Ok, I'll be on my way."

I grabbed my things and ran across the street. He answered the door in his Pajamas and rubbing his eyes. He grabbed a bowl of cereal, and we headed back to his room. He had a new TV in his room, and we laid in bed to watched TV. We cuddled for a while, and before I knew it, we were both sleeping. A knock on the door woke us up. Tyrell answered, "Yeah?" His mom asked if we were hungry, and we both said yeah. We got up and headed downstairs, Tyrell and his mom noticed my cast being gone once we were all in the kitchen. For a second, I forgot, too, until I saw my puny little wrist look back at me. His mom just smiled and served us homemade burritos for lunch. They were ok, a little underseasoned, but I didn't dare complain. We said thank you and went back to his room to finish watching TV. Tyrell was still tired and told me how much work he put in the game yesterday, making sure to mention Sénar did nothing but get in the way. He complained about Sénar and made sure to point out Sénar didn't score any points in the game last night. Tyrell also complained about his job saying that he was getting too old to work at the movie theatre and that he was thinking about quitting, so we could spend more time together. I listened to him go on and on with his list of complaints until I was ready to complain about his complaining. Eventually, he stopped to kiss and fondle each other until we ran out of things to do. I wanted to ask him why we haven't had sex, but I was scared to bring it up, I figured it would happen when the time was right. I told him about my doctor's visit to get my cast off, and he clowned my little wrist until we couldn't laugh anymore. I didn't tell him about the other doctors visit, I was too embarrassed. The sun was starting to go down, and we had spent the whole day watching TV and talking, so I kissed him goodnight and went home. Once inside, I saw Sénar and his girlfriend lying on the couch like they owned the place. I just rolled my eyes and went up the steps to my room. Cassidy wasn't there, and I was so overjoyed, I read my new book *God Still Don't Like Ugly*, as the first one was good enough to get the sequel. I read until I fell asleep.

There was not much time left in the school year, and everyone was preparing for the summer to come to get a break from the hustle and bustle of school. Chino was preparing to graduate and was making some serious moves in the last couple of weeks. I saw him studying vigorously, looking into different career choices, and what college he would attend. He would let Sénar distract him sometimes with his little groupies, but one thing was for sure, London was one of them that was there faithfully with one of her little friends for Chino. With everyone having their distractions, I had the house to myself quite a bit lately. I had to get a life as it seemed I was the only one that didn't have a life outside of my relationship with Tyrell. Sénar made it very clear he was preoccupied with something and that he would deal with me when he was done, whatever that meant. I was relieved it was less pressure for me to have to worry about and gave me the chance to build on my relationship with Tyrell. It was hard to convince him to believe me when I didn't even believe myself when it came to Sénar. With Sénar occupied, I had more confidence in my relationship, and was able to be a good girlfriend, totally focused on Tyrell's emotional needs.

Sénar and Tyrell just completely ignored one another since their disputes could not be rendered; they just tolerated one another for team purposes in basketball. They used their hate for each other to fuel their talents in sports. Sénar was ready to put games aside and play basketball, but his true desire was playing football. Since in his words, "*I can legally fuck people up,*" and only played basketball to annoy and compete with Tyrell. Unlike Tyrell, who absolutely loved both sports and never complained about the effort it took to maintain grades and his performance. Tyrell was so driven and focused that sometimes it turned me on. I hated going to his practices because the whole cheerleading team was like his own personal fan club, but I would go to the games because those are really important to him. After winning the last game without me there to witness it, Tyrell made it very clear that for the championship game, I had to be there, so I had no choice but to go. The next couple of weeks flew by with all the finals, yearbook pictures, and graduation kickbacks everyone was throwing every other week. I did not attend any as I was not invited to any, but everyone else seemed to get an invite. I didn't care; I was trying to finish the school year drama free, and I was not going to let anyone mess that up for me.

The big day was finally here, with only two weeks left of school everyone was preparing for the big championship game. I was going through my things looking for an outfit when Cassidy and her friend Nevaeh came in laughing. I had a feeling in the pit of my stomach at the sound of her voice that alarmed me to start the cooling process of the anger brewing in me before it seeped out. Nevaeh looked at me like I was a contagious disease, and Cassidy ignored it and kept talking. To avoid an argument, I grabbed whatever I could find in a hurry. I did not want to use my newly healed hand to lay hands on her, and I wasn't talking about prayer either. I found some apple bottom jeans that had my butt looking like Beyoncé's and a sparkling red apple shirt with slits on the shoulder, that hugged my voluptuous breast. I was satisfied with my outfit; I gathered my things and went to take a shower. As soon as I was done undressing, I heard a knock at the door.

I was skeptical and asked, "Who is it?"

Chino answered, "It's me; I have to go really bad; please open the door!"

I was reluctant, but I quickly threw my clothes back on without my undergarments to save time. I stuffed them inside the towel and quickly opened the door. Chino ran in like he was going to explode and slammed the door behind him. There was music and giggling girls in their room, I wanted to be nosey, but I decided not to be. Sénar opened the door to his room; I could hear the music and girls grabbing for him as he was walking out, he closed the door behind him. I quickly turned my back to him, hoping Chino would hurry, it was like Sénar had x-ray vision, he cupped my unholstered breast and moaned in my ear, sliding his hands down over my body. I stopped his hands before he could touch my coochie, pushing him off me and turning around to confront him, "Stop it!" I snapped at him.

He laughed and put his hands in the air and asked, "Damn ma, you don't miss me?"

I looked at him with an attitude and quickly replied, "No!" Looking at him like he was shit on a stick. Still noticing he had no shirt on and half his basketball uniform, he looked so damn fine. He chin upped me before turning around to go back to his room, where they did miss him. Chino came out, he looked embarrassed.

I asked, "Are you ok?"

He blushed before responding, "Yeah, I'm ok. Are you ok?"

I sighed, "I'm fine. Now move." I said playfully. He went back to his room where apparently the party was at. I showered and got dressed, I put my hair in a high bun and threw my sparkling gold earrings on that Tyrell bought me. The earrings went perfect with the gold neckless that had Tyrell's name spelled out in cursive linked to it that sparkled against my glistening chocolate skin. Upon coming out, I ran into Sénar with his full uniform getting ready to leave, stopping him dead in his tracks.

His eyes widened, "Damn girl."

He said inching closer to me, as I moved back, he rushed in with a quick kiss, "Wish me luck ma." He said as he turned to leave in a hurry.

Annoyed, I wiped my mouth; I knew he was late because Tyrell had already left to practice and would not ever be late like Sénar was. I went to my room and when I entered Cassidy and Nevaeh looked at me like they saw a ghost. I quickly grabbed the rest of my stuff and headed out of the room. I laughed in my head at their silence, I called for Chino, and he came out with a guilty look as Cassidy and her friend piled out of the room. Had I known they were riding with us, I would have never asked him for a ride earlier, he knew it too. I sat in the front while Nevaeh and Cassidy sat in the back, running their mouths about which of the basketball players were the finest. They were actually acting their age for once, even though they were having sex with grown-ass men. When Nevaeh started to talk about how fine this guy was and that she heard he might go to the pros, Cassidy had a look of shock on her face and asked,

"What guy? What do you want with a schoolboy, all of a sudden?" Cassidy sounded skeptical and a bit irritated.

Nevaeh giggled and said, "I don't know some dude named Tyrell I met at a party. Shit if he goes to the pros, he gonna be ballin!" She said it with excitement.

Chino purposefully turned the radio on to tune them out, and I gave him a silent thank you with my eye contact. I only knew one

Tyrell she could be talking about and that Tyrell belonged to me. Thinking to myself, I smirked at her stupidity, and the fact her girl Cassidy didn't school her. Listening to the music and tuning out the thirsty girls in the back, we finally pulled up to the school.

I couldn't help but look at Nevaeh and correct her, "Oh, the Tyrell that you were so excited about belongs to me. So, you should probably look for a different meal ticket."

She looked me up and down before responding, "Oh, I didn't know, but I am willing to wait my turn." She said with a matter of fact attitude and rolled her eyes at me. Cassidy knew I was passive, but the one sure way for a female to get punched in the mouth was when it came to Tyrell.

Before I could respond, Cassidy cut me off, "No Nevaeh seriously, that's her dude they have been dating for like two years or so."

Nevaeh looked at me like I was nothing and responded, "And?"

I was ready to wring her neck. People were already being nosey as I was ready to slap her silly. Chino grabbed me before I could reach her and said, "Treasure, No!"

Nevaeh smacked her lips and rolled her eyes; she appeared to be unbothered by the ass whipping she was about to experience in front of a million nosey ass bystanders. Chino firmly held my arm, and we walked to the long ass line with Tweetle Dee and Tweetle Dumb following behind us. When we got to the line Cassidy and Nevaeh boldly stood in front of us; Chino quickly stood in front of me to break my and Nevaeh's stare-down competition. I was already tired of Tyrell's groupies, but now this heifer was coming for my man too, I was ready to beat her to smithereens. Hearing all the whispers and gossip around us, I remembered the band Tyrell gave me earlier, knowing it would be a long line to get in. Finding it in my purse, I grabbed Chino and brushed pass Nevaeh, causing her to stumble back, dropping her phone. She yelled, "This bitch!" She bent over to pick up her phone pieces after it burst apart. I laughed as we passed everyone up and reached the front of the line; the security guard knew me already and said, "Hey there Treasure." He said playfully. I showed him my band and said, "This is Sénar's brother, he forgot his band." He told everyone to move back and let us in while Cassidy and Sabrina look dumbfounded, standing there waiting in line.

The game was super intense; everyone was on the edge of their seats. Chino was nice enough to save Cassidy and Nevaeh a seat because I wasn't saving them nothing. Nevaeh was salty having a crack on her phone, if looks could kill, we would both be dead. I saw Tyrell's parents jumping up and down when they spotted me, they waved, and I waved back. Nevaeh rolled her eyes as I smirked at her and Cassidy's skinny asses. The clock was running down, and the other team was up by nine points. It was a good game, but the other team wanted it bad, and their teamwork was phenomenal. There was tension on our team, and it was visible. Everyone seemed to be playing to shine instead of as a team. There was lots of testosterone coming from our team as the young men were flirting and showing off. The coach called time out for our home team to give the boys a tongue lashing and used several choice words to explain his frustration. We could see all the guys' faces drop at his disappointment in their obvious lack of teamwork. He pumped them up to bring their spirits back up, telling them to use it in the right areas and play kiss and makeup later.

They all yelled in unison like a pack of wolves and jumped back on the court with the ball in their hand. Tyrell ran down the court for a layup scoring two points, and the crowd screamed along with his parents. The other team tried the same move, but Sénar snatched the ball smooth out of his opponent's hand, with no foul called because no contact was made. Sénar was too far to shoot, the only open and trustworthy teammate was Tyrell, Sénar had no choice but to throw the ball to him. Tyrell shot the ball, scoring a three-pointer, all net. The other team had the ball now, feeling the fire coming off Tyrell's hands and drove the ball aggressively down the court, knocking Sénar to the ground, a foul called giving Sénar two free throws. He made both shots, and the ball went back to the other team. With one minute and thirty seconds left on the clock, the star player on the visitor team shot a three-pointer but missed. Sénar grabbed the ball and ran down the court, dunking the ball on the player named Josh that knocked Sénar down on the earlier play. Tensions were growing between Sénar and Josh, they were of the same cloth, and they were not feeling each other. Josh had the ball, and Sénar was blocking him, unable to get around Sénar. He flinched at Sénar, thinking he would move back, but Sénar stood his ground. The crowd was booing as Josh was running the clock down intentionally, he tried to go around again and got swiped by Sénar. Pressed for time, Sénar was going to throw it to Tyrell again but instead tried to shoot the ball from the three-point line when he was flagrantly fouled by Josh.

The referees blew their whistles, waving their arms violently in the air calling flagrant foul on Josh. All the teammates from both sides rushed in between the two of them as they were eying each other viciously. Sénar was smiling, but I knew that smile, and it was not a friendly smile. Sénar got three free throws and appeared frustrated, as it was a lot of pressure with only 30 seconds left, he made the first two shots but missed the third. The crowd, "Awed," in disappointment, but the ball was now a jump ball from the center court. The clock started, and the ball was thrown in the air, Josh and Sénar both jumped up to grab the ball. Sénar snatched it, throwing it down to Tyrell on the three-point line. Swish was the sound it made when it went in, all net giving them the lead and causing the crowd to go wild with only six seconds left in the game. The visitor team desperately tried to get the ball passed mid-court to attempt a shot when the buzzer went off, giving our team the win for the champion game. The crowd went crazy, and all our players rejoiced while the other team had temper tantrums. Josh walked up to Sénar, and they had some words before being snatched up by other players to prevent a fight. Tyrell searched the crowd scanning for me, when we made eye contact, his smile grew so big, I couldn't help but blush as he waved and blew kisses.

Tyrell then looked for his parents and waved at them before all the cheerleaders rushed to hug and congratulate him. I looked at Cassidy and Nevaeh, they were observing the crowd, trying to pretend they didn't see Tyrell blowing kisses at me. I started to go down when everybody started to clear when I spotted Sénar gazing at me in the middle of what seemed like a thousand girls. The world grew silent, and it almost seemed we were the only people in the gymnasium for a second when we caught eye contact. I saw all the girls throwing themselves all over him as he watched me walk down the steps. Before anyone noticed, I broke eye contact to see Tyrell following Sénar's gaze to me and becoming extremely agitated. When he looked to me, my eyes were on him, and he was relieved but still appeared angry. I tried not to show any other emotion but happiness as we finally met up on the court. He grabbed me and kissed me like he wanted the whole world to see.

He looked me in the eyes and asked, "How did I do baby?"

I smiled, "You're kidding, right? You were amazing, as always!" I hugged him and told him how proud of him I was. He put his arm around me and high fived his teammates everyone except Sénar, but Sénar flashed his famous smile more so at me than at Tyrell. His grip grew tighter as Senar approached us.

Sénar walked up to us, "Aye bro, good game." He said humbly and kept it pushing.

We were both shocked, but Tyrell kept walking towards his mom and dad. His mom grabbed him like he was a kindergartner on his first day of school and told him how proud she was. His dad high fived him with a smile of approval. They both acknowledged me, and we all headed for the door. Tyrell asked me to ride home with his parents and that he would meet me at his house. He kissed me and told me to wait for him in his room. A little confused, I agreed, only because I knew he wanted to celebrate with his friends. When we arrived at Tyrell's house, his mom asked if I wanted something to eat, and his dad just said goodnight with a smile. I didn't want to trouble her, but I also didn't want to pass up the opportunity to get to know her a little better.

I answered, "Not if it's too much trouble." She smiled and told me she would make me a sandwich. She got the condiments and some turkey and asked if I wanted my bread toasted. I couldn't resist toasted bread, so I told her, please.

She smiled at me and said, "You know, you and Tyrell reminded me of Robert and me when we were young. We met in high school too." I smiled because she fell right into the palm of my hand, allowing me to get to know her.

I asked, "Really? Tell me more." I said in a dreamy state.

She laughed and responded, "Oh darling, you guys are so young. We were a little older when we met, but dating a jock is pretty hard, but it's worth it if you really love one another. They have so many options and to be the one, is amazing. There are ups and downs like any relationship; you just have to know if it's love and what you're willing to take."

I almost felt like she was trying to say something without saying it, but I couldn't tell. The only real conversation I ever had with her was when my wrist was broken. She asked me how my wrist was; I looked at it, almost forgetting it was ever broken for a second. I answered, "It's ok; I'm glad I went to the doctor." I didn't want to talk about my wrist. I wanted to talk more about love. She smiled and gave me my sandwich. Longing to talk to her since my mom was so distant, I asked, "How did you know it was love?"

She sighed and replied, "Hahaha, that's a good question. You just must wait, darling, because love is crazy, no love story is the same." Robert called for her, she quickly said good night and hurried up the steps much like my mom when Ken called her name. There I was alone. I finished my sandwich and went to Tyrell's room to wait for him.

He took so long I fell asleep. He came into the room clumsily, startling me awake. I called his name, and he jumped back, trying to see who or what I was. He smelled like alcohol and was stumbling all over his room. When he finally came to the realization of who I was, he smiled and grabbed me. He kissed me and asked me what I was doing there. I looked at him like he was crazy.

I crossed my arms and whined, "Tyrell, you told me to come here and wait for you." Not wanting to hear it, he put his finger to his mouth to shush me, then hugged me like I was a crying little girl and patted me on my back.

I He then said, "Thanks for coming, babe, but I am faded. We all had enough fun for the night; trust me. You should be safe to go home now."

I was confused by his statement. He got in the bed, squeezing my booty before he passed out. Disappointed, I left quietly and crossed the street to go home. I snuck in as quietly as possible, tiptoeing up the steps and to my room. I laid in my bed with Tyrell's remark repeating over and over in my head. Still not able to understand what he meant, I went to sleep, not knowing how to feel.

Chapter 15

The last two weeks went by so fast; my head was spinning. Before I knew it, I looked up, and Chino was getting ready to graduate with the biggest smile on his face, I have ever seen him have. We were all dressed to impress to support Chino on his big day. We were all running around after Chino left to practice making sure we were looking sharp to go see Chino's life change forever. When we were all done with running around, we all piled into Ken's expedition and drove to the graduation together. I sat in the back row by myself, looking out the window, thinking of how it felt to be graduating and moving on into adulthood. We pulled into the crowded parking lot, upon getting out of the car I noticed Sénar's tie was crooked. It was annoying me, so I told him it was crooked, causing him to look down and him being unable to see it. I started adjusting his tie, immediately feeling his temperature rise, I quickly fixed his tie in time to turn around and see Ken observing the situation. Feeling watched, I moved as far away as possible from Sénar and looked for Tyrell in the crowds of people knowing he would be there for his teammates that were graduating. Tyrell and I made eye contact as he walked towards me with a big goofy smile on his face while avoiding eye contact with Sénar.

Ken saw Sénar tense up and looked around to see Tyrell and I holding hands. Tyrell was telling me how beautiful I looked when Ken approached us with a stern face and introduced himself as my mother's fiancé. Ken put his hand out to shake Tyrell's hand, saying, "So you are the infamous Tyrell?"

Without giving Tyrell the chance to introduce himself. Tyrell beamed a bright smile being under the impression he was referring to his athleticism. Ken quickly assured him it was not by saying, "Well, nice to finally meet you. Hopefully, this next school year, there will be no more fights or injuries."

Tyrell's smile quickly faded into embarrassment as I grabbed his arm, whispering, "Don't mind him, babe, everything is ok. Don't take it personally."

I wanted to assure him of that so he wouldn't hate Ken too. We watched Sénar walk into a group of girls waiting on him to arrive until London came out of nowhere and shewed them away. Tyrell and I giggled as London was not playing with those little hussies. Tyrell joked, "Damn Treasure, you should be like that, and you wouldn't have to miss my practices."

He said laughing, but I didn't find it funny. I just smacked my lips and responded, "Well, you almost got Nevaeh beat down at the championship game, did you not hear Ken's expectations?"

He tensed up, and we both were a bit agitated with each other as everyone segregated themselves before entering in the graduation ceremony. Cassidy appeared to be saving a seat for two people while the rest of us filled the row of seats. Tyrell and I sat at the end, with him on the end seat as he whispered, "I am not trying to be blocked in a row with the Reject Brady bunch." We both giggled, diffusing the tension between us from earlier. Cassidy sat next to me, keeping two seats empty for her invisible guest. London and Sénar sat next to my mom and Ken. We all sat down with anticipation as the ceremony had begun with a heartfelt speech on how to succeed in life despite obstacles. Everyone nods their heads in agreement, and a couple of amens were yelled. As the ceremony continued, people were still piling into the ceremony late, Sabrina and an unknown lady tagging along behind her were some of them. Cassidy waved to get their attention, and they headed over towards us. Sabrina smiled at Tyrell flirtatiously and ignored me, not even saying excuse me as she shuffled through us to get to her seat next to Cassidy. The white, middle-aged woman said hello and excuse me, as she shuffled passed to get to her seat next to Sabrina, before waving at everyone else in our row. They were beginning to call names; everyone was getting their vocal cords and ears ready for the intense screaming that was about to take place.

Our row was on the edge of our seats as they were ready to announce Chino's name. The big moment was here as Mr. Bell stood there smiling before handing Chino his diploma and said, "Very special young man, Chino Brady!" Our row went crazy, screaming and flailing hands in the air, while Tyrell just clapped excitedly. We clapped for all the graduates and screamed for some of the people Tyrell knew. Now it was winding down, after all the speeches and names being called, they had some awards, and it would finally be over. Mr. Bell gave a lengthy speech before presenting his last award, "And now for our Valedictorian a young fine man with a very bright future. Congratulations on all your hard work and determination, Mr. Chino Brady!"

My mother almost fainted as Ken rose up and screamed, "That's my boy!" Our row and auditorium roared in celebration for Chino. I was so proud of him all his reading and hard work truly paid off. Chino took the microphone thanking everyone, with a shout out to his dad and his family for all the support. His smile was priceless as he received his reward. The ceremony ended, and all the family members rushed their graduates with hugs and smiles. Ken's booming voice carried over the noise as he instructed everyone to meet at King's Table Buffet. Tyrell and I made our way out of the ceremony after finding Chino congratulating him for both his award and graduation. We left before the crowds and drove to King's Table. Knowing it would be a lot of people, I told Tyrell to wait for me as I checked to see about the wait for ten people. There was a cute young boy at the front that was nice enough to save a table for us. I went back outside to tell Tyrell we got a table, and we waited in the car until we saw my mom and Ken pull up. We all congregated in the parking lot, awaiting everyone to arrive. Sénar and London were the last ones to arrive as they were fixing their clothes as she was reapplying lipstick to her used mouth. Ken whispered something to Sénar, when Ken was done, Sénar looked like a little kid that got in trouble. We all headed into the restaurant, having our own conversations. My mom and Ken now looked worried when they saw the crowds of people waiting to be seated. I grabbed the boy from earlier as he approached us and walked us to the table that I asked him to reserve for us earlier.

Ken put his hand on my shoulder, "Quick thinking Treasure, those looks come in handy."

I know it was supposed to be a compliment, but it really rubbed me the wrong way. We all found seats that we were comfortable with, as many of us either didn't want to sit next to someone or really wanted to sit next to someone in particular. The adults were on the end, and we all sat next to our significant others. The seating arrangement was important as we did not need any unnecessary tension that would cause drama or a loss of appetite. The first row went as followed; my mom, Ken, Chino, me then Tyrell, on the other side was Sabrina's aunty Carol across from my mom, Sabrina across from Ken, Cassidy across from Chino, Sénar across from me, then London across from Tyrell. Sénar and Tyrell avoided sitting across from one another, neither Tyrell or London wanted Sénar and me to sit across from each other, but they also knew they didn't want to sit across from either of us. The tension was still there as Sénar's girl couldn't keep her hands off of him, Sénar couldn't keep his eyes off of me, and Tyrell couldn't keep his hatred of Sénar concealed.

A young lady came to our table to get everyone's drink order and then swiftly came back with our drinks. Sénar totally ignored Tyrell and was unbothered by London, and it was making me uncomfortable. Ken's voice caused everyone's wondering attention to come to a halt. He cleared his throat and raised his cup in the air to say,

"Congratulations to my Valedictorian, Chino Brady! Let's have a good time tonight enjoy our dinner without anybody being in their feelings."

He was addressing everyone at the table, being that everyone appeared to be in their feelings about something or someone. Sabrina and Cassidy rolled their eyes, Sénar smirked, Chino smiled, Tyrell ignored Ken's demands, London sized me up, I rolled my eyes, my mom and Carol appeared to agree, and everyone dispersed to get their food. Tyrell and I were the last ones up as he grabbed my hand and said, "Treasure your mom's dude is getting on my nerves. I don't have to listen to him. I am not a part of the Reject Brady Bunch!"

I quickly responded, "Please, babe do this for me. Don't mess this up. Just ignore everyone else and be here for me."

I kissed him on his cheek and begged him with my fluttering eyelashes until he softened up. We could not afford any drama after already being warned, and this being Chino's big night. We went to make our plates in silence. There so many choices, but I wanted a big juicy salad to go with whatever I chose for my main course. For my first plate, I compiled a delicious salad with cucumbers, boiled eggs, green onion, tomatoes, cheese, and bacon. When I was done, I went back to sit my salad on the table, and London was sitting down already with a fancy salad as well, eyeing me as if I was copying her. I smirked at her bougie ass because I was going back to get my main course too. Sénar passed me with a gigantic plate full of different meats and veggies.

Tyrell came up to me with a full course meal with meat, veggies, and potatoes then asked, "Where are you going, babe?"

I responded, "I have to make my real plate; my first plate is just a salad."

He nodded his head in acceptance and went back to the table. I was musing over all the different foods when I felt someone brush up against me, thinking it was Sénar I turned around with an attitude, to see Markese cheesing at me.

He then asked, "Damn, girl, why you disappear like that?"

Taken aback and not knowing how to respond, he continued, "Shit, I been asking Cassidy about you; she hasn't told you?"

To get rid of him, I quickly responded, "Look, I am here with my boyfriend. I can't talk to you." I walked away from him, trying to find my food and tried my best to look normal as my heart was beating out of my chest. I didn't want Tyrell or Sénar to see Markese, but he followed me anyway and said,

"Aye, I don't care about your chump ass boyfriend. I am going to give Cassidy my number to give to you if you say you will call me. I'll leave you alone."

He said this as Sénar was walking up, and Tyrell was observing from the table, feeling pressured, I agreed so he would leave me alone before Sénar approached us. Markese laughed, "Aiight then, cool." He said as he scanned my body with his lustful eyes and mad dogged Sénar before walking away.

Sénar's veins looked like they would pop out of his neck when he asked, "Treasure, who the fuck is that nigga?"

I pretended like I didn't hear him and made my plate, frustrated Sénar grabbed a plate and headed towards Markese as Tyrell got up to confront me next, "Treasure, who is that dude you were talking to? That is a grown-ass man!" He said in a whisper, trying not to cause a scene.

I was trying to remain calm as I could feel the tensions rising. I could only imagine what Sénar was up to. Cassidy looked back to see what was going on and quickly got out of her seat to intervene with Sénar and Markese as I tried to calm Tyrell. Cassidy was trying to pull Sénar back to the buffet and told Sénar she knew Markese, thinking it would keep him from wanting to beat his face in. That just made it worse because he realized that he was one of the guys at the house the night I ran home for safety. Cassidy begged Sénar not to react as she knew it would get her in trouble. Sénar wanted to confront Markese before he walked back to the table with his boys. Cassidy begged him to let it go; he snatched his arm from Cassidy. Sénar reluctantly made his plate as he was fuming because he wanted to catch a fade with Markese for what happened the night I ran home. Tyrell was only concerned with why I was talking to him, not knowing the level of drama that could have unfolded. I assured him I was not interested in that guy and dismissed him immediately when he came to me to prove it. I begged Tyrell not to make a big deal out of the situation, but he now seemed to be focused on Sénar's response as well. He waited for me to make my plate before going back to the table and watched Sénar and Cassidy argue.

Tyrell still agitated asked, "Why does Sénar care so much? Hell, he beat me over here?"

He shook his head in frustration while I made my plate and acted like I didn't hear him. We went back to the table together, and I sat my plate of food down, hoping I would be able to eat before losing my appetite. Tyrell just watched me eat; he wasn't in the mood to finish his food. London ate like a bird while watching me eat too. Hell, even Sénar was watching me eat. I felt like I was the main course and got up to go to the bathroom. Sénar and Tyrell in unison asked, "Where are you going?"

Silence befell the table, and I retorted in a calm voice, "I'm going to the bathroom, geesh." I looked at Cassidy like she owed me, catching the hint she said,

"Oh, I'll go with you, I have to go too."

Relieved, we left the table together. As soon as we were in the bathroom, Cassidy asked, "What the hell Treasure you're going to get us all killed!"

In my defense, I answered, "I am not the one who took me to a house full of grown-ass men like Markese who wanted to screw my brains out!"

She looked at me with jealousy in her eyes and spat her response, "Well damn, it's not my fault everyone wants to screw your fucking brains out!"

Not even knowing how to respond to her remark, I shouted, "I dress appropriately, I don't throw myself at anybody, and I have a boyfriend!"

I almost started crying before Sabrina and London came into the bathroom, instantly I went from sadness to rage. I glared at both Sabrina and London with a threatening tone and said, "Don't say shit to me!" London started to come after me, and Cassidy stopped her.

I could hear Sabrina ask, "Why did you stop her, Cassidy?"

I didn't care why, I was ready to whip Sabrina and London's ass, but I knew it would be a mess and they would probably try to jump me. Sénar and Tyrell were impatiently waiting on me to return. I tried not to appear upset when I arrived back at the table.

Tyrell asked, "What took you so long?"

He then looked at Sénar and said, "I'm sure Sénar wants to know too."

Sénar responded, "Aye man, I got a mouth, so I'll speak for myself homeboy."

He looked at Tyrell like he was ready to jump across the table. London came back to the table and mouthed something with bitch under her breath. Sénar looked at her and said, "Aye, London chill out."

She didn't say another word. Tyrell was fed up, he stood up and said, "Treasure, let's go!"

Ken looked down at our end of the table and replied, "If you belong to my household, you're not leaving until we are all done. If you are not from my household, you are free to leave at any time."

He made it very clear and dared anyone to try him. Tyrell sat down; I rubbed his leg and pleaded with him to stay. I tried to eat, but I was not able to eat like I wanted to. I still felt like I was being watched like a television screen, now that everyone seemed to have some type of issue with me at the moment. Tyrell loves ice cream, so I asked him in a flirty voice to come with me to get dessert. He was still mad, but he went with me. He pouted about everything that had happened between him and Sénar. Then pouted about the guy that came up to me, he turned into a big baby. I told him I would make it up to him in whatever way he wanted me to, and he stopped whining. I was actually hoping he took advantage of the opportunity, he had access to me, and it was like he was scared to use it. He was so worried about everyone else that he used his energy in all the wrong ways when it came to our relationship. It made me wonder if he was going elsewhere to get his rocks off. He was the same age as Sénar, and yet he wasn't trying to screw my brains out. Tyrell not having much of an appetite didn't get dessert, but I did. I got a chocolate ice cream cone and headed back to the table, trying to fill my stomach with my dessert, since I wasn't able to eat all my food.

Tyrell watched Sénar as he watched me eat my ice cream cone with a smile on his face, London looked like she wanted some too, so I asked, "Damn, why don't y'all just get your own ice cream?"

Since they were both watching me, I was hoping Tyrell would think it was just the ice cream. London asked Sénar if she wanted her to get him one, never taking his eyes off me, he responded, "Yeah, I want chocolate."

Tyrell had enough and demanded, "Treasure finish that shit already! Damn, this dude is buggin'!"

I felt rushed; I couldn't eat anything in peace. I offered him some, and he took the whole damn cone and devoured it. London came back with a cone for herself and one for Sénar. They enjoyed their ice cream while mine was just a memory. Tyrell and I were both waiting on him to watch London eat her ice cream, which didn't happen, but she watched him lick his ice cream like a pro while still maintaining his masculinity. Tyrell was ready to go; he was getting impatient and was not able to hide his hatred for Sénar.

Feeling frustrated, I started to drift into my own thoughts when Ken's voice startled me, "Ok, dinner was lovely." Ken said sarcastically looking at our corner of the table. He continued with, "Goodnight."

And everyone dispersed. Tyrell drove me home with an attitude and refused to talk to me. I wanted to throw a tantrum and go back on my word to Cassidy by throwing myself at Tyrell, just to see if he would catch me. I was tired of trying to convince him I was his when he didn't act like it anyways. We pulled into his driveway and sat there in silence. We beat everyone home because Tyrell drives like a NASCAR driver when he's mad. I pleaded with him, "Tyrell let's go upstairs. I'll give you a message before I go home."

He looked at me like I was one of his groupies. Tyrell answered, "Nah, yo boy Sénar might want his first."

That was the last straw, I got out of the car, grabbed my things, and slammed the door. He didn't bother to get out to chase after me until I was already at the door to my house. Tyrell yelled, "Treasure!" I turned around, trying not to burst into tears. Before he could say anything, Ken and my mom pulled into the driveway. He kissed me on my forehead and left across the street to go back home. I went inside before I had to face everyone else. I put my nightclothes on and went to bed, crying myself to sleep again.

What can I say, the first week of our summer break was officially starting off terribly wrong. Tyrell was always acting funny because of Sénar and the mystery man that came out of nowhere to ruin all the progress we've had in the last couple of weeks. Sénar and Cassidy were still beefing over her not letting Sénar get revenge at the buffet. Chino was packing up, getting ready to go off to college. It was an emotionally draining week. London added to the drama as she was not secretive of her disdain for me. She made it very clear when Sénar was not around that she would make my life a living hell next school year. She was a senior and very popular; I knew she would keep her word. I just couldn't get a break! She would always brag about how much money her family had and how Sénar was working for her dad. Sénar was irritated with her mouth; he didn't want anyone knowing his business. I heard him talking to her one day,

242

"Damn, girl, shut your mouth sometimes. You talk too damn much. Telling everyone my business." I am sure she made it up to him with her mouth as she did not respond with words.

I needed to figure out a way to ensure Tyrell understood that Markese was a nobody, without exposing what took place the night I ran out of Markese's house. While trying to figure out how to erase the reality of Markese's existence, Cassidy came barging into the room, throwing Markese's number on my side of the room and accused me of being a drama whore. She didn't even let me defend myself before walking back out of our room and slamming the door in her tantrum to go wherever she spent her summer days. I looked at his number and tossed it into a drawer, just in case I needed to tell him to leave me alone in the future. With Chino leaving and Cassidy and I being on bad terms again, I was already overwhelmed. I happily signed up for as many summer classes they would allow me to have, so I could avoid my house. I also wanted the extra credits to help towards my own graduation credits. I even investigated college courses that may be available for me to take, as I needed to plan my future escape from this hell hole.

Tyrell and I didn't break up; he was just distant. He didn't call me as much and busied himself with his dad. When we did hang out, there were several awkward silent moments where we would both be lost in our thoughts. I started my summer classes and was hoping to spend my weekends with Tyrell, but I was never sure what mood he would be in.

Within the first week of summer, Chino moved out to Northern California, choosing Stanford University to major in social sciences. I was so proud of him and was going to miss the normalcy he contributed to the household. Sénar was sad about Chino leaving but appreciated having his own room. I couldn't help but think about how nice it would be to have my own room instead of sharing it with my arch enemy. Everyone pitched in to help Chino pack up his belongings over the weekend, which left me unable to see Tyrell. I called him, but he was either busy when I called or not home. Over the next week, we talked on the phone some evenings when I got back from school, but he just didn't seem to want to see me as much. I was starting to worry because I was used to him being eager to see me and not wanting me to be home as much with Sénar being there. I was not giving up; I called him every day to let him know I loved him or that I wanted to see him. He would tell me he just needed some time to think to himself.

Saturday morning, I was determined to see Tyrell. I woke up early, hoping to catch him before he made any plans or busied himself with his dad. The phone just rang and rang until I hung up. Disappointed, I sat on the couch to watch some early morning TV since the house was still quiet. It wasn't long before I fell asleep to be awakened by Cassidy slamming the door as she left. I just laid there and resumed watching TV. My mom and Ken were the next to come down the stairs giggling like school children as they left out the front door. They didn't even acknowledge me or let me know when they would return. I was envious and started to wonder why me and Tyrell were having so many problems all the time. I mean yeah Sénar can be completely out of line, but Tyrell made it so obvious that Sénar was a threat to him. It completely baffled me how Tyrell had full access to my body and was so insecure, but Sénar, who totally should not have any, be so confident in taking advantage anyway. Just as I was contemplating my million-dollar question, I saw Sénar appeared in the shadows of the hallway of the front door. I thought he was leaving, and I would have the house to myself, but he was just checking the locks. He turned to me and flashed his famous sadistic smile as if he had the answer to my question. As he approached me, I narrowed my eyes at him as I was fully aware of what that stupid smile meant and prepared myself to fight. He stared back at me with his intense stare and inched closer. The closer he got, the more tense I became. I was ready to fight; I was exhausted from trying to hold on to Tyrell, and my innocence at the same time. He wasn't the least bit bothered by my stance; I had my hands up ready to punch him in the nose if I had to. He moved briskly toward me with my heart beating against my chest in fear, I closed my eyes, and when I felt him touch me, I swung with all my might. I felt the impact of my fist connecting with his forehead; he yelped in pain, "Ouch!" Feeling remorseful, I opened my eyes to check if he was ok,

"BOO!" He yelled.

I screamed as I jumped back in shock. He was rubbing his forehead and looked at me like I was crazy. Sénar laughed and said, "Damn Treasure!" He left me there feeling crazy and walked to the kitchen. I could hear him opening the fridge or freezer, probably grabbing ice to put on his forehead. I was stunned and still standing in the same spot, not knowing what to do. My heartbeat was accelerating more by the seconds as I racked my brain for what to do next. I thought about whether I should run to the bathroom and lock myself in there or go check to see if he was ok. I quickly chose the bathroom, running towards the steps, "Treasure!" Sénar yelled my name from the kitchen. I froze like I was playing freeze tag.

He asked, "What are you about to do, go hide in the bathroom?"

My heart almost stopped as I continued to run up the steps before he tried to stop me. Running into the bathroom and quickly locking the door behind me. Not stopping to grab anything, I just paced the bathroom, still not knowing what to do. I eventually sat on the toilet and tried to calm myself, so I could come up with a plan. I was sitting there for almost twenty minutes with no idea of what to do next. When I smelled the aroma of food creep from under the space of the door, I wondered how Sénar was feeling, and whether he was mad with me or not. I started to feel bad because what if he wasn't going to do anything to me this time, and I overreacted? I cautiously opened the door to smell the air and felt my stomach violently growl. I crept back down the steps cautiously and peeked around the corner into the kitchen. Sénar was standing there, holding a bag of frozen veggies on his forehead while cooking.

I felt so bad, I immediately let my guard down, when he turned to look at me, I asked, "Did I hurt you?"

He looked at me like I assaulted him and then nicely asked him if it hurt. I slowly walked into the kitchen still cautious I just stood there in case I needed to run back up the steps. He was agitated and responded, "Yo' ass only came in here because you smelled food. You don't care that you tried to make me into a baby unicorn."

I laughed because his statements were true and, at the same time, extremely funny. He giggled too as he continued to multitask with holding the bag of veggies to his forehead and cooking breakfast.

He said, "You better hope there's no knot, or I'm going to be mad as hell woman." He put the veggies back in the freezer and finished cooking. I took the opportunity to ease into one of the chairs and asked out of curiosity,

"You are making me some too, right?"

His expression suggested he felt used when he replied, "Excuse me, you want me to feed you after you punched me in the forehead?"

With no shame, I truthfully answered, "Yeah." We both laughed, but he quickly asked in return, "Well, what are you going to do for me? You aren't crippled anymore and very combative. I have to charge for my services."

Sénar was serious, that quick, I became uncomfortable again. Remembering we were the only ones in the house, I avoided his question. He complained, "Damn Treasure, your ass is stingy!"

He finished cooking and gave me my plate. Neither of us took our eyes off one another for very different reasons, and we ate in silence. He left his plate there to insinuate that I needed to wash the dishes and quietly retreated up the stairs. I have never been so relieved just to wash dishes; I almost felt like my punch to Sénar's head was effective. I took my time washing the dishes. Realizing I hadn't heard the phone ring, I finished up and called Tyrell again.

Tyrell answered, "Hello?"

I was so happy but wanted to sound as normal as possible when I said, "Hey babe." There was silence. Waiting for him to respond, I said, "Hello?"

He took his time responding, "What's up?"

Not sure of his mood, I answered, "Nothing much, I just wanted to come by and spend some time with you."

He quickly responded, "I am busy, maybe tomorrow."

And hung up. Both dumbfounded and angry, I called back and yelled, "Tyrell!"

Angry, he answered, "What!"

I whined, "Why are you acting like this?"

There was a silent pause before he asked, "Like what?" He said in an agitated tone.

I was desperate now; he was acting so childish, so I asked, "Well, what are you doing today that is so important?"

He replied, "Look, I told you I am busy, and maybe I'll see you tomorrow."

He said it like he was mad that he had to repeat himself. I was so confused I didn't even know how to respond. Before I could say anything else, I heard a click in my ear and then a dial tone. It was like Deja vu after he broke my wrist and then broke up with me. I slammed the phone down with tears burning my eyelids, and I ran to my room, slamming the door behind me. I grabbed my diary; my mom bought me for my birthday and wrote with my heart instead of just my hand. It was like my heart was controlling my hand's movements, without having to think, my hand moved wildly across the page as my emotions were in a whirlwind. I heard my door open as tears were streaming down my face while my hand moved rapidly across the pages of my diary.

Sénar asked, "What's wrong, Treasure?"

I snapped at him, "Nothing. Leave me alone!"

He closed the door leaving me to wallow in my sorrows. My hand aching from writing so much, I stopped to gather my emotions. I was so enraged at this moment I was afraid of myself. I laid on my back, closing my eyes and cried out to the God my mom always taught me about in my younger years. When there was no answer, I turned over and took my anger out on my pillow, screaming into it to release my anguish.

Sénar came back in and said, "Come on, Treasure, let's go."

With tears streaming down my face, I looked at him, confused, and asked, "Where Sénar?"

He responded, "Let's go to the backyard."

I wiped my tears, now curious I asked, "The backyard, for what?" He sighed and said, "Come on, Treasure."

I got up and followed him to the backyard. When we got outside, he pulled out half a blunt, and my eyes widened. He lit the blunt and puffed it twice, and then passed it to me. Still trying to pull myself together, I hit it and coughed uncontrollably. I held on to it until I was able to hit it again, but I still didn't pass it back, I was going to hit it again when Sénar snatched it from me and said,

"Damn girl, save some for me."

We both laughed because I was going to smoke it all if he had let me. He hit it once and gave it back to me before it was too small for me to smoke. I hit the blunt again and felt like I never cried. I was so relaxed and happy for no reason. I was smiling as Sénar was finishing the blunt. I started to giggle when I looked at the slightly red spot on his forehead.

He looked at me and asked, "What's so damn funny, Treasure?"

I snorted when I laughed and exclaimed, "You look like a baby unicorn!" I laughed so hard, I thought I would pass out from the lack of oxygen I was losing from not being able to stop myself from laughing. I laughed until I stumbled forward, having to hold on to Sénar to keep from falling. He wasn't laughing, but he did look at me and smile, a smile I had never seen before. I cocked my head to the side, mesmerized by his face and his new smile as I held on to him for balance. It was a nice smile; I bit my lip and almost kissed his face before the doorbell rang. We both snapped out of our trance and Sénar made sure I was balanced before we both ran inside. Sénar ran to get the door, and I stood in the kitchen, waiting to see who it was.

It was London, she pushed the ajar door open and came in. "Hey daddy." She said seductively and kissed him. She saw me standing in the kitchen, looking like a total goofball. "Sénar baby, let's go get something to eat." London said in an attempt to get him to come with her.

Sénar quickly replied, "I already ate. Why didn't you eat before you came?"

She saw his facial expression and changed her tone, "Well, I can wait, let's watch some TV then."

She eyed me, probably wondering why I was still standing there. I started to wonder the same thing; I was pretty high. I couldn't even remember blinking, so I needed to sit down somewhere. I snapped out of it; I couldn't help but float by the two of them to go sit on the couch. They both watched me as I floated by on cloud nine until I sat down on the couch. Totally ignoring the two of them, I decided to watch some TV, knowing whatever I watched would be satisfying. I put on reruns of Martin so I could laugh. I could hear their voices over the TV, I couldn't tell what was being said, but I knew I was high as hell. As the tension grew between the two of them, I started to visualize a scene from my birthday and realized she was the girl from the beach! It was an actual light bulb that came on in my head when I realized she was the same girl Sénar was arguing with then. No wonder she hates my guts! Feeling confident in my mystery-solving capabilities, I heard London yelling at Sénar and the door slamming. Sénar looked stressed as he walked to the couch to sit down.

Sénar was annoyed when he said, "Damn, she almost blew my high." If blowing a high means not being high anymore, I felt sorry for him because she definitely didn't blow mine. I was feeling superhuman; I could enjoy TV, play scenes in my head, observe my surroundings, and solve mysteries all at the same time.

Sénar saw me drifting off into my own thoughts, "Treasure?" Sénar called my name, summoning me back to reality.

I responded, "What?"

Wanting to continue using my superpowers, he licked his lips and asked, "What are you thinking about over there?"

Too embarrassed to reveal my actual thoughts of me having superpowers, I replied, "Um, nothing."

He reached for my hand and pulled me from the other side of the couch onto him. I was so relaxed when he pulled me; I landed on him, fitting perfectly like a puzzle piece. I could feel his member jump against my thigh as he grabbed my legs, spreading them apart to straddle him. I resisted and tried to get up when he pulled me back down, firmly gripping my butt in his hands to maintain his grip on me. He put his hand behind my neck, guiding my face to his, then stuck his tongue into my mouth, kissing me passionately. I felt forbidden sensations throughout my body as he picked me up and laid me down on my back.

I tried to get up and told him, "Sénar, I can't do this; please don't –" He stuck his tongue in my mouth, kissing me to keep me from talking. I, even while he was kissing me, thought about biting his tongue, but I knew he would probably kill me. I pushed his chest to give myself space, so I could continue to tell him why I couldn't do this again. When he moved down towards my thighs, I tried to pull him back up to talk to him. He resisted and took a grip of my shorts and pulled them off along with my panties in one swift move. I quickly reached for my clothes, and he held them up as I covered myself. I was starting to get nervous and continued to cover myself, desperately asking him for my clothes back. He threw them behind him and spread my legs apart. "Now, give me my Treasure." He said.

I gasped, begging him, "No, no, Sénar .."

I used my energy to squeeze my legs as tight as I could back together. He pried them apart, putting his mouth on the hottest part of my body, leaving me in sheer shock. It felt so good, I bit my bottom lip and tried to breathe before my next attempt to escape his strength. Pleasure riddled through me, causing me to shiver as I locked my legs onto his head, saying, "Sénar, no, um, no, ooh awe."

He kissed and licked my hot spot until I was at lost for words. He pulled me down closer to his face, sticking his tongue deep inside of me and licking his tongue all around my coochie. I thought I would pass out when he put his fingers inside of me, twirling them around while thrusting them in and out of me until I begged him to stop. He grew more excited and shook his head like a wet dog while nibbling on my little man in the boat. I almost burst into a million pieces as my body shook violently. He pulled himself up, pulling out his member and grabbing my hand to feel it throbbing. He positioned himself in between my legs and entered my quivering insides, that he had once again caused. Taking my breath away as he delved deep inside me and slowly gyrated himself inside until I thought I was going to pass out. He moaned in my ear as he thrusted himself deeply and then slowly in and out.

He whispered in my ear, "Ooh wee, Treasure; I love this shit!" I couldn't even speak my mouth was so dry my tongue felt like sandpaper, and the more he thrusted the dryer, my mouth got. It was like all the liquid left my mouth and traveled to my coochie, where Sénar fit like a glove as he maneuvered around my insides. Feeling like I would faint from the sensations going through my body, I yelled, "Oh my Gosh!"

He started to pump faster and harder until I screamed so loud, he stopped, pulling out of me and pouring his man juice all over my stomach. Gasping for air, feeling like my throat would collapse, he ran to get paper towels to clean up his mess. I couldn't move; he cleaned my stomach off and handed me my clothes before running upstairs. I sat there for a moment, trying to gather my thoughts, wondering how I let this happen again. I put my clothes on ashamed at my inability to avoid this situation and tried to run up the steps as Sénar was coming back down.

He asked me plain as day, "Where are you going, ma?"

I looked at him like he was a stranger and replied, "I'm going to my room."

He sighed and said, "No, let's watch TV for a little bit, and I'll make us something to eat." Not having the energy to dispute his request, I turned around like a good girl as the damage had already been done, what more could he do to me?

Chapter 16

Sunday morning, I woke up feeling guilty. Sénar, with his conniving ways, not only had me partake in forbidden pleasures, we watched TV after and lounged on the couch as he would often do with London. Then he made me a five-star meal with dessert. I was literally torn between reality and a fantasy world. I loved Tyrell, and the more I wanted to be with him, the more he pushed me away. I wanted to call him, but I decided I would get dressed and just show up at his house, so he could not dismiss me by just hanging up the phone.

Not wanting to be Sénar's sex experiment, I stayed in my room for as long as possible Sunday morning. I didn't even go downstairs when I smelled the tantalizing aroma of breakfast. Cassidy was going through her clothes to find something to wear. I could feel her occasionally looking over at me to see if I was awake. I didn't budge, I just laid in my bed like I was sleeping, when I was really thinking extremely hard about my life. I was trying to keep my tears trapped behind my eyelids for as long as possible to prevent Cassidy from knowing how horrible I was feeling at the moment. I felt lost with nowhere to run and no one to talk to. How can I tell anyone what I was going through without incriminating myself too? Who was to blame? Sénar? Tyrell? Or me? Either way, we all had our star roles in this drama called life. Maybe Cassidy was right. Maybe I was bringing all of this on to myself. I was starting to feel like I was losing Tyrell and submitting to Sénar's intentions for my body. I hated myself for being so weak and stupid. I just wanted to run far away and not look back. I felt even more pathetic when I realized I had nowhere to run to.

I had to stop swimming in my thoughts as I was going into the deep end, and I didn't want to drown. I gathered my things to take a shower, wanting to clean off any evidence of Sénar lingering on me. I felt dirty, even though I showered before going to bed last night, after watching a million episodes of Martin with Sénar after he violated me. Then ate the most marvelous meal I have ever had in my life, with a decadent dessert to finish our coerced date. I couldn't for the life of me figure out why he didn't just save his lust for London. I never saw him wine or dine her. He never looked at her like she looked at him or looked at her like he looked at me. I was confused about why I was having these experiences with Sénar instead of Tyrell. I couldn't think anymore. I turned the water on ashamed to even look at the showerhead. I vigorously scrubbed my stomach, trying not to think of all the crazy emotions prancing around in my mind. I washed every place I felt dirty or lingering evidence of yesterday's reality intensely, in hopes of washing away the shame with it. I got out of the shower and stood in front of the mirror; I saw Tyrell's name sparkling on the chain against my skin. I ran my fingers over it, longing for him and wishing it was him that I was with yesterday. Not feeling like my body belonged to Tyrell or me, I quickly dismissed yesterday as if it never happened to keep at least my sanity.

I lost the confidence I had to just pop up at Tyrell's house after looking at my pathetic image, so I called Tyrell hoping and praying he picked up the phone. Tyrell answered. Happiness temporarily filled me up as I blurted out, "Hey Tyrell, baby, I really miss you and want to see you! Can I come over?"

Not wanting to give him the option to say anything other than yes or no. He was quiet for a second before he responded, "Why Treasure?"

Frustration threatened to take over the feeling of happiness as his stupid question settled in. I didn't want to give him the opportunity to cop an attitude and hang up, so I humbly replied, "I really need to see you. Hold you, hug you, and kiss you."

He was reluctant to respond, "Yeah, you can come over, but you can't stay long. I have to pack."

He quickly hung up before I could ask him what he needed to pack for. I fought the anger that gripped me at the sound of him hanging up in my face, not wanting it to interfere with the ability to win Tyrell's heart back when I got there. I quickly ran across the street to Tyrell's house. Tyrell answered the door fully dressed, looking so handsome. He appeared to be in a rush, but I ignored his impatience and hugged him. I tried to kiss him, but he avoided me. Overwhelmed with his rejection, I started crying. He just stood there and looked at me like he wanted to hug me, but his pride was in the way.

"Why are you crying Treasure?" He asked with a cold tone.

I didn't answer him; I was tired of his stupid questions. I was tired of him ignoring me. I wanted to turn around and run home, but I didn't want to lose him again. I just wanted him to hold me instead of staring at me like I was an unwanted guess in his house. I started to get angry but suppressed it so I could salvage whatever was left of me and Tyrell's relationship. I was desperate and mustered up the strength to ask, "What is happening between us, Tyrell? I can't keep going on like this."

I stared desperately into his eyes to search for emotion. He hesitated and replied, "Like-" Before he could ask like what and send me into a rage, I cut him off, saying, "Look, I came here because I miss you, I love you and want to be with you. If you don't want me, then I will go home."

He smirked at me as if to dare me. I wanted to slap the smirk off his face or punch him in the forehead, hoping it would be effective in him loving me correctly. He saw the rage in my eyes and developed his own.

He yelled, "I'm tired of this shit! I'm tired of Sénar; I'm tired of wondering about shit I can't control. I am going to visit my cousin in

Jersey. I need to get away and prepare my mind for next year. I need to think shit through, because I'm not trying to mess up my future. I love you, but I love myself more."

I looked at him, thinking of the poem my mother wrote in my diary for my birthday gift. I laughed like a madwoman and said, "Well, I sure hope you love yourself better than you have loved me lately!"

I opened the door to leave, and he slammed it closed.

He angrily asked, "What the hell is that supposed to mean?"

Shocked and not wanting the situation to turn violent, I chose my words carefully, replying, "I thought you loved me, but I guess you're right to love yourself more makes sense."

Realizing he was still holding the door, preventing me from leaving, I just shook my head in disbelief of our current situation. I stared in his eyes, pleading with him to still love me.

He asked, "Well, who loves you better?"

Totally confused by his question, I replied, "What are you talking about?" Instantly feeling confused and guilty all at once, I felt the urgency to leave. His eyes were red; it looked like he wanted to cry.

"Fuck!" He screamed and punched the front door.

I flinched in fear of his rage; my heart started to race when he looked at me like he hated me. His mom came out of her room, rubbing her sleepy eyes and then asked, "What is all the commotion, Tyrell?"

She saw Tyrell hovering over me and instantly became agitated. "Tyrell?" She called his name impatiently, waiting on him to answer her.

He responded, "Nothing, mom. Everything is fine."

She folded her arms while demanding him to get his things packed and went back to her room without saying a word to me. Hurt and embarrassed, I quickly turned around then ran home. I was devastated, I didn't know how to feel or what to think. I just wanted to disappear.

I opened the door like I had the boogie man running after me. Sénar and London were laying on the couch in the same spot we were in yesterday. Hurt and disgusted by Tyrell's rejection and Sénar being there lying with his boo, while mine hated me. I wanted to scream at the top of my lungs. Instead, I ran up the stairs and slammed my door. I threw myself onto my bed and grabbed my pillow and screamed so loud, I thought I would pass out. My door room opened, I looked back, and it was Sénar.

He came in and stood in the doorway and asked, "Treasure, are you straight?"

I thought deeply about my answer because I didn't want him to ask any questions. Annoyed, I replied, "I'm fine; worry about your company!"

He replied, "Damn you a cold piece. Do you want me to send her home?"

My stomach turned at his question. I quickly responded, "Sénar, I'm fine. Thanks for asking. Please do not send her home. I was letting you know I'm good."

I tried with all my might to convince him to keep her here. I didn't know where everyone was, it was early, and I did not want to be alone with him. He bit his bottom lip and flashed his sadistic smile; I quickly jumped out of my bed.

He laughed and said, "Oh, so you gonna beat me up again?"

I didn't laugh as it was not funny to me, and it did cross my mind. Instead, I tried to convince him she needed to stay by saying, "I didn't mean anything by it, Sénar. I am going to write for a while and mind my business. She needs to keep you company."

He almost came in the room, but London called for him from downstairs. He looked irritated and flashed his smile and said, "Ok." And closed the door. I was relieved but quickly gathered my things to take a bath, not wanting to take any chances. It was still early, and I knew I couldn't stay in there forever, but I was going to try. I ran the water for my bath; I didn't even want to look in the mirror as I undressed. I was disgusted with myself and everyone else. I dropped to the floor and listened to the running water so my tears would flow at ease. I felt stuck and broken, but I got up and forced myself to look in the mirror. I felt so pathetic, I quickly looked away. I slid my foot in the water to check the temperature; it was the only thing perfect in my life at this very moment. I got in the tub letting the water run until it was filled. I turned off the water and leaned back, closing my eyes. To keep my thoughts from badgering me, I hummed a Lauryn Hill song, 'Killing Me Softly'. I just zoned out, allowing my body to relax in the steaming water until I fell asleep.

Not caring how long it had been until I was jolted out of my sleep with a knock at the door. Waking up to cold water and Sénar's demanding voice, "Treasure!"

Agitated to be awakened from my slumber, I responded, "What?" He said in a regular voice, "Get out."

I ignored him and turned the hot water on, thinking I would warm the water up and stay in here forever. I looked at my shriveled fingers and the white film that had glazed over my body, taking the appearance of lifeless skin. I reluctantly turned the water off after I washed up and got out. Praying that London was still here, I put on the baggiest pair of jeans I owned, a belt, and a baggy T-shirt. I left my hair a wild mess, purposely hoping Sénar would look at me and be as disgusted with me as I was with myself. I opened the door cautiously and saw Sénar standing there waiting for me to come out.

Sénar looked at me and said, "Come on, man, you been in there forever."

I snapped at him, "So!"

He stared at me as I walked to my room and put my clothes away. He stood in my doorway and said, "You know your ass is hungry."

Annoyed with him and the fact that I was starving, I replied, "So, I can eat a sandwich or some cereal."

He laughed, "Aiight, so you don't want what I'm about to cook?"

I looked at him and yelled, "No!" He shrugged his shoulders and walked back downstairs, I was hungry, but I wasn't falling for that. I laid in bed and wrote vigorously in my diary until the aroma of fried chicken seeped under the door from the kitchen. I thought, *how can I eat a sandwich or cereal with his chicken smelling so good.* My stomach growled as I thought about calling Tyrell and asking if we could have dinner before he left. I went downstairs to use the phone to call Tyrell. Sénar came from the kitchen and leaned on the wall across from me.

Sénar smirked and said, "That nigga ain't home."

My first thought was how creepy it was that he knew he wasn't home. I ignored him and called anyway, and the phone just rang. He had his sadistic smile on his face when I slammed the phone down, making me want to punch him in his face. He put his hands up as if to surrender and turned around, going back into the kitchen. I observed the empty living room, hoping London's face would be staring back at me when I entered the kitchen. I was disappointed when I saw it was just Sénar in basketball shorts and no shirt in the kitchen.

Now aggravated, I asked, "Where's London?"

Sénar responded quickly with an attitude of his own, "Why?"

Tired of being asked stupid questions for the day, I quickly replied, "Because, why didn't you have her join us for dinner?" I said sarcastically looking around our empty house.

He smirked and replied, licking his lips, "Because you are my dessert."

Distressed, I yelled, "Why didn't you have her for dessert?" I was upset and unable to control my anger. I thought about how it should be her he was cooking for, and how he was doing the same to her, I felt like Tyrell was doing to me.

He shrugged his shoulders and answered, "I only eat your chocolate pie."

He said with his lustful eyes. Apart of me wanted to run out of the kitchen and back to my room, but the other wanted fried chicken. He continued, "I don't do that shit for nobody else but you, Tyrell's ass is crazy for not partaking in all that chocolate. So, I'll be having you for dessert until he realizes what he has."

Perplexed at his response, I snapped, "No, your ass is crazy!"

I was upset that he didn't consider that I was not giving him the option, and he was acting on his own behalf. He laughed as he gazed at me and said, "Yeah, crazy about your ass." I didn't say another word. I was really uncomfortable now and decided I would starve myself before dining with my offender again. I started to leave when he said, "Hey, you asked, so I told you, now help me with the food."

I looked at him, defiantly, and responded, "No!"

He sighed before he asked, "Why did you come down here, acting like that? You don't want to help me?"

I crossed my arms, thinking to myself; *this must be the season for stupid questions* and replied, "No, I don't."

He prepared more of the chicken to go into the fryer and took lettuce, tomatoes, and cucumbers out of the fridge to wash. He grabbed potatoes, washed them, and sat them next to the vegetables and looked at me. He grabbed a knife and laid it next to the cutting board and said, "Here is the stuff for you to do your part."

I looked at him like he was stupid, embarrassed I replied, "I don't know how to do that." I thought he would say a smart-ass remark, but he genuinely offered, "Well, come learn because it would be a lot faster."

I got up and grabbed the knife, Sénar looked at me nervously. He quickly responded, "You know what, put that shit down, or better yet, let me help you."

I was holding on tight to the knife when he cautiously grabbed my hand with the knife in it. Never letting my hand go, he organized the tomatoes to cut and then moved behind me to guide my hand, showing me how to cut the tomatoes into squares for the salad. He did the same with the cucumbers. I could feel the warmth from his body as he tried to look over my wild Afro to see what we were doing. We got to the potatoes, and he showed me how he liked his fries cut. He even went into the details of why he leaves the skin on. I was impressed with the detail and his knowledge of cooking. I was almost comfortable learning until I could feel him getting excited. The closer he got to me, the more tense I became until finally; he smelled my hair and squeezed my hand. I pushed back to get some space releasing the knife and went to sit down.

He finished in my absence and said, "You can at least mix the salad."

I rolled my eyes and got up to grab a bowl, he cut the lettuce and went back to the stove. He gave me instructions on what to do with the salad, and I followed them to the best of my ability. I grabbed a piece of chicken before I quickly sat down to observe him in his expertise. He was so much taller than last year; his hair was longer and wildly curly. He was muscular, but not as muscular or as tall as Tyrell. I thought about Tyrell and wished he were the one here with me, even as I ate the best chicken I ever had. I was in my thoughts as I devoured the poor chicken leg and sucked the seasonings out of the bone. When I realized Sénar was watching my every move, I put the chicken bone down.

I was annoyed when I asked him, "What are you looking at?" It was a damn shame; I couldn't even eat a piece of chicken without being observed.

Embarrassed, he responded, "Nothing. You know there is more chicken, right?" He asked before going upstairs for something.

He came back downstairs with a shirt on and some jean shorts. He combed his hair back, pulling it into a forced ponytail, it was barely long enough to fit into one. Feeling like a wild woman with my crazy outfit and hair, I started to feel silly. He reassured me, "Don't worry; you look beautiful. Let's eat." He said it with excitement as Ken, and my mom came in having an argument.

Ken sounding irritated when he said, "I have to go woman. What do you want me to do?"

My mom whined, "Well, take me with you this time. I don't want to be here without you."

He sighed as he walked into the kitchen, noticing me and my attempt to ward off Sénar. He laughed to himself and grabbed a beer with my mom on his heels; he watched me just stare at them both.

My mom asked, "Treasure, what is wrong with your hair?" She paused and looked at my outfit and then at Sénar looking like a decent human being and continued, "Goodness you look like-"

Ken cut her off and said, "Get me some of that chicken, and I'll think about taking you with me."

She pouted then looked at Sénar and me before she grabbed two plates out the cabinet. She barely ever spoke to me, and the one time she did, it was going to be her criticizing me. I thought about being happy with my one piece of chicken and going upstairs, but Sénar handed me a plate to make my own food. My mom complimented Sénar on his presentation of the food and made her and Ken a plate before we made ours. The presentation of the food did look nice and neat; my salad even looked professional. We sat down at the table with my mom and Ken. Cassidy walked in the front door and said hi to everyone, then quickly grabbed a couple of pieces of chicken before running upstairs. I made my plate with plenty of chicken, fries, and a salad, not caring what anybody else had. I still noticed my mom had the smallest plate out of all of us. Which explains why we all were eating, and she was there watching Ken devour his food.

Ken ignored her and asked me and Sénar, "What are y'all doing this summer?" He asked like he really cared eyeing me to gauge my response.

I looked at my food and answered, "I am going to summer school for extra credits." I ate my food to busy my mouth, and Sénar answered, "I am working with London's dad." He said nonchalantly.

Ken raised his eyebrow with suspicion and said, "Oh, I thought you were gonna say cooking."

He and my mom laughed at Ken's wack-ass joke. Sénar smirked without a response and ate his food. Ken continued, "Damn boy, you fried this chicken? Or did you Treasure, since you over there looking like an old 70's housewife?"

My mom slapped Ken's arm, and he laughed as he consumed his food. I was uncomfortable and looked at my plate, not wanting to converse with any of them. My mom took her and Ken's plate to the sink and was nice enough to wash them while Ken continued to pry. Sénar answered his dad having a feeling why he was asking then answered, "I did pops, you know Treasure did not cook this bomb chicken."

Ken looked at Sénar and then at me, asking, "Well damn, did you help at least Treasure?"

I looked at Ken as he had a smile similar to Sénar's mischievous smile, and I tried not to have an attitude. I shook my head no and offered to wash the dishes, not wanting to expose our previous cooking classes.

Ken added, "Well, at least I know y'all won't starve if I take your mom on the road."

I was mortified at the thought of them possibly leaving. I almost wanted to beg Ken and my mom not to leave when I noticed Sénar pleading with me not to say anything. I could barely finish my food as I was in my thoughts about what it would be like if they left on the road. I got up and washed my plate, and Ken talked to Sénar about what he expected if he left. I overheard him telling Sénar to behave as my mom asked me if I would be ok if she left like she really cared. I thought to myself it was like she was never there anyways.

Feeling like a little girl for a second, I asked, "Do you have to go?"

She looked into my eyes and asked, "Do I need to stay?"

Ken got up from the table, rubbing his belly with a big smile on his face and said, "Damn boy, that shit was good, now it's time for dessert." He grabbed his beer, and my mom acted as if she heard her name and walked away before I could even answer her question. He said, "Get me some more beer, babe."

Before she could make her way to him, she turned abruptly to grab her bottle, his beer, and they went up the steps, leaving Sénar and me in the kitchen. I wanted to run after them and beg them not to leave me when Sénar said, "You are doing the dishes, right?" Before walking out, saying, "Damn, I didn't even get to get any dessert."

He shook his head and left the kitchen, leaving me there to do the dishes, since I had offered earlier. I put the rest of the food up and scrubbed the dishes furiously. I was scared, angry, and didn't know what to do. I was overwhelmed and thought about Cassidy feeling a little relieved, knowing she would at least be here. I could not stand her either, but I would literally rather spend it with her than being alone here with Sénar if they really left on the road.

I finished the dishes and headed to my room to see Cassidy crying on the bed. I asked her what was wrong, and she looked at me and asked, "Why do you care?"

Not wanting to make my situation any worse as I needed her to be on cool terms with me, I responded, "I just want to make sure you're ok." I sat on my bed and wanted her to confide in me.

She looked at me with tears in her eyes, and reluctantly answered, "Me and Tony broke up." I wanted to confide in her about me and Tyrell's situation, but I didn't want her to encourage Sabrina to continue her attempt to steal Tyrell away from me. To make her laugh, I said, "Guys are just stupid."

She looked at me and laughed. She continued, "Now what am I supposed to do all Summer? I ain't trying to be here all day; I will probably go visit Sabrina."

Any other time I would help her pack her bags, but I was desperate when she said that. I begged her, "Don't go! We can hang out on the weekends or when I get back from school."

She looked at me like I was crazy and asked, "All of a sudden?"

Not wanting it to be obvious, I just wanted her to stay so I wouldn't be alone with Sénar. She saw me in my thoughts and said, "You will have Tyrell and Sénar to keep you company." She sounded bitter and annoyed with my attempt to use her. She turned off the light, and I reluctantly turned off mine. We both cried ourselves to sleep for different reasons.

I woke up the next morning and got dressed for school. I was leaving when I saw Tyrell's car in the driveway across the street; I instantly became sad. What was I going to do without him? My mom and Ken were leaving to go on some big trip across the country, and Cassidy might go visit Sabrina. I would be alone with Sénar. I was so terrified of what he would do; I was considering telling my mom and ruining everyone's life instead of just my own. The thought was satisfying for a second until I realized Tyrell would know too, and he would have a reason for his jealousy. It was a lose-lose situation for me either way. I had to choose whether it was me that would suffer or everybody that would suffer. I just didn't want to ruin everything for everyone. I just left for school and tried to focus on my work.

The rest of the week went by quickly. Sénar seemed really busy, and Cassidy was home more. I started to relax a little and not worry as much about my mom and Ken possibly deserting us for a couple of weeks. Cassidy moped around the house and Sénar was gone most of the time, leaving me with false hope of normalcy. It was Thursday; I was happy that the whole week was incident and argument free. I was done with my classes walking home in the scorching heat. I tried to keep my mind off the heat by thinking of ways to busy myself besides summer school when I realized someone was following me. I looked back to see a black mustang with loud music following behind me slowly. I couldn't get a good look at the driver, so I sped up my walking and clasped my books tightly in case I had to run. It pulled up on the side of me, I panicked, and I was ready to run when the window rolled down.

"Treasure!" Sénar yelled my name; I looked back, holding my books tightly. He was smiling ear to ear and said, "Get in, with your scary ass."

I was almost relieved, but I was still afraid the outcome could still end the same as it could have if he were some strange horny man instead. I wanted to say no, but it was so hot it only took me a second to make a choice. I got in, and he was still cheesing from ear to ear. I rolled my eyes at him, then asked, "Who's car do you have?"

He smirked and replied, "This is my shit, girl, you like it?"

I looked around; it was nice and clean. I almost jumped out of my seat when he put his hand near my leg, thinking he was going to grab me, but it was some type of gadget he used to operate the car.

He laughed and said, "Girl, you are so silly, it's a stick shift." I looked at him, confused; he sighed and tried to be patient with me. He then explained, "It's a manual car. You use this," he nodded at the stick, "to shift gears as you increase speed, instead of the car automatically doing it for you." I was surprised at his knowledge of cars as he went on, "This is a 1999 5.0 mustang SVT Cobra R V8, and it's fast! You wanna see?"

Before I could say no, he peeled out with his car roaring as he shifted from gear to gear. I almost died, having flashbacks of Tyrell driving in his rage. Sénar saw my expression and tried to reassure me by saying, "Girl calm down, why are you so scared? I'm not even going that fast."

Not wanting to go into details, I nicely asked, "Can you please just slow down?"

He slowed down a little as we pulled on to the block of our house. When we pulled in front of the house to park, I was still a little shaken up, and I jumped out happy to have made it home in one piece. Sénar ran to catch up to me and said, "Damn, your ass is trippin!" We opened the door to see Ken walking down the steps with my mom on his heels.

Ken saw Sénar still cheesin' from ear to ear and saw my expression of relief and asked, "What's going on here?" Sounding almost concerned.

Sénar responded, "Treasure is scared of my fast car." He said it laughing, I smacked my lips and folded my arms as Ken made it to the door to look out as my mom looked too. He smiled when he saw Sénar's car.

Ken asked, "Is it a stick shift?"

Sénar smiled before he answered, "You already know, yes, sir!"

Ken gave him a high five and replied, "Nice!" My mom chimed in, "It's a really nice car Sénar. How did you get that?"

Ken looked back at my mom and appeared to be irritated by her nosiness. Before Sénar could answer, Ken said, "Shit, it's cool with me. I don't care; you saved me some money, and I don't have to leave my keys with your crazy ass!"

I guess everyone knew his ass was crazy because he wasn't even offended, they just went outside to get a closer look at Sénar's car.

My mom looked at me and asked, "Treasure, are you ok?"

I just stared out the door blankly and responded dryly, "I am fine, Momma."

I turned to walk up the steps when she placed her hand on my shoulder to stop me before telling me, "Tonight, Ken and I are leaving. Ken is going to leave money for groceries and some money for you guys to get school clothes for the upcoming school year."

I forced a smile and replied, "Ok, Momma, thanks."

Ken and Sénar walked back in, laughing and smiling. Before I could go upstairs, Ken looked at me and said, "Cheer up, girl, you look like you lost a puppy. Your day will come for you to get a nice ride too."

I shook my head, thinking that was the least of my worries. I started to go upstairs to put my things away, and Ken stopped me to give me 300 dollars, then told me to get some school clothes. He turned and gave Sénar a wad of cash, telling him to take care of the house. He gauged my emotions, then looked at Sénar and told him, "Boy, make me some of those tacos before I get on this road."

He slapped Sénar on the back and headed into the kitchen. I ran upstairs to put my things away to see that Cassidy was taking a nap. I didn't make too much noise and left the room after putting away my things. I went downstairs to watch TV as my mom, Ken, and Sénar talked in the kitchen. I wish I could crawl into the TV and pick a sitcom and character to trade places with, instead of being stuck being me. I watched TV until Sénar's intoxicating food filled my nostrils. I walked like a hungry zombie into the kitchen to make my plate as my mom was making Ken and hers. I sat in silence, eating my food, listening to everyone chatter while trying to keep my tears from escaping.

I finally managed to say, "Thanks for the tacos and the shopping money." I got up and washed my plate. On my way up, Cassidy was coming down to eat without saying a word to me. I excepted I would be deserted in the woods Chino warned me about so long ago.

I went to sleep and woke up to my mom, leaning over me to kiss me on the cheek and tell me she loved me. I wanted to hold on to her and cry my heart out, but I just told her I loved her too. She just let Cassidy sleep and left. I laid in my bed, wondering how I was going to make it for the next couple of weeks. I wondered what Tyrell was doing way out there in Jersey while I was here all alone. I tried to sleep, but I couldn't stop worrying about all the things that could go wrong. Crying always makes it easier to sleep, so I cried until I could go back to sleep. I walked to school in the morning in a daze; I was annoyed, tired, and grouchy. I barely slept, I had to force myself out of bed, and I knew it was going to be a long day. I sat in my math class, and it sounded like he was speaking another language in his monotone voice. He handed us a paper with practice questions for an upcoming test.

I looked at the paper like it was foreign when this girl asked, "Aren't you Treasure?"

I looked at her pretty brown face and wanted to tell her to mind her business, but she looked so happy. I asked her, "Why?"

She smiled and answered, "Because you're pretty, and it would make sense with all the stuff I heard about you."

I was irritated instantly and retorted, "Well, you shouldn't believe everything you hear."

I dismissed her because she appeared to be an annoying dingbat. I needed that push to do my work and look busy. She just stared at me.

Now I felt awkward; what did she hear? I finished my work, and she asked, "Damn, let me see your answers?" I looked at her like she asked my bra size with my hand on my chest. She laughed and said, "Dang, you did it so fast; I didn't think you would care." I rolled my eyes and gave her my paper. She copied the work and answers then gave it back. She smiled and told me, "The last one is wrong."

I stared at her like she was crazy, then examined my paper and I'll be damned, she was right. I fixed it and put it to the side, then I pulled out a paper and scribbled on it until the bell rang for the next class. It was my Spanish 2 class, and this time he was actually speaking another language. I tried not to doze off, hearing people snicker and laugh every time I nodded off. I was ready for the day to be over, everyone seemed to be focused on me, and I was not in the mood. My next class was liberal arts, and we had to work in groups. The same chick from my other class just happened to be in this one. She ironically was in the group I was assigned to. We had to write a play together, and whoever wins gets to put on a show at the end of the summer session. Normally I would be happy to showcase my writing skills, but today was just not my day. Everyone had different ideas, and finally, someone asked me mine. I was caught off guard because I thought everyone was doing fine without me.

I shrugged my shoulders and said, "I don't know, give me until Monday, and I'll come up with something."

Everyone agreed to present their final ideas on Monday. I thought wow, that was easy; everyone just talked about their weekend plans after that. I thought I was getting off the hook when the girl whispered, "Don't you live with Sénar?"

I rolled my eyes at her like she was a pest because she was really on my nerves. I asked, "Look, why do you want to know?"

She smiled and fluttered her eyelashes and answered, "Because Sénar is so fine, I wish I lived with his fine ass." I rolled my eyes again, and she then said, "Anyway, you are one lucky girl." I wanted to scream at her and ask her how she was so sure, but I didn't want her to think I was crazy.

I felt like a broken record when I replied, "Why?"

She smiled again then replied, "You're pretty, you are dating Tyrell, you live with Sénar's fine ass, and you're smart." I wanted to tell her she was lying and had no idea what she was talking about. Those were the same areas of my life that were sucking the life out of me. I didn't exactly feel very smart, either. Instead of bursting her little bubble, I said, "Thanks." And got up when the bell rung. I was so glad I only had one class left, which was reading. I was so happy everyone needed to be reading instead of talking. I read until the class was over. I walked home in the heat, almost wondering where Sénar was. When I made it home, I didn't see his car. I was actually happy and went inside and went to sleep. When I woke up, I woke up to Cassidy packing; I wanted to jump on her back and beg her to stay.

She asked, "So what are you going to do for the rest of the summer?"

I looked at her and said, "I have no idea; I actually wish you were staying."

She sighed and then said, "I can't. I would be bored out of my mind and me and you have been bumping heads lately."

I couldn't even disagree with her. Cassidy actually sounded hopeful when she said, "Well, don't worry, I'm sure you'll figure it out. Plus, Sénar has a car now, and so does your boyfriend."

She finished packing and got ready to walk out the door when Sénar peeped in to see if she was ready. Sénar asked if I wanted to go, and I declined. I sat in my room and debated what I would do for the last hour. I didn't know whether to take a bath or go somewhere, anywhere, just to get out. Before I knew it, Sénar was back. I froze for a second, wondering how he got back so quickly then remembered how fast he was driving yesterday. I just grabbed what I could and planned to run to the bathroom. Before I could, Sénar was at my door smiling but more amused than sadistic.

He asked, "Where are you about to run to, your hiding place?"

Cautious how I responded to his question, I took a deep breath before answering, "Maybe. It depends, should I?"

He smirked then countered, "You can't stay in there forever."

That was all he needed to say before I gathered my things and tried to walk past him to the bathroom. He stood in front of me and told me, "Don't be acting all scary and shit. We could have a really good time."

I took another deep breath and replied, "Sénar, I don't know what your good time consists of, and I-" He kissed me. I kept my clothes in between us, and he looked deep into my eyes. I looked away and said,

"Sénar let me go. I don't want it to be like this. I can't do this."

He picked me up and carried me to the bathroom anyway then sat me on the counter. He took my clothes from me and threw them on the floor. He grabbed me to kiss me, and I pushed him off, then he just stared at me. I looked away, then pleaded with him, "Sénar, please let me take a bath. I just want to be left alone." I said with the sweetest voice I could give, and then I tried to get off the bathroom counter.

He sighed and asked, "Then what?"

I looked at him like he was crazy, but he was serious. I panicked a little before I answered, "I don't know, maybe eat some food, then go to sleep. I mean, I can't do this. What part of that don't you understand?"

I knew he was going to ask a stupid question just by his expression, but he let me down and said, "Well I'm going to cook, come eat when you're done. And don't take forever, or I am going to come to get you."

I shook my head in a yeah motion, not wanting to say anything to make him change his mind about leaving. As soon as he walked out the door, I quickly and quietly locked it then fell to the ground crying. I had no idea what this next couple of weeks would be like, and he was right, I couldn't run to the bathroom for safety forever. I had to figure something out, so I didn't lose my mind. I took a shower instead of a bath because there was no way that I could relax. I just let the shower run until the water was cold. I had no choice but to turn it off and then sit there to wait for it to get hot again. Sénar knocked on the door and said, "The food is ready." I guess that was a nice way of telling me to get out.

I got dressed and crept down the steps. Sénar was fully dressed, so that made me feel better. He smiled when he saw me and tried not to laugh. I was offended and asked, "What's so funny?"

He stared at me and saw that I was barefoot, with baggy sweats and had a T-shirt on from my gym class. My hair was wild, and I was extra ashy. He smirked then said, "Yeah, you funny, trying to dress down that pretty face and body of yours. But you're still Treasure, and you still look sexy as fuck. In a natural, cute kinda way."

I blushed because I really tried to look like a bum and tied my drawstring extra tight on my sweats. I just responded, "Whatever." I rolled my eyes then asked, "...What are we eating?"

It was steak and potatoes with a colorful salad, my eyes widened when he gave me my plate. It looked like we were eating at a restaurant, everything plated to perfection. He even had some wine poured. I smacked my lips and asked, "Why are you doing all of this, Sénar?" He ignored my question and ate his food. I hesitated before tasting my steak. When I put it in my mouth, there was an explosion of flavor, and it made me want to clap my hands. I just pretended like it was just food, and nothing more. I also hesitated before drinking the wine, but I really liked wine. It was yet another amazing moment as the juices from the steak lingered in anticipation of the wine. I was in food heaven and totally forgot about being deserted with Sénar until I realized he was watching me.

I got annoyed with him and asked, "Damn Sénar, why are you so nosey? Let me eat in peace." He rubbed his chin and licked his lips, but didn't say anything, which was more disturbing. I drank my wine and ate my food in silence. When he was done, he opened the freezer and made us ice cream cones. I couldn't help but smile because he thought he was slick. He just wanted to watch me eat the ice cream cone. I wanted to get a bowl to put the ice cream in to be under less observation, but he looked at me like I needed to stay where I was. But

I walked out of the kitchen anyway, and he followed me. I put the TV on and sat on the corner of the couch, and he sat down next to me.

Trying not to be mean, I said nicely, "Give me some space, dang Sénar."

He bit his bottom lip and reluctantly yielded before saying, "I am going to be good because I have plans tomorrow. So, get ready in the morning, we have a long day."

He left me on the couch, eating my ice cream cone and went to bed. I was shocked but relieved. I watched TV until I got sleepy and went to bed feeling like a normal person, well almost. The morning came, and Sénar was up with music blasting from his room. He looked fresh; his hair was thick and curly. I saw him putting a wave cap on to try to get his hair to lay down. He was in a good mood; he had on some dark blue jeans and a white polo shirt.

He told me, "Hurry up and get dressed, so we could leave. And don't put anything silly on, that shit is not going to work. Plus, we are going to the city, so no red and no blue. Shoot, if you got a cute pink shirt, wear that."

I didn't even bother asking questions; I just found some jean shorts and a pink shirt to save any possible issues. I put my silver hoops on and put my hair in a bun. He saw me and licked his lips, then said, "Damn, you look perfect." He smiled, and I dryly said,

"Thanks."

We jumped in the car and hopped on the 10 West to Hawthorne, in Los Angeles. I had never been to LA; I only heard about it in rap songs or from people who pretended like they had street credit out there. I was a little scared and excited because I knew it was dangerous. We listened to music, and once on the freeway, he lit a blunt, I was scared to hit it because we were driving. He assured me we would hit it a couple of times, and then we would put it out. The music was blasting, and the traffic was busy. We went to a place called the alley and shopped for some super dope clothes that I never see in the malls out where we lived. We tried on clothes and were silly as hell, no matter how many Asian store owners may have followed us around. We purchased our stuff and gave them a reason to feel stupid. We ate at a burger spot called Bobo's Burgers, which was so good. He called one of his cousins on his new cellphone he purchased and asked if we could spend a night.

They were all happy to see Sénar and asked about Cassidy, Sabrina, and Chino. He gave them all a run down, and no one dared ask who I was. I could tell they already knew the way they looked at me. Everyone was super nice, even his auntie. I noticed her and Ken favored one another when she asked how he was doing. She told Sénar I was pretty just like my momma and shook her finger at him before we disappeared into the back with his cousins. They clowned each other, drank, and smoked in the backyard while I watched. I was careful not to drink or smoke too much, so I could observe my surroundings. His cousin gave us the couch and some pillows with a blanket. Sénar gave them to me and kept a pillow and slept on the floor next to me. I woke up with him staring up at me along with the rest of his cousins.

I sat up, and nervously said, "Good morning."

And everyone said, "Good morning." In unison. Sénar started to blush, throwing his pillow at a pack of his cousins as they just watched him blush. He jumped up and went to his car, leaving me there with his googly-eyed ass cousins. One of his girl cousins came in and looked at me then asked, "Who is that?" His older male cousin said, "Girl mind, yo dang business!"

Sénar came back with some clothes and towels for us; he even had brand new toothbrushes. He told me to take a shower, and I was not comfortable until his aunty said, "Girl, we don't bite, gone in there and take a shower."

When I came out, Sénar was in the kitchen, schooling them on what and how to cook breakfast. His aunty said, "Boy, I taught yo ass how to cook, so don't come over here telling me what to do."

He laughed and left me in there with his family while he showered. His auntie asked in a whisper, "You must be Treasure? Cuz, that boy crazy about you."

I just smiled as I did not know what to say. One of their neighbors came by; she was about our age or maybe a little older. She came in and said, "Good morning, y'all. I heard Sénar was here. Where is he at?"

She walked through the house looking for him. His cousins laughed and ran to the back. I was eating the grits and eggs his auntie cooked, and they were good. She put a lot of cheese in hers and served it with fish. It was so damn good; I didn't notice the neighbor staring at me. I stopped eating and stared back at her waiting on her to speak, but she didn't, so I just kept eating.

His auntie felt the tension and told her, "Girl, Sénar is in the shower; you can come back and see him before he leaves."

The girl sat down and waited for him; she was cute but a little rough around the edges. She was chocolate and tall with long braids. Sénar got out the shower with some grey khakis and a grey and white Polo shirt with LA in big white letters.

She smiled and said, "Damn nigga, you lookin' fresh. You so big and sexy now."

He rolled his eyes as she ran up to him and hugged him. She asked, "What, you forgot about me?"

He looked at her and replied, "Nope. What's good?"

She laughed and tugged on his T-shirt then asked, "What's up? How long you out here for?"

He passed her up to grab some bacon and some toast and answered, "I'm 'bout to roll out shortly after I smoke this blunt."

She smiled flirtatiously and said, "Shiit, let me hit it; I know you got that bomb."

I was pretty sure she was not talking about the weed at this point, I just watched the two of them like I was watching a sitcom on TV. She was super aggressive, and that was the first time I ever saw Sénar get uncomfortable with a girl, or I should say, woman. She brushed upon him, and he jumped out the way; he smacked her hand away, then said, "Man, Daisy stop playing!"

She looked back at me and asked, "That's your ol' square ass bitch over there?"

Before he could respond, I said, "My name is Treasure."

With my eyebrow now raised at her audacity to refer to me as a bitch and ask him about me. Instead of staring me down, she could have asked me if I was his girl, and I would have told her no. She laughed, and Sénar said, "Aye, man, don't be disrespectful." He even said it nicely; it was shocking to me how he was responding to her. I was ready to go; she was annoying me.

Sénar saw me stand up and said, "Come on, Treasure, let's roll."

She moved to the side and watched us walk away to the back with his cousins, then followed behind us with Sénar in the middle of us. Sénar lit the blunt and hit it three times before he passed it to me, I only hit it twice then Sénar summoned me to leave with him. He said bye to everyone, knowing it was too many folks even to get the blunt back. Everyone followed us out and complimented Sénar on his car. I watched Daisy look at us like she wanted to say something but didn't, we drove off. I was feeling good, I had some bomb food, we smoked, and Sénar hadn't done anything out of line. This was turning out to be a pretty cool weekend. We shopped some more and ate at Bobo's Burgers again since we didn't know when we would be back. I had the pastrami fries with jalapeños. We laughed and talked about all his cousins and how Louie was his favorite cousin. Sénar told me that Daisy was crazy when he told me she was 24; my mouth fell open in shock. I didn't even want to know the story; I could only imagine. We pulled up to our house after our crazy weekend. We both went straight to bed, no funny business, and I slept like a baby.

Chapter 17

I woke up in a good mood; I was humming and smiling. I got dressed and headed to school. I was rested and paid attention in class, ready to take the test coming up on Wednesday.

The nosey girl turned around, saying, "Someone is in a good mood."

I rolled my eyes at her; she was almost getting on my nerves. She introduced herself, "I'm Leah. I came at the end of the school year, so I'm making up credits. What about you?"

All her information was unwanted, and I dryly responded, "I am here for extra credits."

She assumed, "Oh, you need to make up classes too."

I gave her a look to indicate that she was getting on my nerves and replied, "No, extra credits for early graduation."

She asked, "Ooh, you fancy, huh?"

The bell rang right before my rude response that I kept to myself. I got up and walked out of the class, she followed me and asked, "So, you want to hang out sometime?" Shocked, because no one at school ever asked me that, I paused for a minute and thought about it.

I responded, "Look, I have to go, maybe, I'll let you know."

I was at home watching TV, we were halfway through the week, and I was finally at ease. Sénar came in with bags and his cellphone ringing. He put some of the bags down and answered his phone.

I could hear him talking, "Look, woman, leave me alone. I will come see you tomorrow. I've been busy." He rolled his eyes and continued, "If you call me again, I'm not coming tomorrow either!"

He ended the call and put the rest of the bags on the floor, then went upstairs for a second, and then came back down. He looked so stressed. I flinched at the sound of him putting stuff away and rummaging around in the kitchen. I felt bad, but I didn't want to go in there, and he take his frustration out on me. So, I just sat there and watched TV. I was in the best mood I had been in for a long time, and I didn't even want to mess it up. It wasn't long before he came and sat down in the living room across from me on the couch. He laid his head back and closed his eyes. He fell asleep, and I snuck passed him and went to my room. I did not want to be there when he woke up; he looked so drained and frustrated. I went through all my bags we bought back from LA. I smiled when I thought about how much fun we had and how he was really trying to be good. In the back of my mind, I still worried about how long he would last before doing whatever he wanted and not caring about the effects of it. I started to think of what I could do to keep him at bay and remain preserved for Tyrell's return. It was like Sénar could hear me thinking of a scheme way from downstairs.

He entered my room without knocking and asked, "Why did you leave?"

I looked back at him and tried not to have an attitude, even though I should not have to explain myself. I replied, "I didn't know I had to stay down there." I continued folding my clothes, not wanting him to come in any further. I continued, "Besides, you looked really tired and irritated."

I stopped folding my clothes to look at him to observe his facial expression. He was gazing at me with his head on the door. I saw the smile I saw the day we were in the backyard, and my heart started rapidly beating. He walked away without saying anything, leaving me there wondering what was next. Knowing that anything could happen, I sat down to think hard and fast. I could skip dinner and go to bed early or go see a movie by myself. I looked at the time, and

It was already after five, so it might be dark when I came out of the movie. I was in the middle of thinking when Sénar called my name, startling me back to my current reality.

I answered from the top of the stairs, "What?"

He responded, "You know what, get down here and help me with the food."

I tried to be funny but seriously hoped it worked and replied, "Um, I'll pass, thanks." He came way to the stairway to look up at me, with a smirk on his face. I laughed and asked, "Sénar, do I have to?"

He crossed his arms, answering my question with his gesture instead of words. I walked down, not really prepared to deal with this situation; however, it may turn out, I knew I was not ready. He waited for me until I got down to the bottom of the steps. He pulled me into the kitchen so quickly; I felt like I was running to keep up with my arm. It wasn't aggressive; it was just impulsive. He turned around and picked me up like I was a little girl and sat me on the counter. I tried to get down while I complained, "Why do I have to sit here?"

He stood in front of me and put his hands on my lips, I smacked his hand away, and he squeezed my thigh with his other hand. He said, "Stop it, I have a surprise, and I need you to sit here for it."

I wanted to dropkick him and run, but I knew I would not make it very far. He looked for something with his other hand telling me to close my eyes and open my mouth. I looked at him like he was crazy, he laughed then said, "Nah just do it, Damn." He was trying to be patient, but he was excited.

I closed one eye and looked at him with the other and said, "Don't do anything dumb, Sénar."

He smacked his lips and said, "Come on, damn, you might like it." He said it flirtatiously, I opened both eyes, and he quickly demanded, "Close them Treasure."

He was impatient now. I closed them and cautiously opened my mouth. He put something on my tongue, it was cold and wet. I opened my eyes; I was chewing as I asked, "What is this?"

He responded, "Smoked salmon." He then ate some too and told me to close my eyes again. I was still a bit cautious; he then placed something cold and kind of fleshy on my tongue. It had a fresh taste with a hint of green onion, but it was good.

I made a weird face, he laughed, and I asked, "What was that?"

He eagerly answered, "Poke, it's a popular fish in Hawaii." He ate a piece himself; it was red and cut in cubes. I closed my eyes without him telling me to, and he put something else on my tongue with the texture of rice and a creamy filling, it was really delicious.

Sénar said, "Oh, you like that one, huh? That's a California roll."

This was getting to be a little more fun than I thought it would be. The next time I closed my eyes, he put a paste on my tongue, and it started to burn. I thought he was trying to kill me or drug me until he started laughing while handing me a drink out of a shot glass.

He said, "Calm down, Treasure, it's just wasabi!"

I drank the liquid and spat it out on the both of us. He looked like he wanted to slap me, but he just wiped his face and shirt off instead. I quickly apologized for spitting on him, but now I felt like he was playing too much.

He chuckled when I asked, "What was that, Sénar?"

As he wiped me off too, he smirked and told me, "It's Saki, and it's Japanese alcohol."

That explained a little bit, but it wasn't very tasty. I was highly annoyed, but I was also intrigued by tasting all those different flavors. I asked, "How do you be getting all this stuff?"

He smirked and asked, "Why are you so nosey?"

I shrugged my shoulders and answered, "I don't know. I was just curious, that's all." I rolled my eyes at his question.

I started to get down, and he asked, "Where are you going?"

I sighed and said, "Sénar, don't mess the moment up."

He looked at me with hopeful eyes and asked, "What moment?"

He gazed deeply into my eyes, and I quickly responded, "Never mind."

He was satisfied with my answer and told me, "If you get down, you're going to help me or just sit there and look pretty." I rolled my eyes and chose to sit there, feeling it was probably a safer choice. He took his wet shirt off and threw it over the chair, he put his hands out then said, "Wallah, Chef Sénar in the building!"

I couldn't help but laugh; he was so intense and goofy at the same time. He worked his way around the kitchen like a professional and made sure I was sitting pretty. He asked, "So how was school?"

I answered, "It was cool, I guess." He continued cooking, occasionally looking back at me. I was bored, so I asked him, "So, how was your day, Chef Sénar?" I almost regretted asking him, after remembering how agitated he was earlier when he got home.

He smiled as if he was happy that I asked him, he replied, "It was horrible until I saw you." He fluttered his eyelashes, the way I did when I wanted something. He laughed when he saw me squirm a bit, then continued to tell me about his day, "I haven't had none for a couple of days and the one who wants to give it to me, I don't want it from. The one I want it from is playing games."

I got even more uncomfortable and replied, "Maybe because the one you want it from, has a boyfriend." I said it with minimal attitude to avoid him getting angry.

He stopped what he was doing to ask me, "Is that the only reason?"

I sighed and tried not to roll my eyes and asked, "Can we change the subject, Sénar?"

He smirked and replied, "I don't give a fuck about Tyrell, so is that the only reason?"

I looked at him, lost for words. I didn't know how to answer him; there was no right or wrong answer. He came closer to me, and my heart rate began to increase. I looked down and thought hard before answering, "I don't kn-"

He was kissing me before I could even get a sentence out. Overwhelmed, I pushed him back and wiped my mouth, then blurted out, "You didn't even let me answer!" He gave me some space; I thought about my answer and replied, "I love Tyrell. Sénar, I don't know what else you want me to say." I pouted as I looked at him, hoping he would understand.

Sénar glared at me and responded, "That's not a good enough reason." He walked away laughing, he checked his food and grabbed a piece of sushi. He leaned on the counter, frustrated, and said, "He's definitely not the reason I behaved lately." Knowing he had been on his best behavior the last couple of days, I wanted to encourage him to continue, so I replied, "Sénar I-" He cut me off and said, "I don't want to talk about it anymore. I have my mind made up, and he's not enough to keep me from you."

I was silent, he was already frustrated, and I didn't want to say the wrong thing. I was nervous; I wanted to run into the bathroom and lock the door. He looked at me as if he could read my mind, and I knew I wouldn't even make it off the counter, I was stuck. I didn't move an inch as he finished up his stir fry and turned the stove off. He grabbed plates, and even though he was irritated, he still served me. Our plates consisted of the sushi I liked, Beef and broccoli cooked to perfection with white rice. I just ate in silence, trying to figure out ways to influence him to keep up his good behavior. He finished his plate and washed it. He put the rest of the food in containers and cleaned the pans, watching my every move to make sure I didn't runoff. I was scared to move, but I didn't want to appear scared, even though the situation was intense. I got up and tried to act as normal as possible, not wanting him to sense fear and possibly arousing him even more. I washed my plate, dried it, and then put it away. I was going to say something, but I just walked out instead.

I briskly walked upstairs to my room and grabbed some nightclothes, knowing I didn't have much time. I quickly opened my door to run to the bathroom to see Sénar standing in front of the bathroom door. I looked at him like he was Houdini, wondering how he got there so damn fast. He smiled his famous sadistic ass smile, and I grasped my clothes as tightly as I could. I envisioned myself as a football player, holding the ball, trying to make a touchdown, and charged forward trying to get pass Sénar. He effortlessly caught me, picking me up and carrying me to his room. His chest was against my back, with his arms tightly clamped around my upper body. I kicked my legs to no avail as I tried to cause difficulty for him. Once in his room, he let me go locking his door. I held on to my clothes tightly, like they would protect me from him and serve as a barrier between us.

I stood tall and said, "Sénar, this is crazy! Please let me take a shower in peace!"

He licked his lips and looked like he would consider it, but asked, "Let me watch you?"

I gasped in awe of his question, before replying, "What? That is absolutely not happening; I need my privacy."

He laughed and asked, "Let me watch you use the showerhead?"

I was blown away at his absurd request. I answered in disbelief of his boldness, "No!"

He put his head back against the door in frustration and then suggested, "Ok. Well, let me have you for my dessert?"

I thought to myself, *what kind of options are these?* I replied, "No! Sénar stop, you are being unreasonable right now."

He cocked his head to the side in disbelief and asked, "Am I really being unreasonable?"

I quickly thought about his self-control at the moment, and for the last couple of days then felt a little guilty of my assessment of our current situation. I still just shook my head no like a defiant child without looking at him. He sighed in irritation and said, "Look, Treasure, I don't have all night. I have to work in the morning, and I am having some serious withdrawals." He said this as he moved toward me.

I moved back and desperately pleaded with him, "Sénar, everything has been going so well. I just want to take a shower and get ready for school tomorrow."

He impatiently rolled his eyes and asked, "So what are you going to do? Are you going to let me watch you use the showerhead, or are you going to let me have you for dessert?"

This was the second question tonight that I was at a loss for words. There was no right or wrong answer that would remedy this situation. I closed my eyes and wished I could teleport to a safe place and replied, "Neither, I am just going to bed."

I tried to walk out, and he stopped me and said, "Nuh-uh Treasure, I'm not negotiating much longer, I've had enough torture these last couple of days." He was serious and really didn't care about anything but himself at the moment. I almost started to cry when Sénar said, "Let me help you, and you help me."

I sighed and asked, "How?" I was desperate for a realistic compromise. He looked agitated, making me nervous and anxious to get out of his sex auditorium, he used as a room.

Sénar smirked at me and said, "You already know which one I am going to choose." I gripped my clothes tighter and tried to reason with him by saying, "Ok let me go, I'll get ready, and you can come in once I'm in the tub and you could watch from the door."

He smacked his lips as if it was a terrible idea and said, "Nah, that's wack! What about me? You have to do something for me."

I was frustrated now; I didn't want to do either of his suggestions, and I thought mine was the best. I wished I could click my heels together to make a wish and be asleep in my bed, but this was no fairy tale, this was real life. I smacked my lips out of frustration and said, "Sénar, you are buggin'!" I walked toward the door, even though he was blocking it.

He was as frustrated as he was when he came home earlier. He glared at me, anticipating a solution; I shook my head; I was really being held hostage. I was fed up and snapped, "Sénar, move!"

He said, "No!" I got mad and dropped my clothes to the floor. I was ready to jack him up when he saw my fury, his eyes filled with lust. Sénar smiled like he was ready for whatever I was going to do next. The moment he saw fear in my eyes, he picked me up over his shoulder as I was swinging my arms, slapping his back and kicking my legs. He threw me on his bed and wrestled my shirt off me.

I covered myself as he said, "Take your bra off!"

I looked at him and yelled, "No, Sénar!"

He growled in frustration, then yelled back, "Treasure, you're driving me crazy!"

I snapped at him, "You were already crazy!"

He pulled me by my legs, and I kicked him as hard as I could in his chest. He was so mad, I thought he would hit me, but he roared, "Man, get the fuck out!" He was enraged, as I quickly ran out of his room into the bathroom, slamming the door. I fell to the ground and cried so hard, not realizing the door was still unlocked. Sénar came in and glared at me, throwing my clothes at me before slamming the door. I was devastated, now Sénar and Tyrell both hated me. I couldn't do anything right; I cried until I passed out on the bathroom floor.

Sénar opened the bathroom door seeing me sprawled out on the floor and rushed to me. He called my name, frantically, "Treasure?" I jolted out of my sleep, realizing I was still lying on the bathroom floor, in the same spot I cried myself to sleep in last night. I looked at Sénar's face; he was worried and scared.

He said, "Treasure, man, get up!" He commanded as he was kneeling over me. I sat up and looked around to see my clothes all sprawled over the floor next to me, after having Sénar throw them at me. Remembering he was the reason I ended up here in the first place, I got up and ran to my room, slamming the door. I didn't even bother grabbing my clothes from the bathroom, I just threw myself on my bed and cried. Sénar came in with my clothes, including the shirt that he ripped off me last night and sat them on my bed. He combed his hair and got dressed, then came back and stood in my doorway. He eventually came in and laid down on the floor next to my bed.

Sénar confessed, "Damn Treasure, you're driving me crazy. Just give me a chance. I can't get over how I feel about you." He said, sounding remorseful.

I ignored him and buried my face in my pillow. He got off the floor and stood over my bed, watching me lie there still in my bra and shorts. He slowly squeezed in between me and the wall and wrapped his arms around my bare stomach. He said, "I'm not going to do anything but hold you." He squeezed me tightly, and we fell asleep. I woke up feeling something hard, poking me on my behind and Sénar's arms wrapped tightly around my stomach. He was still sleeping so I wasn't as alarmed, I looked at the clock it was a little after nine o'clock. Sénar noticed me awake and released me when he saw the time.

We both said, "Oh shit!" Sénar sat up and said, "Damn, I'm late for work! Get up and get dressed so I can take you to school."

We both jumped up and ran around like Macaulay Culkin did in *Home Alone,* trying to get ourselves together. When we were done, we left the house like civilized human beings, well almost. Sénar slapped me on the behind so hard that I wanted to punch him in his face.

He bit his bottom lip and said, "I'm gonna get some of that, whether you know it or not!"

I took a deep breath to keep my comment to myself so that I would make it to school and not end up in his room again, fighting for my freedom. I was tardy and a little disheveled, but still presentable.

I walked into my first class and didn't even sit down yet before I heard Leah ask, "Damn, girl, why are you late?"

I smiled at her to keep from choking her to death, and then I replied, "Look, little girl, you need to mind your damn business. Ok?"

She snapped back at me, "Damn, what crawled up your ass?"

I smirked and rephrased her question in my head to, *who almost crawled up my ass*? Then I replied, "Well, what do you want to crawl up your ass?"

I had my foot in mind, when she responded, "Shoot, hook me up with Sénar, I'll take that shit up my ass all day."

I took a good look at her for the first time, scanning her from head to toe. Leah had a pretty chocolate complexion and a cute face. She had nice petite breast that was not as full as mine, but just enough, and she was sitting on a pretty nice ass that I could see from how thick her thighs were. I smiled a sadistic smile of my own, then replied, "I'll see what I can do."

I dismissed her by busying myself with my classwork. I went to my next class scheming on how I would hook her and Sénar up to keep him occupied the next few weeks, so that he would leave me alone. My drama class was the longest of the day as I listened to Leah talk about all the stuff that she wanted to do to Sénar and all the stuff she would let him do to her. She was so desperate; she offered to be my slave if I could just get her in good with Sénar. She was a little strange, but I figured that would make her and Sénar the perfect match. I tuned her out and wrote the skit I offered to write for our group while everyone had their own individual conversations. I was done hearing her talk and asked her for her number. She wrote it down inside a heart she drew and gave it to me. I tried not to laugh and told her I would do my best, but I wasn't going to promise her anything. Besides, Sénar being completely obsessed with me and having a crazy ass girlfriend named London, she would be lucky if she even got a chance to talk to him. Nevertheless, I planned to figure something out that would hopefully work out for my benefit.

When I got home after walking in the hot sun, I was so tired. Last night was crazy, it was too draining to even think about it. I didn't get to shower last night, and I felt like I barely slept. I knew Sénar would not be home until later. So, I showered and came out in my towel, relieved to be home by myself for once. I was thinking about how crazy Leah was as I opened my door to see Sénar lying on my bed. I almost screamed when he jumped up to close my door. He smiled sadistically before snatching my towel off me. I quickly covered myself in pure shock.

I asked, "Sénar, what the hell are you doing home so early?" I walked backwards as his eyes grew wider for him to scan my body with.

He was in awe of my nakedness when he said, "Damn Treasure, you are literally a goddess."

He threw my towel on the floor and approached me slowly; I backed up until I couldn't anymore. The dresser supported me as I braced myself mentally for what was next. When he reached me, he ran his fingers down the side of my face then smelled my hair as if I was a flower. My heart raced and skipped several beats before I made a desperate attempt to get out of the situation by saying, "Sénar, there's a pretty girl at school, who totally adores you…"

Sénar totally ignored my verbiage as he was in a trance. His eyes were all over my body and then soon, his hands. I tried to swallow the knot that had formed in my throat as I tried to tell him about Leah's effectuation with him. I continued to tell him, "She has a really nice body-"

He kissed me so deeply mid-sentence, he probably could taste the rest of my words. I held on to the dresser tight, almost losing my balance when he picked me up and sat me on my dresser. I kept talking to him, trying to intrigue him and distract him from his devious intentions. I said, "Sénar, she has a really nice body, and she is chocolate-"

He kissed me again mid-sentence to occupy my mouth, and then pulled out his eager member. Hovering over me and looking into my eyes lustfully, it made me more desperately try to tell him how bad she wanted him, "Sénar, you could do anything you want to her she…."

He plunged himself inside of me, taking my breath away as he filled my insides with himself, passionately thrusting in and out of me until I couldn't even talk anymore. Trying to catch my breath as I was being throttled on my dresser. Sénar cupped his hands under my butt cheeks, bringing me closer to him, so he could go deeper inside of me. I yelled as my coochie was throbbing in unison with his thrust. He picked me up off the dresser, bouncing me up and down while he was deep inside of me, causing me to moan in pleasure. He kissed my neck and my breast as he laid me down on my bed. He mounted me and moaned in my ear, "Oh my, Treasure, I needed this!"

He squeezed my breast and stuck his tongue deep in my mouth as I squirmed to fight the urge to move in unison with his thrusts. He gyrated while plunging himself in and out of me until pleasure completely took over my resistance. He gazed deeply into my eyes and moaned in my ear, saying, "I want this forever and ever!" I closed my eyes as he pumped faster and harder, squeezing my breast while sucking on my neck. I pushed against his chest, causing him to pump into me even harder. As I panted for air and opened my eyes, I saw his eyes traveling all over my body and face. His face was full of excitement until he gazed upon my gold necklace, with Tyrell's name sparkling between my breast. I closed my eyes; I felt like I was going to burst like a balloon while he thrusted deeper and deeper; I could feel his hand graze across my chest. He ran his hand down my neck, thrusting faster and deeper until I yelled, "Sénar, please!"

I sucked in as much air as I could, to keep from passing out from the violent convulsions, I felt rippling through my body as Sénar simultaneously snatched the chain from around my neck, while pulling out to relieve himself all over my stomach and pelvis area. I tried to pull myself together while shivering from the aftershocks of all the sensations that made my toes feel like I had a million Charlie horses running through them, and my back stiffened like a rod was put in place to straighten it. When I was done spasming, I felt for my chain while Sénar wiped me off with my towel and then himself. Sénar took a deep breath and said, "Oh my God, woman!" He left the room, leaving me there to gather myself.

I sat there in a daze, wondering how I let this crap happen again. My body was such a traitor, and Sénar was freaking crazy. I started to recap some of the moments feeling for my chain; I panicked and looked everywhere for it. After checking the floor, the dresser, my bed, and every inch of my room, it hit me that Sénar snatched it off my neck. I just threw some shorts and a top on and ran out to look for Sénar. In a rage I checked downstairs, I checked in his room, and he wasn't there, I was livid with anger. I went to the bathroom, hearing the water running. I banged on the door.

He yelled, "It's open."

As he showered, I opened the door like a crazed woman and asked, "Sénar! Where's my chain?"

He laughed at me and replied, "I don't know what you're talking about."

I rummaged through his clothes and didn't find anything, fueling my anger. Sénar said, "Treasure get in the shower, I might give it back."

I yelled at him through the shower curtain, "Give it back! Now!"

I was so pissed off I snatched the shower curtain back, exposing his naked body dripping with water. I took a deep breath, I already needed to calm myself down; I demanded, "Sénar give me back my chain!"

He looked at my breast and then bit his bottom lip before he replied, "Ooh, your headlights are on."

I looked down to see my nipples protruding through my flimsy shirt; I was so embarrassed I lunged at him. Sénar dodged me, pulling me into the shower with him. I almost broke my neck when my foot slipped after it unexpectedly came in contact with the wet tub, but Sénar's grip on me was so strong it prevented me from falling. He ripped my shirt, exposing my breast, I pushed him so hard he almost slipped. He turned me around and pressed me against the wall of the shower, then snatched my shorts off, sending the button flying somewhere into the bathroom. From behind, he slid into my quivering walls that had not yet recovered from earlier, pressing my face against the wet wall he whispered, "This shit is mine."

He kept going until I was shivering uncontrollably from his lust thrusts, he squeezed my breast and gave me demands, "Now put a skirt on because I didn't get my dessert yet." He pulled out and released his fluids all over my behind and legs, along with my juices that streamed down my inner thighs. He got out of the shower, leaving me in the shower. Before he left, he said, "And, make sure you wash up too." I slid down in a crouching position, my coochie had a heartbeat of its own, it was still pulsating, and my nipples were hard as rocks. I thought I would die from all the stimulation I was feeling. My body was a traitor and just a tool for Sénar's pleasures. Tears streaked my face as I cried, letting the water run all over my body until it was cold. I felt for my chain, and it was gone.

Once I washed up in ice-cold water, I went to my room to frantically look for a skirt and, at the same time, hoped my chain would appear. I wanted my chain back; there was practically nothing else he could do to me. I cried at the thought of not getting my chain back, that was the only piece of Tyrell I was able to hold on to. I just cried until I got the strength to confront him about my chain and stormed down the steps. I stood in front of him as he was sitting on the couch as he appeared to be waiting on me to come down. He smiled when he saw my skirt and said, "Good girl."

Not caring if I made him angry, I asked, "Where's my chain Sénar?" I had my hand on my hip, ready to have a tantrum. Apparently, all Sénar's built-up frustration was relieved; he looked at me with sincerity before he answered, "Look, I don't want to talk, I want to eat. But first I want to smoke this blunt. I had a long week, and finally, I feel like I can relax."

He hopped up off the couch, not even giving me the option to respond. I was infuriated with his little speech. No way in hell could a normal person have the audacity to tell me about his long-ass week or any of his problems after having taken advantage of me in the way that he did. He smiled and said, "Girl, you wore me out!" He walked to the backyard to smoke. As I walked through the kitchen, I thought about grabbing a knife and chopping the smile off his face. I knew I wouldn't get far, but I would at least be justified in cutting him. As if Sénar could read my thoughts, he watched my every move from outside as he hit the blunt. I wanted to go out there to scream to the world how crazy he was and how he was taking advantage of me, but I knew no one would hear me or even care. I went outside to interrogate him about my chain. It was so quiet outside; I could feel the cold air and wanted to go back in immediately. Sénar saw that I was cold and got up with the blunt and walked into the house.

I gasped and said, "You can't smoke in the house!" I followed behind him, closing the door behind me. He walked into the garage, and I followed him. I said, "Sénar, have you completely lost your mind?" He looked at me and rolled his eyes. I hit him in the chest and pointed my finger in his face, then said, "Sénar, you are totally crazy! Give me back my chain now!"

He was high now, looking at me like I was the crazy one and found a box to sit on. He passed me the blunt, but I declined, not wanting it to mess up the delivery of my speech. He held it in the air until I grabbed it, I hit it once and tried to give it back. He put his head down and said, "I'm cool." I hit it again, coughing hard as I tried to pass it back to him again. I hit the weed again, and everything seemed to be in slow motion as I sat down to push his head up to pass it to him. He laughed and said, "Nah, I'm high as hell. That's some fire, I'm good."

As he put his head down again, I hit it and laughed hysterically at the idea of me trying to have a normal life. Sénar lifted his head to look at me, then took the blunt from me to put it out before I could hit it again. He wanted to cook but said, "I would probably burn some shit up, huh?" He ordered a pizza, some hot wings, and a soda.

We sat down in the living room and turned on the TV. I tried to be mad, but *Martin* reruns were on, and it was hilarious as hell as Tommy was trying to convince everyone he had a job. We laughed and giggled while watching TV on the couch; we were high as hell while we waited for the pizza to come. It wasn't long before Sénar scooted closer to me. I got up and sat on the other couch and said, "Leave me alone!"

He giggled then begged, "Come on, let me get dessert before we eat dinner."

I scooted away and replied, "No!" Then I pushed him away from me. It was like he got all his strength back at once and kissed me so long and deeply; I couldn't breathe until he let me go. He got down on the floor, and his hands traveled up my thighs. He quickly pulled on my panties as I tried to hold on to them; he quickly snatched them out of my grip off of me. I squeezed my legs together and pushed his head back as he pried my legs open. I said, "Stop, Sénar!" He pushed my hands off his head and licked and nibbled on my coochie until I screamed for him to stop. As I was having mini convulsions from his dessert session, he almost climbed on top of me, but the doorbell rang. I was so relieved when he got up to get the food. I put my panties back on to keep my juices from oozing all over the couch. He came back to sit on the floor between my legs. I squeezed my knees together, so he got up to wash his face and hands instaed. He came back tot the living room with cups and plates.

He sat on the couch next to me and said, "I guess I had a little dessert. Let's eat!" I stared at him and wondered what I was going to do with him; he handed me my plate with pizza and hot wings on it. We watched the *Fresh Prince of Bel Air* episodes until we both fell asleep.

The sun was shining through the window on my face waking me up. Sénar was passed out on my chest and lying in between my legs, sleeping like a baby. I panicked after yesterday's events flashed in my mind like they were on a projector screen. I quickly felt for my chain on my neck, and it still was not there. I pushed Sénar to wake him up. He woke up and looked at me; he smiled goofily.

I snapped at him, "Get off of me! I'm about to be late for school!" I ran upstairs to take a quick shower and then got dressed. When I came downstairs, Sénar was dressed and ready to take me to school. When I got to school, I was still ten minutes late.

When I walked into the office, the secretary asked, "Treasure is everything ok? This is the second time you're tardy this week."

I ignored her concern and replied, "I'm fine."

Then took my tardy slip and went to class. As soon as I walked in, I sat down, and Leah whispered, "Dang Treasure, you busy, huh?"

I looked at her and smiled, "Yeah, I was up late writing our play."

Leah looked at me like I was lying. A little offended, I looked at her and said, "I take my writing very seriously."

She just rolled her eyes at me and then said, "Right."

I ignored her sarcasm and did my work. The next couple of classes went by quickly; I was focused on my work because these classes were important to my escape in the future. My drama class wasn't so bad as I spent it showing them the play. I wrote, called *Bonquisha Goes to School*. I explained to them the characters and how the girl that was being bullied would go on a talk show with her bully. Everyone picked their parts and were super excited about the play. I ensured everyone would have their roles by the end of the week to practice for the big show next week. Of course, I was Bonquisha, and Leah begged me to be the bully, so I gave her the role. The bell rang, and I left before she could ask me anymore favors. After school, I was ready to walk home when I noticed Sénar's car in the parking lot.

I smacked my lips and asked, "What are you doing here?"

He replied, "Get in."

I got in before people started to notice. When we got home, once inside, Sénar tried to kiss me. I took my whole hand and shoved his face back, then I asked, "Where's my chain Sénar?"

He looked at me with his sadistic smile and said, "What are you willing to do for it?"

I screamed, "What is wrong with you, Sénar?"

He eyed me nonchalantly, then replied, "Nothing is wrong with me. What's wrong with you? You don't like to cum?"

I scrunched my face in confusion then asked, "What are you talking about? Look, I don't even want to know, just please give me my chain!"

He laughed before he replied, "You sure cum a lot not to know what it is. Besides, we have a couple of things to do before they get back, and I might give you your chain, and I might not."

I felt like my head would explode when I asked, "What more do you want from me? You have done everything you can do to me! Just give me my chain!"

He laughed at me; then he smirked before he responded, "Oh no, I have not, there is so much more Treasure. I can show you better than I can tell you."

This was just a game to him, while my entire existence was being toyed with, I was on the verge of losing my mind. I looked at his devious smile and ran up the stairs to the bathroom, but the door was locked. I banged on the door, and there was no answer. I ran to my room and cried like a big baby. I cried until I was enraged and recklessly ran down the steps, ready to beat the shit out of Sénar until my chain popped out. When I got down the stairs, Sénar was on his phone arguing with London. I hit him in the side of his head, making him drop his phone. He smiled like a maniac and snatched me by my shirt, normally I would be scared, but I looked at him like I was ready to die.

He said, "Treasure you are trippin, don't put your hands on me like that. It really turns me on."

He released me and winked at me; he picked his phone back up. I jumped on his back and tried to maul him, slapping him and trying to choke him. He had the phone to his ear and was laughing hysterically. He calmly said, "London, I'm going to call you ba-" SLAP! I tried to slap his mouth off. I took his phone and threw it against the wall shattering it. He pushed me off of him. I got up and tried to push him back down, so I would have the chance of hurting him.

I yelled, "Give me my chain!"

He picked me up and threw me on the couch, then said, "Stop hitting me, Treasure." He was really calm, which enraged me even more. I jumped off the couch, and he pushed me back down. He glared at me and asked, "You ready for another round? So, I could show you some of the stuff that I have not done to you?" He raised his eyebrow and smiled sadistically. I felt heat all over my body, I didn't know if it was anger or excitement, but whichever it was, it turned him on. He snatched me off the couch as I fought him wildly, he threatened, "I'm going to have to get some restraints for your ass if you keep acting like this."

I was mortified because I knew he would if he had the opportunity. I was out of breath and enraged as he carried me to the kitchen with my arms and legs flailing everywhere. He let me go, and I turned around and slapped him so hard, I thought he was going to hit me back. He grabbed my throat instead and slammed me against the wall. He choked me, while I was trying to get his hand off my throat, he was unbuckling my shorts. He slid his hand into my shorts, then stuck his fingers inside me while still choking me with his other hand. When he felt the moisture he was looking for, he eased his grip a little on my neck, allowing me to breathe a little easier. I was exhausted, but not dead yet. I tried to choke him back, but he didn't stop me. He just snatched my shorts down, maneuvering them all the way down with his leg, then moved them out of the way with his foot as we choked each other. He laid me on the kitchen table, neither of us letting go of our grips on each other's throats. He left one hand free in case I got crazier as I tried to squeeze the life out of him, but his rage went inside me as he plunged himself inside of me, it felt like an electric shock going through my body.

His veins were popping out of his neck; as he was straining to keep his neck intact, he continued to thrust himself deeply in me. I thought I would lose consciousness; I was becoming tired and had my breathing restricted by his hand clenched around my neck. My hands were starting to hurt, but I squeezed so hard as he was pumping his fury into me until there was a hot explosion inside of me, making my eyes roll to the back of my head. We both released each other's necks after what felt like an internal bomb went off inside the both of us. We both dropped to the floor, trying to breathe some life back into our lungs, I crawled to where my clothes were strewn over to and laid down next to them. I wanted to cry, but l was furious, and I was still trying to figure out what the hell just happened between us. Sénar was still lying on the floor; I almost hoped he was dead, just for a second. I picked my clothes up off the floor and ran upstairs to my room. I laid on my bed, wanting to scream at the top of my lungs, but my throat was hurting, and my mouth was dry. I got some clothes and went to the bathroom, but it was still locked.

I didn't even wait; I just ran to my mom's room to use her bathroom instead. I almost passed out when I saw all the restraints and sex toys neatly stashed in the corner of their room. I felt nauseated and turned to run back to my room. I could hear Sénar coming up the steps; my heart almost stopped beating. I ran to my room and looked for the shorts he snatched off me to put them on, after realizing I was still half- naked. I could hear the bathroom door open and close. I got my stuff ready to go in there, for when it opened again. He was taking so long I banged on the door. He didn't answer, so I opened it, and he was taking a shower. I wanted to find something to throw in there to electrocute him, as he got out to grab a towel, I looked away.

He walked past me and said, "Your turn." He left the water running, and before leaving, he said, "Damn, girl, you are crazy as hell. Shoot, and I thought I was the crazy one."

He had not seen anything yet. If he didn't give me my chain before Tyrell came back, he would be sorry; I was fed up. I felt like I was losing my mind, along with the control over my body. I wanted to detach from my body to keep my heart and my mind for Tyrell. I was a mess; I was lost, and I needed to find myself, so I didn't end up in Lala Land like my mom. I didn't want to take a shower; I needed to relax in the bath for the rest of my life. I was so exhausted; I laid there for hours until I decided to slide my entire body into the water, including my head and face. The water covered my nose and mouth, and I held my breath, not wanting to come up for air anymore, I closed my eyes. Unable to take it any longer, when I felt myself drifting away, I came up for air and heard Sénar yelling my name.

In a daze, I weakly answered, "What Sénar?"

He pleaded with me, "Come out here, so we can eat and go to the store."

I laughed like a madwoman, "I'll be right there." I said in a happy tone. It sent chills up my spine as I felt like the voice came from an unknown place.

I got out after getting dressed, my body was sore and felt drained of energy. I put some jeans on, a V-neck white T-shirt and put my hair in a bun. I looked in the mirror and rubbed my hand over my chest, where Tyrell's name should be dangling from my chain. The space seemed as vacant as I felt after the chain having been there so long, and now it was gone. I felt rage creeping back into me, and I didn't have the energy stored to use it. So, I just left the safety of the bathroom and entered Sénar's world. I felt like my world was slipping away, having it snatched away like my chain, and the only way to get it back was through Sénar.

Not even feeling like myself as I exited the bathroom, Sénar asked, "You good, ma?"

I just nodded my head, yeah, and went to my room to put my shoes on. He waited for me at my door, watching my every move. I didn't have the energy to fight; I felt like a zombie. We got in the car and drove to the T-mobile store to replace his shattered phone. Sénar offered to get me one, but I didn't except or decline, I was quiet. They did all the paperwork for me to get one, and I just signed, not even listening to a word anyone said. I just nodded my head yes or no to whatever question they were intended for. When we got home, he told me he was going to warm up some leftovers, and we could chill after if I wanted to. While in the kitchen warming up leftovers, he started a conversation.

He said, "I have to make up all the hours I missed this week at work." I stared blankly at him and didn't respond. Sénar asked, "Treasure, what's wrong with you? You been smoking weed without me?" He laughed and then stopped when he realized I was not laughing or responding to his conversation. We ate leftovers in silence.

He asked if I wanted to smoke, I spoke for the first time in hours and replied, "I am really tired Sénar. I just want to go to sleep."

He looked a bit concerned when he took my plate and then cleaned up. I got up and went up the stairs in slow motion. When I got to my room, I fell on my bed and was out like a light bulb. I went to sleep in my clothes and woke up to Sénar sleeping on my floor. I wanted to step on his neck, but he turned over, startling me out of my murderous thoughts. It was like he had an invisible cord connected to my body, and sometimes, even my mind.

He asked, "Treasure, do you hate me?"

I stared at him and got up, ignoring his question to put my shoes on. I left the room and brushed my teeth as that was the least I could do. I left the same clothes on from last night and left out the front door. Sénar ran out after me and said, "Let me take you to school, and why didn't you change your clothes?"

I didn't say anything I got in the car and let him drive me to school in silence. I got out without saying anything and went to class. Leah said, "Dang girl, what's wrong with you?"

I looked at her and asked, "You wanna come over my house after school?"

She looked at me like I was crazy and responded with excitement, "Hell yeah!" I replied, "Cool," and did my work without another word to her. I went through the day like I was in a trance. In drama class, I gave everyone their roles, and everyone was so impressed, it was the first time I smiled for the whole day. Sénar came to pick us up after school, and I introduced the two of them. Sénar was super uncomfortable as she was really into him and didn't hide it.

He turned a different corner, and I asked him, "Where are you going, Sénar?"

He didn't answer, we pulled into the parking lot of a bowling alley and then asked with his sadistic smile, "Wanna go bowling?"

Leah answered, "Hell yeah!"

I was surprised, what kind of crap was Sénar pulling now? We got out and walked into the bowling alley. He paid for us both, we put our bowling shoes on and set up our lane to play. I was still confused, but I eventually figured out why we were there. Leah talked our ears off and made several advances toward Sénar. She was even annoying me when asking him questions about me. It was kind of creepy; she seemed to be interested in both of us at one point. Sénar raised his eyebrow in interest as she talked about how she wanted to try a threesome after she lost her virginity. I was annoyed with them both; they were both nuts. They were talking when it was my turn to bowl, so I threw the bowling ball with all my might, wishing it was the both of them and anyone else that I wanted to hit in my lifetime. I got a strike! I jumped up and down, celebrating my victory and turned around to see both of them gazing at me in a way that made me so uneasy. Sénar smiled first, and then Leah giggled. I was not feeling their little psycho bond; it felt dark and gave me a knot in my stomach. Sénar got up and grabbed a bowling ball and played his turn, he got a strike too, making me even more irritated. Leah got up to bowl, and Sénar checked her out, the same way they probably were when I went for my turn.

Sénar whispered, "Nice try, Treasure, just another toy in my toy box. But you will always be my favorite forever." He said as she walked back over toward us.

She didn't strike, but the way she was smiling, one would think she did. Sénar bought us all some food. We ate and talked while Sénar bragged about beating us in bowling. When we were done, we took her home. Leah offered her number, Sénar said flirtatiously, "I'll get it from Treasure."

She blew kisses at us and then got out. Sénar was cheesing, and I was so irritated because I had no idea what I had just got myself into. He advised me, "I would not bring her to our house ever. Her ass is for real crazy, and you have another admirer in your box too." He said with a dark smile that I had never seen before.

With another one of his brand-new smiles, this was just the beginning of a whole new game. He didn't bother me when we got home, and no matter how long this would last, I was grateful to have a break. I went to sleep, thinking it would be peaceful, but it was not. I had several disturbing nightmares and woke up sweating while gasping for air. Afraid to go back to sleep, I just wrote in my diary until I fell back asleep unknowingly.

Chapter 18

Sénar woke me up in the morning, standing in my doorway, gazing at me. When I noticed him, he warned, "You better get up before you're late again."

I looked at the time, and it was 8:30 am, I had to be to school in less than thirty minutes. I changed my clothes, not even caring that he was standing there. I went to the bathroom and brushed passed Sénar to brush my teeth since he didn't move out of the way. I combed my hair; I brushed my teeth and washed my face with Sénar watching me the whole time. When I finished, I went back to my room to grab my backpack, and Sénar was waiting for me in the hallway; He was like my shadow. He dropped me off at school, and I barely made it before the bell rung. My teacher pretended not to see me slip in the classroom after the bell. Leah saw me and was instantly excited.

She greeted me, "Hey, girl! Shoot, I saw you slip in here, real smooth with it." I ignored her comment as she was really annoying me already. She continued to run her mouth, "Sénar is fine as hell, and he is cool as fuck too! Damn, what is it like to live with his fine ass?"

I dryly responded, "Torture."

She laughed and said, "I bet! It would be hard for me too. I would never leave his bed!"

She seemed to be in a dreamy state; I continued to ignore her and let her think it was a joke. I spent the whole day in my mind, trying to sort out how I would make it through the next week, let alone the rest of my life. I was so messed up, and I couldn't tell a soul, not even

Sénar would understand. I tried to make it through the day and keep my composure as I knew I had one more class with Leah. Drama class was better than I thought, as we were busy practicing our roles for the play. Leah enjoyed her role as the bully and did a really good job. Almost too good of a job.

She had me feeling some kind of way when she then asked, "Are we going to your house after school?"

Totally caught off guard by her question, I had to think hard before I responded, "I am going to the library after this, and I think Sénar is working today."

She wasn't happy with my response, but I didn't care, I had to figure out a way to ward her off now too. She was invasive and needy. I decided to actually go to the library to corroborate the lie I told Leah. I was looking for a book when I thought about whether Sénar had come to pick me up and I wasn't there. I dismissed the thought quickly. Maybe he and Leah would find each other. Quite frankly, I didn't care about anything; I just wanted to find a good book. I chose *Rain* by V.C. Andrews and a book called *Midnight* by Sista Soulja. They both seemed like an interesting read. After spending some time in the library, I walked home. When I arrived home, Sénar's car was there with one parked behind it. When I went inside London and Sénar were arguing. He looked at me, and I knew he wanted to ask where I had been, but London was screaming in his ear. I just walked up the steps to my room without being disturbed. I got to my room and started to read the book, *Rain*. I heard the door slam and jumped up; I quietly opened my door to be nosey.

I heard London refusing to leave, and then I heard several footsteps coming up the stairs, so I closed my door quietly. They went to his room, so I snuck out to listen to his door. I heard London calling Sénar's name and moaning, but I didn't hear anything from Sénar. I snuck back to my room and continued to mind my business. I read a little bit more and wrote in my diary before I went to the bathroom to pee. As I was coming out, London was fixing her clothes and smirked at me, as if to brag.

I did an Indian accent, impersonation, "Come again!"

I giggled, and she glared at me then said, "Oh, I'll be back, little girl."

Sénar looked at me as if he was annoyed; I couldn't tell with whom. I was glad when she came over. I wanted her to keep him occupied, so he would leave me alone, even though it only worked sometimes. Sénar came to my room after he showered, he looked refreshed with his white tee and some basketball shorts. I ignored him even though he smelled good and looked like he was in a better mood than the last time I saw him. He said, "Sorry for the unexpected company. What took you so long to get home?"

I could not believe his audacity, after having screwed a whole person, he wanted to know what took me so long to come home. I answered, "Why?" It came out with an attitude, so I quickly added, "I went to the library."

Before he could say anything smart. He still replied, "You must not want that chain back, with that smart-ass mouth of yours."

I sat up, glaring at him, and said, "Sénar stop playing with me. What more do you want?"

He smiled at me and then answered, "I want it all."

I thought *what he could possibly be talking about*; he pretty much did everything he could do to me. He walked away, leaving me in my thoughts. I grabbed my diary, and vigorously wrote my emotions down as I could not hold them inside any longer. I felt like I was going insane. I wrote until tears fell on the paper of my diary. I was tired of crying, I was tired of being a victim, and I needed to figure something out.

Sénar came back into my room and asked, "What do you feel like eating?"

I couldn't even look at him; I didn't want him to see me crying, I answered, "I don't care whatever is fine with me."

305

He closed the door; I really didn't care. All I was going to do was eat and run into the bathroom after, no matter what crap he tried to pull. I couldn't even depend on my own body; it had a mind of its own. I couldn't trust anyone, not even myself. Tyrell probably had something up his sleeve as well. Leah, I didn't even know her, and she wanted something for nothing too. Everyone wanted something at my expense, and I really just wanted to be left alone. The only person I still wanted to be around was Tyrell, and it seemed like he hated me. If he kept rejecting me, I would eventually reject him back; I was starting to get fed up. I even had some hatred for Tyrell as I blamed him for being an insecure asshole. He was bigger, smarter, and a better athlete than Sénar. He even had the one girl Sénar wanted and was still a loser in the situation. I needed him to man up to protect me and stop leaving me hanging every time he got his feelings hurt. I tried to convince myself that if he had not left me hanging again, none of this would have happened or at least not as much. I didn't know, but someone had to take the blame, not just me. I was in my thoughts when Sénar called for me to come downstairs to eat. I almost declined until I smelled the food.

Sénar made tacos, he had already made our plates and cleaned the kitchen before he called me down. I was already cautious when I saw that he had done all of that before calling me down because that was part of my exit plan, to escape while he cleaned up. I was disappointed that I had to come up with another plan.

We ate in silence until he asked, "I'm about to run some errands. You wanna smoke before I leave?"

I was cautious, but I was hoping it would help me sleep, so I said, "Yeah, I guess."

He asked, "Are you going to be cool while big daddy is gone?"

I looked at him like he was stupid then said, "I am a big girl, the only person I have to worry about is you."

He laughed and said, "Whatever, you don't even believe that."

I frowned at him while he passed me the blunt, saying, "I am not going to be gone long anyway. I just need to get me some more trees and pick up my little ass check."

I shrugged my shoulders to insinuate that I did not care. I hit it again and passed it back to him. He was in his thoughts when he passed it back to me. I hit it two more times and was so high; I started smiling for no reason, Sénar was grinning too.

He said, "I should stay, huh?"

I laughed and answered, "Heck, no, you should not."

We both laughed, Sénar chin upped me and left after making sure I came in the house before he left. I raced upstairs to take a bath. I let the water run and pulled the showerhead down, placing it between my legs, thinking of Tyrell, and all of the fun we use to have in the mornings before school. I pictured him kissing and touching me all over. I was so high everything felt times ten, I moaned freely without worrying about anyone hearing me. It felt so good; the more intense the feeling got, the more my thoughts flashed back to all the things Sénar did to me. I tried to think of something different, but it was so many thoughts flashing of him licking me and kissing me. I started to squirm as I could not control my thoughts any longer. My body was tensing up as Sénar's face flashed, sending a shock of electricity through my body, I squeezed the showerhead and yelled as I climaxed. A new word I learned helped me explain what I felt when I was in the shower or when my body was being handled by Sénar. I also realized there are different levels of pleasure, which was insane. Feeling ashamed of my inability to control, not just my body but even my thoughts, I went to bed wondering how many levels I had experienced and how many was there left.

In the morning, I woke up to the aroma of breakfast and followed the smell downstairs. Sénar was cooking in his typical attire, no shirt on, and some basketball shorts. I couldn't help but compare Sénar's body to Tyrell's. Although I never saw Tyrell fully naked, his body was definitely more developed than Sénar's. He was bigger in every aspect all the way down to their man sticks. Unfortunately, I had more experience with Sénar than I did with my own boyfriend.

I was starting to think way too hard when Sénar said, "Good morning, sleepyhead."

He was smiling like he was super happy to see me. I rolled my eyes, and anxiously waited for my plate. He gave me my plate and said, "So, I shouldn't have any unexpected company today. My bad, you know, she just wouldn't take no for an answer." He said with his hands in the air. Once again, another eye-rolling moment for me, I just ignored him and ate my food. When I was done, I got up and washed my plate. He got up to give me his plate to wash, too; I sighed out of annoyance. He watched me as I washed the plates and then handed me two pots.

Then he asked, "So, what are we doing today?"

I looked at him like he was crazy and replied, "We aren't doing anything. Isn't London by the phone waiting for your call? Or better yet, don't you have a new toy to play with?"

He smirked at me then replied, "I want to play with you; I would give all my toys up for you."

I was tired of rolling my eyes, so I smacked my lips and finished the dishes. When I was done, I tried to walk out of the kitchen, but Sénar grabbed me by the back of my pants. I put my hand behind my back and slapped his hand away, but he wrapped his arms around the top of my body. He squeezed me close to him then smelled my hair. I asked, unable to escape his grip, "What is it with you, Sénar?"

He turned me around to face him and said, "You drive me crazy, Treasure."

I was confused and curious and asked, "Why?"

He shrugged his shoulders and replied, "I don't know." And then walked away. He turned around to say, "Come on, let's go to the movies and see *Rush Hour 2*."

I swear if he had said any other movie, I would have said no, but I loved the first *Rush Hour* movie. I said, "Fine, but when are you going to give me my chain Sénar?"

He laughed and replied, "What's so important about your little necklace, anyway?"

I ignored his question because it was stupid, and I didn't want to give him more reasons to use it as collateral. I just went to get dressed. We smoked a blunt before we left for the movies. He was nice enough to drive our way to Rancho Cucamonga to go see it, so we wouldn't run into a bunch of people we knew. The movie was hilarious; we laughed the whole time. When we got back home, we smoked again and talked for a bit in the garage. I was ready to go to bed, but Sénar wanted me to watch TV with him. I knew that was not the case, so I declined. Then he told me what he really wanted, and I declined that as well. He didn't even bother to fight about it; he let me go to sleep peacefully.

In the morning, Sénar came to my room and woke me up with a treaty. I listened carefully. His proposition and terms were as stated, "If you let me have one night where you let me show you a couple of things my way, I'll give you your chain back before they come home."

I got mad at him and retorted, "No, Sénar! What more can you do to me?"

He had a sadistic smile on his face and replied, "You have no idea."

Disgusted with him, I told him to get out of my room, but he didn't budge. He climbed into my bed and laid next to me. I scooted over, making sure our bodies didn't touch. Then he whined, "Damn, you're so stingy and mean."

I went back to sleep and woke up to him being gone. I was happy he was gone and took a shower, making sure I had everything I needed before going into the bathroom. I didn't want to make the mistake of thinking he was gone, and he wasn't. When I got out of the shower to dry off, I noticed all my stuff was gone. I looked on the side of the toilet to see if it fell, I scanned the floor to make sure I didn't drop it on the way in. I took a deep breath and braced myself because, unless I was losing my mind, my clothes had disappeared. The only way for them to disappear as if someone took them.

I opened the door to the bathroom and yelled out, "Sénar! Where's my stuff?"

I peeked out of the bathroom, and the house was quiet. I ran to my room to open the door, but I quickly turned around after changing my mind. I tiptoed to Sénar's room to throw him off. He wasn't there, so I locked the door behind me and looked for one of his T-shirts to cover my wet body. I quickly searched through his things looking for my chain until I heard his door handle move. I saw some pictures of me in one of his drawers, but I couldn't get a good look at them before he opened his door. He looked irritated and said, "You are funny." He closed the door behind him and locked it. He asked, "Did you find what you were looking for?" I nervously shook my head no. He whispered, "Well, I did." He walked over to me to put his hand under my chin and kissed me. I moved back, wiping my mouth off as he pulled me back toward him, he then sat down on his bed. He lifted his T-shirt that I had put on, he gently rubbed his hand over my stomach and then all over my breast.

I pushed his hand away and asked, "Sénar, where's my chain?"

He laughed at me; I was getting angry again to overcome the feeling of being vulnerable and desperate. He stood up to take his shirt off and then his pants while grabbing my hand to place it on his member. My heartbeat started to accelerate as his member grew in my hand. I tried to snatch my hand away from him unsuccessfully. Sénar then asked me, "How bad do you want that chain?"

I whined, "Sénar, please, just give it to me."

I wanted to cry when Sénar said, "Well, get down on your knees and show me how bad you want it then."

A knot formed in my stomach, contorting my face as I replied, "No, Sénar! I don't even know or even want to know what you are talking about!"

He looked at me like I was being stupid. My eyes almost popped out of my head when I visualized what he was talking about. I snapped, "Hell, no! I don't even know how to do that!"

He pulled me by the back of my neck with his other hand and kissed me, letting my other hand go to put his hand in between my legs. I pushed him off, and he released me. I tried to leave, but he blocked me and then pushed me down onto his bed. He said, "Fine, then let me show you how bad I want you."

He pried my legs open to suck and nibble on my coochie then slipped his fingers inside of me. I muffled my moans as I tried to move away; he pushed my stomach down to keep me where he wanted me. I squirmed and pushed his head back, trying to make it as difficult as possible for him. He spread his fingers, slipping one into my coochie and the other into my butthole; I almost sprang up to a sitting position before he pushed me back down. He moved his fingers in and out so rapidly; I yelled, "Sénar, please stop!" I felt an indescribable amount of pleasure and pain intertwined, rippling through my body that caused me to shiver in sheer shock. He got up to get on top of me, entering me softly as I was still recovering from his double finger stunt.

He slowly thrusted himself in and out of me while whispering, "Damn Treasure, you should be mine; I like it better like this." He took his time stroking me slowly while kissing my breast, my neck, and all over my face. He smelled my hair as I lay there and let him have his way with me. He took his T-shirt off me and marveled at me in my nakedness. I closed my eyes, not wanting him to look into my eyes. He laid back down, flipping me over on top of him while grinding me from the bottom and holding me close to him. My heartbeat was accelerating along with the feeling of my coochie gripping his member tightly, while Sénar pumped his lust into me. I moved in unison with him, feeling pleasure rise to my nipples, as I now gyrated on top of him. He released me in a trance, I sat up arching my back and tilted my head to the back. I moved wildly on top of him until it felt like lightning mixed with thunder was surging through my body. Sénar was struggling to hold himself together as I continued to grind on top of him.

He called my name, "Treasure?" I didn't answer; I kept grinding even harder. Sénar called my name again, "Treasure? Damn. Treasure? Oh, shit!" Sénar tried to get my attention, but I just kept grinding until he screamed my name, "Treasure!" I felt a hot explosion inside of me, my body shuddering from the intense sensations flowing through it until I went limp on top of him. Sénar was at a loss for words as he laid under me and tried to catch his breath; I rolled over and went to sleep.

I innately woke up to the smell of food. I looked around, realizing I was still in Sénar's room, naked and lying in his bed. I quickly got up and left my room to get dressed. I put the shorts, undergarments, and shirt on that I had prepared earlier as they were on my dresser folded neatly when I got to my room. After I got dressed, I headed downstairs feeling ashamed once again. My body was so greedy when it came to pleasure, no matter how much pain it had to endure before or after, especially with Sénar. I tried not to dwell on it because I was hungry and was still trying to digest what happened without guilt. I went to the kitchen as Sénar was putting our plates on the counter. He saw me and smiled the same smile I saw the day we first smoked in the backyard, which was my absolute favorite smile. The only one he had that made me feel safe.

Sénar gazed at me and said, "Hey, Treasure."

Sénar was trying not to blush but made me blush instead. To avoid eye contact, I looked down at my plate that he put in front of me. I must say it was beautifully prepared. The plate had grits, eggs, bacon, and sausage cooked to perfection with some toast he sat on the side. He even had the nerve to have some fruit on the side with a flower in the middle. There was some Donald Duck orange juice already poured in our glasses. I was so impressed by the presentation; I had to voice it, "Awe, this is awesome!"

He winked at me and said, "And, so are you." I smiled, bashfully, and rolled my eyes as it was starting to get uncomfortable again. We ate and talked about the movie *Rush Hour 2* and how it didn't disappoint, being just as funny as the first one. For a minute, I put all my thoughts on the side to embrace the moment. He listened attentively to me tell him all about the play that I wrote and would be rehearsing for. I was so excited to tell him that the play was picked for the final act on the last day of summer school this week.

He smiled proudly and asked, "Oh, so you got writing skills, huh?"

I looked at him confidently and answered, "Oh, most definitely."

He looked at me like I was doing too much and then shook his head. We avoided talking about what happened this morning as we were both embarrassed, for our own reasons. We just chilled the rest of the day and made and ate the next two meals together, not even bothering to go anywhere. Sénar's phone rung the entire day, and he just ignored it. After dinner, Sénar asked, "Where's your phone?" I left it on my dresser and totally forgot about it. He came to my room and then sat down on my bed to show me how to set up and work my phone. He gave me his number and told me to call him if I needed anything because he would be working a lot during the week; to make up the hours missed from last week. I smiled nervously when I thought about why we're both deemed irresponsible last week.

He said, "So, I won't be here to wake yo' sleepy ass up. I am not going to be able to take you or pick you up from school either, but I'll see what I can work out."

I replied, "It's cool; we can't get used to that anyway."

He looked a little disappointed, but chin upped me before leaving my room to go to his room. The day was strange but somehow awesome. Monday morning, I used my cellphone as an alarm to wake me up on time. Without the alarm, I probably would have overslept, being I haven't slept that well in a long time. I grabbed my clothes and took a shower to avoid the urge to masturbate. As I was feeling a little feisty with all the energy, I restored from sleeping so well. I used the toilet before leaving the bathroom and noticed some red spotting on the tissue. I didn't know whether to be happy or sad. Happy because having a period was a good sign, or sad because it was a gross process that I absolutely hated for many reasons. I got a pad from under the counter, and it was the only one left. I panicked, thinking about how I would get more. I didn't want to be late to school, so I grabbed my things and left out thinking that I would figure it out later. I was full of life when I got to school, and Leah noticed right away.

She blurted out, "Damn, girl; you are cheesin'! Looking all bright-eyed and bushy-tailed."

I ignored her over-exaggeration and paid attention to the teacher until she asked, "What, you got some bomb D over the weekend, huh?"

I looked back at her, both curiously and annoyed. I asked, "What are you talking about?"

She laughed until she realized I was seriously waiting for her to elaborate. She again asked, "You know, bomb D?"

I shook my head, trying not to seem too lame. She continued, "You know, bomb dick, Schlong, wang, wood, swipe, cock, beef?"

I winced to get her to stop elaborating and then responded, "Um no, and why is your mouth so vulgar?"

She replied, "Girl, please, that's what it is, what do you call it?"

Annoyed with her questions, I answered, "I don't know. I don't talk about it to call it anything."

Feeling a little stupid for not knowing what I referred to it as, other than member or man stick, or its intended name, "*penis*," which she didn't even mention. I wanted to change the subject, so I said, "I don't know, sheesh. Leah, can we change the subject now?"

She wasn't satisfied with my answer and asked, "Well, you got a pussy; what do you call that?"

Now I was frustrated; I just ignored her until she named off her nicknames for it. She again elaborated, "Pussy, punanny, Squase, cooter, Poon-tang, cunt, taco-," Cutting her off.

I said, "Ok, I get it! Dang, I call it coochie, I guess. Damn, since we are talking about coochie now, do you have a maxi pad?"

She looked at me with a disgusted look on her face and responded, "Girl ugh, hell no. But I got a tampon, though." She went into her bag and gave me one, and I looked at it like it was a foreign object. She laughed then said, "Girl, you are a square. How do you deal with the finest niggas in the universe and not even know these things that I am talking about?"

Offended, I snapped, "Um, to be a virgin, you sure know a lot."

She replied with an attitude, "Yeah, but I didn't say I was retarded or that I ain't ever gave no head?"

She was really tripping me out, what the hell was she talking about? She saw my expression and asked, "Oh, so you never sucked a dick now? Or what do you call it a blow job?"

I was blown away, the girls sitting in front of us started snickering. That was it; she was going too far; I was done with our conversation. She was completely out of line at this point. I totally ignored her question and did the work the teacher passed out to help prepare us for the test this coming Wednesday. She smacked her lips when she realized she was being ignored and reluctantly focused on her work. When the bell rung, I ran out of there so quickly; she couldn't even get out of her seat in time. I went to my next couple of classes and tried to erase our conversation out of my brain, but I wanted to know more about things that I was not as aware of. I would do my own research and not take advice or information from someone like Leah, who was completely obnoxious. Drama class was next, and I really needed to prepare myself for Leah as she was getting on my nerves. Everyone was excited about rehearsal and playing their roles.

As everyone practiced their part, Leah whispered in my ear, "How do you have a boyfriend like Tyrell, and you are such a square?"

Offended, I answered, "Maybe, that's why I do have one."

I rolled my eyes at her and self-consciously wondered if I even had one anymore. She was really on my last nerves before she could say anything else, I asked, "Are you going to practice your role or not?"

She smacked her lips and rehearsed with malice in her voice while she practiced bullying me with pleasure. When the bell rang, she asked, "So, when am I going to your house?"

Not wanting this to end awkwardly, I answered, "I am going to the library after school, and I really never had anyone come over for me at my house before. So, I gave Sénar your number, and he will call you eventually, I guess."

She looked at me with an attitude and said, "Sometimes I think you're trying to keep him for yourself!"

My mouth fell open in shock of her accusation. I was ready to snatch her by her fake ass ponytail when she turned away and walked off. That was it; after this summer session, I was done with her crazy ass. Sénar was right about her; she was crazy as hell. I didn't have time for her little games and mood swings. I went to the library to pick some more books to read that would advance my slang terms and knowledge of our anatomy.

When I got home, I was still irritated, but I just opened my book *Midnight* by Sista Soulja. I read very attentively to any sex scenes or verbiage regarding sex. I immediately noticed things that I may have read and just never paid attention to before. I even got aroused while reading some of the sex scenes thinking about my own experiences. I was really into the book when I was startled by my behind vibrating. I felt around my pocket, grabbing my phone and answering it.

Sénar's voice was full of anticipation when he asked, "What's up, ma?"

I tried not to smile and just answered, "Hey."

Sénar then asked, "I am about to go to the store you need anything?"

I quickly answered, "No," but then I remembered that I had to take the nasty tampon I stuck up my coochie earlier out eventually. I said, "Wait, um yeah."

"Aiight, what you need?"

I was embarrassed to ask, but I really needed it, so I reluctantly hinted around "Um well I need somethings, that I ran out of, but if you take-"

He cut me off, "Treasure what you need some maxis or tampons or something?"

I was so embarrassed. I almost hung up, "Treasure?"

I was reluctant to answer, "Yeah, but no tampons."

He laughed and said, "Ok, I got chu ma. Shit, I rather buy those than a pregnancy test!"

He chuckled, and I hung upon him. It was not funny, and it was already a difficult conversation. I went back to reading my book. Sénar knocks and then comes in. I thought to myself, oh how sweet of him to knock. He came in and saw me all into my book, lying in my bed. He stood there until I acknowledged him.

I finished reading my last sentence and put the book under my eyes and said, "Hey, Sénar."

He looked at me and asked, "Damn, what are you reading? It must be good."

He came in and put the bag on my bed and rolled his sleeves up on his uniform that I had never seen before. He went through the bag, and I snatched it from him. He looked at me like I was nuts and said, "I was going to show you the different ones I got you."

I laughed then said, "No thanks, spare me the details."

He snickered and sat next to me. I opened the bag and laughed when I saw morning, noon, and night pictures on three different packages of Playtex Wings. They were really good ones too. I looked up and said, "Thanks Sen-"

He kissed me and rubbed my hair. I pushed him back gently, "Sénar, stop. My goodness." I said, trying not to make him mad and, at the same time, ignore my coochie pulsating as a result.

He smiled at me, "Next time, if it makes you feel more comfortable, just ask for band-aids for your kitty cat." He joked and giggled before leaving.

I threw my pillow at him and missed. I picked the nighttime maxi since it was almost night time and went to the bathroom. I looked for the string and couldn't find it. I panicked and was seconds from asking Senar for help as I thought I lost the tampon until I finally found it after a very uncomfortable search. I was so relieved when I found it; I pulled it out like it would try to escape. I vowed never to use once again as I wrapped it in tissue and stuffed in the empty maxi bag, I tied it and ran to take it outside. When I came back in, he was waiting for me by the door. Seeing Tyrell's car made me think about my necklace that was being held, hostage.

I walked in and asked, "Sénar, when are you going to give me my necklace back?" I asked with my arms crossed.

He looked at me and became instantly agitated when I asked. He stared at me and said, "When I feel like it."

I walked away, irritated. I went to sit on the couch with an attitude. He went into the kitchen, ignoring my attitude, and started to make dinner. It was way later than we normally eat, it was close to eight o'clock at night, and we would be done eating by seven o'clock or seven thirty at the latest. He called me to the kitchen. I almost didn't go, but I went just took my sweet time instead.

I pouted, "What?" He raised his brow. I looked at him with an attitude as I was still upset about my necklace. He ignored my attitude and told me to cut the fries. I huffed and puffed, but I tried to remember how he liked his fries cut. I washed the potatoes really well to make sure the skin was clean, then cut them in slices of four, and then cut them into lines. It took way longer than Sénar would have taken, but I still had all my fingers, and I think I did a good job.

He looked over his shoulder and started cheesing, "Look at you, Chef Treasure. Ooh, you gonna put on a show." He said with a sadistic smile and bit his lip.

318

I rolled my eyes at him, ignoring his comment and his devious behavior to rinse the potatoes I put in a bowl. He came up behind me as I was washing the cut potatoes startling me, making me jump wasting water on my shirt and the top of my pants. He whispered in my ear, "Well, you are a fast learner."

He wrapped his arms around me from behind and smelled my hair. I froze for a second and nudged him with my shoulder before saying, "Move Sénar." He lifted my wet shirt over my head and used it to dry off my stomach like he would do when he made a mess of it. I took a deep breath when he whispered, "You can keep your pants on, though." He laughed while taking the bowl from me; he then poured the water out correctly. He seasoned the potatoes, and then gave instructions, "Ok, now you can sit pretty."

I started to go put another shirt on, but he made it obvious what he wanted me to do. I still tried to go sit on a chair when he called my name, "Treasure?" I ignored him calling my name and sat on the counter instead to avoid an altercation of any sort. He flipped our burger patties and toasted the bread. He got the lettuce and tomatoes for him to cut; he said, "I can't risk the tomatoes." He laughed.

He made the burgers and didn't ask me what I wanted on mine; he just made it with cheese, lettuce, tomatoes, mayo, and mustard. It was delicious and juicy. Damn, if he did nothing right, the boy could cook that was for certain. We both had to get up in the morning, so we went to bed after he tried to bribe me to stay downstairs to watch TV. I was bleeding like a gutted pig and wanted no parts in his shenanigans. He didn't seem to care to try to bribe me into his traps. I declined to say, "Umm, thank you for dinner, but I am going to bed." I ran up the steps before he could say anything.

I used my alarm clock again, as it was really effective for getting me up on time. I went to school in a good mood and totally focused on my work, not giving Leah the chance to distract me in with her chatter. The day went quickly, as I focused on my work and rehearsed in drama class, not letting or anyone else distract us from practicing. I walked home and looked across the street at Tyrell's house, and it seemed empty. I read and wrote in my diary until I was bored. I was starting to get hungry when my phone rang.

I answered, "Hello?"

Sénar responded, "Hey ma, sorry I didn't call earlier, you need anything?"

I answered, "No."

He said, "I am working over, and I won't be home 'til later, but there is some chicken salad in the refrigerator."

I tried not to show my excitement and responded, "Ok, Sénar, you don't have to check-in."

He responded, "I know that just like I know your ass is hungry right now. Anyway, see you later, ma."

I ate the chicken salad and was in food heaven for a minute before taking a shower. I tried to think of everything, but Sénar, when I was masturbating, I even tried to think of the chicken salad that was so pleasurable to my mouth. Nothing worked as it always ended with Sénar's face or his actions that was able to carry me over to a climax. It was late, and it was a little lonely, so I crawled in bed to read until I could fall asleep. Sénar was gone until like 10 o'clock I was already in the bed when he got home.

He let me know he was back; he looked so tired when he said, "Good night, ma." We went to bed without any shenanigans.

I was focused every day this week as it was the last week and needed to pass all my classes with flying colors. It was Wednesday, and I was excited we only had one day for our big show. Leah didn't say much to me in math class because we had a test. I went through all my classes and tied any loose ends finishing any extra credit assignments and even got grades for some classes. My day went by so quickly I was home before I knew it. Lying in bed and reading when Sénar called me again to let me know he was working late. This was a lucky week. I just took a bath and masturbated every-time I had the house to myself for the last two days. I was getting prepared to deal with my sexual frustration in the future in a more appropriate way until me and Tyrell were to the level where could help fulfill each-others' sexual desires. I was hoping he would be out of his feelings when he returned, so we could move on, and I could put all these unadulterated sexcapades behind me. I just had to figure out what I was going to do with Sénar's crazy ass and how I was going to get my chain back. I took a bath and made me a fancy chicken salad sandwich for dinner since chef Sénar was so busy working this week. I got in bed and read until Sénar came home and said good night to me before going to bed.

It was finally Thursday, and my week was definitely going smooth compared to the last two weeks. I was excited to get my grades and have our last rehearsal before the play tomorrow. I sat down in morning class, and Leah acted like she didn't see me walk in, and I was totally fine with that. I just listened to the teacher tell us we would receive our grades for the summer session tomorrow. Every other class I got my grades for, and I was pleased that I had all As I just needed math to be an A for a perfect summer session. I went home and thought of Tyrell when I saw his car parked there and just hoped he would be back soon. I read in my room for a while until I was bored and took a bath. I was hungry, and Sénar hadn't called, so I figured he was probably taking my advice that he didn't have to check-in. I made myself a fancy Peanut butter and jelly sandwich and watched some TV too excited to sleep. Sénar came in a little after 9:30 pm and saw me sitting on the couch watching TV. He came to the living room and sat down on the couch. He looked tired and frustrated as he set his phone down on the table.

He said, "What's up, ma?"

I looked at him and said, "Hey."

He put his head back and said, "I would have called you, but someone blew my phone up until it died"

After his third day of working over, I almost felt sorry for him as he looked drained. I replied, "Hey, Sénar, what's up with the uniform?"

I didn't care that he hadn't called or that he had a crazy girlfriend. With his eyes closed, he answered, "I got a different position, and it requires me to wear this uniform for the different jobs I do there."

I was curious to know what he did, so I asked, "What do you do there?"

I was nosey, but he tried to be patient with me and answered, "I am being trained in mechanics, I transport cars to different locations, and do maintenance on different machines." He looked at me, "Enough about me. Did you eat?"

I answered, "Yeah, I ate something."

He laughed and said, "I bet, what did you eat?"

I confidently said, "A peanut butter and jelly sandwich."

He replied, "A PBJ? Damn, I failed you tonight, huh?"

I wrinkled my eyebrows at him and responded, "Um no, my sandwich was very satisfying trust me. Well, since you are so fancy, what did you eat?"

He sighed then answered, "Nothing yet, I'll figure something out"

I snapped at him and asked, "What, you don't eat peanut butter and jelly sandwiches?"

He closed his eyes again then answered, "I'm mean yeah, I guess, but It's been a while, sweetheart."

I rolled my eyes at Sénar and then asked, "Well, do you want me to make you one?"

He smiled his special smile for me, then said, "Awe, you are so cute. Yeah ma, I'll take one, but I have to go shower and get out of these clothes. I'll be back." He showered and then and came back down. I was sitting on the counter, waiting for him to come down and jumped off the counter when he came down. His eyes lit up as he bit his bottom lip and said, "Where's my food, woman?" He laughed and tried to grab me.

I slapped his hand away and put my hands out and said, "This is Chef Treasure's show!"

He laughed at me when I said, "Now sit pretty."

He smiled at me and hopped on the counter to watch me. I toasted his bread and Sénar made a face and asked, "Girl, what the Hell are you doing?"

I looked at him and gestured my hand for him to shush before saying, "This is the Chef Treasure show, Sénar." He sat on the counter, confused, and watched me. I put the peanut butter on the toast while it was still hot and spread the jelly out evenly on the other toast as they cooled. I cut the two sandwiches in half and served them to him on a plate. I poured him a cold glass of milk and gave him a napkin.

He laughed and said, "Well, I have never had a toasted PBJ, but hey, we only live once."

I rolled my eyes once again and watched him eat his food. His first bite, he was shocked at how good it tasted toasted. He drank his milk and looked like a happy camper to me. When he got to his last bite, he looked at me and asked, "You want some?" He laughed and threw it in his mouth, then drank the last of his milk. He rubbed his stomach and said, "That was the best peanut butter and jelly sandwich I ever had in my life, Treasure." He pulled me in between his legs and said, "Thanks," Chef Treasure." He tried to grab my coochie and said, "Is your kitty cat still wearing a band-aid?"

I slapped his hand away and said, "Stop weirdo!" He jumped down from the counter, and I walked into the living room to watch TV before he asked. We laid on the couch to watch TV, and I let him lay his head on my stomach if he promised to be good, he was sleeping within fifteen minutes. I fell asleep not too long after too. Before I knew I was being woke up by my alarm.

I got up, and my cellphone rang, I answered, "Hello?"

Sénar replied, "I am just making sure you're up for your big day."

I assured him I was up and went to get dressed. I put on a cute jean skirt and a pink top with my pink Saucony shoes to match. I put my hair in two buns and looked like a black Chun Li from *Street Fighter*.

When I left to walk to school, I looked across the street, and it looked like Tyrell's car had been moved, but I quickly dismissed the thought as wishful thinking while I continued to walk to school. When I got to my math class, I was nervous and excited as we all anticipated getting our final grades. When the teacher passed me my grade, and I saw that I got an A, I was super excited and noticed Leah was happy with her B as she did not appear to care.

Leah's rolled her eyes at me and stated, "I passed, shit who cares; it's just summer school."

I guess she was practicing her role as a bully to prepare herself for our play tonight. I, too, just rolled my eyes and ignored her hating. The day went quickly, being that our last class was used for rehearsal. Everyone practiced their short skits, and we prepared for our final play. We all decided it would be cool to interact with the audience as part of the scene for the talk show. We were all super excited as Leah had already taken on her role early on in the day with her little attitude. I ignored her as she was already on my last nerve. We did perform our play and involved the audience and let them give input scanning the crowd I saw Sénar in the midst of the people cheesing. I was happy to see him as I was not expecting him to be there. I, even for a moment, thought I saw Tyrell. I was tripping ever since this morning, I kept feeling he was somewhere lurking but never was really sure. Leah definitely added to her lines and used the opportunity for personal attacks against me during the play, but I stayed on course, not showing her any reaction to it. The audience loved the show so much; we received a standing ovation as we all bowed. After the show, I spotted Sénar again, making eye contact with him and smiled at him. People made their way over to me after the show to congratulate and encouraged me to pursue a writing career. While everyone stopped to encourage me, Leah made her way over to Sénar. I finally made it to Sénar as he watched me the whole time until I made my way to him.

He clapped his hands and said, "Great show Treasure." He had a goofy smile on his face.

I rolled my eyes as he messaged my ego when Leah chimed in and said, "Umm, she wasn't the only one in the show."

Sénar acknowledged her, "Leah, your performance was superb, best bully ever!" She smiled, not aware of his sarcasm. He turned his attention back to me, "Come on, let's go celebrate!"

Leah got excited, "I can come, right?" Me and Sénar looked at her, answered at the same time: Sénar said, "Yeah." And I said, "No."

Leah replied, "Well, I guess I'll go with Sénar's answer."

She smirked at me and crossed her arms. Sénar looked at me like a little kid that got in trouble when I cut my eyes at him. We headed out to his car; I got in on his side to sit in the back seat. Leah rode in the front seat, now she was really feeling herself. Sénar took us to Denny's to eat where we talked about the play and some of the plans for the next school year. I wasn't really in the mood to eat, and every chance Leah got to cut me off, she took it. She made several advances at Sénar and tried her best to appear knowledgeable in every subject bought up. I could tell by Sénar's facial expression that he regretted bringing her. We left and pulled up to Leah's house, leaving her highly disappointed she was being dropped off.

Leah asked, "Sénar, Treasure gave you my number, right?"

For a second, I really did feel like a hater because I had not given him her number. Sénar looked at me in the rear-view mirror and then responded, "Oh yeah, she gave it to me, but I have been working a lot. I'll hit you up sometime soon."

Leah looked at me with a nasty smirk on her face and said, "Goodnight, Bonquisha, I'm mean Treasure."

I rolled my eyes and waved my hand at her saying, "Girl, bye Felicia."

She got out and walked to Sénar's side of the car and kissed him on the cheek. He said goodnight to her and told me to get in the front seat. I declined and folded my arms with an attitude. Sénar asked, "Why are you pouting?" He then added sarcastically, "Aren't you the one who was playing Cupid?" I ignored his question, and he pleaded with me, "Awe,

Treasure, don't do me like that ma." He watched me in the back seat as I sat quietly. When we got home, he pulled bags out the trunk and told me, "Our real celebration and dinner is in these bags."

I was glad to hear that we both barely ate at Denny's as we both ordered a salad and barely finished it. He pulled out steak, potatoes, and asparagus. He bragged about his boy getting him some bottles of Alizé because he was old enough. He prepared our food while I drank some Alizé and watched the Chef Sénar show. He was so goofy and happy. I felt like we were in a temporary dream world. We ate and laughed as we talked about Leah's crazy ass. When we were done eating, we cleaned up together and hit a blunt. We smoked in the backyard, not knowing when Ken and my mom would return instead of the garage. Our bellies were full, and we were high as a kite after a long day, but we still played and chased each other through the house. He threw me on the couch playfully, getting on top of me and said, "Let's play a game called Sénar says."

I pushed him off of me and said, "No!"

He laughed but still took my clothes off, starting with my shirt. He stood in front of me, gazing at me, and said, "I want some dessert, and I could be yours."

I saw his member grow before my eyes, and I got quiet before I responded, "No. I told you I don't even know how to do that."

I looked away, feeling embarrassed and ashamed for even being in the situation in the first place. Debating my next move, he interrupted my thoughts when he spoke, "Well, I will be your tutor. I hold classes on-"

I cut him off and said, "Boy shut up."

I rolled my eyes and pushed his body from in front of my face. He got down on his knees; I was starting to get nervous and said, "Sénar, we should not be doing this."

He sighed and said, "Girl, just sit back and enjoy the ride."

He slid my panties off from under my skirt and kissed me passionately as he removed my bra. I couldn't help but cover myself, knowing I should not be participating. He spread my legs to nibble and suck on my hot middle, sliding his fingers inside of me while rubbing all over my body with his other hand. He pulled his two-hole two-finger stunt again while he sucked and licked all over my stomach. I was in a world of pleasure as he handled my body and pushed all my buttons. I was really tipsy from the Alizé and the blunt we smoked, making me feel a sense of euphoria as he caressed every part of my body. He stood up and pulled me off the couch while my body quivered with unbearable sensations and switched spots with me, he took my skirt off as I stood in front of him and pulled me down to the ground onto my knees. He bit his bottom lip as he scanned my naked body and then said, "Senar says lick it and suck on it, like you did that ice cream cone you were eating."

He winked at me, and I felt the throbbing of my coochie start back up as I positioned myself to follow his instructions. I wanted to ask about my chain first, but it was like he could read my mind and said, "Don't say a word."

He grabbed my neck and stuck his tongue in my mouth and kissed me deeply before guiding my head to his hard member waiting for the wetness of my mouth. I closed my eyes and opened my mouth, feeling the warmth of the tip on my lips before I felt his whole member fill my mouth up. He moaned as I went forward, not knowing what to do. Next, he pulled me up when he felt my molars grinding the tip of his member. Sénar quickly stopped me and said, "Oh no, you definitely need a tutor ma. I'm available for tutoring whenever you want, but I want to get some without injury, so come here."

Worried, I asked, "Did I hurt you, Sénar?"

He smiled and said, "Nah, but it was a little too risky."

He then helped me up off the floor. Embarrassed now, I almost wanted to call it a night because this was not even supposed to be happening. I was naked and standing in front of him while he gazed at me until I asked, "What are you doing, Sénar?"

He eagerly answered, "I am taking in the moment. I don't know when I'll get this opportunity again." He got up and kissed me and then turned the TV off. He gathered our clothes and went upstairs. He took me to my room, and we played a game of Sénar says.

ABOUT AUTHOR

Born and raised in California, I grew up in the Inland Empire during a time where families were strong and thriving. I went to what I think some really great schools with really great teachers. All my memories and experiences molded me into who I am today. Right along with my close-knit family and friends, I managed to make it out unscathed. I had my experiences in life, but through them all, I am here.

I met some pretty phenomenal people on my journey to becoming who I am today. I have been in the nursing field for over 15 years, from one end of the spectrum to the other. Lastly, working in mental health as I was drawn to that population to bring hope and the desire to recover. I worked hard to get through school and build a career that would sustain me and my family. After having one of the most traumatic events in my lifetime happen to me, I thought all that I had worked for would be snatched from me in a blink of an eye. On the brink of losing everything, even myself at one point, I thought I would never be able to overcome my situation. I survived the chaos, pain, and suffering, through God's love, I was able to be resilient, and that is why my motto stands: Resilience Breeds Brilliance. I am a living testimony to that motto and plan to bring others to hope to be resilient at all costs!

As for my reason for writing, it is my passion! I want to shed light on many things and have forums to speak about them. I want to encourage people they can heal and move forward with the right help. I do not encourage any of the behavior in this book or in any other book. Things happen and just because we don't talk about it, doesn't mean that it goes away. I hope my books/forums help people make better choices and be aware of how our actions can affect others. How suffering in silence affects the one suffering and liberates the person causing the suffering. Please do not suffer in silence, speak up and for anyone who needs to be spoken for.

Sneak Peek

And now a sneak peek into the epic
conclusion of Pleasure vs Pain Vol 2!

Chapter 1

I woke up in the morning with no clothes on and lying in my bed with a slight headache. I sat up and felt something fall from my chest to the V- shape crevices between my thighs. I looked closely at the glimmering object and realized it was my gold chain Sénar had held captive. I could see Tyrell's name tangled in the chain-links as it lay on the top of my coochie. It was a horrifying reality that it would land on the very place that was supposed to be Tyrell's but had been ravished by Sénar. I felt a knot in my stomach as guilt came over me. I grabbed the chain holding it close to my heart and cried like a baby as I realized all the bad decisions I had made. I took my necklace and hid it under my mattress, where I thought it might be safe. My heart was racing, as my reality was starting to set in. What was I going to tell Tyrell? How could I explain my necklace being broken? Was he going to believe me? I was devastated as I badgered myself with questions; I did not know the answers to. My emotions were spinning in a whirlwind, and I felt like I was being flushed down the toilet. Feeling like I would drown, I quickly got up and grabbed some clothes to take a shower. In the shower, I tried to scrub off any lingering evidence of Sénar on my body. I scrubbed and scrubbed until I couldn't bear it anymore.

After I got out of the shower, I had to hold my head to keep from losing it; I felt like I would throw up. When the phone rang after not having heard it for weeks, my heart felt like it stopped beating. I ran downstairs, almost slipping from the momentum I accumulated as I ran down the steps.

I answered, "Hello?" Trying not to sound out of breath as my heart resumed beating and was now threatening to beat my chest open from suspense.

Tyrell responded, "Hey, Treasure."

I wanted to make sure I was not hallucinating by asking, "Tyrell?"

He quickly responded, "Who else would it be?"

I shook my head as I did not want the conversation to end up in an argument, so I tried to convince him by saying, "Nobody Tyrell, I am just shocked to hear your voice, that's all." Feeling like I had already messed up, I tried to get the conversation back on a better note and asked, "How was your trip?"

He was quiet on the other end for a second before responding, "Come over, and I'll tell you all about it."

Sénar came down the stairs and glared at me when he saw me on the phone. I felt like a piece of crap, as I hung up the phone in a trance. Before I could even snap out of it, Sénar grabbed me. I closed my eyes as I literally felt like I would faint from being overwhelmed.

Sénar said, "You can do better than him."

I glared at him and instantly filled with rage asking, "Like who? You think you're better?" I pushed him off me and ran upstairs to grab my chain and put it in the pocket of my shorts. Sénar tried to stop me from going out the door so that he could talk to me. I pushed him away and opened the front door to see Tyrell ready to knock. As I opened the door, Tyrell and Sénar locked eyes; I quickly tried to close the door to prevent an altercation. Tyrell looked different; he was taller, bigger, and had a look in his eyes that gave me chills. My eyes were all over him when I called his name, "Tyrell?"

He scanned my body before he spoke, "Hey, Treasure, are you busy?"

He acted like he didn't just call me. Both scared and confused, I responded, "No. I was on my way to your house."

Sénar snatched the door open, and mad dogged Tyrell before walking to his car. Tyrell appeared unbothered but still asked, "Your little boyfriend got a new car, huh?" His voice was deeper, and his speech was pressured. Before I could answer, he said, "Let's go!"

I followed behind him like a little puppy to his car while trying to gauge his emotions, but he avoided eye contact with me. We got in the car, and he pulled out of his driveway without saying a word. I was nervous but didn't want to show it, so I asked, "How was your trip?"

Trying to keep the conversation light. He responded, "It was cool." He looked at me, searching my eyes then asked, "What did you do the whole time?"

I held my composure despite the tension in his voice, so I cautiously answered, "I went to summer school and the library a lot."

He looked at me, then mockingly asked, "Oh yeah, is that right?"

I felt like he was sarcastic, so I replied, "Yeah, that's right."

He sensed my agitation and then asked, "Why do you have an attitude?"

I didn't want to make him mad, so I let my attitude go and responded, "I don't have an attitude Tyrell, I just want you to be happy to see me like I am happy to see you." He looked at me and asked, "You're happy to see me?"

I smiled at him genuinely, "Yes, I am happy to see you, looking all grown up and stuff." I said, blushing. He smiled for the first time since he came to my door to get me. I felt like I could relax a little bit.

Eyeing me as he scanned me up and down and said, "Shoot, you lookin' kind of thick over there, what have you been eating?"

I was almost offended, then I thought about all the food I ate, and I guess I did put on a couple of pounds. I was feeling a little pressed in my shorts too. I laughed instead and said, "Food. Sheesh, thanks, I guess."

We both laughed until he asked, "Is that it." I felt uncomfortable again, and then I countered, "Damn, what else would it be? You put some weight on too, so what you been eating?"

He just sighed and ignored my question before he replied, "Anyway speaking of food, do you want to get some tacos?"

My mood changed instantly. I eagerly answered, "Yeah, that sounds like a good idea." We pulled up to the taco truck, and we got out to order some tacos. Tyrell sarcastically asked, "What, you want six now?" I slapped his arm, immediately thinking how much bigger his arms were now. He looked at me and our eyes filled with lust, "How can I help you?" Our gaze interrupted by a rude Hispanic lady rushing us to take our order. Tyrell ordered twelve tacos instead of eleven to be funny, but he ate the extra one. They were so good we didn't talk much while we ate.

We pulled up to the park and sat in the car for a minute before Tyrell asked, "You want to go for a walk?"

I thought about the extra pounds I had put on and shrugged my shoulders, answering, "Yeah, I guess I could use the exercise." We both laughed and got out. He came around to my side and grabbed me, pulling me close to him. I clung to him and waited for him to kiss me; in case he wasn't planning on it to avoid being rejected. He gazed deeply into my eyes and asked, "Do you still love me?"

I quickly answered, "Of course I do. I never stopped loving you Tyrell." I thought this might be the time to bring up the necklace before he noticed it. I said, "Tyrell I wanted-" He kissed me and wrapped his arms around me. I melted in his arms, allowing him to caress me, not wanting him to let me go. He let me go to grab my hand; then, we walked the path for runners while holding hands. I wrapped my other arm around his arm and listened to him, tell me about his trip. He talked about the weather being so different from our sunny California weather and how it was overcast a lot, making him appreciate our hot summers.

He laughed and then said, "They love sandwiches, or should I say submarine hoagies and hot dogs. Shit, I wanted some tacos or some Chinese food. It was not happening when I first got down there, but my cousin took me to some spots eventually."

I laughed because we both love our tacos. He talked about their accents and how they said he had one too, which had him chuckling to himself. I asked, "You didn't have a bunch of groupies out there, did you?"

He smirked at me, then he quickly responded, "Not like you do." I rolled my eyes and realized I set myself up for that comment. We found some tables under a gazebo, and I sat on one of the tables. I looked at him, wondering if he missed me like I missed him, despite my weeks of misery and passion. He looked like he was wondering the same thing as he stood in front of me. He softened up a bit and reassured me by saying, "There were a lot of girls, but none of them were as fine as you." He kissed me passionately and rubbed his hand down the side of my face and neck. He stopped kissing me, and I could see his facial expression change.

He asked, "Where's your chain?"

I looked down as I nervously pulled it out of my back pocket. I took a deep breath to prepare myself to be ridiculed for whatever lie I chose to tell to explain the situation. Before I could say anything, he asked, "Why isn't it on your neck?"

I opened my hand slowly to reveal the broken chain links to my necklace and then said, "I broke it when you rejected me and didn't call me for weeks. I thought you didn't love me anymore. I was hurt and angry." I looked down as I unwillingly started to cry; the tears streamed down my face. I was ashamed of how it really broke and that I had to lie about it. My answer consisted of a mixture of lies and my real emotions combined. He was angry but remained calm, I continued to try and console him with my apologies, "I am so sorry Tyrell, I regretted bre-"

He snatched the chain out of my hand and barked, "Look, baby girl, I love you. You are special to me, but I don't want my heart to end up like this damn chain!" I heard every word he said, but I still felt anger surpass my guilt.

I asked, "Well, does that mean you can just break mine whenever you want?"

Now we were both upset and just glared at one another until he answered, "No, but damn Treasure, I need to know you are mine. All mine. That nig-"

I grabbed him and kissed him. I wanted him to know that I loved him and missed him. He pushed me off of him, gently enough to not hurt me but hard enough to not let me continue to kiss him. Tyrell confessed, "Damn Treasure, you're driving me crazy! I just don't know what to do with your ass!"

He sat next to me on the table and put his face in his hands. He then looked at the chain in his hand and maneuvered the broken chain links that surrounded his name. I could tell his feelings were hurt. I grabbed his arm and laid my head on it, feeling sorry for the both of us as we were both so emotionally impaired at the moment for different reasons. I said, "I am so sorry, Tyrell. I love you so much. It hurts me when you just give up on us and leave me hanging. I never know what you feel until you're already mad. Then you just shut me –"

He cut me off and yelled, "Don't make it seem like it's all me! Your ass is not innocent!"

I looked at him, debating if I wanted to argue my innocence at a time like this or salvage what was left of our relationship. I chose to salvage what was left and pleaded with him, "Tyrell look, we made it through this year, and it was crazy. Let's make next year the bomb! Let's not let anything break our bond or trust for each other. We need to be confident in each other. Please, I need you, Tyrell."

He dropped his head in silence and then spoke, "Look, I just got home, I need to square away a couple of things, but I wanted to come to see you first. I need to prepare myself for the next school year and think hard, but I think we will get through this." He stood up and took a deep breath, and I got up to hug him. He held me tight in his arms and kissed me on the forehead. "You're my Treasure no matter what, and now I have more to love." He squeezed my booty and laughed as I playfully pushed him away. He joked, "Jump on my back, and I'll give you a piggyback ride."

I laughed at his smart-ass joke and then jumped on his back, kissing his face as he carried me to the car. We drove back to the house and pulled up to see Sénar and London outside of the house, arguing. Tyrell rolled his eyes and parked the car. Not wanting to return to my captivity, I asked, "Well, can we watch TV and chill for a while before I go back to my hell hole of a house?"

He looked at me and shook his head, rubbing his waves of hair forward in frustration before he answered, "My mom is really tripping right now, ever since that day I left for Jersey. I must square away some stuff first, but maybe tomorrow we will get together. I have to unpack and get situated; we will see."

I was disappointed; I asked, "Well, can I call you?"

He just looked at me and said, "If I can, I'll call you, but if not, we will talk tomorrow."

I was devastated, not only did I have to win Tyrell's heart back, I had to try to get back in good standing with his mom. She was not happy to see us arguing that day, especially after believing our lies the day my wrist was broken. I was really lost, not knowing where things would end up, and all I could do was believe him that we would get through this. I got out of the car, and he met me on my side as I tried to hold back my tears. He hugged me and kissed me before going inside, and I reluctantly walked back across the street to my house. I avoided looking at Sénar as I know he was watching me and Tyrell as we hugged and kissed. I heard London refer to me as a bitch. I ignored them both as I went inside with no chain, no confidence, and not knowing if my relationship with Tyrell was broken like my chain.

I laid in my bed to cry as I felt the vacant area of where my chain once lay on my neck. I wondered if Tyrell would ever want to give me back something I had allowed to get destroyed. My guilt made me feel like I didn't even deserve it. I was lost; my heart barely felt like it had a heartbeat left. I wanted to write, but I couldn't stop crying. I smelled food, but I didn't bother to eat or see what was being cooked. I didn't even shower, I just stayed in my room and cried until the next morning.

www.ingramcontent.com/pod-product-compliance
Lightning Source LLC
Chambersburg PA
CBHW020918110726
47900CB00001B/205